THE FAITHLESS

Martina Cole

WINDSOR
PARAGON

First published 2011
by Headline Publishing Group
This Large Print edition published 2012
by AudioGO Ltd
by arrangement with
Headline Publishing Group

Hardcover   ISBN: 978 1 4458 2835 0
Softcover   ISBN: 978 1 4458 2836 7

British Library Cataloguing in Publication Data available

Printed and bound in Great Britain by
MPG Books Group Limited

For my Freddie Fling Flang.

Love you, darling

Dolly R

xx

In loving memory of Wade Purvis,
a true fan.

Prologue

'Ain't It Grand To Be Bloomin' Well Dead'

Leslie Sarony
Song title

'You are not going to make me listen to this shit, Gabriella. You are wrong, *very* wrong. Use your bloody head, girl! I loved that little boy with all my heart . . . and, as for your brother . . . I don't believe a word of it—they must have the wrong person.'

But Gabby could see the fear in her mother's eyes, and she knew that it was true. Every word of it.

'I met your old mate, Jeannie, today. That's how I know everything—she told me *all* about the house in Ilford.' She could see her mother's head working, trying to figure out exactly what she was saying, could almost hear her brain whirring as she tried to lie her way out of what they both knew was the truth.

'What the hell have you been taking this time, eh? What the fuck are you on, Gabriella, to make you come out with this shit?'

Gabby found she'd picked up a large bronze statue of a cat. As she held it in her scarred hands she felt the weight of it. Her mother kept talking. The world according to Cynthia Tailor who, along with God Himself, was almost omnipotent in the lives of her family, who ruled everyone around her with a rod of iron. She could see her mother's mouth moving constantly, but she couldn't hear what she was saying any more; all she was conscious of was a rushing noise in her ears. Then she struck her.

She lifted the bronze statue back over her head and hit her mother across the face with it, using all the force she could muster, and enjoying the feeling of total retaliation. She was determined now, determined to shut her mother up once and for all.

Cynthia fell sideways on to the white leather sofa. The spray of blood that came from her mother's face was like a crimson mist. Gabby hit her again and again, each blow easing the knot inside her, each blow seeming to calm the erratic beating of her heart.

She looked down at the bloodied form and, for the first time in years, she felt almost at peace. Her mother's face was unrecognisable, a deep red gash that was pumping out blood at an alarming rate.

Gabby looked at the woman she had hated nearly all her life. Then she sat down on the ladder-backed chair her mother was convinced was an antique, put her face into her bloodied hands and cried.

Book One

Long is the way
And hard, that out of Hell leads up to light

Paradise Lost (1667)
John Milton, 1608–74

For the love of money is the root of all evil

1 Timothy 6:10

CHAPTER ONE

1984

'Come on, Jimmy, have another one. I'm celebrating.'

Jimmy Tailor grinned; he had an easy-going nature that some people took advantage of. He was a big man, big in all ways—over six feet and well built. Before his marriage he had been a body builder, and he still held traces of his former physique.

'Nah, better get home, Cynthia's waiting for me.'

It was Friday night and all his pals were going to have a few more pints before meeting their wives and girlfriends later on in a wine bar in the West End. He would have loved to have joined them, but he knew that Cynthia wouldn't come.

'Fucking hell, Jimmy, you're married, mate, not joined at the hip.'

This from his best friend Davey Brown. Davey thought Jimmy was a mug and that he should put his foot down with Cynthia, but Davey didn't understand her. No one did it seemed, except him. He smiled, but it was a tight smile. 'We're saving, what with little Gabriella and all.'

''Course, mate, you get yourself off.' Davey seemed immediately sorry for his jibe.

Jimmy left the pub a few minutes later, reluctant to go if he was honest, but even more reluctant to stay where he was. He walked along the road, feeling the cold hit him, making his face sting and, pulling up the collar of his overcoat, he made his way slowly home.

3

CHAPTER TWO

Cynthia Tailor was pleased with herself. Her house looked lovely and festive—just how a home should look at Christmas time, from the scented pine tree, decorated in what she felt was a tasteful manner— no tinsel and no coloured lights—to the neatly wrapped presents underneath it. It couldn't be further away from the house she grew up in, with the dirt, the smell of frying bacon, and the garish, cheap hanging garlands. She shuddered inwardly as she thought of her mother's house. She had escaped from that life and there was no way she was ever going back.

Cynthia's sitting room was painted a pale cream, and the carpet was a thick Axminster. It had cost the national debt, but looked wonderful against the walls and the luxurious chocolate-brown velvet curtains at the windows. She knew her home was beautiful, and she never tired of cleaning it, or enhancing it. This was the first step on the ladder for them; they would go on from here, make their money on this place, and get bigger and better houses each time. She sighed with contentment at the thought.

James was a decent man, boring in some ways, but she knew that with his accountancy job in the city they would always be all right for money. And he was expecting some big news about a promotion any day now. Cynthia had come from a council estate in Hackney, and she had been determined from a young age that she wouldn't be staying there for longer than she had to. Now here she was, with a lovely semi in Ilford, and the chance to go onwards and upwards.

She walked out into her kitchen, and checked on the casserole she had bubbling on her new halogen hob. The kitchen was like something from a magazine, all white doors and stainless steel sinks. It was Hygena, and she knew it was far too good for the house, but she saw it as an investment. James had baulked at the price but she had won him over. He always saw the sense of her arguments in the end; after all, she was the one stuck here all day, and she was entitled to have what she wanted around her—at least that was what she thought, anyway. And she had her ways to make sure he knew who was the boss under *this* roof.

She heard her daughter's cry and, sighing, she left the kitchen and made her way up the stairs.

Gabriella was a handful, and this was the only bugbear in her otherwise perfect life. She should be clean at night by now. The other kids at Gabriella's playschool were all clean, so why was her daughter so late?

She went into the child's room. It was decorated as a girl's bedroom *should* be decorated, with pale pink walls, and cream carpet. Cynthia loved this room. She had been brought up in a flat and had had to share her bedroom with her sister. It had been scruffy, cold and damp and she had hated every second she had spent in it.

The small night-light cast a rosy glow in the room. Kneeling down beside her daughter's cot, she looked at her child.

'What's wrong, Gabriella?'

The little blue eyes held a plea, and she knew immediately that her daughter had wet the bed

5

again.

'Oh, Gabriella, why don't you call me, and I'll take you to the toilet.' She lifted her daughter out of the cot with a heavy sigh, and set about cleaning her up, without another word.

Gabriella allowed herself to be stripped, washed and re-dressed in a clean nightie without saying a word either. As young as she was, she could feel the tension filling the room. The unspoken disapproval and the knowledge she had done some-thing wrong was enough to quieten her. She knew her mummy was cross, and she knew better than to aggravate her.

Ten minutes later, Gabriella was once more alone in her cot and, closing her eyes, she tried hard to get herself back to sleep.

CHAPTER THREE

Jimmy came in as his wife was putting their daughter's pyjamas and bedding into the washing machine.

'Dinner smells good, Cyn.'

She didn't answer him. She could do that, just blank some-one, make them feel an outsider in their own home. It unnerved Jimmy. He was from a family who were boisterous, noisy, happy—not that Cynthia allowed him to see them any more. He wasn't used to long silences that had some kind of accusation in them, even though nothing was actually said. He wasn't sure how to deal with them. Turning abruptly, he went into the hallway and removed his coat. Careful to hang it up *properly* to make sure it didn't look untidy. Why this was a necessity when they were locked away in a cupboard under the stairs he wasn't sure. But Cynthia wanted everything perfect, so he did it anyway; it was easier in the long run.

As he went into the sitting room, he smiled at Cynthia's efforts. The room looked lovely, and he reminded himself how lucky he was to have a wife like her. She was not just pretty, she was like sex-on-legs. With her stunning blue eyes and thick sovereign-coloured hair, she turned heads every-where she went. He knew that other men envied him his gorgeous wife. Everywhere she went men looked at her, and she noticed them looking, he knew that. It pleased her, because it showed her that she was still attractive, even after having a child. It was important to Cynthia that she was wanted. Not that sex was her top priority, unfortunately, but because she liked the power it gave her. She was a strange woman, cold—even towards their daughter. She only smiled when the child was doing what she wanted, acting as she felt a child should. Like him, poor Gabby had to behave just how Cynthia believed a daughter should, and not show her up. His wife had no room for reality, and that really worried him. Cynthia had two beliefs: that she was right, and that everyone else on the planet was wrong.

Now he had to give her some bad news and he wasn't looking forward to it. Not at all. No matter how he dressed it up, she frightened him; her colossal temper could erupt at any moment, and when it did she was like a madwoman. Most of the time she *acted* like a lady, he had to give her that. She was perfection personified—until you crossed

7

her and told her something she didn't want to hear. Then she could swear like a docker and fight like the Irish. But then her family *was* Irish—not that she bragged about that.

He glanced at the TV set, but didn't put it on. Cynthia didn't think watching telly all the time was something *nice* people did. A good film or a documentary was fine, and *News At Ten* of course. But gameshows or comedy programmes were beneath her radar. She saw those as common, and common was what really sent her off her head.

It wasn't easy being married to her and, even though he told himself that he was lucky a girl like her chose him, it was getting harder and harder to keep up that pretence. They were over-stretched in every way—every half-penny was accounted for and, as much as he appreciated her housewifely acumen, he knew they were way over their heads in debt. Not that she wasn't good with money—she was—but, all the same, he felt they could have lived much better if she didn't feel this almighty urge to be something she wasn't. She had such exacting standards and, though he knew she wanted a better life for them all, he felt at times they'd be much better off if she spent the money in other ways, like on a night out or a day at the seaside, not just on *things* she felt were needed for the home. They had the best house in the street, but still that wasn't enough for her. She would never be content, he understood that now. The kitchen alone had cost a bloody fortune, and the carpets and curtains, all paid for on the weekly, were another drain on their resources.

Now she had the Christmas bug, had talked about having a goose and all other manner of

8

expensive frippery. He knew she wanted the best for them, but it had to be stopped. She had to understand they couldn't go on like this.

Cynthia came into the room, slipping in quietly, as if she had materialised out of thin air. Her quietness had been what had attracted him; she had seemed so self-contained, yet so vulnerable. Not that he really believed *that* any more. It was getting harder and harder to convince himself that she was anything other than what she really was. A bully. His mother had warned him, but he had not been inclined to listen to her. Now he wished he had. But, as his old mum also said, hindsight was a wonderful thing.

Cynthia stood before him, her head slightly at an angle, and that tight little smile on her face. 'I'm dishing up.'

He sighed heavily, and barely nodded in reply.

'Are you all right?'

He sighed once more. 'Not really. Brewster got it.'

He saw her face freeze, and could see in her eyes, not pity for him—he could have coped with that—but disgust. Veiled disgust, but he saw it all the same. He knew what was going on inside her head. He tried to talk himself out of those kind of thoughts, but it was no good.

'And you just let him, I suppose.'

She was still standing there, only now her back was rigid, she was looking at him as if he had done it deliberately. He felt the air leave his body as if it had been punctured. He had been dreading this.

'I can't make my boss give me the position, Cynth. Be fair, love.'

She sighed heavily, her face set in a rigid mask

9

of acceptance. ''Course not, I mean why would he give it to you, eh? Hardly setting the fucking place alight, are you? You know your trouble, don't you? You're weak. Weak as a bloody kitten.'

She left the room then, and her animosity went with her. The quiet was like a balm to his tortured spirit.

Willy Brewster was five years younger than him, and he was a dynamo. Jimmy liked him, you couldn't not. He was fun, clever and popular; he *did* set the place alight all right, with his energy and wit. Jimmy wasn't like that, and he didn't begrudge Willy for being something he wasn't.

He walked out to the kitchen, feeling better now he had actually said the words out loud. Had told her.

She was standing at the sink. Her shoulders were slumped and her hands were gripping the stainless-steel draining board so hard her knuckles were white. Her head was hanging, and he knew she was biting her lip. He could almost feel the hate coming off her in waves. Looking at her now, he felt a great sorrow for her, because he knew that there was a terrible kink in her nature. It was a mixture of loathing for her start in life, and a covetousness that made her envy everyone in her orbit. She would never be satisfied, because it wasn't in her nature. He hated that part of her, but he also pitied her for it. He understood that she had never known one happy day because she was always convinced that everyone else knew the secret of happiness, and it would always elude her. Yet if she could just once let herself be content with what she had, he knew she could find the thing she craved. If she could only understand that happiness had nothing to do with an expensive kitchen, and designer clothes, or being better off than the neighbours.

He placed his hand gently on her shoulder, willing her to turn to him, to just once let down her guard. He could feel the heat of her body through the thin material of her dress, and then when she turned towards him he felt his heart soar. He placed his arm around her slim waist, wanting to pull her towards him, comfort her, but she threw him off her with a strength that belied her slim frame.

'You fucking useless ponce.'

She was spitting out the words with fury, and the vitriol in them stunned him, as it always did when she exposed this side of herself. She never swore in front of the neighbours of course, she felt she was above that. But in private it was as if the swearing was a vent for her pent-up aggression. When she was angry with him or little Gabby her repertoire was never far away.

'You do realise what this means, don't you?'

She was looking into his eyes now, and he could see the first glimmer of fear amidst the anger and the disgust.

'Look, Cynthia, we won't starve.'

She pushed him away from her and, sighing, she shook her head sadly. 'No. No, you're right, we won't starve, but then again we won't be living the high life either, will we? It's make do and mend, it's thinking through every purchase. It's making ends fucking meet, and robbing Peter to pay fucking Paul. It's the life I grew up with, never being able to do anything . . . Never being able to just have what you want, when you want it. It's like admitting I've failed . . .' She turned from him, and her whole

11

body seemed to have shrunk, as if the enormity of what she was saying had broken her somehow. 'It's being no one, no one and nothing for ever, that's what this all means to me.'

Jimmy looked at his wife, his heart in pieces. He couldn't understand why she was so upset. He looked out for her, he looked out for his family. 'You're wrong, Cynthia. We have a good life. The trouble with you is, it's never enough, is it? You always want more than you can have. You should never have married me; I can't give you what you want.' He had finally said it to her. Had finally said what was on his mind.

She laughed, a derisive little laugh. Then, facing him once more, she said quietly, 'Well, you got that much right anyway.'

For a split second she thought he was actually going to strike her and, in her heart, she knew no one would blame him if he did just that. Instead, though, he placed his hands by his sides, clenching his fists as if to stop himself.

'Maybe you're right, but do you know something, Cynthia? No one in the world could ever give you what you want, because it would never be enough. You want, want, want, and then when you get it you lose all interest in it, and you start wanting something else. Well, now you know the score, I'll have me dinner.'

He had never spoken to her like that, not once since she had set her cap at him, and she knew then and there that she would make sure he never spoke to her like it again. But she was trapped, trapped in this house, with his kid, and with his name. And, as if that wasn't bad enough, she had a terrible feeling she was pregnant again.

12

CHAPTER FOUR

'Oh, for fuck's sake, Cynthia! Cheer up, girl.'

Mary Callahan looked at the hard, set face in front of her and suppressed the urge to shake her daughter. Where she had got this one from she didn't know. Cynthia looked down her nose at everyone around her, had done since she could sit up on her own.

Gabby, bless her heart, was the antithesis of her mother. She looked like a little angel with her halo of blond hair and huge blue eyes. She was a gorgeous, loving little girl, but Mary knew that the poor child would not get that love returned from her own mother. Mary had accepted years ago that her daughter was capable of a lot of things, but love wasn't one of them. And as for that poor sap she had snared, and who she still had by the nuts . . . Mary wasn't an advocate of violence against women, but if ever a man should slap his old woman, poor Jimmy was that man. Cynthia rode him like a devil, and he let her, the poor bastard.

Mary glanced around her home; it was scruffy, granted, but it was clean enough. She was of the belief that a home was to be lived in, not just admired by fucking strangers. Unlike her daughter's gaff. She acted like fucking royalty was due round any minute. Cynthia's house was like the fucking library, you felt like you had to whisper, creep around it, as if noise of any kind was against the law.

She inwardly shook her head in sadness; her daughter would never know a really happy day in her life, she wasn't built for joy. Still, that didn't mean little Gabriella shouldn't be happy. Not if Mary had any say in the matter, especially on Christmas Day. Turning to her granddaughter, she said cheerfully, 'Come on, Gabby, let's see what Santa left for you, shall we?'

The little girl ran to her nervously, worried as always that her mother would stop her in her tracks, give her a lecture about how little girls *should* behave.

Mary Callahan doted on her granddaughter. She was a little darling. Good as gold and pretty as a picture, with a lovely nature to boot. How her Cynthia had produced something so sweet she didn't know, but she had, and Mary prayed daily that her daughter didn't destroy this little girl's confidence with her constant criticisms.

Gabby sat in front of the plastic Christmas tree, her eyes glowing with happiness. She loved this house, from the garish tinsel everywhere, to the smell of cigarettes that permeated everything around her. She loved the whole 'Nana Mary experience'. And the constant noise—the TV was always on, as was the radio in the kitchen, and the record players upstairs. It was a jumble of sounds and smells. It was always full of people, there was always laughter, and any arguments were good-natured—unlike at home. She knew her mummy *liked* to leave her here sometimes and she knew, somewhere deep inside herself, that her mummy left her here for all the wrong reasons. But, for Gabriella Tailor, being here was enough.

Mary Callahan followed her daughter into the kitchen, wondering why she was even asking the question she knew her daughter would resent.

'Have you any idea how lucky you are, Cynthia? That man worships you, and he'd give you the earth on a plate if he could. Yet you still walk about with a face like a fucking wet weekend in Margate. What's your problem?'

Cynthia gritted her teeth in annoyance. 'Give it a rest, Mum, eh? You don't know the half of it.'

'Then tell me, child, maybe I can help?' It was a plea, and they both knew it.

Cynthia was tempted to turn to her mother and throw herself into her arms. She knew that, even after every—thing, she would be accepted, would be enveloped in her mother's love. But she couldn't do it. She could never admit to anyone, let alone this woman in front of her, that she had failed. Had made a grievous mistake. Had married a man who she had never loved, for a so-called decent life and who, nowadays, she had no respect for whatsoever, let alone any kind of warmth. He had let her down badly, and she was frightened of what the future held for them.

The worst of it all was she knew her mother would think that her feelings were not justified. She thought the sun shone out of James's arse. They all did. They thought *he* was a saint for putting up with *her*, and that rankled. They looked down on her for trying to get herself a better life, a decent life. James Tailor had promised her that, and he had reneged on his promise. At least that was how she saw it anyway. Instead she plastered a smile on her face. 'Nothing to tell, Mum, I'm just tired that's all.'

Mary Callahan grinned suddenly. 'You're pregnant again, aren't you?'

Cynthia closed her eyes slowly and nodded. 'Yeah, I think so. Just my fucking luck.'

Mary hugged her, even though the hug wasn't returned. 'That's what life is about, Cynthia! It's about having babies, and living your life as best you can. Millions of women do it every day.' She laughed then and said gently, 'And you, Cynth, have it easier than most, love.'

Cynthia shrugged nonchalantly. 'Well, that's as may be, but I want a bit more than this, Mum. I never signed on for cheap and cheerful, and I'm not settling for anything less.'

Her daughter's words wounded Mary, as she knew they were directed at her and the life she lived. The inference was that she had failed somehow, because the Callahans weren't rich or important enough for her elder child. Oh, she was itching to slap that beautiful face, but she wouldn't because she knew it would be pointless. She'd have a fleeting feeling of satisfaction, but it would also mean she wouldn't see her beloved grandchild until her daughter felt she needed to get away from the poor child once again. So Mary took a deep breath and said matter-of-factly, 'You got more than most women. Your trouble is you want the fucking earth on a plate. Well, as my mother used to say, you've made your bed, you better get used to lying in it.'

Looking around the kitchen as if it was the local dump, Cynthia replied, 'Well, you would know more about that than I would.'

Mary wanted to punch her daughter's lights out so badly she could almost taste it. Instead she said as coolly as she could, 'Do you know something, Cynth, one of these days you are going to push me too far, and when you do . . .' She was poking a finger into her daughter's face now, the anger rising inside her like a tide.

16

'Nana Mary, Granddad's here!'

Gabby, having run into the kitchen, was beside herself with excitement. After her nana Mary, her granddad Jack was the next best thing in her world.

Mary took a deep breath to calm her anger before she turned to Gabby, saying with forced joviality, 'Ah, sure, he'll be thrilled to see you, young lady!'

But Gabby could feel the tension in the small kitchen and, as always, it frightened her. She hated it when her mummy was like this, grim-faced and hard-mouthed. She wished her mummy would laugh more; she had a lovely laugh, like she had a lovely face.

'You better run, Mum, your better half just got home from the pub early. That must be a fucking first for you, eh?' Cynthia couldn't resist another jibe.

'Oh, you're a bitter pill, girl. At least your father *wants* to come home. More than you can say for poor Jimmy, I'm sure.' Mary knew it was a cheap shot but she couldn't help herself; sometimes Cynthia pushed you to the limit. Job himself would have struggled to be patient around her daughter.

CHAPTER FIVE

Jimmy Tailor liked all his in-laws. In fact, he was thrilled to be spending Christmas with them— anything was better than the silent dinner he would have had at home, with Cynthia sending him sneering, reproachful looks over the table. At least here he'd have a bit of fun and so would

Gabby. Jimmy was especially fond of Celeste, his wife's younger sister. She was a really nice girl, not as beautiful as Cynthia, but still very attractive. She had a generous nature and kind heart too, and that made her a joy to be around.

'Hi, Jimmy, you look well.'

He grinned with pleasure. Celeste was always glad to see him. 'So do you, love. In fact, you look wonderful.'

She almost shone with pleasure at the compliment. Jimmy would never understand his wife's animosity towards her sister. It was beyond his comprehension. Jimmy didn't have a jealous bone in his body, so he never understood the naked envy in his wife's eyes when she looked at her little sister.

'Don't start her off, her head's big enough as it is.' He could hear the nastiness in his wife's voice.

Celeste smiled at her sister and said sweetly, 'You'd know all about that, Cynth. It's a wonder you can leave the fucking house!'

Everyone laughed. Cynthia watched them as they laughed at her expense. She hated that they were her family, hated that these people were her blood, hated that she needed them, that they were the only people who really knew her. It was the last place she wanted to be on Christmas Day but, then, she never missed an opportunity to lord it over them and look down her nose at them.

'Ha bloody ha ha. What are you so done up for?'

Celeste grinned once more, she was always so good-natured it made Cynthia want to hit her.

'Don't you mean for *who*? Didn't you tell her, Mum?'

Mary flapped her hand with feigned discretion.

18

'Why would I? It's your news to tell.'

'Come on then, Celeste, out with it.' Cynthia sounded bored now, as if anything to do with her sister was beneath her. Which, as far as Cynthia was concerned, pretty much summed up how she felt about Celeste and her excuse for a life.

'I'm seeing Jonny Parker, have been for a couple of months.'

Mary watched Cynthia as she digested this little bit of information, saw the shock as it occurred to her what that statement actually meant in real terms.

'He's too old for you.'

Celeste laughed, a happy, loud laugh, a natural laugh that made her look prettier than she actually was. She too had the arresting Callahan blue eyes and blond hair, although she didn't have the striking glamour of her sister. She might be a pale imitation in looks but Celeste's beauty came from within, from her nature. She had a wonderful lust for life, and she honestly believed that everyone was nice and kind, like her, and that if you treated people decently they would reciprocate.

'What you talking about, Cynthia? He's twenty-seven, and I'm nineteen. Eight years ain't much now, is it? It ain't like I'm thirteen and he's twenty-one. He's such a nice bloke, Cynth, treats me like a queen.'

Cynthia forced a smile on to her face; her sister couldn't know how this news was really affecting her. 'Well, you make sure he carries on treating you like that, OK?'

Celeste nodded happily, and Cynthia saw the genuine pleasure on her face. She turned to her father. 'What do you think about it, Dad?'

19

Jack Callahan shrugged. He was already half cut, having been down the local pub for the best part of the day. He tried to focus on his elder daughter for a few seconds before saying amiably, 'What's to think? He's a nice enough fellow, and you can tell he thinks the world of her. Did you know he's bought the bookies on the high street? He's a dark horse, that one. He already owns a couple of pubs. This one here will be living the life of Riley if she plays her cards right!'

'Oh, Dad!'

Celeste was crimson with embarrassment at her father's words, and they all laughed at her discomfort at being the centre of attention, but knowing that she loved it really.

'Gabby can be your bridesmaid, she'd make a gorgeous little attendant!' Mary's voice was loud, and she watched her elder daughter carefully; if Celeste decided to settle down with Jonny Parker, and it looked more and more like that was going to be the case, Cynthia needed to accept it as soon as possible. Jonny and Cynthia had a history, not that Celeste knew that, but Mary knew that Cynthia had set her cap at him years ago. He had not been averse at first—no bloke was when she looked at them with her lovely face—but he had realised very quickly that Cynthia was seriously high maintenance and had dropped her so fast it had made her head spin. She was now hoping Cynthia would not feel the urge to enlighten her younger sister of that fact. Not that Celeste would be all that bothered, but Mary suspected from her reaction that Cynthia had never quite got over Jonny. And, as much as her elder daughter aggravated her, she still wouldn't like to see her hurt. But, more than

20

that, she didn't want her younger child's happiness compromised because Cynthia was jealous. And jealous she might be, because Jonny Parker was going places, and that meant that Celeste would be going with him.

Mary Callahan looked at her granddaughter, the light of her life, and wondered, in the glow of her Christmas tree, what the future held for them all.

Knowing her elder child like she did, she knew that her younger daughter's life could be destroyed in an instant. But, if that ever happened, Mary would retaliate in a heartbeat because, if push came to shove, her younger child would win hands down. Cynthia had been given her chance with Jonny Parker many moons ago, and she had played it all wrong. Now he was fair game, and her Celeste was welcome to him. If Cynthia felt the need to challenge that, then Mary would be only too happy to put the fucker wise. Cynthia needed a wake-up call, and this might just be it.

Mary had two daughters, and she loved them both in her own way, but she wouldn't let one of them walk all over the other.

CHAPTER SIX

'He's so handsome, Cynth!'

Mary wasn't surprised that her daughter didn't answer her, it was par for the course, but sometimes, like now, it grated. She looked down her bloody nose at them all, yet she still dumped the children on her parents on a regular basis. 'He's the image of Jimmy, but I can see you in him as

21

well.'

Cynthia smiled but it wasn't a real smile. She was just going through the motions.

'We love having him over. Little Jimmy Junior!'

'He's James, Mum, he'll always be James.' Her daughter said it as if it was a matter of life and death. Which of course it was to her.

'Well, that's your call, love. He's your son after all.'

Cynthia nodded in agreement. 'Can you keep Gabriella for a few more days, just until I get into a routine?'

Mary nodded silently. She had been looking after Gabby for nearly six weeks now and, apart from Jimmy popping in most evenings to see his daughter, she might as well be an orphan, because Cynthia didn't bother with her at all.

James Junior was now a month old, and it looked like Cynthia was going to be the same with this child as she was with poor little Gabby. She fed him, changed him, and washed him, he was immaculately turned out, and well cared for in every way—outwardly that is—but she never picked him up unless she had to. Cynthia only did what she felt was expected of her. It was frightening to admit that his own mother, her daughter, had no real love for him. Because she knew that she didn't. She didn't truly care for either of her children. It was as if love was beyond her. Mary wished she knew how to stop it, how to make her daughter see the mistake she was making. Tell her how she saw through her—her life, her marriage and her sorry attempt at being a mother. She never comforted or played with her children, showed them any love or maternal instinct. Yes, she catered for their

22

welfare, but she always kept her distance from them somehow. Cynthia always seemed to be on the periphery of their lives, never at the centre of it like she should have been.

Cynthia had always been a cold fish, she had never grasped the meaning of happiness. It seemed to have eluded her somehow, and Mary wondered at times if that was her fault. But she knew logically it wasn't anything she had done—in the beginning she had loved Cynthia as much as she had Celeste. She had loved both her girls with a deep and abiding passion from the minute she had given birth to them. But Cynthia had always had this wall around her, and nothing Mary had done had ever broken through it. So she had eventually accepted her daughter's personality, accepted that her Cynthia was not built for big displays of affection— in fact they troubled her, bothered her. Cynthia had always been a law unto herself, and it had been hard for Mary, a genuinely warm person, to be rebuffed by her own daughter from a young age. From then on, Cynthia had been a child who was difficult to love, really love. Mary had even disliked her sometimes, and now she wondered if that was why her daughter was such a hardcase. She'd tried to understand her daughter's personality but, if she was honest, it was beyond her. Cynthia had never been an easy child, and she was not an easy woman.

But now, her daughter's aloofness, and her complete indiffer-ence to her own children really worried her. She knew she couldn't do anything about it, because outwardly Cynthia was the perfect mother—who would believe her? But Mary worried that her grandchildren would suffer one day for their mother's lack of genuine affection.

Jimmy tried to make up for it, she knew, she saw that every day, and she wished she could tell him that she understood what he was going through. But voicing her worries would be tantamount to treason, would be criticising her own flesh and blood, and she just couldn't do that. It would be different if Jimmy came to her, and said it out loud. But she knew he would never do that. Cynthia had him well and truly under the thumb.

'Are you all right, Cynth? You look so down, love.'

Cynthia looked into her mother's eyes, the same deep blue eyes that her daughter had inherited, and she said in genuine bewilderment, "Course I am! Why wouldn't I be?'

Mary smiled sadly. This was hard for her, really hard—she didn't know how she was supposed to deal with any of this.

CHAPTER SEVEN

Jimmy looked around the kitchen and made sure there wasn't a cup out of place. He wanted Cynthia to come home from her mother's to a spotless house and a nice meal. He had even cooked for them. He was looking forward to seeing her and his new son, of course. He just wished his daughter was coming home with them too.

Jimmy found he was shaking, and he *hated* that he was so nervous about something so normal. His wife had only been for a visit to her mother's—it wasn't as if that was something outrageous. But she was so difficult these days, even making a cup

24

of tea was like a military operation around her. He loved his new son and he adored his daughter, but Cynthia made everything awkward, he felt unable to enjoy being with his own family. He hated that he was so weak, and he knew that *she* hated that he was so weak. But he didn't know how to fight her, he had never known how to fight for anything. That was the trouble.

He had always been the type of person who would do anything to keep the peace. That was all he had ever wanted, peace and quiet. How had it turned out so wrong? When did he realise that his life was a sham, and everyone had known long before he had that his wife was a nightmare?

As he heard the taxi pull up outside, he walked out into the hallway and said a silent prayer that his wife would be in a good mood for once. That she would walk into their house with a smile on her face, and tell him how much she had missed him.

But he didn't hold out much hope.

CHAPTER EIGHT

Jack Callahan was watching *Rainbow* with his granddaughter on his lap. He loved this little girl, and he was loathe to send her back home to her mother. He didn't think Cynthia was strange—he thought she was a complete fucking nut-job. And he was very vocal about his opinions, much to his wife's chagrin.

'Listen, Mary, the trouble with Cynthia is she's self-obsessed, always was, and always will be. There is nothing you can do about it, so let it go, will you?'

Mary didn't answer her husband; she knew from experience that he had said all he was going to say on the subject. Unlike her, he never made any allowances for his elder daughter, in fact, he was quite happy to denigrate her on an almost hourly basis. He had no time for Cynthia whatsoever and, as she had no time for him either, it was a very mutual arrangement. But it hurt Mary, because she loved her family, and she hated that her elder child had ruined everything with her toxic personality. She had left this poor child with them and, as much as she loved her, she knew that Cynthia should have wanted her own daughter at home with her, along with her new son. But Cynthia had never wanted Gabby, not really, and Mary knew she mustn't think about that too much. It just hurt her feelings, hurt her inside.

Thankfully she had her younger daughter to take her mind off it. Celeste had just got in from work, and she was beaming, as always, with happiness. Smiling widely in response, Mary looked at her younger daughter and said with determination, 'You look happy!'

Celeste grinned back at her, and Mary decided that this child at least was going to be all right. Celeste was the antithesis of her older sister—she had no side to her, what you saw was what you got.

'I'm all right, Mum. I take it Cynthia hasn't taken poor Gabby home?'

Mary shook her head. 'I think she's still a bit tired after the birth of young Jimmy . . .'

Celeste frowned then, very theatrically, in a perfect imitation of her older sister, said 'Don't you mean *James*, Mum!'

They both laughed. Cynthia hated the child being

called 'Jimmy'. She had given birth to a James, and James was his name, that was the end of it.

'Yeah, James! Like anyone will ever call him that.'

Celeste stopped laughing and said seriously, 'Cynthia will, Mum, you know what she's like.'

'That's true. Like anything else where the kids are concerned, we can only do what she wants.'

The laughter stopped completely then, even the pretence of it. They had often laughed about Cynthia and her ways, mocked her even—behind her back, of course—but suddenly it was as if they had decided to stop playing the game, as if they had all realised that, in reality, none of it was actually very funny. In order for Mary to see her grandchildren she had to go along with Cynthia's rules—they all did. She used the children like a weapon. And they let her, they *allowed* her to do it, because they knew that without them in the background the children would have nothing.

'Do you think she'll ever be all right, Mum? Because she seems to me as if she's getting unhappier by the day.'

Mary flapped her hand in annoyance. 'She'll never be happy, Celeste, it's not in her nature.'

'Well, that's as may be, Mum, but at least she has a husband, and a family who care about her.'

Mary smiled sadly. 'Well, for the time being anyway, eh, love?'

Jack Callahan, who had been listening to this exchange with half an ear, looked at his wife and daughter and shook his head in disbelief. Gesturing at Gabby, whose eyes were still glued to the TV, he said loudly, 'Look at this little one here, would you two rather she went home with that hard bitch?'

27

Celeste sighed heavily at her father's words. 'I think you should think a little about what you say in front of the child, Dad, you know.'

Jack Callahan laughed uproariously, amazed at his daughter's stupidity where her elder sister was concerned, and he said as much. 'Oh, fuck off, this little one here knows the score. For fuck's sake, she spends half her life here with us! As small as she is, she knows the score with that mad fucking whore.'

Mary Callahan shook her head in exasperation and, looking at her husband, she said seriously, 'Will you ever stop calling your daughter a *whore*?'

Jack Callahan took a deep breath and, after exhaling loudly, he said in a very quiet voice, 'And would you two ever fuck off? This child knows that she's safe here with me. Because her father, God forgive him, is as frightened of her mother as everyone else is. Well, *I* ain't, and I told him, poor fucker that he is, that if he was any kind of man he would batter her on a daily basis. Women like Cynthia need that. They are like poison, and you have to sort them out from the off. She looks down on us, and she looks down on *everyone* around her. If he had any fucking gumption he'd leave her, and do you know what? I'd be the first one to shake his hand if he did.'

Celeste looked at her mother and shrugged in resignation. Then Jack Callahan dropped his bombshell.

'And you, Celeste, had better watch your back because, mark my words, she doesn't like what's going on between you and Jonny Parker. As long as she leaves this little one here with us, I'll swallow me knob, but I'm telling you now, I wouldn't trust her as far as I could kick her.'

Gabby looked up at her granddad and smiled happily. She knew that he would always stand up for her. As young as she was, she knew, deep inside, that her mummy didn't love her properly. She only felt truly loved and cared about when she was with her father, or her grandparents. Her daddy, she knew already, was too nervous of her mother to be trusted completely. Her granddad, though, would fight for her with everything he possessed. It was a good feeling, cuddled up with him, because she knew that he was the only person in her little world who wasn't scared of her mummy.

CHAPTER NINE

As Jimmy watched Cynthia kneel down at the altar, ready to receive Holy Communion, he wondered at how they had ended up like this. They were like strangers. She avoided him at every opportunity, slept in their spare room, and tried to convince him it was because it was easier to see to their son. She shrugged off any attempt he made to discuss their financial situation—which, thanks to her, was dire—and she continued to spend money at an alarming rate.

Looking at her like this, from a distance, he understood how he had fallen in love with her. She was still beautiful, her body was hardly changed by childbirth. If anything, she looked lovelier. She had filled out somehow, and her curves were all in the right places. But now he knew her properly, and that, in all honesty, meant he knew that inside she wasn't in any way beautiful. In fact, as far as her personality went, she was ugly. Ugly and hateful. Dissatisfied in every possible way with her life. And with him. She told him over and over again, how bored, disenchanted, and completely disillusioned she was with him and the life he had tried to give her. She made him feel as though everything he tried to do for her was pointless.

Now, as he watched her accept the communion host and look up at the cross of Christ, he wanted to slap her across the face. Of course he never would, he knew he wasn't capable of that kind of display of emotion, not outwardly anyway. He seethed inside though, and imagined slapping her across the face again and again. Oh, how he dreamt of that, how he dreamt of putting her firmly in her place. But he didn't know how to.

He waited for her to come back to the pew beside him and, kneeling down, he prayed to God to give him strength. The strength to fight against this wife of his, and the strength to fight for his children, because he knew that, if he wasn't careful, she would hurt them too, just as she had hurt him.

CHAPTER TEN

Jonny Parker looked at Celeste as she walked back to the table and sat down and wondered at how much his life had changed through meeting this girl. She was lovely, really lovely. It wasn't so much her looks—though she was certainly the prettiest in the pub tonight—but she was lovely *inside*. There wasn't a bad bone in her body. He loved that she saw the best in everyone, even that leech of a sister of hers.

30

What a narrow escape he'd had there!

All those years ago he had been blinded by Cynthia's beauty, but then so had a lot of men. She had been cold-blooded though, so he'd had to get shot of her. In the end she went for a man she believed would give her the life she craved. Unfortunately, it seemed, she had made a serious fuck-up in that respect, and now she was tied to that poor bastard come hell or high water. But that wasn't his problem—he'd wiped her from his memory. His love for Celeste was completely different. Of all the women he had met, slept with, and gone through, she was the only one who had kept his attention, kept him interested, and kept him enthralled. He loved her with every fibre of his being. He just hated that he had been with her sister first, that Cynthia was a part of his life still, because she was there whether he liked it or not. And he didn't like it, not one bit.

He was making a name for himself, becoming a Face of sorts, making himself important to the right people. He could give Celeste a good life, a good home, and a good seeing-to as and when she needed it. He also knew that Celeste was the kind of girl who would appreciate that—and welcome it. She didn't have any hidden agenda, she just loved life itself. And he loved her for that.

His mother was a drama queen. He loved her of course, but he knew that he could never live with all that himself. Celeste was a real woman, as innocent and unassuming as she was. Jonny knew she would never understand how marvellous she really was. He also knew that Cynthia, her older sister, would never accept that he had chosen Celeste over her. But he had, and he would never regret

31

that decision. Cynthia still bothered him though, if he was truthful. For some reason he knew that Cynthia would make them pay for their happiness. He didn't know how, or why, but he knew Cynthia would somehow extract her pound of flesh. It was in her nature. He had fallen for Cynthia, sexually and mentally, for a short while, but he never wanted Celeste to know that. Cynthia was poison, she was not someone anyone in their right mind would have kept in touch with. And she was dangerous, because she had no real care for anyone or anything, except herself. He had realised overnight how one person could change your life, not for the better, but for the worse. Because that was what people like Cynthia did, they tainted everyone around them, and they made sure that everything and everyone they touched would be as broken as they were.

Back then he would never have dreamt that he would one day meet her sister and fall so deeply in love with her. To be truthful, if he had known the connection that first night he met Celeste, he would have walked away. But it hadn't happened like that. He *had* met her, and he had fallen for her. And now he couldn't imagine being without her. If Cynthia caused any aggravation whatsoever, if she made his relationship with Celeste a problem in any way, he would happily wipe her off the face of the earth. Because, unlike Celeste, he knew the *real* Cynthia, and he had no intentions of making any kind of excuses for her.

She had nearly got her claws into him once before, and he would never ever let her do that to him again.

CHAPTER ELEVEN

'Come on, Cynth, let's go out for a couple of hours? Your mum's happy to have the kids.'

Cynthia looked at her husband and stifled the urge to take him out once and for all. She pictured herself taking a knife from the wooden block she had paid so much for, and running him through with the boning knife. She knew she would never use the boning knife otherwise; after all, why would she ever feel the need to bone a piece of meat? That knife was obsolete, she would never use it, no more than she would use most of the other knives in the set. She had bought them because they were expensive, and would give her kudos should anyone visit her kitchen. But sometimes, like now, she felt that she could happily use a couple of the knives on her lawful husband.

She was getting more and more worried, because he had no idea about how much debt she was actually in. He didn't understand how hard it was for her when she wanted something new, because he couldn't earn enough money to keep them afloat. Oh, it was so unfair! Here she was laden down with two children, a house that had a kitchen worth more than their car, and a husband who was never going to go up in his world because he didn't have the fucking brains he was born with. She was now lumbered with a moron, who she had never really even liked, if she was totally honest, let alone loved, but who, until recently, she had believed would give her the life she craved. The life she had *deserved* because, after all, she was very beautiful and very shrewd, and she had made a point of looking out for a man she was certain would give her what she wanted—a life of luxury and ease.

Now, it seemed, she had sacrificed herself to a man who had no real ambition, and who was happy to stay at the bottom rung of the ladder of life. He actually thought that their son would make them happy—that having a second child made them some kind of family! And perhaps they would have been if he had reached his full potential. But he hadn't—James had lied to her, he had told her he would make something of himself, he had promised her he would give her the world. Instead, he had let her down spectacularly, while her little sister had snagged herself a fucking real grafter. A grafter *she* had actually been attracted to. How was it that fucking Celeste, that fucking stupid, senseless, brain-dead idiot, was swanning around with Jonny Parker, like she was important or something. Celeste! Who was another fucking moron, who had the brains of a gnat. Who had no personality to speak of and no looks either really. Nothing to write home about anyway.

Cynthia looked in her bedroom mirror. She saw herself as a stranger would see her, looked at herself without any bias whatsoever, and she knew she still looked good. She had been lucky—most women after two children looked exactly like they had given birth to two children. She didn't; there wasn't a mark on her. That pleased her, because she knew that she would have to look around at some point for another husband.

Because there was no way she was going to stay in this marriage, no way she was going to waste herself on someone as pathetic as James.

34

CHAPTER TWELVE

Celeste was happier than she had ever been, since Jonny had asked her to marry him. And it was obvious to anyone who knew her. She was genuinely thrilled at the direction her life had taken. As she looked at Jonny sitting at her mother's dining table, she felt the happiness well up inside her. Her love for him was so strong it was as if she could hold it in her hands.

She knew that Jimmy was thrilled for her; he was a really nice man, too good for her sister of course—not that she would ever say that out loud. But Cynthia somehow made you think awful things about her. It was as if she was only there to make you dislike her. She dumped her children here, at her parents' house, for weeks at a time. Not that she minded; in fact, like her mum and dad, Celeste actually felt happier when the kids were there, because Cynthia didn't seem to care about them really.

Now, though, as they all sat around the table for Sunday lunch, Celeste suddenly felt sorry for Cynthia, and that was a new experience for her. She had always felt she was beneath her elder sister somehow, because in many ways she was a hard act to follow. For a start Cynthia was movie-star beautiful, a head-turner, a real stunner. It had been difficult to grow up in her shadow, a watered-down version of Cynthia. People had often pointed out her sister's lovely face and perfect figure, and they had never realised how hard it had been for *her*, because no one ever talked about her in that way. It was as if, to them, she didn't exist. But, in fairness, she had understood why they had singled Cynthia out.

Things were very different now. With Jonny loving her like he did, and her life being so tremendous, Celeste felt for the first time ever that she could pity her sister. Because, no matter what, she knew that Cynthia wasn't happy at all, she was desperately *un*happy, and that saddened her. At the end of the day Cynthia was still her sister, she was still her flesh and blood. And she *did* want her to be happy. She wanted her sister to be as happy as she was, she wanted her sister—just once—to have a smile on her face that wasn't forced.

As Celeste looked at Jonny and saw his handsome face beaming at her, as she looked at little Gabby, all nervous twitches and tension, she wondered how anyone could give birth to a child, and not care for them in any way. It was clear to her suddenly that her sister didn't care about anyone, least of all her little daughter.

'What you thinking about, Celeste?' Cynthia's voice was low, but the question was serious. Everyone around the table went quiet, each interested in the answer.

Celeste shrugged nonchalantly, embarrassed as always to be the centre of attention. 'Nothing really, Cynth, nothing you'd be interested in anyway.'

Cynthia grinned then. 'Listen, Celeste, an original thought in your head would die of fucking loneliness.' She laughed at her own joke, a loud, harsh laugh.

Celeste couldn't help herself. She said loudly and honestly, 'If you're not careful, you're the one who'll die of loneliness, Cynth.'

Cynthia looked around the table, and she saw the shock on everyone's faces at her sister's words, a shock that was quickly followed by genuine laughter, and she knew then what they really thought about her.

'That told you, Cynth! The truth hurts, girl, don't it?'

Her father was looking at her with such loathing it made her realise just how disliked she actually was in her family. It was a real shock for her because she had been under the impression that she was better than them somehow, and she had believed that they had thought that too. She glanced at her husband, and saw the triumph in his eyes, even though he wasn't looking directly at her, and she knew then that, if she wasn't careful, she would be sidelined by this sister of hers.

She was the elder sister, *she* was the one who had dragged herself out of this dump, and *she* was the one who had bettered herself. And she would carry on bettering herself, because there was no way she would settle for anything less than the best.

CHAPTER THIRTEEN

'Oh, for crying out loud, James, are you stupid or what?'

Jimmy looked at his wife and wondered, not for the first time, how he had ended up tied to a woman who he had nothing at all in common with. In fact, he knew somewhere in his heart that she had nothing in common with anyone else in the world. She was a one-off, a complete enigma.

37

No one liked her. Once that had saddened him, he had thought she was misunderstood and seen her as someone he could protect. Now, though, he knew that if anyone needed protecting it was him— him and his children. He had married a bully, an emotional bully, and he could no longer pretend otherwise. The last few months had shown him what his life was really like, and it wasn't pretty. He had finally admitted to himself that he *had* no real life, nothing even remotely resembling one. All he had was Cynthia and her wants and her moods. She had taken away everything from him: his dignity, his self-respect, his children.

He was also not blind to Cynthia's reaction to her sister's husband-to-be. Cynthia was almost ill with jealousy at Celeste's obvious happiness and, even though he hated his wife at times, hated her for her coldness and her complete disregard for everyone around her, there was still a part of him that longed for her to love him. Look at him in the way she looked at Jonny Parker. But he knew it would never happen.

They lived in this expensive mausoleum, and the saddest thing of all was that this house, which he had bought because she had loved it so much, was now her prison. They couldn't sell it, couldn't make their money back—she had spent so much on it that to try and sell it now would mean they would be thousands of pounds out of pocket. The expensive kitchen, which he had known at the time was too good for a semi-detached house in Ilford, had been paid for with what amounted to a second mortgage. When you added in to all that the carpets, curtains, the fitted wardrobes, the bathroom with its cast iron bath, and the new central-heating system, they

38

were up to their eyebrows in hock.

'No, Cynthia, I ain't stupid. I *was* stupid, though, when I let you borrow money like it was going out of fashion. But I wanted *you* to be happy, and *you* were only happy when you were spending money. Well, we can't sell this drum and make a profit on it because the designer kitchen and bathroom that cost the national debt hasn't actually put a fucking bean on this place! It's still just a semi in Ilford, in Essex. *And* we still have to pay it all off. So, thanks to you, and your fucking wanting, we'll still be here when we're fucking seventy.'

Cynthia looked at her husband, and she felt the hatred rising up inside her. She looked at his weak features, his pale eyes, nondescript brown hair and his doughy body. She'd thought him handsome once. Now all she saw was that he was useless, useless and weak. She felt like her life was over. She had tied herself to a man who would never ever be even remotely important to her, or anyone else for that matter. She had two children, children who had half of this man inside them, children who, if she wasn't careful, would grow up to be as useless and nondescript as he was.

'We're insured, aren't we? I made sure of that much. Use your fucking loaf for once in your life!'

Jimmy looked at his wife and felt overwhelmed with despair. Life could not get much worse, surely? His children lived at his mother-in-law's and his home was a permanent battleground because his wife no longer hid her disdain for him. He was earning a good wage, but it still wasn't enough for what they owed. He had allowed her to do what she wanted, and he had stood back while she sunk them further and further into debt. He had not been man

39

enough to put his foot down—in fact, he had not even thought about curbing her spending. But, now she knew he wasn't on the fast track, now she knew he wasn't going to become the boss of bosses, she treated him like dirt. Like he was nothing. And it hurt.

CHAPTER FOURTEEN

'Oh, Celeste, you'll look stunning in that, babe. I'm so proud of you.'

Jonny was thrilled at his fiancée's choice of dress for their engagement party. It wasn't cheap but, in fairness, it wasn't really expensive either. It was just like Celeste in many respects—quietly beautiful.

'Do you like it really, Jonny?'

He grinned happily at her and she caught her breath. He was so good-looking, with thick dark hair, and dark blue eyes, well built and always well dressed. Celeste wondered every day how she had been lucky enough to catch his eye.

Gabby grabbed her hand and she laughed delightedly. 'Don't worry, you. You'll be the chief bridesmaid.'

Jonny picked the little girl up, and threw her into the air. Gabby screamed with delight and, as he placed her back on to the ground, she said happily, 'Can I live with you two when you get married?'

Celeste looked into Jonny's eyes and she saw the sadness in her own mirrored there. She knelt down and hugged her little niece tightly. 'You can stay with us any time you want, right?'

Gabby nodded seriously, understanding that she

wasn't being invited for any real length of time. But already in her short life she understood that people came and went. And often let you down. One thing she had learned was that everyone eventually let you down, *that* was real life, that was how it all worked. But it hurt her, because she would love nothing more than to become a part of her auntie's life. She would love to be a part of something that she felt would last for a long, long time.

She knew her daddy loved her, but he never came to get her any more from her nana's, and her mummy *never* came to see her, never gave her the time of day.

It was as if she had done something wrong and her mother was punishing her for it. But she hadn't done anything—she had tried her hardest to be a good girl. She tried everything in her power to make her mummy want her again, but nothing had worked in any way, shape or form. It was hard for her, because she didn't know what she was supposed to do. She didn't know *how* to make her mummy love her. She didn't know why she wasn't wanted by her mummy.

Her nana loved her, of that much she was sure. Because, no matter what happened to her, she always ended up back at her nana's, which was strange because, according to her mummy, her nana's house was a filthy shithole that she wouldn't let a dog live in. Gabby supposed that was why she couldn't have a puppy, though she would love one dearly. Her nana's house wasn't clean like her mummy's, but it felt better than her mummy's house because she didn't have to be on her best behaviour all the time. And the nicest thing of all was she never wet the bed at her nana's. Her granddad said that was because she could kip in peace without her mummy watching her every move. Her granddad also said that her mother was a stuck-up bitch, who needed a right-hander, and that her dad was a lovely bloke but he needed to toughen up and stop letting his old woman walk all over him like a second-hand carpet. He was funny, her granddad.

As she saw her auntie smiling and laughing, she felt warm inside. She loved her auntie Celeste, and she loved her uncle Jonny, and she wondered why her mummy didn't like them very much. She had the idea it was something to do with Uncle Jonny. Her mummy always tried to get Uncle Jonny's attention, but she guessed that, like most people, he didn't want anything like that from her. She could understand it too—*she* didn't like being in her mother's eyeline either because all she did if you were was moan and complain.

Gabby pushed away the thoughts that troubled her and tried to bask in the sheer happiness of being with her auntie. So many of her thoughts worried her, and she didn't know how she was supposed to make them go away. As she forced a huge smile on her lovely face she suddenly felt the urge to cry, because times like this, the really good times, only made her more aware of the sadness inside her, the sadness that was always there.

'You all right, sweetheart?' Celeste knelt before her little niece and, seeing the tears in her eyes, she said brokenly, 'What are you crying about, you silly mare? You're with family, darling, family who love you.'

But Gabby couldn't tell her auntie that *that* was what was wrong with her. That was why she felt so sad. With this part of her family she felt loved and cared for, and she was always terrified that one day this would all stop.

Gabby realised then that she didn't want to go home ever again. She was far too happy here.

CHAPTER FIFTEEN

'You're not taking them, Cynth, and that's that.'

Cynthia looked at her father and sighed heavily. They all knew she had no intention of taking her children home with her. This was a game they played all too frequently; Cynthia faked a maternal interest and her parents pretended to talk her out of taking her children home with her. It was tedious, but they all saw it as a necessary evil. Cynthia could go back home content in the knowledge she had done her bit, and that her parents would be heartbroken if she removed the children from their care. It was a win-win situation as far as she was concerned.

Mary joined in the argument. 'I'm taking Gabby to the market with me tomorrow, and then we're going to get her fitted for her bridesmaid's dress. So it's not convenient really, unless you want to take her to that?'

Cynthia shook her head as if her mother had asked her to do something completely outrageous. 'No, thanks! Like I haven't got enough to do!'

This was another part of the pretence; that Cynthia had a busy life, that she was somehow too busy to do the usual things other women did like take her daughter for her fitting for her bridesmaid's dress. And yet this was the woman who wouldn't get a job if her life depended on it.

'They're all right here then, Mum, if you're sure.'

Mary Callahan barely kept the sarcasm from her voice as she replied casually, 'Oh, I'm sure, Cynth.'

Cynthia looked around the home she had grown up in, at the scuffed paintwork, and the old-fashioned wall-paper, and shuddered inwardly. How had these people spawned her? It was a question that had always baffled her, and always would. All her life she had wondered at how she had been brought up in this dump, and yet had somehow known the proper way to dress, eat and live. Her childhood had been all slapdash; it was beyond her how she had grown up so refined. She believed that somewhere, way back in the bloodline, there must have been someone just like her and, generations later, she had been the recipient of those good genes.

Cynthia looked at her daughter and saw her own beauty reflected in her face. She was a good-looking child, true, but she was too much like this lot. Happy with nothing, happy to eat crap and spend her life watching telly.

It even smelled, this house—all overflowing bins and dirty ashtrays, washing-up and bacon sandwiches, everything she had hated growing up here. It never changed—the smell of her father's work shirts and her mother's cheap perfume seemed to permeate the very walls. And then there was the gas fire that popped all night long, leaving its residue on the walls and the doors, the constant noise of a radio or the TV, no real conversation unless it was about someone they knew, never about what was going on in the world. It was like

44

being caught up in a soap opera, except the people in the soaps had personalities—this lot had nothing of any interest going for them at all. Her mother was bad enough. She spent her whole life smoking her fags, drinking her tea and living for the next episode of *Coronation Street*. Her mother knew more about Emily Bishop than she did about her own family.

And now her sister was lording it up with a man who was a right Face, and a right earner. It was so unfair. If only she had used her loaf, waited a while, kept her options open. But, back then, she had been so *sure* about James. Now look where she was; stuck in a vicious circle of debt with two kids hanging round her neck. If James had kept his part of the bargain she would have had a nanny, or at least an au pair, to take the brunt of the work off her. She closed her eyes in frustration. She had to work out a way to get rid of the house and still come out quids in. Once she sorted *that*, they could get back on track. If she left it to James, they would still be in that dump of a street when they were drawing their pensions—if she could stand him for that long.

Now, here was Celeste, about to hitch up with a man who was obviously going places. It was like a kick in the teeth.

Her father lifted his leg and broke wind loudly, and she pursed her lips, knowing it was for her benefit. Her father enjoyed her discomfort at what she regarded as common behaviour. If she wasn't going to be so busy the next few days she would take Gabriella home with her just to teach him a lesson.

'Here, Cynth, do you want to stay for your tea?

45

Jonny's coming round, and Jimmy Boy could come here as well. Be a nice family get-together.'

Her mother was smiling as she said it, and Cynthia realised that she genuinely meant it. Still, she was going to refuse because seeing Celeste and Jonny together made her feel even more depressed than usual.

'I would, Mum, but I've made arrangements . . .' Her voice tailed off and she forced a smile. 'Maybe another night, eh?'

Mary nodded, wondering why she had bothered asking Cynthia in the first place. Mary Callahan could see that this daughter of hers was eaten up with jealousy about Celeste and Jonny, and she also knew why, though she wouldn't bring it up in front of her husband. He'd love to go on about it, to use it as another stick to beat his daughter with. It was strange really because Cynthia had always been his favourite—until she was about thirteen. Then the fastidious ways that they had laughed at and her determination to act like the lady of the manor had ceased to amuse them. Jack had suddenly realised that his daughter was ashamed of him. Not only that, but she also despised him. Despised them all and wanted to be nothing like them. She had only stayed a Catholic because the nuns had beaten the religion into her, and it was the one thing she knew would cause a complete break from her parents. Jack Callahan was a lot of things, but he was a devout Catholic and there was no way he would countenance his daughter turning her back on her faith. And Cynthia, for all her airs and graces, was secretly frightened of having this front door closed on her once and for all. Mary could see that. And, deep down, she needed them more than they needed her.

Cynthia saw a momentary flicker of sadness on her mother's face, and stood up to put her coat on; she didn't want or need her pity. Just because she wouldn't settle for less than what she deserved didn't make her a bad person. In Cynthia's book it made her a winner, a fighter, a survivor. A council house and making do would never be her life, she was determined about that much anyway. She would sort out their financial problems, and put all this behind them.

When her mother left, Gabby sighed deeply. Her mother could even make the air seem heavier with her presence, but Gabby hadn't understood until then the force of certain people's personalities.

She was beginning to understand that only too well now.

CHAPTER SIXTEEN

Jimmy was tired and it showed. A lot of it was to do with being married to Cynthia; she had worn him down to nothing. It saddened him that none of his friends visited any more. Cynthia could cook a beautiful meal, pour them good wine, but her very nature stopped people from wanting to be in her company for any length of time. She only bothered with people she thought were class, with people she thought were a cut above. Unfortunately, those were the very people who saw through her like a pane of glass, much quicker than her own kind anyway. She was neither fish nor foul as his old grandmother used to say. She didn't really fit in

47

anywhere.

Now, as he sat in the warmth of a pub in Dean Street, he wondered why he didn't come here more often. It was a great place, full of people, full of laughter. He was with Jonny Parker and his cronies and he was having a really fantastic time—he liked Jonny, and he liked Jonny's mates. He couldn't understand Cynthia's almost pathological hatred of him and all he stood for. Jimmy knew Jonny was a bit of a lad, but that was *his* business, certainly nothing for him to concern himself with. He swallowed another Scotch, and felt the warm glow as it hit his empty belly.

'How you doing, Jimmy Boy?'

Jonny was smiling at him, but Jimmy could feel his concern.

'I'm all right, Jonny, just thinking, mate. Drink can do that to a body.'

Jonny sat beside him and, leaning across the table, he grabbed his own drink and sipped it. Lighting a cigarette, he casually waved towards the bar for another round of drinks. They appeared only a few minutes later. Jimmy was very impressed; it was as if Jonny owned the place, and that's how it had been all night long.

'Here, Jonny,' said one of his mates, 'you heard about Black Micky?'

Jonny nodded and said nonchalantly, 'He knew the score. I warned him, but he wouldn't listen to me. He'll get an eighteen if he's lucky.'

The other men at the table all nodded sagely, the conversation had suddenly turned serious.

'His old woman's to blame,' someone else pitched in. 'Fucking want, want, want. She could spend money like a fucking Russian oligarch, or

48

whatever they're called! That's what alerted the Old Bill—fucking BMWs outside the front door, the kids in private school, and him without a legal fucking earn to his name. Got to attract the wrong attention.'

Jonny nodded once more. 'I told him five years ago when he was first on a good earn—I was working for *him* then, I was only a kid meself—but I said to him, buy a few houses, rent them out, get a shop or a café, something to look like you're grafting. But you know him, thought he was sorted because he had a few Old Bill on his payroll. It was the serious crime squad who gave him the capture, not local fucking plod.'

Jimmy listened in amazement at the men's conversation.

'The SCS are all over the place lately. Someone, some-where is earning a fucking wedge of some description from them, either getting a pass for their own dirty dealings, or picking up a serious rent. Either way, there's skulduggery afoot.'

Jonny laughed nastily then. 'Well, whoever it is, I wouldn't want to fucking be in their boots when it all comes floating to the top. And it will. You can't get away with that for any length of time. Someone will stumble eventually, that's the law of the streets.'

Trevor Carling, a small, dark-haired man, with eyes that were a deep violet-blue, leant forward and said conversationally, 'I hope I get first fucking refusal on the cunt. I'd keep him screaming for days—within the hour I'd have the ponce praying for a quick death.'

All the men laughed now, and Jonny grinned as he said, 'Fucking hell, Trevor, you'd grass your own

49

granny if she owed you a fiver!'

Trevor laughed good-naturedly then, lightening the mood once more as he said, 'Nah, I love me granny and she's too intelligent to borrow money from me in the first place!'

Jimmy sat back in the chair, shocked at the conversation around him, and frightened now of the men who had welcomed him into their company and who he had liked and admired only a few minutes before.

Jonny saw the way Jimmy was reacting to their banter and he put an arm around his shoulders. Then, winking at the men around him, he said loudly, 'Enough! This is my soon-to-be brother-in-law, and he's straighter than a copper's parting.'

Trevor leant towards Jimmy and said with a chuckle, 'Oi, son, remember the old wartime slogan, careless talk costs lives!'

It was a serious warning, and Jimmy knew it.

'He won't say a word, he's sound is Jimmy.'

Jimmy saw that, with those few words from Jonny, he was accepted without a murmur. And he also thought he understood now why Cynthia had such a problem with her sister's intended. Jonny Parker was going places, and even Jimmy, who was as green as the proverbial grass where the criminal life was concerned, could see that much. It was also obvious that Celeste would be going with him, and that must be what was really causing Cynthia sleepless nights.

Jimmy knew then that Jonny Parker wouldn't be getting an eighteen any time soon. He was too shrewd for that. Jimmy also knew that he liked him, even if those last few moments had surprised him. Still, whatever he might be, Jonny Parker was a nice bloke.

CHAPTER SEVENTEEN

'You all right, Jimmy Boy?'

Jonny Parker was laughing as Jimmy emptied his stomach into the lay-by. He rubbed Jimmy's back and, when the retching eased off, he opened the boot of his Mercedes and got out a bottle of water.

'Here y'are, mate, get that down you, you'll feel better.'

Jimmy drank the cool water gratefully. 'I don't drink that much normally.'

Jonny laughed delightedly. 'I should fucking hope not and all, your liver must be praying for a transplant.'

Jimmy smiled and Jonny wondered at how this big man, who was a lump in many respects, had lumbered himself with someone like Cynthia. But he knew the answer to his own question; Cynthia was a looker, and she had that stuck-up way about her that attracted men. Jimmy had fallen for her, just as many a man before him had fallen for a prize bitch; it wasn't till they were safely married that they showed their true colours. Jonny should know—his own mother had been a ball-breaker, and his father, a Face in his own right, a hard man, had still never been hard enough to put her in her place. She had dripped her poison in his earhole all day, every day and, eventually, that kind of treatment could bring down even the toughest of men. This poor sap didn't stand a chance.

Jimmy sat on the kerb and took a few deep

51

breaths; the world was finally coming back into focus, and he was grateful for that much at least. 'I really enjoyed tonight, Jonny, but I think the strippers had best be kept a secret if you know what I mean!'

'Well, I won't be broadcasting it to the nation, mate. Celeste is an easy-going girl, but she ain't that easy going!' Jonny lit a cigarette and pulled on it deeply before settling himself beside Jimmy on the dirty kerbside.

'She's a lovely girl, Celeste, you got a good one there, Jonny.'

'I know that, wouldn't be marrying her otherwise.'

Jimmy sighed heavily. 'She's kind is Celeste, very kind-hearted. My Gabriella loves her, which is just as well, because she spends more time with her than she does with her mother.'

Jonny could hear the bitterness in Jimmy's voice, and felt ashamed for the man's weakness. 'Well, Jimmy Boy, that's not really any of my business, is it?'

Jimmy shook his head; he appreciated Jonny's tact, but the drink had taken its toll and he wanted to talk to someone. *Needed* to talk to someone, say it all out loud, and he knew that Jonny would listen and not hold it against him.

'I know that, Jonny, but tonight I realised how much I've lost out on. You lot together, having a laugh, a few drinks. I miss that. Not that I ever did anything like tonight, but I used to meet the blokes after work in the West End, you know. Not any more, though, Cynthia has me on a bloody schedule. She knows my movements better than I do, plus I'm not running the firm, not even going upwards if truth be told. I haven't got what it takes for the office politics. I congratulate men younger than me when they get promoted over my head. My kids live at their grandparents' house. Not that *my* parents ever get a look in with the kids—they've never been allowed to see them. I just don't know how this all happened to me. I don't know how to make it all right.'

Jonny threw the cigarette into the road, and immediately lit another one. He was genuinely sorry for the man, even though he couldn't help feeling that the situation was all of his own making. Having been brought up by a woman who was like Cynthia, having seen the damage someone like her was capable of causing to the men who were unlucky enough to love them, he could understand the man's predicament. And he had been on the receiving end of Cynthia himself, when he had been enamoured with her and her lush body for a while. But, unlike James Tailor, he had seen her for what she was before it was too late. His father's example was always with him, and he knew that a big part of Celeste's attraction was that she was the complete opposite to Cynthia. He knew that with her he wouldn't have to fight for supremacy in the relationship; all he would have to do was love her and take care of her. That would be more than enough for her, and she would be loyal to him till her dying day.

'Look, Jimmy, I know the score, but you have to sort this out yourself. You have to put your foot down, let her know who's boss.'

Jimmy laughed then, and it was almost as if he really found the conversation hilarious. 'Easier said than done, Jonny! She has this knack of saying

53

things in such a way you have to believe she's in the right. We are in so much debt, she spends money like it's going out of fashion and, when we discuss it, *I* end up feeling like *I'm* the one who's in the wrong. She convinces me that it's not *her* getting us into the debt in the first place that's the problem, but it's *my* inability to pay said debts which is.'

Jonny knew exactly where Jimmy was coming from; he could write the script. 'Well, Jimmy Boy, you either sort the debts out, though in my experience she'll just run up more, or you put the foot on her neck and rein her in once and for all.'

Jimmy didn't answer him.

Then Jonny said quietly, 'There is a third option, Jimmy.'

Jimmy looked up. 'What's that, Jonny?'

'You could do a bit of moonlighting. You're good with other people's money, and I could do with a creative accountant, if you get my drift?' As he said it, Jonny could have kicked himself. He blamed it on the whisky. Scotch always made him sentimental.

'Really, Jonny, could I make decent money from it? I mean real money?'

Jonny realised he had just answered this man's prayers. And ruined him into the bargain. 'If you can hide a good percentage of my earnings and still make it all look legit, you'd be an asset, mate. But before you go making any quick decisions, remember that you'll be breaking the law and if we ever get a capture you could go down for it. You'll be expected to keep your trap shut, and do your time without a whimper to anyone, especially not the Filth. I work for some very heavy people, so think long and hard about what you'll be getting

54

involved in. Because if you step out of line, you'll be wiped off the face of the earth. Family or no family connections, you fuck up and I'll come after you meself.' Jonny hoped this advice, delivered with a threat and a promise of trouble to come, would be the decider for Jimmy Tailor, and make him see that this wasn't the life for someone like him.

Jimmy, though, saw this man as a saviour and saw the chance of a good earn doing what he was good at—working with money. Jimmy, in his desperation, believed that if he worked for Jonny Parker nothing bad could ever happen to him. After all, he would only be keeping the books, it wasn't as if he would be a real part of the business. He conveniently forgot about the conversations he had heard earlier in the evening, chose to forget that those were the very people whose money he would be responsible for. All he could see was a way out of the enormous debt they were in, and the look on Cynthia's face when she realised he had finally sorted it out.

'Thanks, Jonny. But I don't need to think about it. I'd be honoured to come and work for you. You won't regret it, I'll work my fingers to the bone . . . Twenty-four seven if needs be.'

Jonny held his hand up to stop the man's excited chatter. It occurred to him that Jimmy was not exactly *au fait* with what the job actually entailed, and he also knew that he would have to test the man's abilities before he gave him any kind of real money to work with. 'Hang on a minute, Jimmy Boy. You have to keep the day job, mate, that will be your blind for the future. Mr Respectable and all that. You'll do my number crunching in your spare time and keep it under your hat—don't even tell

55

Cynthia until it's a done deal. I'll take you on trial for two months to see if you can do the job how I want it done, and to see if you can handle what the job entails. That way we can both decide if it's not what either of us want, OK?'

Jimmy nodded then as if he finally understood the situation, and Jonny Parker wondered how the fuck this idiot would cope with the stress that this new world he was becoming a part of would inevitably place on his rounded shoulders. But the damage was done now, and all Jonny could do was make sure he kept a beady eye on the situation.

As if he didn't have enough to fucking do.

CHAPTER EIGHTEEN

1988
Cynthia was beside herself with annoyance, but she held her temper as she had learned to do over the last couple of years. Seeing Celeste with her detached house and her flash little sports car was bad enough, but that contented smile that was always on her moon face was the real bugbear.

Cynthia had finally got herself and her family out of the house in Ilford—and she had made sure they made their money back on that place. *Not* that she had ever told anyone the long and the short of *that* story—even that prat James was still none the wiser where that was concerned. He wasn't capable of understanding her logic. Also he was like all villains and, when all was said and done, he *was* now a villain, albeit a minor one. He believed you should never publicly break the law. It brought the

Filth down on your head, and made them look at you a bit closer than you'd like. And, though they weren't exactly rolling in it, they were in a much better financial position than they had thought they would be—all thanks to her, of course. That prick would have sold at a loss, and they would never have got out of the debt. But, seeing how they were now getting an extra few quid courtesy of Celeste's husband, the high and mighty Jonny Parker, she had to watch herself these days and it was getting harder and harder to keep her opinions to herself.

Now, as they walked into the restaurant for another expensive party, to celebrate yet another feather in Jonny Parker's cap, Cynthia felt she could easily scream in utter frustration.

She caught a glimpse of herself in a mirror, confident she was easily the best-dressed and the best-looking woman in the place. That wasn't difficult—the competition wasn't exactly Crufts standard. She smiled at the simile. She could stop an articulated lorry in its tracks when she was wearing the right top and the right make-up. Yet she knew that to Jonny Parker she might just as well be invisible. He spoke to her, he was polite to her, but she knew that he didn't see her in any way that meant anything.

She, on the other hand, was always conscious of his presence; and he had just that—presence. It was no wonder he was doing so well in his chosen field—men as well as women were drawn to him. He was charismatic, dangerous and he knew the score better than the people around him. It was the one thing she could never get out of James, because no matter how much she kicked off, no matter how much she created, he would not, under any circumstances, tell her the extent of Jonny's businesses. In fact, he told her absolutely nothing. He was another one getting too big for his boots; since he had started working full time for Jonny he was getting far too clever for his own good.

Cynthia sat at the table beside her sister, aware that she looked much better than her, and the knowledge was like a balm. She saw a lot of the men giving her the once over on the quiet. She was wearing a plain black silk dress that had looked like a rag until she slipped it on, and then it hugged her ample curves in such a way it was almost obscene. But that was the whole point of it; she acted as if she had no idea of the way she looked, and she enjoyed the way the women reacted to her even more than the men. She knew they all envied her— two kids and she still looked better than any of them. She smiled tightly as her sister poured them both a glass of white wine.

'What do you think of Jonny's restaurant, Cynth? It's lovely, ain't it? Really upmarket.'

Cynthia nodded and forced herself to answer her sister. 'Beautiful, Celeste, really smart.'

Celeste knew that her sister was putting on an act, but she didn't mind; after all, this was preferable to her causing murders, and Cynthia was more than capable of doing just that. To Cynthia, a good fight was all in a day's work, and it was wearing at times. Celeste was a great believer in a quiet life. She could never understand her sister's need to make everything a drama. She had a mouth on her, and she knew how to say things so they were not just hurtful, but also seemed to hold a modicum of truth. That was how she justified what she said. She was a hard task-master—she could destroy a person's reputation with her insinuations.

She was vocal in her opinions on how kids should be brought up, and how women should act as mothers and wives, even though she never bothered with her own kids. She had an opinion on everything and everyone, yet she couldn't see herself clearly or how people perceived her. If Cynthia only knew how disliked she was by both women and men, she would be genuinely surprised—not that she had ever cared what women thought of her, Celeste knew. But she was aware that her sister assumed every man she encountered found her as fascinating as she herself did. She loved herself all right, and it was a shame that love didn't extend to the other people in her life. Maybe then she would be a happier person. Still, Celeste was shrewd enough to keep those thoughts to herself; she knew that everyone liked her because she didn't express the majority of the thoughts that came into her mind. She had learned very young that it brought you nothing but grief.

Cynthia, on the other hand, saw it as her God-given right to tell it like it is in a vicious and demeaning way. Cynthia didn't care if someone took it badly; she loved upsetting people, loved the negative vibe she created wherever she went. But it left a bad taste in everyone's mouth, and Cynthia was now basically *persona non grata* with just about everyone in her orbit.

'I wouldn't eat here if you weren't my sister, to be honest. It's a bit ostentatious for my liking.'

Celeste replied amiably, as always, 'Well, people seem to like it, Cynth, so I think we'll do all right.'

Celeste smiled as she spoke, and Cynthia felt the rage at her sister being the beneficiary of all this money and kudos. As the wife of a man of means she would always be afforded a great deal of respect, and it was that respect Cynthia wanted more than anything else. It was that respect that would have afforded her the life she felt she deserved, the life she should have demanded. But all she'd been given was boredom, a firm belief in the power of a good insurance policy and hope for an early death for the fucker she'd lumbered herself with. If it was left to her, James would have a massive heart attack and she could start all over again. Properly this time, and with the hindsight she wished she'd had at the outset.

'Well, Celeste, people always want what's new and different, although it soon wears thin. Still, in fairness, he's done a good job.'

The naked envy was evident and Celeste felt a deep sadness for this sister of hers who, if she would only relax and stop wanting the impossible, could enjoy her life like everyone else. Celeste smiled once more and suddenly hugged her sister to her. She said happily, 'Thanks, Cynth. If you like it then it must be good!'

Cynthia preened at the praise and, feeling magnanimous, said kindly, 'You're getting there, Celeste, so don't let it bother you too much.'

'I won't. Thanks for coming, mate, it means a lot.'

Cynthia was thrilled at how her sister saw her as the yardstick for her husband's new enterprises. It was another balm to her tortured soul. She felt she should be the one enjoying all this, not her younger sister. If only she had seen the truth of the situation years ago, she wouldn't have let him go, whatever the circumstances.

It never occurred to Cynthia that her sister was actually in the know where all that was concerned. Celeste was clever enough to keep that information close to her ample chest. Jonny had never said a word—he wouldn't, he was too nice a person—but she listened to gossip. It *had* bothered her that her sister had been there before her, but now she knew, deep inside, that Jonny loved her, *really* loved her, and she was woman enough to accept the truth of that. She only worried that her sister would find out that she actually knew the score, and thereby feel the humiliation of realising that Celeste knew and didn't care. With people like Cynthia you told them what they wanted to hear, because it was so much easier that way. If they ever saw themselves as everyone else did, it would be too much for them to take onboard. They lived in their own little worlds, it was what made them into the people they were.

Jonny Parker walked deliberately to the table that held his lovely Celeste, as always feeling the pull of her. She was worth fifty of any other woman in his world.

'You enjoying it, babe?'

'Oh, Jonny, it's wonderful.'

He looked into Cynthia's eyes as he said seriously, 'She chose all the décor, what a star, eh?' Tonight he wanted to get his first conversation with her out of the way, and he wanted it to be in front of his Celeste. He had nothing to hide and he wanted to make that plain.

Cynthia smirked as she answered him. 'That explains a lot, Jonny.'

The insult was clear and he knew it. More to the point Celeste knew it but, as ever, she chose to ignore the implication. Jonny loved her for her kindness and the fact that she only ever saw the good in everyone, including that ponce of a sister.

Cynthia looked at Jonny with her heavily made-up eyes; she could eat him as he was. Every time she saw him she could kick the fuck out of herself. What she could have had was evident in every move he made. She wanted him more than ever. If she had only known he would have achieved what he had, and in such a massive way, she would never have let him slip away from her. Unfortunately, she had believed he was no more than a fucking wanter, she had never believed he would be a getter. Just proved how wrong a girl could be. But Cynthia wasn't going to give up—she still believed she could change the future, and she wanted Jonny Parker back badly. She felt that if she fought hard enough she might just get him. After all, what was she up against? Her sister Celeste wasn't exactly a hard sell where she was concerned. She was a prat, and a prat of the first water.

Jonny watched the thoughts flicker over Cynthia's face and he could read her mind. He had no intentions of giving this vicious bitch what she wanted, what she expected. True he had felt something for her once, well, her body at least—that had been spectacular and what she had promised him and eventually delivered had been the best of the best. But it had not lasted. She had expected too much for far too little. She had been a great fuck, but even then that was only because he had been her first, and *that* had only happened because she had wanted what she *thought* he might have to offer. Cynthia was like a robot, she would fuck a table if it got her what she wanted. And, as luck would have it, he had realised that

62

about had some kind of basis in fact.

As she looked around her, saw the people fawning over her sister and Jonny Parker, she was already wondering how she could bring them down and, more importantly, when.

She knew she could easily take them out without a second's thought if she opened her mouth to the right people, at the right time. She didn't know enough yet. But she would, eventually. She would bide her time and she would learn what she needed to know. And then bring them down she would, if it was the last thing she did in her life.

CHAPTER NINETEEN

'Stop it, Cynth, we're earning a good wage. He gives us more than anyone else would.' Jimmy watched as his wife rolled her eyes dramatically and shook her head in abject disbelief.

'Huh, only you would say something that fucking stupid. *They* are the ones on a good earn, not us! They are making fucking mugs of us. You might be content with fuck-all, but I'm not.'

Jimmy looked at his wife and, for the first time in years, he knew he had to fight her, had to make her see sense. He knew that if he wasn't careful she would queer their pitch once and for all. This had been coming for a long time, and he knew he had to nip this latest tantrum in the bud. She was getting too outrageous even for him. If only she could understand their world like normal people, but he knew that was never going to be the case. So now he had to finally stop her in her tracks.

Jonny Parker had already said as much and, in fairness to him, he had a point. Cynthia was a liability, and he knew that better than anyone. She had a trap that was dangerous, she never knew when to *shut the fuck up*. He also knew that if he didn't sort her out then Jonny would have to make sure someone else did the dirty deed. They were all in it up to their necks, and he had no interest in being sidelined because his wife was a loose cannon.

'We are on a seriously good earn if only you would see that. We get a percentage of everything, Cynth. Where else would we get that, eh?'

Cynthia laughed derisively as if he was a complete fool, then shouted angrily, 'Oh, have a day off, James, will you, for fuck's sake! You're such a mug! We're not earning fuck-all in comparison to that lot, you're a fucking joke . . .'

'Don't, Cynth, not tonight, don't start now . . .'

Cynthia was shaking her head slowly and deliberately as if she was in the presence of the greatest moron since Benny off *Crossroads*. But Jimmy shook his own head then, and she suddenly realised that she was pushing him too far. Looking at him now, his face contorted with anger, his heavy body taut with rage, she saw that her constant criticism had finally hit home. He looked menacing and dangerous; after all, he had had a good teacher and she forgot at times how his life had changed. He was playing with the big boys now and picking up their bad habits. He was looking at her with distrust, with an anger she didn't know he possessed. He looked capable of anything, and she knew it was in her interests to leave it for a while. That she should temper her barbs, not make her anguish so plain.

After all these years she understood that she had finally pushed him too far. For the first time ever she actually felt afraid of the man she had married, felt the strength of him, saw the anger in his eyes. In fairness, she knew he was providing for them more than adequately, not that she would ever tell him that, of course. But that was not enough for her, would never be enough for her; she wanted what her sister had. The lion's share was all she would ever be content with, was all she would ever accept. Even she admitted to herself that at times her jealousy got out of hand, but she couldn't help the feeling that life was pissing on her from a great height. That seeing that mousy little sister of hers getting one over on her was all she could ever think about. She should have been the one to have achieved it; she had more brains and more savvy than Celeste would ever have. It was unfair, it was so unfair. Not that he would ever understand that, of course.

But as he looked at her now, disgust and dislike in his eyes, she knew they had somehow crossed a line. Never before had he fronted her up like this, it had always been the other way round. Something had given him some courage that he'd never previously had, and she had a suspicion what that something was.

'You, calling me stupid?' he said. 'You, who wouldn't know how to earn a crust if your life depended on it? *You*, who can't even bloody get yourself together long enough to take care of your own kids! *You* dare to question me, and what I do for this so-called family?'

She didn't answer him, didn't know how to.

'I fucking get up and go out twenty-four seven. And do you know what? *That's* why Jonny looks after us, you stupid mare. He offers me a taste, a bit of what he's doing and I am thrilled to take it. Because without him we'd be scratching a living, like we were before. So you had better wind your fucking neck in, shut your trap and be grateful for what you have got, instead of constantly harping on about what you think you *should* have. I've had it, Cynth. I've had you and your fucking wants till I'm dizzy.'

Cynthia looked at her husband in complete amazement; if someone had told her he would turn on her like this she would have laughed in their face. But she shouldn't have been so shocked; she had watched him getting too big for his boots, saw him blossoming as he became more and more successful in his chosen field. She had seen him become a man of renown almost, knew he was respected because he could hide a few quid from the tax man and the law. Now it seemed he thought he was better than her, the mother of his children. She also suspected that he had acquired a habit of sorts—a severe case of the sniffles. In fact he was often assaulted by a case of Colombian flu. She was pretty sure her goody-two-shoes husband was a bit of a cokehead.

Oh, how times changed.

'You can't talk to me like that! I won't swallow *you* of all people treating me like a fool.'

Jimmy laughed then and, pushing her backwards on to the sofa, he said seriously, '*Fuck you*, Cynth, do I look like I care what you think these days? I'm over you and your viciousness. You bring my kids back home or you can fuck off. I've had you up to

68

my eyebrows. You're a vindictive cunt, and a bully. But I ain't swallowing no more, so you better sort yourself out.'

Jimmy couldn't believe what he had just said, let alone that it was to Cynthia! All the things he had dreamt of saying he had finally said. He knew it was because he had partaken of a few lines of cocaine. Lately he had found that he liked the way it made him feel. He didn't care what anyone thought of him after a few lines, and he felt invincible. He felt that he could do no wrong. He also knew that if Jonny Parker found out about it he would go ballistic. Jonny didn't like drugs, especially not in his personal circle of friends; he might sell them of course, and in large quantities, but that was just business as far as he was concerned. As long as Jonny didn't know about his newfound habit, Jimmy knew he was OK. He also knew that his wife, who he still loved after everything, was a woman who needed a serious slap. And, if she wasn't careful, the chances were she would get just that. He had had enough, in more ways than one.

Cynthia realised that it was not in her interest to pursue this conversation, and her instincts were telling her it was much better to retreat on this occasion. But she knew that if her husband had access to drugs—and he had to be on drugs otherwise he would never have dared to say the things he had—it was something she could use against him in the future. Oh, he was on the old Persian rugs all right. And he had been on them for a while. That had to be something to do with Jonny Parker and, as such, she knew that it could only be to her benefit in the long run. She would dig and dig until she found the truth, and then she would use the knowledge to her advantage. She had access to James's clothes and his wallet. Sometimes it was so easy, all you had to do was sit back and wait. Eventually it just came to you, without any real graft.

Her sister thought that her life was so fucking special, so fucking great. Well, Cynthia could end it with a phone call. One call and it would be over. That knowledge alone made her feel so good.

CHAPTER TWENTY

'Well? What's happening then?'

Mary Callahan was annoyed. She hated this weekly argument—Cynthia acting like she had arranged to take the children out for the afternoon when everyone knew that was never going to happen. Cynthia never had the kids for more than a day, and even then it was as if she was doing them a favour in some way. She couldn't cope with both her children for more than a couple of hours anyway. She palmed them off on her parents with a relief that was almost tangible.

But today Cynthia seemed determined to cause some kind of aggravation, it seemed as if she had an agenda, and it was not the first time she had acted this way in the last few weeks. It bothered her mother. She knew this daughter of hers better than anyone else. In many ways she hated her daughter if truth be told. She knew that Cynthia was capable of great hate, and great treachery. She also knew that Cynthia was not averse to using her children to get what she wanted. She had been doing that since

70

they had been born. But lately she wouldn't trust her daughter with anything—she knew that there was a hidden agenda, there was *always* some kind of hidden agenda with Cynthia. This time she knew exactly what that was.

'Look, Mum, if you don't want them, I'll take them back home with me . . .'

Mary was already holding her grandson in her arms, and her granddaughter was clasping her around her legs. She knew she was never going to let them leave now.

'I never said that, Cynth, did I? But you seem like *you* don't want to leave them.'

Cynthia sighed heavily, rolling her large blue eyes, and Mary Callahan saw just how lovely her elder daughter really was. And it hurt her, knowing that this beautiful girl had no real care for anyone in the world, least of all her two children. And they needed her. James Junior had developed a bit of a temper lately. Every time Cynthia left the kids behind he threw a tantrum.

'Oh, Mum, I'm worried that's all, I know they are safe with *you*.'

Mary didn't react to her daughter's words, but she could hear the drama in them. Instead she said to her granddaughter, 'Come on, you, let's go and see Granddad.'

Cynthia looked at her mother and said seriously, 'Is that it, Mum? Are you not going to listen to what I've got to say?'

Mary looked into her daughter's eyes and said quietly, but seriously, and everything she really thought about her elder daughter was there for anyone to hear, 'No, Cynth, I'm not, and neither is your father or anyone else. The Old Bill has told

71

Jonny about your little chat, and they have decided to overlook it. But I'm warning you now, girl, you've crossed the line. You want to be a grass you do it on your own because none of us are even remotely interested. In fact, if you were anyone else you'd be dead. So you listen carefully, and you listen good. You've gone too far this time. I wouldn't start celebrating just yet, if you get my drift.'

Cynthia walked from the house without another word. For the first time ever, she didn't know how to react. She knew she had been rumbled and she was frightened—she knew she had gone too far. Her hate had caused this situation. She had hoped Jonny and his cronies would all be taken away, so she never had to look at them again. She had tried to bring them all down, had tried to make them all see how vulnerable they really were. But instead she had found out how deeply entrenched they were with the police, and now she finally understood how dangerous a position she was in. She had wanted to take them out, her husband included—*especially* her husband if truth be told— but now she knew she had no chance of making that happen. They were involved in some deep shit, and she knew exactly how deep that shit was. So she'd told the Filth all she knew—for a price, of course. Instead *they* had served her up, the *Filth* had served her up like a fucking sacrifice. She would never get over the fact that the people who should have been hanging on her every word, who had been given the information they'd need to bring down some serious crooks, had turned it all around and had left her hanging in the wind, at the mercy of the very people she had tried to bring down.

She was now an acknowledged grass, a woman

who would never be trusted again. Someone who would be a dead body if her sister had not been Jonny Parker's other half. She knew that she was tainted, knew that she would have to really prove herself at some point and, worst of all, she knew that she had brought this on herself. She was a jealous, vindictive bitch. She knew that better than anyone. But everyone around her knew that too. And that really irked her.

She felt sick with apprehension and she realised that feeling would never leave her.

CHAPTER TWENTY-ONE

'You've asked for it, Cynth, all of it. You would have taken us all out—even me. Or should that be *especially* me?'

Jimmy Tailor had long ceased to be in awe of his lovely wife's tongue. Since she had brought the Filth breath—ing down all their necks, he had been decidedly rude where she was concerned, and with what he thought was good cause.

Cynthia put on her best, please-why-don't-you-believe-me voice as she said sadly, 'Look, James, I believed at the time I was doing it for the best. You were taking cocaine like it was going out of fashion! I was worried about you . . .' Cynthia was still trying to prove herself a year later, but she wasn't making any kind of inroad and they both knew it. 'I just want what's best for my family. I know you don't see it that way, none of you see it that way . . .'

'Oh, change the record, Cynth! Like you ever cared about me, or anyone come to that.'

Jimmy was fed up with her. He was already putting on his jacket, and she knew he would be out of the house having a good time while she sat here alone wishing she could be a part of it all once more. She was desperate to be a part of it, if she was really honest with herself. She needed some serious brownie points to get herself back in with the big boys.

'I was frightened for you, James, whatever you might think . . .'

Jimmy rolled his eyes in annoyance. 'You nearly fucked us all up. You know what you did and you also know if it wasn't for your sister you would be dead.'

Cynthia had tried to get the sympathy vote from her husband, but it wasn't working. In the last year she had been treated as a pariah—in fact she had hardly left the house. Watching her back had become part of her daily routine—even Celeste had given her the cold shoulder. The worst of it was she missed her sister. She actually physically missed her. Who'd have predicted that? When all was said and done, Celeste had always been there for her, and it had taken a year of being blacklisted to make Cynthia realise that.

In that year, her sister and her husband had become the local celebrities, always in the local papers, opening a new boxing gym, or attending a charity auction. They were like the poor man's Burton and Taylor. Cynthia understood that if she had not been so vindictive, she would still have been a part of that. Would still have had some kind of a real life. She missed the social aspect of it all, missed the nights out, the reflected glory of being Celeste's sister. If only she had understood then how lucky she had been.

To compound all that, James was doing really well. They were living better than ever before, and she knew that she was walking a thin line with him. She still didn't understand why he had never left her—even she wouldn't have blamed him if he had.

It never occurred to her that he might actually love her, care for her as the mother of his children and as his wife. All she saw was that James was loving his new role in the family set-up. He was the main breadwinner, but he was also finally the head of his own household, as hard as that was for her to admit. He came and went as he pleased now.

Cynthia couldn't kick up too much fuss—she needed him these days, far more than she had ever thought possible. In fact, it was outrageous just how much she now needed him. She had played a hand that she had believed was a winner only to find out it was the opposite. The Old Bill had listened to her and then served her up without a second's thought for her welfare. She should have guessed that Jonny would have them in his pocket; he was too shrewd not to.

If Cynthia had achieved her objective, her sister's husband would be banged up now for the duration, and she would have felt a distinct satisfaction about that. She would have watched them fall, and from a fucking great height at that. Instead, she had inadvertently sabotaged any kind of life that could have come her way. She had, in effect, chewed her own foot off, because she was paying a terrible price for her treachery.

Celeste, in fairness, *wanted* her to have nice things, *wanted* her sister to have money in her bin and Celeste, most of all, wanted her to be content.

As if she could have ever accepted that, especially coming from her of all people! But now, though, Cynthia knew she had to make some kind of amends, she had to prove herself worthy in some way. And she would do just that. She had to put herself on the line, make sure she was seen as a person of worth—not to the Filth, but to her sister and her sister's husband.

It was all that was left to her.

CHAPTER TWENTY-TWO

'Have a guess who I just saw?'

Jack Callahan shook his head, uninterested in his wife's yammering.

'Shaw Taylor, that's who.'

Shaw Taylor was the star of a programme called *Police 5* from the early sixties, where he would ask the public nicely to grass up various members of their families or their communities. Shaw Taylor was also the nickname they'd given Cynthia since she had caused all the trouble a year before. If she knew she would be mortified.

'Was she on her way here?'

''Course not, she would have been here by now, stupid. She was going into the train station, so I assume she's going up west.'

Jack Callahan didn't answer; they all knew she didn't shop or go anywhere local any more. Her name was a byword for treachery and so it should be. Every time he thought of what she had done he felt a murderous rage that he had fathered her. If she wasn't so like his own mother in looks he might

76

have accused his wife of all sorts after his daughter had grassed everyone within her orbit. That she was capable of something so fucking heinous, so disgusting . . . He shook his head once more in absolute disbelief.

'Poor old Celeste. She still feels guilty about it—after everything she still tries to make excuses for her sister.'

Jack Callahan didn't even bother to reply; Cynthia had been nothing but trouble since she could open that big painted trap of hers. He didn't want her anywhere near him now. As long as she left the kids here regular like, he couldn't give a toss whether he ever saw her again. Good job she didn't know what was going on now, or they'd all be up shit street. His son-in-law Jonny was coining it in, and sailing a bit too close to the edge, even by his standards. Truth be told, even Jack was getting a bit shirty at the lad's audacity. But Jonny seemed to know what he was doing. He had a knack for skulduggery, and he had the sense to temper it with legitimate enterprises, so he could at least explain where the houses and cars came from. But sneaking over to South London was a daring little escapade, and it could cause nothing but grief to everyone concerned. Not that anyone involved seemed to be bothered about that. It was as if the old standards had died, and anyone who still believed in them was classed as a dinosaur.

Well, maybe Jack *was* a dinosaur, but he felt that the old guard, with their boundaries and their guidelines, had it right. You can't go around taking other people's earns without a fight, no matter who you were. It was the principle of the thing. He had a bad feeling about these new premises. The men on the receiving end of Jonny's new enterprises would not take it lightly, he knew that much.

Jonny Parker was a clever boy, and Jack thought the world of him, but he believed he had crossed one too many lines with this latest rigmarole. Bloody drugs, they caused no end of trouble, whether it was for the dealer or the buyer. Look at Jimmy, he was snorting up that white powder like his life depended on it. Although living with that fucking daughter of his, he could feel sorry for him in many ways. But drugs were drugs, and Jack didn't like them, and he didn't like the mayhem they caused for all concerned. But he would keep his own counsel for now and see what occurred. The problem was, his Celeste was in the firing line if it went tits up, and that was what was really worrying him.

In Jack's day, there was honour among thieves, as much as that sounded like a contradiction in terms. Not any more though—now it was every man for themselves. And Jonny Parker wanted it *all* for himself, every pavement, and every earn.

It was nothing more than a recipe for disaster.

CHAPTER TWENTY-THREE

Jonny Parker was not as worried as he probably should have been, and that fact pleased him no end. He was taking a big chance and he knew it; he was putting his life on the line. But if he didn't do this, he knew he would regret it one day. He had always gone with his instincts and they, so far, had never let him down. He could only hope that this was another one of his more lucrative ideas.

His instincts now were telling him the time was right. It worked on paper, admittedly, but paper never allowed for the reactions of the people involved. He was *always* wary of the reactions to his more outrageous business enterprises. But, where this one was concerned, he would do murder if necessary, because he was determined to see this one through to the very end.

He was a much harder fuck than people realised. But after this next coup—and it was a very audacious and dangerous scam—his real intentions and his real personality would be known to all and sundry. He had bided his time, and this was the moment he had been working towards. If he was honest, he was still a bit nervous about it but, as far as he was concerned, that nervousness was all to the good. It would ensure he didn't take anything for granted. Didn't let his guard down. It was when people became too sure of themselves that they tended to make mistakes, and he had no intention of fucking this one up.

'You all right, Jonny?'

Celeste looked worried, and he forced a smile of nonchalance on to his face.

'I'm fine, sweetheart, just thinking that's all.'

Celeste grinned then. 'You're always thinking! What's on your mind, mate?'

He cupped her face in his hand, amazed at the force of the love he felt for this woman. 'Nothing for you to worry about. Now are you sure you'll be all right tonight? I won't be out longer than necessary, I promise.'

'Stay as long as you want. I'm going round me mum's anyway—she's got the kids.'

79

Jonny grimaced and the look made her grin again.

'She's always got the fucking kids!'

Celeste was serious suddenly. 'Not any more. Be fair, Jonny, she doesn't have them half as much as she used to.'

It amazed him how this woman—because she was a woman when all was said and done, despite her childishness and her naivety—could still stick up for that sorry excuse of a sister. But, as his old mum always insisted, blood was thicker than water. Bollocks of course, but women seemed to think it was a valid excuse for their family's treachery and skulduggery. Personally, he thought her sister should be six feet underneath a golf course somewhere. But that was only his opinion and, where her piece of shit of a sister was concerned, his wife was not going to listen to any arguments he might put forward, no matter how valid they may be.

'I'll retreat on this occasion, darlin', because I don't want to row about it. She ain't worth rowing about, is she?'

Celeste shook her head, but he knew she was upset.

'So I'll see you later then, eh?' He kissed her and, as always, she responded to his embrace with all her being.

'I'll hold you to that!'

When the door shut behind him, Celeste sat down and lit a cigarette from her secret stash. Jonny hated her smoking, but she needed it to calm her nerves. She knew something big was going down tonight, and she feared in her heart that it was something that could go very, very wrong. She trusted Jonny, but she knew he was taking some big risks these days—at least as far as her dad was concerned he was, and her dad wasn't a spinner. If *he* was worried, there was something to worry about. Her dad might not be the sharpest knife in the drawer, but he heard anything that was worth anything, and her husband should listen to him now and again. In fact, he ought to understand that he *should* listen to the truth sometimes even if he wasn't in the mood for hearing it. She felt personally that it was always worth a quick listen to the local gossip. Nine times out of ten, they knew more than the Filth ever would and even more than the people involved in a scam. Gossip was a serious thing where they came from; it was the forerunner to a serious nicking. If it was known outside their workforce, it was dangerous to everyone involved. It meant that it wasn't as secret as they all assumed. In fact, it meant it was common knowledge, in the public domain, and that meant that someone in his personal circle had a big mouth and that big mouth could cause more fights than John Wayne. She couldn't talk to her husband about any of this because he saw local gossip as nothing more than fabrication, stupidity and idiocy. Those being his exact words.

Celeste loved her husband more than life itself, but she knew he wasn't exactly kosher. In truth, she knew a lot more than he gave her credit for. She also understood what he was capable of, and that frightened her. Not for herself—he would never hurt her, of that she was sure. But he was capable of murder, she had no doubt about that at all.

She smoked the cigarette with shaking hands. Tonight was going to be a long one.

CHAPTER TWENTY-FOUR

Jonny Parker was excited, but the excitement was tinged with worry. He might be a Face to be reckoned with, but he knew he was dealing with people who would never give him a second chance if he didn't achieve his goal straight off. And the goal was to get what they had; he wanted every bit of it. He was legitimate enough to pass off his affluent lifestyle as above board. He also had a cache of fall guys who worked for him, unaware that if it went pear-shaped they would be the ones in the frame. That was the brainchild of his dear brother-in-law who, if it ever did go off, would be the first one nabbed by Lily Law. Jonny had enough safety features in place to keep himself out of stir. What he *didn't* have, at least not one hundred per cent, was the guarantee that he wouldn't be taken out before he achieved the more outrageous of his goals. But he was a planner and he was a plodder in many respects; he waited and he watched, and he thought through his business moves with precision. Still, you always had to allow for eventualities, such as the people you were dealing with being a bit fucked off that you were intending to wipe them out. That tended to give people the raging hump.

Jonny was respected for doing the majority of his dirty works himself; that was so people knew what they were dealing with. He never left a trail though, he was far too shrewd for that. But tonight was about some serious money, and meant having to cross some serious people. He was confident he could make the transition from supplier to managing director with no real trouble. If he took out the main men, he was laughing all the way to the bank.

It was the taking them out that was the tricky thing. Taking them out and making sure the people who worked for them understood the economics of the deal. After all, his education had taught him that as long as people earned, they would happily work for whoever provided that earn. They lived in a Thatcherite society; you give me a good wage, and I'll swallow my knob and work for you instead. It was the way things worked now. It wasn't the sixties any more, and the sooner people realised that, the better off they would all be. It was like living in a fucking bubble; the old values were all right in their day, but this was the eighties, and anyone with a sawn-off and a few quid could walk in anywhere and get a decent hearing. The days of gentlemen villains was long gone; they were banged up, and wouldn't see the light of day until the fucking Jews returned to Zion, that's how remote their release dates were. They had been put away for the duration, judges had taken it upon themselves to rid the country of some of its best earners. Legal earners at that; for all their skulduggery they had been proper earners as well—good, decent taxpayers. None of them had ever signed on the dole or asked for a fucking handout.

It was a new world, with a whole new set of rules and regulations; the old guard were gone and forgotten. This was really about the survival of the fittest, and Jonny Parker knew he was fitter than most. He was going to play them all at their own game, and they would understand that this was not a dress rehearsal, this was the real thing.

He had planned it down to the last detail, and all he had to do now was make sure it was executed with the minimum of fuss and the maximum of terror. Fear was the best way to ensure the complete devotion of everyone concerned. Fear had its own rewards—that cunt of a sister-in-law had learned that the hard way. Without realising it she had taught him a good lesson: it was the people nearest you who were the real danger. It was something he would never forget. The shock of her revelations to the Filth had made him take a step back and look at his workforce and their relatives very closely. In her own way, that two-faced ponce Cynthia had shown him the chinks in his armour. He had understood then just how easy it was for outsiders to know far too much about his businesses.

Not any more, though. It was now common knowledge that anyone who talked outside of their working circle would be treated with the response that such treachery deserved. Wives and girlfriends were now treated as scornfully as the Filth, were seen to be as dangerous as the law courts. They were not party to anything even remotely pertaining to the business of their husbands or partners. It was working out wonderfully. Jonny told his wife, the love of his life, fuck-all as well. She was a great girl but, like every woman, the less she knew the better.

Tonight he would be well and truly blooded; he was going to make his mark once and for all. He didn't want to do this because it would be bloody and callous and it would become legend. He *needed* to do it because once he had, no one would be in any doubt who was the main earner in the Smoke. Now it was time. Every businessman comes to a crossroads, where they decide what route they'll take—either the easy option (always the less lucrative), or the hard option, where they have to fight for what they really want. Well, he was going to fight, and fight with everything he had. He was going to make sure that no one, no one at all, would be left to queer his otherwise perfect pitch.

This was make or break time, and he was determined to break them, little by little, bit by bit.

CHAPTER TWENTY-FIVE

Joseph Makabele was a large Rastafarian, who had not been near Jamaica even once in his long and eventful life. He was actually a Nigerian, who knew that his heritage would not help him in any way, shape or form. Not in the world of drug-dealing anyway. He knew the real Jamaicans were suspect about him, and that the white boys were even more so. Mainly because they had gone to school with the Jamaicans and the Tobagonians, and every other Caribbean boy in the neighbourhood; he had never gone to school with anyone who was worth anything. He looked the part and he talked the part, but he didn't have the creds.

Joseph knew that meant he would not get the loyalty he needed; people worked for him, but they didn't really trust him. He offered a good wage, but nothing more, because no one knew him years ago and, in London, unless you were able to hark back at least three generations, you were no one.

He understood that now, he also understood that if he didn't win tonight with Jonny Parker, local hero, and all round likeable cunt, he was finished. But he had allowed for something like this, and he was sure he had enough get-out clauses to last him at least one lifetime. Joseph was handsome, he was charismatic, and he could supply enough drugs to keep the whole of the South East high until the next millennium, and at half the usual going price. But he also knew that being the outsider would always be his weak spot.

People in the south of England had a blind spot, and that was for others of their ilk. If Joseph had been born and bred here, he knew he would be all right. But he wasn't, and he also knew that his pretending to be a Jamaican Rasta meant nothing to the people he had to deal with tonight. Jonny Parker was going to challenge him and that, in itself, was a serious challenge by anyone's standards.

Joseph had seen this coming for a long time, but he had hoped, like many before him, that a good earn and good fringe benefits would see him safe. He had played the Rasta man, but it was an act and, deep inside, he was aware that everyone who worked for him knew it.

He was frightened. Tonight was the real deal, and how he reacted to it all would affect the rest of his life. But he was ready for the fight. He had surrounded himself with the best of the best, paid them more than they were worth, and now he had to hope that that would be enough.

He shrugged. He was letting the demons get the better of him, as his old grandma used to say. He wondered wistfully if she was still alive. He had been brought over to England by his mother, who had swiftly abandoned him and, eventually, he had ended up a Barnardo's boy. Another reason he wasn't trusted; after all, if your own family didn't want you . . . Another East-End saying that he had to admit had the ring of truth to it.

He mentally shook himself. He had got this far, and he had the nous and the guts to get wherever he wanted to be. He had told himself that all his life, and it had worked up to now. He reassured himself that he had the right men beside him, and that they were paid enough to ensure their loyalty. That had to mean something. They knew as well as he did that Jonny Parker was not really meeting him to arrange a large shipment of drugs—he was meeting him to tell him that from now on his services would no longer be required. Well, Jonny Parker had a big shock coming to him, and in a way he was sorry about that, because he liked Jonny Parker, he was a nice bloke.

Joseph got into the back of his large black BMW. For protection he had a driver and two outriders, one of whom was his right-hand man, Linford Fargas, who had been his number two for over three years now and was the nearest he had to a real friend. The men were well versed in what they had to do this night, and were well armed.

'Shall I go straight to the depot?'

Joseph nodded almost imperceptibly. 'Is everything arranged?'

The driver nodded, even the back of his head had an arrogant look to it. Like him, the man was black, dread-locked, and spoiling for a fight with the white boys. Joseph felt himself relax. He leant forward and pulled a large machete from under the driver's seat; it would take off a hand or a foot easily, the perfect weapon for incapacitating the enemy. It could also take a man's head off his shoulders if the blow was powerful enough. A machete was the weapon of choice for most of the Yardies except, in England, unlike Jamaica where it was classed as a work tool like a screwdriver or a pair of pliers, it was illegal to walk along the road with them.

'You nervous, Joseph?' asked Linford.

'Not at all. I feel good about it all. This was needed, even I saw that.'

Linford nodded sagely.

'Besides, I'm gonna take that fucker out.'

The driver then laughed heartily, saying loudly, 'A-fucking-men to that! You take the fucker out, boss.'

That caused them to start laughing, but they were all aware it was a nervous laughter. It occurred to Joseph that his men were even more nervous than he was, and he knew he had no choice but to show a true hand to them tonight. Then maybe, just maybe, it might go some way to making them see him as one of them after all. The thought pleased him, and he was glad now that this was happening; it might be just the thing he needed to ensure his place in this London black boy society. All of the men were well versed in the art of fighting, both with their fists and with weapons. And none of them were in the least frightened of guns—they'd been around them for the best part of their lives.

Joseph realised he had been worrying about nothing—in fact he could already taste his victory as he drove into his depot in Croydon. This was where he kept the majority of his arms, this was where he was safest, because only a few people knew he even owned it. That was another thing; he liked to keep his private dealings private, and that could only hold him in good stead at times like these. Only four people knew about this depot, and they were all in this car.

Linford jumped out and opened the gates, unlocking the huge padlock. Joseph looked around the yard and smiled grimly at its sameness. As they drove in, he saw Linford opening the door of the Portakabin that served as his offices. He had a good bottle of Irish whiskey in there, and he was going to pour himself a large glass before setting off for the festivities.

There was still two hours to the deadline, to the meeting with Jonny Parker that would determine the rest of his life. As he put his foot out of the car, it suddenly occurred to him that neither of his other men had moved, but it was only when he felt a boot shove him in the back and saw the dirt floor of the yard coming up to meet him that he realised something was amiss.

Then Jonny Parker was standing over him with a machete that made his own look like a penknife.

'Sorry, Joe, but you didn't honestly think I was going to negotiate, did you?'

The first blow took off the top of Joseph's head; the other blows were entirely unnecessary, but the brutality of the attack was what made the statement for Jonny Parker. When word got out about Joseph's demise, and get out it would, he would be seen in a new and entirely different light, and that is exactly what this whole exercise was about.

Linford Fargas watched the events with a nonchalant air; he prided himself on always backing the winning pony. Truth be told, poor old Joseph had never had a chance. He wasn't fish nor fowl. Now he was nothing.

Linford went inside the Portakabin and picked up his twenty grand—not bad for a night's work. If Joseph had used his considerable loaf and paid out over the odds for his loyalty, he might have been in with a chance tonight.

Now, though, Jonny Parker was king of the hill, and there would be no one capable of stopping him for a good few years. It would take that long for a new little crew to grow and develop, but he had a hunch that Jonny P, as he was now known, would still be a match for them. Jonny had what they called back in Jamaica the devil's want, and he wanted it all. Well, he was welcome to it, and the problems that came with it. Because this first hurdle might be over but he now had to deal with Kevin Bryant, never a man to cross lightly.

But time would tell; by tomorrow night one, or all of them, would be dead. That was Linford's opinion anyway.

CHAPTER TWENTY-SIX

Kevin Bryant heard the news of his business partner's untimely demise with his usual closed features. His expressionless face was his trademark in his world. He never looked angry, rarely looked pleased and had never in living memory laughed out loud at anything. Hence his nickname, Kevin 'No Face' Bryant. He liked the moniker, felt it put him above most of his contemporaries. His countenance, coupled with the fact he never spoke unless it was extremely necessary, only added to his criminal mystique.

His wife Sojin, a thirty-something living doll, told all and sundry that he was a different person at home with her and the kids, that he never stopped talking, but no one actually believed her, much to her chagrin. They thought Sojin was with him because of *who* he was; it never occurred to anyone that she might actually see a different side to him than everyone else. It grieved her that no one saw the ebullient, funny man she loved and adored, because adore him she did. From his size twelve feet, to his balding, endearingly ugly, head.

Kevin's second-in-command, a tall, frighteningly skinny man called Bertie Warner, was trying desperately to gauge his boss's reaction to the outrageous news that Joseph Makabele had been hacked to death by Jonny Parker and the Anthill Mob from Brixton.

'Do you hear me, Kev? They fucking nutted him, he was chopped up like a fucking Friday night fish! Do you not have any interest in what the fuck I am telling you?'

Shrugging disinterestedly, Kevin said quietly, 'He's dead then?'

'Hello, earth to fucking Kevin! He is dead as a fucking dodo! For fuck's sake, *Monty Python*'s parrot has more life in it than him! He's a human fucking paper chase. Get onboard, for fuck's sake!'

Sometimes Kevin's attitude could be severely aggravating, and this was one of those times. Their main supplier was now scattered to all corners of the country, loaded into bin bags and dumped like a fucking treasure hunt for the Old Bill, and here was Kevin unconcerned and, to add insult to injury, not even remotely disgruntled about it.

'He had our protection, Kev, we fucking owe

him, and everyone else who thinks we are watching their fucking backs.'

Bertie was realising how this would look to outsiders; everyone, including that cunt Jonny P, knew that Makabele worked ostensibly for them—it was his ticket to the big time. That meant they had to be *seen* to be doing something about it—otherwise they could kiss goodbye to their stranglehold on South London, that much was a fucking definite.

Kevin shrugged nonchalantly once more. 'And?'

It wasn't a question, it wasn't anything. It was annoying that's what it was. 'And! Fucking "and"? Is that all you've got to fucking say? We are fucking being mugged off like a pair of prize cunts, and all you can say is fucking *and*!'

But Kevin Bryant wasn't listening to his friend any more; he was already planning his next step, and he knew better than anyone that he had to box very clever. If Jonny P had made it this far then he was armed and extremely dangerous. Obviously he was being protected, and he would have made sure that this little exercise was going to work out in his favour. Anger was a fruitless exercise—not that Bertie would see it that way, of course. What was needed now was a long, hard, sensible *think*, and he wasn't going to be able to do that with Bertie wittering on like a fucking old fishwife.

'Bertie.'

'What!'

'Shut the fuck up.'

Bertie did as requested, but he was seething inside. If Jonny Parker was allowed a walk on this kind of calumny then the London they knew and loved would be his for the taking. This was a direct affront to them and everything they had achieved, and if Kevin didn't strike quickly it would be their turn for the machetes next. Fucking machetes! What was wrong with a common or garden sawn-off? Were these people fucking animals or what? Bertie shook his head in utter disbelief at the skulduggery of some people.

Unlike Bertie, Kevin Bryant knew exactly why the man had been taken out with machetes. This was a statement as well as a killing. It was telling him and everyone else that Jonny P had the black vote of confidence. That meant Brixton, Tulse Hill, Norwood, et al, were happy to be on his payroll. He was carving up the city and, in fairness to him, he was doing it very well. Credit where credit was due, he had worked a fucking blinder, and Kevin Bryant admired a shrewd business head. So few Faces possessed one; most were daydreamers who never saw the big picture, were shocked and outraged when they were taken out by a more superior intelligence. Anyone could get a decent earn—it was keeping the fucker that took the time and the trouble. A good earn was like an unfaithful wife; you loved them, you fucked them, but you kept watch on them twenty-four seven. Otherwise they fucked you over in more ways than one.

But Kevin Bryant wasn't finished yet; he still had a few miles to go on his clock, and when he retaliated, he would retaliate big time. But it had to be perfect, it had to be well planned, it had to be executed with the minimum of fuss and the maximum of aggravation. He could put on a show as well as the next man, and he was determined to do just that.

CHAPTER TWENTY-SEVEN

Jonny P was euphoric. He had taken out Joseph without any real resistance at all. But that was all well and good—now he had to either take out Bryant completely, or try to negotiate some friendly terms with him, whatever seemed the most viable option.

Personally, he felt it was best to take the man out. Kevin was a loose cannon. He was a hard fuck in his own way, and that was to be taken into consideration. No one *ever* knew what Kevin Bryant was thinking, so it was difficult to negotiate with him. No one played cards with him any more either, he had a legendary poker face. Years ago, Jonny had watched Kevin take a twenty-grand pot on a ten high. He had also been playing those cards with some very naughty boys, the very same bad boys they had both overtaken on their quest for the pavements of their youth.

It was important to run your own neighbourhood. It meant a loyalty that was almost guaranteed, providing, of course, you looked after your own, and they had both done just that. But, whereas Jonny was a likeable fellow, Kevin Bryant wasn't. Respected, yes, but liked? That was a different kettle of fish altogether. No one approached Kevin, he wasn't that kind of bloke, whereas Jonny was accosted wherever he went. He always made sure people had a few quid in their bins, and was known for paying for the endless rounds of drinks his hangers-on and supporters expected. He mediated between warring factions, and was known to give out rough justice to the less salubrious of his neighbours—burglars, nonces, liars and the like. He was a hard taskmaster with his workforce, but paid them well, and they understood he would not, under any circumstances, tolerate bullying, thieving off him or their own and, most importantly of all, he would not countenance slackness in either word or deed. He paid well, and expected the best they could offer him, and he saw to it that he got just that.

But this latest deal he was going after was as audacious as it was dangerous. It could either bring him untold riches, and untold power, or it could mean he was on his last few hours on God's good earth.

Jonny took a deep breath and exhaled slowly; he had read somewhere that it calmed the nerves and, despite appearances, he was actually as nervous as fuck. He looked up as his new best friend and confidant on this latest scam, Linford, walked into the small office quietly.

'Any news?'

'Not a fucking murmur anywhere on the pavements. News has got round, of course—you're the hero of the hour. No one liked Joseph anyway. But nothing yet from Kevin Bryant and nothing from his mouthpiece Bertie.'

So they were scheming, and that was to be expected. Jonny nodded and sipped at his whiskey. They had paid off the best part of Bryant's workforce, guaranteed them a bigger and better earn and, more to the point, they had put the fear of Christ up half of London with their antics this night. He had done all that could be done.

He could hear the riotous laughter coming from

the pub he owned on the Mile End Road. He was surrounded by his best workmen and his most trusted friends. They were tooled up and ready for anything. All he could do now was wait, and he had a feeling on him that the wait was going to be a short one.

Kevin Bryant was a lot of things, but a mug wasn't one of them.

CHAPTER TWENTY-EIGHT

Bertie was fast getting the raging hump.

Kevin was so laid back he might as well be in a fucking coma for all the good he was doing at this moment in time. Bertie's old woman had made more noise in the sack and that was saying something. His Deirdre was a lovely girl, an exemplary mother, and an all-round decent bird, but she wasn't exactly what you'd call a live-wire in the fuck department.

Bertie, on the other hand, was a doer by nature; if anyone fucked him over, he done them, simple as that. It was a credo he had lived by and which had kept him alive and kicking this long in a very dangerous game. All his instincts were telling him to go after Jonny P mob-handed, guns blazing, pickaxes swinging, and maybe even a few fucking machetes thrown into the mix just for the irony factor. And that was exactly what he was going to suggest to Kevin. He couldn't sit here like a fucking Victorian mistress any longer. It was, in effect, doing his head in.

Bertie liked Kevin; he probably knew him better

than anyone else, and he respected him, and saw his good points as well as the bad. But this fucking silence was deafening; he could almost hear his own brain turning over, and at every little noise he expected to be overrun by a mob wielding giant machetes.

Kevin was watching Bertie placidly; he knew exactly what was going through his mind and, in a way, he could sympathise with him. Bertie didn't have the patience of a three year old, and when a bit of chastising needed doing he was the man to call on. Unfortunately, he had the brains of a fucking gnat and, whereas Kevin had never been that loquacious, Bertie could talk for England. He never shut his fucking trap from the minute he got up till the moment he fell into a fitful sleep. Kevin would like to bet he was still talking even then.

'Get your coat.' As he spoke he stood up and his considerable bulk seemed to fill the small room to capacity.

Bertie smiled, this was more like it!

In the small outer office of his scrap-metal yard, Kevin opened the arms safe and, taking out a semi-automatic he had purchased from an old acquaintance, he proceeded to arm himself to the hilt.

'Shall I call the boys?' The excitement was already overflowing in Bertie's voice. He was thrilled at this turn of events; there was nothing he liked more than a good tear-up, a serious fucking straightener was always something to be enjoyed. Violence as far as he was concerned solved *everything*, there was nothing like a good fucking tear-up to sort out the men from the wannabes.

Kevin shook his head. 'Not yet. Make a cup

of tea.'

CHAPTER TWENTY-NINE

Jonny was half-pissed and he was annoyed with himself because of it. But it had been a very strange night so far, and he knew that if his calculations were correct it could only get fucking worse. Much worse. He glanced at his watch—it was twenty past one and no news yet. But there was plenty of time; he would sit and he would wait. He could feel the sweat trickling down his back, and he wondered at how this night would eventually pan out.

Linford had poured himself a large brandy, and he downed it in one gulp. 'I needed that, bwoy,' he said, reverting to his Jamaican patois.

Jonny grinned. 'You're about as Jamaican as I am fucking Irish.'

Linford laughed happily, he knew the truth of that statement. 'I left Jamaica as a baby. My mother came here looking for me father—she still hasn't found the bastard. But I grew up in a Jamaican household and, believe me, that's as good as being brought up in the home country. A bit like the Irish, eh?'

They laughed together, pleased that the change of topic meant that they were not waiting in silence any more.

'Very much like us actually. I feel more Irish than English at times. Catholic school will do that to you.'

Linford nodded sagely. 'That's the truth.' He took a ready-rolled joint from his jacket pocket and lit it ostentatiously, as only a true Rasta could. Toking on it a few times, he breathed the smoke in deeply before saying seriously, 'You know you've got to kill him, right?'

Jonny sighed deeply before he said sadly, 'Knew it from the off, mate.'

Linford grinned through the thick blue smoke. 'You know it makes sense. He can't be left standing, he's too proud a boy. Eventually he would have to come a-knocking.'

'Shame though, Linford. I always respected Kevin Bryant.'

Linford shrugged. 'Don't mean he ain't a bad mother-fucker. Mark my words, you don't cancel him out this night, he'll just wait for his opportunity. Stands to reason. Now Bertie has to go either way—holds too many fucking grudges for his own good, that one.'

Jonny didn't answer; there was nothing more to say, the decision had been made.

CHAPTER THIRTY

Celeste felt ill with worry, and couldn't settle at all. Why she had come to her sister's she didn't know— she just supposed that at certain times in your life, you needed your own. Even with family like hers. She couldn't go to her mum's, what with her father muttering away about Jonny's front and her mother offering endless cups of tea. Instead, she had found herself on her sister's doorstep.

Her sister seemed both amazed and pleased to see her, that much was obvious, even at this late hour.

'Oh! Hello, sis.'

Cynthia had taken to calling her 'sis' and it sounded more false each time she heard it.

'All right, Cynth? I thought I'd pop in and give you a quick hello.'

Cynthia's eyes said 'not at this time of night you haven't', but she didn't question further. Instead she said brightly, 'Come through to the kitchen, I'll make a cuppa. Or I've a nice bottle of wine if you'd prefer that?'

Celeste followed her sister into the pristine kitchen and asked frankly, 'Got any vodka?'

Cynthia turned to face her sister and, smiling sadly, she said sympathetically, 'That bad?'

Celeste nodded.

Cynthia responded, 'That's why I'm still up and about too, James is on the missing list as well.' She poured them both large vodkas and, gulping deeply from hers, she grimaced in a comical manner before saying, 'I know you can't tell me what's going down, but I can guess from the fact you're here it's important. I know I done a wrong one, but it was only because I was frightened for James. He's a cokehead, you know that, don't you?'

Celeste didn't answer her, she didn't know what to say.

'He snorts it up like it's going out of fashion—out of his nut most of the time, he is. Now I know better than anyone that I'm not the greatest wife, or mother come to that, but I was jealous of you, and frightened for him. Does that make sense? I know now that what I did was wrong, was disgusting, and I'm paying the price for that. But you're still my little sister and I can see you're not right. You

100

can confide in me if you like, or we can just sit here and talk about nothing. It's your call, Celeste. Either way, I'm here for you, OK?' It was said with honesty and humbleness.

Celeste knew that her sister really meant what she was saying. Her time in the wilderness had obviously hit her hard, but she knew what Jonny would say if he ever found out she'd told Cynthia *anything*. 'I can't talk about it, Cynth, I wish to fuck I could. But I just *can't*.'

Cynthia plastered a smile on her lovely face and said in a resigned manner, 'Fair enough. We'll talk about something else. Have you seen the dresses in that new shop in Ilford? I treated myself the other day.'

Smiling gently, Celeste listened as her sister prattled on, grateful for her company, and glad that they were back on some kind of even footing. But the worry was still there, and she wondered when this bloody night would ever end.

CHAPTER THIRTY-ONE

Bertie was getting worried. He couldn't track down anyone of note on his payroll. He realised after the second phone call that they had been poached. All the minions were available, but the real deals, the hard men they relied on to administer their commands, were nowhere to be found. At first he had refused to believe it, hadn't wanted to doubt that he had their loyalty. Now, though, it was an absolute certainty and he felt the unfamiliar feeling of dread lying in his stomach like lead.

Kevin wasn't as surprised as Bertie; he knew that everyone had their price, and that no one was really a hundred per cent loyal—not in their game anyway. Everyone wanted to play for the winning side—that was human nature. But he was a bit fucked off that it had been done so easily and so sneakily. Neither he nor Bertie had even sniffed anything untoward going on, so that showed it was well planned and had been well executed. It also told him that they were on a losing streak. They had one chance to rectify this situation, and that was by taking out Jonny P once and for all. This was no longer just about revenge, it was about absolute survival, and that put a completely different complexion on things. This was now a fight to the death. And it was going to get dirty, very dirty indeed.

Kevin looked at Bertie Warner and he could see the fear and the disbelief in his eyes. Bertie had always believed that their blokes were sound, were unwavering in their loyalty.

'He's done us up like kippers, Bertie. We have to accept that. But if I'm going down, then I'm taking something of Parker's with me.'

Bertie had never seen Kevin Bryant look so human in his life, and that worried him. For the first time in living memory he could see emotion on the big man's face. But it was his friend's words that really chilled him. He knew that Kevin, like himself, was not going out without a fight, and that was something he could understand.

'I'm right behind you.'

CHAPTER THIRTY-TWO

'Thanks for coming home with me, Cynth. I know it's silly but I get nervous here by meself.'

Cynthia didn't answer her sister. Instead she busied herself making a pot of tea. She wanted to be seen to be the administering angel when her brother-in-law arrived home. She wished she knew what was going on, but she knew better than to ask too much about it. If she played her cards right, she could at least start to get back into the family and their way of life.

That Celeste was this anxious told her that something big was going down. For the first time that night she wondered if her James was involved. She hoped so—whatever it was would be a big earn. All this worry wasn't for a lousy couple of quid, of that much she was sure. Her quick brain worked out that it had to be about taking something from someone—that was the only way a true Face could go forward in life. It was how you spread your workforce and made sure everyone was getting a nice earn.

Cynthia was a born criminal. She had the innate cunning needed for the job, and she also had the hard core inside her that was necessary when the time came to take out those who had outlived their usefulness. She didn't know that, but her instincts were nearly always spot on. Except when she was blinded by jealousy—then her instincts risked being overpowered by revenge. She had a taste for revenge, she had since a small child. In a man these would have been traits that could have taken her to the top of her game; in a woman they were seen as a weakness. Men in her world believed that women were ruled by their hormones, and they could never respect a creature that had no real will of their own—it was as simple as that. Yet Cynthia knew she was ten times more intelligent than most of the men in her orbit, especially her ignoramus of a father, and that imbecile of a husband she had tied herself to.

As she looked round her sister's home, saw the luxury and the expense, she could once more kick herself metaphorically in the head. This could have been *hers*, this could have been *her* life. This *should* have been her life. Because, all that apart, Jonny Parker was the only man to ever ring her bells. When he had taken her she had finally felt whole, poor James couldn't compete with that. No man could compete with that. She had chosen respectability and where had that got her?

She had imagined herself presiding over dinner parties, where her James, not Jimmy, *James*, would bring his minions, and she would patronise them while stunning them with her food and her witty repartee. Instead she had chosen a man who couldn't decide whether to wear a tie without a fucking twelve-day postmortem on the subject.

She closed her eyes in anger and frustration. She hated her life so much, and the fact she had been the instigator of her own downfall was doubly frustrating.

Cynthia took the teapot to the table, and looked at her little sister. She was all eyes, all big blue eyes and anxiety. Even in her anger she felt a stirring of pity for her. 'He'll be OK, Celeste, stop worrying.'

'It's three in the morning and not even a phone

call.'

Cynthia sat down and sighed heavily. 'James does this all the time. It's the nature of the game, nightclubs are called nightclubs because they are open at night!'

Celeste smiled then. But she was still guarded, not saying anything that might give the game away. But Cynthia acted as though she didn't care about any of that and was once more the solicitous sister.

'Shall I make you a bit of toast? You need to eat, love.'

Celeste shook her head. 'I couldn't, Cynth, thanks.'

'How about a biscuit? You always had a sweet tooth.'

Celeste stood up abruptly. 'Did you hear that?'

'What?' Her sister's panic was spreading to her now.

'That noise, there's someone outside.'

'You stay here, Celeste, and don't move.'

Cynthia walked silently from the big kitchen and checked all the downstairs rooms. As she looked out of the front-room window, she saw a large man walking towards the front door. Running back to the kitchen, she said to her sister in a whisper, 'Get down to the cellar. Don't argue, just go.'

'What's going on, Cynth?'

After dragging her sister none too gently, Cynthia pushed her into the back kitchen and, opening the cellar door, forced her inside. Following her, she bolted the door and groped around in the gloom till they reached the bottom of the steps, where they crouched as quietly as they could. It was almost pitch black, the only light coming from under the door above them.

'Is there a torch anywhere in here?' Celeste was clearly terrified now. Shaking her gently, Cynthia whispered, 'For fuck's sake, Celeste, is there a torch in here?'

Celeste walked unsteadily to a row of shelves and took down a small hand torch. Giving it to her sister, she waited like a young child to be told what to do next.

Turning on the torch, Cynthia looked around the unfamiliar space and, seeing a door that was obviously once the coal hole, she went towards it and made sure it was secure.

By now they could hear people walking around above them. It wasn't Jonny that was for sure—they could hear the doors being wrenched open upstairs, and they both realised that whoever it was wasn't visiting for any kind of social reason.

'What's going on, Cynth?'

Celeste's voice was rising and Cynthia went to her and said quietly but forcefully, 'Shut up, Celeste. Whoever it is mustn't know we are here, OK?' But even in the weak torch light Cynthia could see the hysteria rising in her sister's eyes and marvelled once more at how such a fucking coward could ever be enough for Jonny. She hugged her to her tightly saying in a soothing voice, 'Calm down, Celeste, we'll sort this out. Now, has Jonny any weapons hidden down here?'

Celeste was shaking so badly she could barely talk. 'I . . . I don't know . . . Probably . . .'

Cynthia looked around the large room and, spotting a large steel trunk, she went over to it. There was a large padlock protecting the contents. She sighed heavily. Looking round again, she grasped a large spanner from one of the shelves and attempted to break the chain with it. It was a fruitless exercise and the noise would alert them as to their whereabouts, but she tried anyway.

She could hear the men at the cellar door now, and she knew that the still-warm teapot would tell them that they might still be in the house somewhere. And now they knew where. She guessed they had come through the French doors in the lounge; they wouldn't risk the neighbours hearing them kicking in the front or back doors.

The cellar door was another thing altogether though. It was well inside the house, and they were now kicking at the lock with a ferocity that told her they would be through at any moment.

Celeste was crying openly—she wasn't even attempting to be quiet any more. Terror had taken her over and Cynthia knew that if they were to get out of this it would be down to her. Panic rising inside her, she gave the locked box one last wrench and, even though it didn't open, she saw that if she lifted the lid there was a four-inch gap—just wide enough to get her hand inside. She did that and, feeling around, she gripped the first thing that came to hand. A few seconds later she was holding a small calibre gun. Whether it was loaded she had no idea, but in her blind panic she pulled the safety back and then, leaving her sister crying in fear, she walked deliberately behind the stairway.

She was shaking herself now, she felt as if she was going to pass out. She took a few deep breaths and, when the cellar door finally crashed open, she waited for the visitors to come down the stairs.

The man was like the anti-Christ. His anger was so consuming he looked willing to rip them limb from limb with his bare hands.

Emerging from the stairway silently, Cynthia pointed the gun at the back of his huge head and fired.

He dropped to his knees, and she felt the bile rising inside her as she saw the gaping hole that was left after his skull and brains had been ripped open.

Twenty seconds later she heard a muttered 'Fucking hell', followed by the sound of the other man leaving the house as quickly as possible. She went over and looked down at the man's body. He wasn't quite dead yet and, kneeling down beside him, she removed the heavy shotgun from his reach. Then, pointing the gun once more at his head, she pulled the trigger again.

That was when Celeste started to scream.

Going to her sister, Cynthia slapped her as hard as she could across the face. Seeing that the girl was calmer, she walked her slowly up the stairs back into the kitchen. Then, the gun still in her hands, she closed the now-open front door before pouring both herself and her sister large brandies. She gulped hers and made sure her sister did the same. Next, she walked out into the hallway and, picking up the telephone, she rang around until she located James, only telling him that she was at Jonny's house and that Celeste needed her husband as soon as physically possible.

Then she sat at the kitchen table and waited, all the time talking calmly to her little sister and assuring her that everything was going to be all right. She wasn't sure she believed any of that herself, but she knew it was all she could do until the men arrived.

CHAPTER THIRTY-THREE

'I still can't believe it.' That much was evident in Jack Callahan's voice.

'Your daughter shot Kevin Bryant in self-defence, and she saved our Celly's life by all accounts.' Mary Callahan's voice choked up as she once more relived her daughter's close escape from death. There was no doubt in anyone's mind that Kevin had been going to take out Celeste to get back at Jonny P. A few of the more sceptical said he might have only used her as a hostage, but Mary strongly suspected his plan was always to wipe her baby out like a little boy would stamp on an ant. 'Well, you better believe it, she's the fucking hero of the hour by all accounts, and our Celly won't have a word said against her.'

Jack Callahan could hear the fear in his wife's voice and decided to keep his opinion to himself; she might be stunned by Cynthia's actions but he wasn't. She was like a bloke in a lot of respects, oh, not in her womanly body, but in her mind. There was something missing in his elder daughter, and he knew that, as hypocritical as it was, had she been a boy he would have been proud of her. Males could be like his Cynth and it would be seen as strength, in a woman it was seen as suspicious.

His daughter a murderer! Because that's what she was. She had waited behind the cellar steps and done Bryant from behind, using her sister as bait. That was the action of a man, that was a cold-blooded reaction. If she had had a lump of pipe instead she would have hammered his head in,

109

he was sure. That his daughter had knelt down and finished the fucker off, was so distasteful to him he felt a moment's sickness in his belly. She was a fucking strange cove and no mistaking. 'How does Jonny feel about all this?' he asked curiously.

'Pretty much the same as everyone else.'

Mary was as amazed as her husband about the turn of events. In fairness, Cynthia had saved the day; if it wasn't for her the chances were Celeste would be dead now and the thought upset Mary so much she had to swallow down the urge to cry.

The mess had been cleaned up at the house by all accounts, but Celeste still refused to go back there. Well, she could understand that—what she couldn't understand was why Celeste was staying with Cynthia and not with her? They were like Siamese twins nowadays—where Cynthia went, Celly followed.

Jonny Parker was too wise to do anything about that just yet; he knew that Celeste needed time to get over what had happened to her. Plus, Mary guessed shrewdly, he would be grateful to have Celly off his hands while he cleaned up the mess he had caused by his greediness. For once Mary agreed with her husband. This was something that should have been avoided at all costs. It had left a bad taste in a lot of people's mouths.

Kevin Bryant might not have been liked, but he had been respected. It was only the fact that he had gone after a defenceless woman that had stopped the other crime bosses in London from retaliating on his behalf. She bet they were watching their backs now. They would need to and all; Jonny had half the Smoke at his disposal. Kevin Bryant was dead and his business partner Bertie Warner had disappeared completely. She suspected they were sharing the same grave somewhere and she hoped they would rot in hell for what they had tried to do to her poor daughter. Bastards, the pair of them. No one went after wives or kiddies—it was the unwritten law.

CHAPTER THIRTY-FOUR

'No one has seen him, Jonny, it's like he dropped off the face of the earth.'

'What about his wife and kids?'

'House is empty, hardly even any clothes packed. I've got people keeping an eye out in Spain and Portugal but, in reality, he could be fucking anywhere.'

Detective Inspector Jones was as bent as a nine-bob note, and he knew that he was expected to give his main benefactor Jonny Parker something substantial for the money he was paid on a weekly basis, but there was nothing. It was the gospel truth—he had not been able to locate the man, or his family.

'Bertie would have a fallback plan, he probably had passports, et cetera waiting for just such an eventuality. All we can do is wait and see if anyone recognises him, or he commits a crime somewhere and we get wind of it. As I say, Jonny, he could be anywhere. South America, maybe? They would welcome the cunt with open arms—look at Biggsy.'

Jonny Parker knew the truth of this, but it wasn't enough for him. He wanted Bertie Warner's balls for this outrage and he wanted them now. If there

111

was one thing he knew, it was not good practice to let Bertie have a swerve on this. It would make Jonny look weak and it also meant that someone was out there and they would have him and his family in their sights. It made him uneasy, even though he knew they were well protected. He had made the mistake of assuming his family was out of bounds, and he would never make that mistake again. Celeste was in bits, and why wouldn't she be? After what she had seen, he was surprised she wasn't in a nut-house.

But it was Cynthia who had amazed him the most. She had taken out Kevin Bryant and, from what he could gather, she had knelt down and finished the job. Either way, she had fucking scared Warner off—he must have thought they were waiting down there for him and wasn't prepared to take the chance of a bullet in his own bonce. None of it seemed to have affected Cynthia that much, she seemed a bit unnerved but that was about it. As he had looked at her comforting his wife, it had crossed his mind that she would have been a worthy mate for him, and he had hated himself for that thought even as he had acknowledged the truth of it. She was like a modern-day Boudicca, all hair and fiery sexuality. He was ashamed at how she had affected him, because he knew she was a two-faced, conniving whore, but somehow that just made her seem more intriguing.

Celeste was like a ghost of her former self; he had taken her to a doctor in Harley Street who was known to keep a closed shop, but all he had said was that she was suffering from shock. Well, Jonny could have fucking told the doctor that much, and *he* wouldn't have charged five grand. But the doctor

112

had given her some happy pills and some sleeping tablets—both of which Jonny could have purchased in any pub in London for a millionth of the price—and sent them on their way. Still, Jonny felt better for having done *something* for her.

It was Cynthia who was on his mind, though—and the fact that she had taken Bryant out in such an audacious way. She had shown her mettle and, even though she had been an outcast over her last carry-on, she was now number one in everyone's books. She had more than redeemed herself; she had killed someone, and not just anyone either—she had killed the man who had been going after his wife, after Jonny P's wife, and that counted for a lot in their world. She had been a ruthless and efficient killing machine and for some strange reason that turned him right on. He liked a bit of fire in a woman, and she had it in abundance. Cynthia was a stroppy mare, she was arrogant, and she was dangerous. All those things in a man would have been great, but in a female they were a worry. Females bled every month, they lived on their emotions, and they were as unreliable as a bent Filth, so what was the attraction suddenly?

He knew what it was all right, she was a goer in every way was Cynthia Tailor, and it was Cynthia Tailor he wanted under him. Not Cynthia Callahan. He wanted the woman she was now, not the girl he had bedded all those years ago. Her face that night it had happened had been a revelation to him; she was almost triumphant she had killed a man and she was determined not to let it affect her too much. He could see her forcing the terror out of her body, saw it being replaced by pride, and she had never looked lovelier to him than at that

113

moment when she had conquered her fear. She had stared him in the eyes and it had been a challenge; she was daring him to turn away from her, and she knew, and he knew, he couldn't. She had protected his most treasured possession, his wife, and she had seen to it that the person who had been a threat to them was no more.

Even Linford had been impressed and, though the clean-up operation had been long and laborious, they knew it could have been much worse. It had been a long night, but it had been a lucrative one. More than that, it had been a night that had given him an itch, a terrible itch that he knew he could only assuage by bedding his wife's sister. Even though he knew it was a madness inside him, he couldn't deny the strength of it. Every time he thought of her kneeling down and putting one right in Bryant's ugly face he felt a tightening in his groin, and he knew that he would get no relief until he had her under him and crying out his name. It was madness but, like many a man before him, any caution was all but gone to the wind.

Jonny forced his mind back to the matter at hand and, looking straight at DI Jones, he said seriously, 'So I am paying you a serious fucking wedge to be told sweet fuck-all? Bertie Warner could be hiding under this table for all you know, is that it?'

Jones sighed heavily, he knew he was on borrowed time. 'That's about the strength of it, yeah. As I say, unless he shows up somewhere . . .' His voice trailed off, it sounded futile even to him.

'Get this fucking muppet out of here.'

Jones didn't need telling twice, he couldn't wait to get out the door.

Linford was laughing as the man left the room

shame-faced. 'I hate bent Filth, worse than a fucking grass. They fuck up their own. Give me a straight copper and a fair nick every time.'

Jonny nodded his agreement, most of his associates felt the same.

'How's Celeste?' Linford asked.

Jonny shrugged. 'How'd you think? Scared, frightened, timid.' Even he could hear the irritation in his own voice, and Linford raised his eyebrows but didn't comment.

He knew Jonny blamed himself and a man would not forget that he, and he alone, was responsible for his wife's condition. He had left her hanging in the wind, and that was something no man could live with easily. Of course, luckily, Cynthia had come up trumps. Linford found what she had done admirable but distasteful, if he was honest. A woman who could do that and not even feel remorse was not a woman to him. Jimmy Tailor was welcome to the hard-faced bitch; he wouldn't want to lie beside her of a night—who knew what she was capable of if you fucked her off? No, thank you. He thought Jimmy should out her at the first available opportunity. After all, she wasn't a wife who inspired love and affection, and she had the mothering skills of a fucking demented hyena. At least hyenas looked after their young; by all accounts Cynthia dumped hers at her mother's for weeks at a time. Jimmy was a fucking cokehead, and that was because he had nothing to go home to. That pristine mausoleum was not a home, it was a show place. Linford had been there twice and each time he had felt as welcome as a sausage at a Bar Mitzvah. No, he didn't envy poor Jimmy Tailor in the least.

Linford liked his women clean and uncomplicated; he also liked them living at a separate address so they never got too big for their boots. Once they started cleaning his drum up after a night of revelry they were out the door and gone from his life. He had too many things to do, places to see, and strangers to bed for one woman to do anything for him. He looked after any kids of his that arrived, and he saw that they were looked after very well, but there was no way he was tying himself to one woman. That, as far as he could see, was a mug's game.

It was cut and dried to him; he saw, he conquered, and he came. Then he went home. Unlike Jonny, he liked to keep his life as uncomplicated as possible.

CHAPTER THIRTY-FIVE

'Come on, Celeste, have a bit of lunch—you'll feel better for it.'

Celeste smiled gratefully, and dutifully ate her salad sandwich. She liked it at Cynthia's house; it was clean, and it was orderly, and best of all she couldn't smell the blood here. She couldn't get that smell out of her nostrils and she couldn't get the picture of Kevin Bryant out of her mind. The fact that her sister had killed him didn't bother her one bit; she knew Cynthia had done it to save her life, and that she could brutally kill a man wasn't something she thought about. Cynthia was her saviour and that was that.

Today, with her mum there too, and the kids

116

squabbling on the kitchen floor, she felt the best she had felt since it had happened. Gabby got on to her lap and Celeste hugged the child to her tightly. She needed the warmth of these children to make her believe that life was normal once more, even though inside herself she knew it could never be normal again.

Jonny was looking for a new house for them because she refused to ever set foot in that other one again as long as she lived. She knew that Jonny was annoyed with her, not that he said anything of course, but she could feel his impatience with her. But she wasn't like him, she couldn't shrug this off as if it was an occupational hazard—it might be for him, but for her it was a nightmare he had brought on her and she didn't know if she could ever forgive him. She hoped so, because she loved him with all her being. But his actions had caused this turmoil and upset, and she couldn't quite get over that yet.

Gabby seemed to sense her auntie's upset and she snuggled into her like she was trying to take it on herself. Celeste hugged her little body as if it was a life raft. James Junior watched them silently, and Celeste felt the tears prick once more, at the innocence of these children. The same innocence she had once possessed, and now it was gone from her. She had seen death in its rawest form, and it had blighted her life.

Crying silently, she didn't see the look that was exchanged between her mother and sister. She didn't understand that they thought it was time she let it go and sorted herself out. Celeste had never been strong like them, and that was why she couldn't forget the sight of Kevin Bryant with half his head gone, the blood seeping out of his body and making a heart shape on the concrete floor. For the thousandth time, she wondered what his wife and children were going through, and how they would ever come to terms with his disappearance. Four little children and a wife. Everyone said Kevin Bryant's wife was a nice girl. Why was it always the nice girls who had their hearts broken?

Gabby was trying to wipe her auntie's eyes, as she felt herself being lifted off her lap. It was obvious her nana was going to take them back to her house, but Gabby wanted to stay here. So did James Junior, who was beginning to kick up his usual fuss. For once though her mum was being nice to him and wasn't shouting at him. In fact, her mum was being nice to everyone and they were calling Cynthia a 'Brahma', and she knew that the way they said it meant it was something good. But Gabby allowed her nana to put her coat on, and take her and her sobbing brother back to her house. After all, she was a kid and she had to do what she was told.

Whether she wanted to or not.

CHAPTER THIRTY-SIX

'Come on, Celeste, you have to at least look at the new house.' Jonny's voice was gentle but there was a steely undertone that wasn't lost on anyone in the room. He had stopped the cajoling weeks ago, and he was getting more and more aggravated by the day. But Celeste, as weak as she was in many ways, was adamant about this one thing. She would not leave her sister's house for anything. She had not stepped across the door since she had entered it that night, the night Bryant had been taken out.

Jimmy Tailor was heart-sorry for his sister-in-law, but he knew it would be futile to interfere. Also, in a selfish way, he wanted her gone from his home. It had been nearly three months now, and he wanted his wife back, though he never thought he would ever be saying that.

'You go, Cynthia,' said Celeste. 'You go and then come back and tell me about it.'

Cynthia looked at her husband and shrugged. 'It doesn't matter what I think, love, it's what you think that matters.'

'No, you go, Cynth. I'll wait here with the kids, and Jimmy, Jimmy will stay here with me, won't you?' She didn't want to be alone.

Cynthia walked out into her hallway and Jonny followed her. 'If I go with you, we can come back and tell her how lovely it is, and then I can get her to come with me tomorrow, I'm sure of it.'

Jonny looked into her eyes and knew, as she did, that if they went to the house together they wouldn't be doing much looking at it, not at first anyway. He felt the excitement in his groin and wondered at how such a change could come over a man.

'If you think so.' His voice was noncommittal; no one listening to them would ever guess at the turmoil inside him.

Cynthia was elated, she knew he was prepared for what was going to happen. 'I'll go and freshen up, get my coat.'

He nodded, not trusting himself to speak.

Thirty minutes later they were naked, they were sweating and they were both aware that no one else would ever fulfil the strange need that they both shared.

'Tell me, tell me what it was like to kill him, Cynth.'

As she bit into his shoulders and spewed her filth into his ears, Jonny Parker felt, for the first time in years, that he was well and truly, *finally* home. That he was betraying his wife, the so-called love of his life, didn't bother him one iota. Every time he looked at Cynthia's full breasts and long legs, he saw her kneeling down beside Kevin Bryant and taking him out once and for all. There was no woman on this earth who could compete with that, and they both knew it. They were a match made in hell, and the knowledge only made them desire each other more.

CHAPTER THIRTY-SEVEN

'It's lovely, Celeste, I bet you're glad you came home, aren't you?' There was genuine warmth in Cynthia's voice and it wasn't lost on anyone in the room. Even Jack Callahan was beginning to warm to this strange daughter of his. Jonny and Celeste's house was like a mansion and, where normally that would eat at Cynthia like a cancer, she seemed to be genuinely pleased at her sister's good fortune.

''Course I am, Cynth.' It was forced and everyone ignored that fact.

Cynthia was like a different person, everyone remarked on it. She was almost playful with the kids, and she was always in a good mood, even Jimmy didn't get the tail end of her tongue as often

120

as he had before. She seemed happier than anyone had ever seen her, and it made their lives so much easier. She still left the kids with her mother for weeks on end, but these days she was happy to have them around during the daytime. She had started taking a Cordon Bleu cookery course, and Jimmy was eating better than ever. She never questioned his late hours any more. She saw him off to work with a cheery wave and a big smile. It was as if she was born again, and this time God had given her a heart. Celeste loved her with a passion and Cynthia seemed to reciprocate those feelings.

But Cynthia lived for the stolen time with Jonny Parker.

That her killing Bryant had appealed to him so strongly was a real eye-opener. If she had known that, she would have gone on a fucking killing spree a long time ago! Kevin Bryant's death didn't bother her, it wasn't an issue where Cynthia Tailor was concerned. It had got her the one thing she wanted more than anything in her life, Jonny, so she saw it as a good thing—nothing to lose sleep over. She enjoyed telling Jonny all about it; it turned her on as much as it did him. She relived it over and over again, and she didn't feel the least bit sorry about it.

She had never questioned that she was capable of great violence. Inside she had always known it; from a child she had been consumed by violent rages. When she was really angry she knew she was capable of almost anything, she knew she could easily stab someone if they thwarted her. She saw it as part of her strength and now she saw it as part of her allure. She looked like butter wouldn't melt when, in reality, she was capable of carrying out serious harm.

That Jonny Parker loved that about her was the bonus, of course. She had always known they were meant to be together, she had made a big mistake once by letting him get away and she wouldn't be making that mistake again.

The strangest thing of all was she realised she loved Celeste—really loved her. Now she wasn't a rival any more, Cynthia could find it in her heart to pity her. With her big house and her endless supply of dosh, *she* now had the one thing Celeste really wanted. She had Jonny Parker, and she was not going to let him go.

She would kill him first.

CHAPTER THIRTY-EIGHT

Gabby watched in amazement as her mother laughed and joked with them all. She was like a new person, and it was wonderful.

Gabby had at last stopped wetting the bed, and stayed Sundays and Mondays at her mum and dad's house. It was wonderful. They ate a lovely meal together then watched the telly. Sometimes her mum still got impatient with them, though never too much, even when James Junior was really naughty. She loved her school, and she was making friends and, all in all, life was good. Now she had Christmas to look forward to as well. Everyone was going to come to their house! Her grandad said it was unheard of, though somehow Gabby knew she mustn't say that to anyone or it would cause trouble. There was a big tree up, and the mantelpiece was decorated with a huge piece of pretend holly. Her nana said it looked like a Victorian Christmas card, and her mother had liked that so it must have been a compliment. Never had Gabby looked forward to something in her life as much as she looked forward to this coming Christmas Day. The turkey was massive, the veg was all prepared, and her nana was going to bring the Christmas pudding. She had actually helped her mum ice the Christmas cake, and she and James Junior had been allowed to make a chocolate log. It was magical.

As Gabby lay there wondering at how lucky she was, her mother came into her bedroom and sat down on the side of her bed. This was something else she was beginning to like—her mother had started chatting to her like a real person, like the mummies in the books at school. She didn't just tell her off all the time.

'You comfortable, love?'

'Yes, thank you.' She still knew enough to watch her Ps and Qs.

'Looking forward to Christmas, I bet?'

She nodded, her face shining with happiness.

'Well, remember that Santa only comes to good boys and girls.'

'I will, Mummy, and I've been good. Sister Angela said I had been impressive, that was the word.'

Cynthia laughed then, a real laugh. 'I remember her—tall, ugly old cow.'

Gabby grinned at this blasphemy. 'She said I looked just like you at the same age.' She had also said that her mother was a heart-scald if ever there was one, and that she had been nothing but trouble from the day she walked into the Sacred

Heart School. But Gabby wisely kept that bit of the conversation to herself.

Cynthia looked down on her lovely daughter— she really was lovely, she was beautiful. 'You're a good kid, Gabs.'

This was another new thing, the shortening of her name to 'Gabs', this from her mother who always insisted everyone got their full title.

Gabby felt the tears sting her eyes then, it was not often her mother was this kind to her. 'I try, Mummy.'

Cynthia smiled. 'I know you do, mate. I know you do.' She kissed her daughter's brow then and, making sure the bed was tidy, she left the room, whispering, 'Good night,' softly before shutting the door behind her.

When Cynthia went into her front room, she sat down and sipped at her wine. They would both be off to sleep soon, she had made sure of that—she had crushed half a sleeping tablet into their hot milks. James was off out, overseeing the books in a club in Romford, and she had a small lamb casserole in the oven simmering away ready for when Jonny got here. She felt the pull of him already, hence the drugged children; nothing or no one would interfere with her time with him.

It was strange the way it had panned out. She felt a sorrow for Celeste that was so deep, and so sad it was almost tangible. She knew that Jonny could never leave her sister, and she was content with that for the moment. All she wanted was him, inside her, in her bed where she gave her husband a mercy fuck often enough to allay his suspicions. All she wanted was what she had. And that was tonight, because there was no way they would be able to get

124

together over Christmas.

She had put on her new underwear, she had made her face up so it looked more exquisite than ever, and she had put on her old clothes, because there was nothing that turned him on more than ripping them off her as he walked through the door. She felt the thrill of him inside her once more and, settling herself in the comfortable armchair, she awaited his arrival.

Life didn't get much better than this; a drink, a sit and the anticipation of a good fuck into the bargain. This was what she lived for, what kept her going. This was the stuff that dreams were made of.

CHAPTER THIRTY-NINE

Jonny Parker was on his way to Cynthia's with a bottle of Dom Pérignon, and a diamond pendant that she would dismiss as a knock-off from the market like she had everything else he had bought her. He felt the tug of her as he drove sedately through the London traffic.

He liked to savour the journey to her house— always *her* house, never Jimmy's. He liked the knowledge that she would be waiting for him, would fuck him like an animal, and then feed him a wonderful supper and talk as if they were no more than good friends. She knew what a man wanted, a real man, and he felt sorry for Jimmy Tailor, who would never be enough for the woman who was his wife.

Jonny was the king of the world; he had outed Bryant, he was now the main man in the Smoke, and all that was left for him to do was find that cunt Bertie Warner. And find him he would, if it was the last thing he did in this life. He would find him, and he would crush him like a fucking beetle under his shoe. He owed Celeste that much, if nothing else. He had put her in danger and, if it hadn't been for Cynthia, she would be dead. Then he would never have found out what really made him tick.

No woman had affected him like Celeste— she was pure and clean and good. But, thanks to Cynthia, he saw that she was not enough for him. Without *her* he would never have understood that he had a real lust for blood, and that blood lust would take him places he had never dreamt possible, both mentally and sexually.

London was his, and he was going to own it all. The man who could take it off him hadn't been born yet. He had a slice of everything—from blags to betting shops to nightclubs, market stalls, shops, even the bingo halls, the list was endless. He had finally made it, was finally the top banana, and now came the hardest part of all.

Staying there.

Book Two

The half is greater than the whole

Hesiod, ca. 700 BC

CHAPTER FORTY

1994

Cynthia was tired after her long day's work but happy; these days she was working for Jonny along with her husband and she loved it. They were getting a serious earn now, and if her husband wondered at the change in their status he was either too shrewd or too stupid to say so. She had a feeling it was the latter, but she never asked him, she didn't really want to know the answer. Jonny had gone from strength to strength in the last few years and was now the undisputed and, more importantly, the unchallenged king of London town. He was the main man, and he was loving it. That Cynthia was the main woman thrilled her even as it worried her. It was a miracle they had not been found out and that made her think people knew but weren't talking about it. Jonny Parker wouldn't look kindly on any gossiping, and she was not about to let her life be ruined over it either.

She was known as a killer in their circle, and she felt the respect from the men, and the fear from their women. The story had been repeated and built up over the years until it was nothing like the real events. The younger ones even thought it had been planned. It amused her how stories really did get stretched in the telling, and how a story, true or otherwise, could impact on a person's life. Everyone was wary of her these days and that helped her in her new-found career.

All except Celeste, of course. Celeste was still treating her like she was the second coming or

129

something and, though she was sorry for her little sister, she didn't feel in any way guilty. She now believed that what had happened was inevitable, believed that she and Jonny Parker were meant to be. Like all great loves, theirs had not been an easy road.

She tolerated poor James, and she knew that he was grateful to her for her affection, scant though it was. His attempt at being the head of the household was long over; now he deferred to her as he always used to, only these days she didn't provoke him as she once had. In fact, she believed he was happy in his own way. Jonny saw to it that they were well looked after, and well compensated, and who would have thought she had a knack for the betting shops? She ran them all with military precision, and the percentage she took was no small amount.

All in all life was great—except for one thing. As good as she looked, time was beginning to take its toll on her. Lately she had noticed that Jonny, while still as ardent as ever when they were together, wasn't as eager to meet up as he used to be. Whereas once it had been every day, sometimes twice a day, often a quick coupling in the back of a car because they only had an hour, now he seemed as if he was stepping back from her somehow, and that was not something she was prepared to accept. That he had a lot more on his mind she understood and accepted, but what she wouldn't accept was another woman in his life—other than Celeste, of course. Celeste was no threat, but the advent of the lap-dancing clubs had made Cynthia aware that, unlike the nightclubs where young girls were in abundance but ultimately looking for a man on a permanent basis, the lap dancers were all out for what they could get. Their brazenness alone was something that would appeal to her Jonny. *She* should know, she was brazen enough herself, and that was what he wanted from her. She knew that this was a jealousy brought on by insecurity; she was still a good-looking woman, but she was just that—a woman, and these were girls. Very *young* girls at that.

Jonny had embraced the lap-dancing clubs and made them the jewel in his rather large crown. He also spent a lot of his free time in them, though he said it was work and she had to believe that, didn't she? But, as good as life was, she felt that he was somehow slipping away from her, and that was something she could never countenance.

No one, not her kids, her family, nobody on this earth meant as much to her as Jonny Parker, and she would see him dead before she saw him with someone else. That wasn't even a threat, that was a promise. Without him she would wither away and die. He was like a drug to her and, though she knew it was unhealthy, that their attraction was wrong in so many ways, she embraced it because she could not live without it.

CHAPTER FORTY-ONE

Jonny Parker had changed over the last few years, and he was as aware of it as the people who worked for him. He would not be gainsaid and he would not listen to advice from anyone; he was unable to take any kind of criticism and he severely punished those who he felt were being disrespectful. It was said by

131

a few that he was getting far too big for his boots—but not within his earshot naturally. Nevertheless, there were the beginnings of dissent, and it was something he should have been aware of, and should have done something about.

The old affable Jonny P, always ready to buy a round of drinks, always the first with a good joke, and always the first to arrange a big party, was long gone. He was a serious, rather dour man now, who occasionally reverted to his old ways while in his cups. He had still never touched a drug—alcohol being his only real vice—and he took his job and its responsibilities very seriously indeed. As his father-in-law always said, getting to the top was the easy part, it was staying there that took the real hard graft.

The truth of the statement was not lost on Jonny now as he sat working. He had fought to get the top prize and it was getting harder and harder to hang on to it. London in the nineties was run by him and a few other Faces—they had minor roles, of course. But it was being swamped by Eastern Europeans, Russians, and the like. They were like no other adversary seen on these turfs before; they had unlimited money and they were ruthless, and that meant *he* had to become more ruthless. That was the law of their game, but it was a hard graft all the same.

The girls in many of his clubs were Eastern European. The men he dealt with had a constant supply, and the girls were brought over, relieved of their passports, and then told they had to work off their debts. Jonny also had fingers in more than a few pies concerning some Eastern-European brothels. These were constant money-spinners and,

132

though he had found the whole thing distasteful at first, he knew if he didn't become a part of it some other enterprising fucker soon would. That would mean a serious rival for him and he could not allow that.

All the same he didn't like the business—but then he didn't bet and he still had plenty of betting shops. Betting was a fucking mug's game as far as he was concerned; only fools and bigger fools thought they could really beat the odds. If they had a win, it was rarely enough to cover the years of spending in his shops that preceded it. Still, each to their own and if the Good Lord had not invented lust, greed and all the other vices, he would not have been able to live the life of a biblical king. And live like a king he did, though he was clever enough not to live *too* ostentatiously. He did though have property all over the world, and that was thanks to his Eastern-European connections. They were masters at the long game and he was learning shitloads of stuff from them.

Jonny bought properties for cash, and laundered the money by remortgaging them, not just in England but all over the world; it was like a licence to print legal dosh. He was also amazed at the amount of money to be made in whoring, because it was the whoring that had been the most lucrative of all his new ventures. The only real drawback was that he had no real control over the money and, if caught, the sentences were heavy. That was because the girls were there against their will and that often led to charges of white slavery—even though many of the girls were West African—and kidnapping. It was costing a fortune to grease the right palms but, thanks to his connections, they were pretty safe. At least as safe as those kind of deals can be. It was taking its toll though, and he knew that the happiness he should have been feeling from all he had achieved was not there.

The reason for this was his Celeste. Yes, she was better than she had been, but she was still scared of her own shadow. In fact, the only time she was remotely happy was when they were out in Spain. She loved their house in Majorca and she seemed to relax there. It was up in the mountains, and the greenery and the dramatic views seemed to calm her soul. Personally, he liked it for the first week and then felt he was going stir-crazy, but he knew she needed the time there.

They had not yet had children, though Celeste had suffered miscarriages, and they both said there was plenty of time, but he guessed that deep down she was frightened of it all. He wanted children, but he was in no hurry. And perhaps that was just as well because he couldn't see how Celeste would cope with a baby. He loved her with all his heart, and he still cared for her, but now she was more like a sister. Although, in all honesty, that could be the result of the guilt he felt for what he was doing with her sister . . .

Now *there* was a woman, though she was getting harder and harder to keep in line. She was like a man in many respects; she thought like one, she worked like one, and she could fight like one when the fancy took her. The only downfall was her mouth. Cynthia never knew when to let something alone, and she would push an issue to the hilt. Lately, that had begun to irritate him; he had enough going on without having a five-point crisis every time he saw her. He understood her loathing of the lap-dancing clubs—most women disliked them. And yet the brothels didn't bother her one iota. She was a strange, contradictory creature. He cared for her deeply, but she was hard work; 'high maintenance' was the expression men used about women like her these days, and it described her totally.

All the same, when he was with her, deep inside her, was the only time he really felt content, the only time he felt fulfilled. He didn't analyse these thoughts, he just knew them to be true. What it was about her he could never put his finger on. All he knew was she drew him to her like a moth to a flame. And he hated that it was being spoilt by her constant wanting for more and more of his time.

He shrugged the thoughts away and concentrated on what he was doing. He glanced at his watch and realised he was already late for a meeting. Where did the time go, and why was he still working fifteen hours a day? But he knew why; he didn't trust anyone around him to do the job properly. He was wary of delegating too much of the big stuff; once you took your finger off the pulse you lost the beat of the world you were in, and that was a dangerous situation to be in. You only had to look at the likes of Kevin Bryant to see the truth of that statement.

CHAPTER FORTY-TWO

Gabby hated her life. She hated school and she hated the nuns there. She was thirteen, and her whole existence was a big drag, at least it was this week anyway.

But there was one high spot, and his name was Vincent O'Casey. He was seventeen and he was gorgeous. She had met him at Chrisp Street Market last Saturday and she was seeing him again tomorrow. She couldn't wait.

Like all her friends, Gabby's Saturdays were for doing the markets—the Roman Road, East Ham, Chrisp Street, Romford of course and, occasionally, Soho Market—not that they bought there, but it was wonderful to look at all the strange things. Sundays were for 'the Lane', as Petticoat Lane Market was called. Romford was Gabby's favourite though; she loved that it was far away from her mother, because her mother was a giant pain in the arse.

She frowned as she thought this, and she wondered at how on earth she had been lumbered with such a woman. These days, she went home for whole weekends, when she would prefer to be there only on Sundays and Mondays as it used to be. But her mother wasn't stupid. She wanted her there because she wanted to make sure she didn't go '*out* out', as she called it. That meant with boys, although it was never actually stipulated. It was fine for her to go with her friends to the markets—it was what her mother had done, after all—but when the evening drew in she had to be indoors like an errant school kid.

Well, she would be fourteen soon—she wasn't a baby any more. With her already ripened body she knew she could pass for eighteen with the right clothes and make-up. Christ Almighty, she could get in to see any film she wanted, and that was no mean feat. Some of her friends still looked younger than they were, but she was like her mother—

136

all tits and legs, as her grandfather was forever saying. Gabby knew that she was pretty, knew that boys looked at her. Men did as well, though they made her uncomfortable. But they looked all the same—even some of her friends' dads, and that was absolutely gross.

Her dad was great but, as always, he had to do what her mother wanted, so Gabby got no support from him. She felt sorry for him, because he seemed so sad a lot of the time, and yet her parents lived in a lovely house and, to an outsider, it would seem they had a nice life. But Gabby knew instinctively that her mother didn't love her dad, not like he loved her, and that was why he was so sad inside. It was in his eyes, and it was tragic to see. Sometimes she looked at him and felt the urge to cry, he looked so forlorn, so lonely. But how could he be lonely when he had her and James Junior?

Her dad knew that they preferred it at their nana's house—at least there they could be themselves. He knew that their mother was sometimes inordinately hard on them both, and he tried in his own way to make up for that. He ruined them, according to her mother, gave in too quickly, but she saw her father was sensible enough to appreciate that if you let a child be free, they would come back to you of their own accord. All her mother's draconian measures seemed to do was make her want to break away, get away, as far away from the source of her unhappiness as possible.

But now she had Vincent to think about, and he was absolutely gorgeous, from his dark hair, his blue eyes, and his muscular physique, to his great big feet. She felt her pulse race as she thought of

137

his body and wondered why she felt suddenly so shy and awkward. She knew she wanted to kiss him, but she would not let her mind imagine any more than that. She did think about him all the time though, alone in her bed at night, and the feelings she had then were exciting and frightening. She knew her mother would have a heart attack if she knew about them! Her biggest problem at the moment was how she could swerve her mother so she could meet him one night. Like her mother, she was very resourceful and very determined. And, like her mother, she would not, under any circumstances, be thwarted.

Unlike her mother, Gabby had a truly kind heart, and an even kinder nature. She was happy in her own way, and enjoying the act of defiance that meant her meeting up with her heart-throb Vincent O'Casey behind her mother's back. She couldn't wait.

CHAPTER FORTY-THREE

'The sap's rising in her, she's just growing up. She wants to be with her friends and not have us standing over her the whole time.'

'She's only thirteen, Dad.'

Celeste sounded upset and Jack Callahan retreated on this occasion. Celeste agreed with everything her sister said, and if Cynthia said that her daughter was not to move across the doorstep then that was that.

Personally, he felt sorry for the child. She was like a caged lion, and eventually caged animals

138

turned on the person who caged them in the first place. He could see the dislike and the irritation in his granddaughter's eyes for her mother, and he felt deeply sorry for her. Plus, she was a nice kid and a trustworthy kid at that, which was more than could be said about her mother at the same age.

Cynthia had been round the turf more times than a National winner by the time she was fifteen, although he wasn't supposed to know about that, of course. That was the problem with daughters, they got into trouble; boys were just the cause of their downfalls. Even in these so-called enlightened times, a girl in trouble was still looked down on where they lived; the doings of a load of braless fucking lesbians and their shouting about equality didn't cut much ice in the East End of London. Fucking feminism! A load of old cobblers as far as he was concerned. All it meant was that girls were getting like men, and what good would that do in the long run? Bullshit baffles brains all right, but where his granddaughter was concerned he hated to see her locked up like some kind of prisoner. Jack hated Cynthia at times, really loathed her. She was a piece of work. He knew about her and Jonny, but what could he do? If it ever came out it would be like one of those IRA bombs exploding in the heart of his family. And Jonny was *not* a son-in-law he could give a tug to, pull to one side and put the hard word on. Jonny was the local fucking Face— and how Jack would like to shove his fist into Jonny's face at times. He knew Jonny loved Celeste, loved her deeply, but he also knew that his Cynthia was in his blood. A woman could take a man like that and get under his skin. Jack had seen it before; when it hit a man he was helpless to fight it. Some

139

women had the power to make a man go against all he believed in, go against his basic instincts, walk away from his family, his job, his life. And the worst thing of all was that these women were never worth it. Hindsight was a wonderful thing, as Jonny would one day find out. For now, as long as Celeste didn't get hurt, Jack had to go along with it.

He wondered how much his old woman knew. Mary was a shrewd old bird, and she could also keep her own counsel; she wouldn't air something so potentially dangerous unless she had to. She *had* to know but, like him, her first thoughts were for Celeste and her fragile state of mind.

All that mess years ago had left its mark on them, and the seed of hatred that he had always felt for his elder daughter had grown into something much deeper. He hated feeling useless, hated that he was in no position to do anything for his family. Jonny paid for all their lives now, he had them in the palm of his large and treacherous hands and, at bottom, that was what really bothered Jack. He was helpless to do anything and, for a man like Jack Callahan, that was a terrible position to be in. But one day Jonny would get his comeuppance, of that much he was sure.

CHAPTER FORTY-FOUR

Mary Callahan was watching her grandson James Junior as he gazed at the television. She liked to think she had a special bond with him, but she worried that he wasn't *right* somehow. He could barely count to fifty, and he struggled to read the

140

comics he bought by the dozen. He seemed to be away with the fairies half the time, and spent hours staring at the TV screen. Lately she had begun to wonder if he actually took in what he was watching. All he seemed interested in at the moment was getting a kitten. They couldn't have one here—she was too old for all that palaver—and there was no way Cynthia would have one in that surgically clean house of hers. But it was all James Junior went on about. His schoolwork was clearly suffering, though she had a feeling he just couldn't do it and that it was too advanced for him. He needed a private tutor or something.

Mary had broached the subject with Cynthia who had shrugged and said he was 'as thick as shit' and 'he'll snap out of it'. At nearly nine, James Junior was larger than other lads his age, but he hardly spoke a word unless spoken to first. Unless he *really* wanted something—then he would pester and annoy everyone till he got what he wanted. Look at all that about the kitten. James had flown into such a rage when he was told he couldn't have one. They had been amazed at the intensity of it. And the language! Kicking and spitting out filth the like of which she'd never heard before. Jack had eventually given him a good clump, and that seemed to have sorted him out. But again, the ferocity of his anger was all wrong, too deep and too hateful for a child of his age.

He seemed to have no friends either and she believed it was because he didn't seem to want any. That, to her mind, was unnatural in a child, and she knew that someone should address these problems but she didn't know who that should be. It wasn't as noticeable to everyone else, they just thought he

141

was quiet. But Mary felt instinctively that there was something radically wrong with the boy, and that frightened her. If only she could talk to Cynthia, voice her concerns about his schoolwork, his indifference to other people. A kitten might be just what he needed, a little friend of sorts, something to love.

The doorbell rang, and she got up to answer it, leaving the young lad with her husband.

Roy Brown, their neighbour for over twenty-five years, was standing there with his little grandson Tyrone and, in his arms, he was holding a dead kitten and a Tesco carrier bag, blood everywhere.

Her evident surprise turned to shock when Roy Brown, his huge face twisted in disgust, said angrily, 'Get young James out here. Look what he did to the kitten. He cut the little fucker's throat.' He was roaring in his anger, and this brought Jack out into the hallway.

'What the fuck's all the shouting about?' He was looking at Roy Brown and the crying Tyrone in utter amazement.

'Your grandson, that fucking weirdo James, has cut my Tyrone's kitten's throat. Cut the little cat's throat, the wicked little bugger.'

Jack Callahan was looking at his old friend as if he had just grown another head in front of his eyes. 'What the hell are you on about, man?'

Little Tyrone Brown was only five years old but, with the acumen of men ten times his age, said tearfully, 'He did, he did, I saw him, he made me watch . . .'

Jack was staring from one person to another in utter disbelief. 'That's bollocks! Our James loves cats. For fuck's sake, he's been driving us mad

142

about getting one for weeks.'

Roy interrupted him then saying, 'That's why he did this.' He thrust the dead body of the kitten towards Jack who instinctively stepped backwards. '*He* couldn't have one, so he didn't want my Tyrone to have one either, the murdering little fucker.'

Jack was shaking his head; he refused to believe his grandson was capable of such an act. He was stunned into absolute silence.

Roy handed him the carrier bag saying, 'Open that, go on, see whose knife it was that cut the animal's throat.'

Jack opened the carrier bag and peered inside. There, blood-stained and covered with the cat's tabby hair, was their bread knife. He knew it was theirs because it had a white bone handle—it had been Mary's mother's and she treasured it. Sometimes, as she cut up a loaf, she would remark at how long the knife had been in use and how it must never go into the dishwasher, but be cleaned lovingly by hand.

Now it had been used to kill this poor child's little pet and, staring into the blood-stained carrier bag, Jack Callahan felt the rage boiling up inside him. The wicked, feral little bastard. That he was capable of something so heinous, so barbaric was unthinkable. Yet the knife was there, and the only person who could have taken it out of this house was James.

Young Tyrone was looking at him with the sad, soulful eyes of an honest boy, and Jack knew he was telling the truth. Where was the culprit though? He must have heard all this commotion. Jack called his name out loudly and, when the boy didn't appear, he went into the front room. Lifting him bodily from where he was crouched on the sofa, he physically dragged him into the hallway.

'Did you do this? *Did you?*'

James was terrified and, for a few seconds, even Roy Brown was almost sorry for the boy. Jack Callahan's temper was legendary in their street—he didn't go often but when he blew, he really lost it.

Snatching the dead kitten from Roy, Jack pushed the corpse into his grandson's face, smearing him with blood and hair, all the time shouting, 'You did this, didn't you? You vicious little fucker . . .'

Pulling away roughly, James screamed, 'It's not fair! *I* wanted a kitten, that should have been *my* kitten! Not his bastard kitten . . . But no, I couldn't have him, could I? Not me, I never get fucking anything off you bastards . . .'

The blow, when it landed, knocked James across the hallway and into the small table where they kept the phone. The table collapsed, and the phone was sent sprawling along with the boy, who was now attempting to cover his head, protect his skull from the rain of punches that was being administered by his granddad.

Eventually, Roy Brown stepped in and pulled Jack off, shocked at the severity of the beating. He could see that if it went on for much longer Jack would surely kill the child. The hallway was spattered with blood. Roy looked at Mary Callahan and, seeing the utter horror on her face, he wondered if he could have perhaps handled the whole situation better somehow.

Young Tyrone Brown was watching in morbid fascination, knowing this was wrong even though to him it felt right. His little cat Bullet had had its throat cut by James and he felt he should pay for that. Being too little and too young to fight James, he had gone to his granddad because he knew he was big enough to do what he couldn't. He had loved his little cat, and he didn't want to see it die like that. He started crying then, a high-pitched keening that seemed to jerk Mary Callahan to life.

'Come here, child, come to me.'

But Tyrone had had enough, and he left the hallway sobbing, his granddad following him in a bewildered state, shocked at the day's events, and wondering if he had any hard stuff in the house.

Picking up the dead cat, Jack Callahan threw it at his now inert grandchild and said scathingly, 'Clear this lot away. You'll bury that little lad's cat for him, and you'll do it properly and with an apology, you rotten little fucker. The shame you've brought on this house today, you murdering little bastard. You're your mother's son all right.'

It wasn't until much later when he went over the events again in his mind that it occurred to him that his wife had not once leapt to her grandson's defence. That alone spoke volumes.

CHAPTER FORTY-FIVE

'It was a fucking cat, Jonny. Anyone would think he'd murdered Mother Teresa the way they're carrying on.'

Jonny had heard the story—it was all people were talking about. The school had got wind of it and had said that James Junior should see a psychiatrist. The general consensus was that the school was right; cutting a kitten's throat wasn't exactly a boyish prank for all Cynthia tried to make it out like that. It also seemed that her boy James was getting a name for himself as a weirdo, for want of a better word. The school had been concerned about him for a good while, and he knew that was what was really getting up Cynthia's nose. She didn't have any real interest in the children unless they were reflecting well on her—then she was proud, or at least acted proud. She played the part of an exemplary mother and housewife, but it was all a façade. Now this latest incident had brought out the mother lioness in her, and she was determined to make sure it was seen as a youthful indiscretion and no more. But even hardened criminals were shocked at the child's antics. Cutting that poor kitten's throat because he couldn't have one of his own was seen as something sinister, not quite acceptable. Not for a nine year old anyway.

'Still, Cynth, it's a bit OTT don't you think? Cutting its throat with a bread knife? Not exactly tit for tat, is it?'

Cynthia could feel the anger burning away inside her and she held it in check. 'I should have let him have the cat, I didn't realise how much it meant to him.'

Jonny knew she was genuinely bewildered and believed that the reaction to James Junior's antics was overboard. 'Well, if you want my opinion, he needs a shrink now, before it's too late.'

Cynthia laughed then. A harsh, derisory laugh. 'Oh . . . hark at Doctor fucking Spock! What you know about kids I could write in block capitals on the back of a postage stamp. He's nine, fucking nine and, like any nine year old, he overreacted . . .'

Jonny was laughing now, really laughing.

146

'Over-reacted? For fuck's sake, Cynth, can you hear yourself? Use your loaf and let this die down. Get him help—that's what normal people do for their kids.'

Cynthia knew that Jonny was trying to help not just her but James Junior too. But she couldn't accept what he was saying; she felt strongly that the general consensus was way off base. He was a kid, and kids did stupid things. Somewhere deep inside her she knew she should be worried; it wasn't because she believed it, but her common sense told her that when the opinion of the majority was against you, the chances were you were wrong. But he was a child, and children were cruel—how many times had she heard that expression? What was annoying her more than anything was that this man, who she actually loved in her own strange way, was also ridiculing her and calling into question her mothering skills. She knew she would never win any awards, but she prided herself on having the cleanest, best turned-out children anywhere.

She would not be criticised by *anyone* about *anything*—especially not where her kids were concerned. But what really rankled was Jonny talking about psychiatrists for her son, when his wife, her sister, was madder than a box of frogs. Not that she would ever point that out to him of course; she knew he blamed himself, and so he fucking should.

Celeste wandered around that big house like the Orphan of the Storm. She could barely leave the house these days, not that anyone pointed that out, of course, but there was a word for it— agoraphobia. Still, in all honesty, it made their lives easier and that suited her down to the ground.

The only time Celeste left the house under her own steam was to go to Majorca and their house there, but even that was getting harder to achieve. He should leave her out there, let her enjoy the weather and the different surroundings.

Cynthia knew that she had to save this situation from getting out of hand, so she hid her true feelings and forced a smile on to her lovely face. 'Well, not a lot I can do. You'll be pleased to hear he's going to see a shrink on Tuesday, the school's insisting on it.'

Jonny felt the relief as a physical thing. Cynthia had to understand that *her* problems were not *his* problems, even though at times like this he felt he had to try and talk some sense into her. It wasn't easy reasoning with Cynthia. She had a knack of sounding right all the time—he assumed that was because she believed with all her heart that she *was* right all the time.

'Well then, darling, how about a drink?'

Cynthia smiled her assent, but the magic had gone out of the night and they both knew it. James Junior's so-called escapade was having far-reaching repercussions, and both suspected that the shrink would not be the end of it.

CHAPTER FORTY-SIX

Celeste was worried, but then that was nothing new. She was permanently worried these days. Since the night of Kevin Bryant's death she had never been the same. Every time she closed her eyes she saw his face, every time she opened her eyes she saw his face. And it was a horrible face, twisted up in anger and agony. Over the years he had grown in size, until now, all these years later, he was like some kind of giant in her mind.

She crept around her house, her lovely big house that should have made her happy, half-expecting his ghost to be behind her, expecting at any moment a tap on her shoulder and his decaying, rotten hand to touch her.

She poured herself another glass of vodka and downed it in one gulp. Alcohol was the only thing that stopped her from hearing the whispers and the noises that she was convinced came from the grave, the grave of Kevin Bryant. A constant whispering sound, it was reminiscent of when she had been a kid on a school trip to St Paul's Cathedral, and they had dutifully listened to the teacher in the Whispering Gallery, hearing the words travel around the structure, and all pretending to marvel at such a device in such an old building. She had not liked it in there with dead people everywhere you walked. So what if they were poets? They were still fucking dead and she was sure they would have much rather been buried in peace—somewhere a crowd of bored school kids wouldn't be taking the piss out of their names, and sniggering about their lives.

She closed her eyes against the negative thoughts. She had read somewhere that you had to force negative thoughts from your mind and think positive. But think positive about what? What did you think about when there was nothing positive in your life? When your whole world was built on quicksand and could be snatched from you in a millisecond?

Her husband loved her, that was a positive she supposed, but he could be shot dead, stabbed, maimed or disappear at any given moment. She knew better than anyone that that was the kind of world they lived in. So it was hard to think positive about that. She had a nice home and a caring family, but then so did a lot of people, so that wasn't really that big a positive when you analysed it properly. That was more of a human right, surely?

Celeste sighed heavily and looked at herself in her bedroom mirror. It was a large, very expensive mirror from France, and it made you look slimmer. But she knew it was just a trick of the glass so that, too, was built on a lie. Her whole life was built on lies and deceit, and she was powerless to do anything about it. She studied herself for a few moments. It was rare she ever looked at herself; she loathed what she was, what she had become. Outwardly she still looked OK. If she was on a bus—not that she ever got buses these days—she knew she would fit in with people's general opinion of someone normal. They couldn't see the blackness inside her, the rottenness that was at her core, and that bothered her. Really bothered her. It proved to her that you could never really trust anyone, because you couldn't see inside of them. You couldn't really ever know what was in their minds or, more importantly, their hearts.

Like James Junior killing that poor kitten. He looked like an angel that child, but he was filthy, putrid just like the rest of them. She was relieved now about her miscarriages, that she didn't have any children. How would you ever know what they were really like? Imagine having a baby which grew

150

up to be a monster, a killer? By then you already loved it, had made plans for it, and then it turned around and kicked you and all your hard work right in the teeth.

Oh no, that wasn't for her—that was for the likes of Cynthia. She had the strength to deal with things. Cynthia was the only person Celeste trusted. Cynthia would always look out for her, would always save her from danger. She was like a modern day Penthesilea, an Amazonian woman who could fight like a man, and think like a man. She could always depend on her, she knew that much. Like she would sort out little James, and steer him towards the right path.

Celeste was surprised to find herself in the kitchen, and wondered vaguely how she had got there. She opened the huge fridge and took out a chunk of cheese. She bit into it and savoured the strong cheddar taste, the saltiness on her tongue. Then, replacing it, she went to the countertop and poured herself another vodka. It occurred to her that she had not left the house for over a week, but she shrugged off the thought. Inside the house was bad enough, but it was nothing compared to the dangers on the streets.

She settled herself at the kitchen table and began to peruse the papers they had delivered every day. She looked for stories of death, pain, serial killers and genocide. These stories made her feel safe, made her feel that her take on the world was the true one. Even Spain, her beloved adopted country, wasn't immune. It was filling up with gangsters and murderers, including Majorca where she had believed life was simpler and therefore better. The papers were full of it nowadays, all kinds of death

151

and destruction, the whole world over.

Those facts, those stories she read, assured her that her thoughts were not wrong, that her life as it was could not be any other way. It was comforting to know that the world outside was just as she believed. That was the only positive thought she possessed, and she hung on to it like a dog with a bone.

CHAPTER FORTY-SEVEN

Jimmy Tailor was understandably upset at his son's behaviour and, what was worse, he didn't know how to address it. He could see that the hiding had meant nothing to the boy. To compound these feelings of worthlessness, he was aware of the look of contempt for his family in the boy's eyes too. It was a strange thing, but he really disliked his son now. Knowing he was capable of something so shocking and so heinous, and was not the least bit concerned about his actions, had shown Jimmy the true state of the boy's mind. He knew that in his hands he was now holding a potential threat to society.

That Jimmy could have fathered a child so devoid of love, so devoid of care, bothered him. In his heart of hearts he feared that while the boy may resemble him physically, the personality of his mother had come to the fore. The fact that Cynthia didn't think that the event was in any way catastrophic, really brought home to Jimmy just what he had tied himself to. Like Cynthia, James Junior looked as if butter wouldn't melt, whereas inside him was a seething cauldron of hate and viciousness. The school had regaled him with his son's other sins which had all come out after the affair with the cat had become public knowledge; from bullying to stealing, it seemed his James was capable of anything. No wonder he didn't have any real friends.

As he sat in the psychiatrist's waiting room, Jimmy looked at his son properly. He was reading a comic—always a comic never a book—and he looked unfussed about his surroundings and the reason why he was even here.

Most people here at the clinic looked like throwbacks from the sixties, all long hair and abundant moustaches. The rest were the opposite, well-tailored clothes and iron-grey hair, their countenances unreadable and their eyes cold and appraising. Not the most auspicious beginnings for the saving of this son of his.

A young girl sat opposite them. She looked to be about fourteen, with dyed hair and make-up. She smiled at him as he caught her eye and said, as if in answer to a question, 'I'm old enough to come on me own. Anyway, me mum's never up in time.' She shrugged as if this was a normal, everyday conversation.

Jimmy looked at her, wondering how the hell he had ended up in a place like this. He had been brought up in a nice home by nice people, and he had been happy in his job—the job which had displeased Cynthia because it had not provided enough for her and what she wanted from life. When she had chosen him—and he made no bones about it, *she* had set her cap at *him* and she had got him—he had envisaged a lovely life like his own

153

parents had, a nice, secure kind of life. Holidays every year, and a couple of nice, normal kids.

Instead, he had become a criminal. He had been sucked into a world he would never understand although, in fairness, he sometimes quite liked. It was glamorous at times and it was lucrative. Once Cynthia had realised he would never run the company he worked for the rot had set in, and she was not a woman to compromise from what she wanted.

He wiped a hand over his face. He needed a line but he guessed this was not the place to have one. He knew he had a problem with the coke but it made him feel invincible, made him believe that he was living a good life. At least these days he got acceptance, if not respect, from his wife. She didn't go on at him like she used to and, now she had her own 'career' as she referred to it, they were financially better off than they could have ever hoped to be. In a way he wished she had never been invited back into the fold; after her attempts to bring the family down, his life had been much easier. She had needed him then, she had needed what he could offer her.

Now she was like a phoenix risen from the ashes; she had all but become the main person in the businesses. He knew that Jonny liked her and her acumen. He said she was perfect for their world— she looked like an angel and thought like the devil, a simile that had made Jimmy shudder inwardly. It summed his wife up perfectly, and it also summed up his son.

When they were finally taken into the office and introduced to Dr Wendell, Jimmy started to relax. She looked like someone's nan, not at all as

154

intimidating as he had expected.

After a few preliminary questions she looked into young James's face and said seriously, 'Why did you cut the kitten's throat, James?'

To which he answered truthfully, 'I don't fucking know, do I? That's why I was sent here.'

It was obvious to everyone in the room that the boy thought there was a moron among them and it certainly wasn't him.

CHAPTER FORTY-EIGHT

Gabby was watching Vincent from inside the Golden Egg Café as he walked in to meet her. He looked very handsome and a little bit vulnerable. It was their third date and, thanks to her brother, she was now well and truly dispatched back to her nana and granddad's house—her mum didn't seem to want anything to do with either of them now. Though she hated what little James had done, she couldn't help but take advantage of the situation it had left them in.

Gabby liked Vincent even more when he wasn't trying to impress her, when he wasn't trying to act older than he was and more knowing. Inside, she knew he was as bewildered as she was about the feelings they had for each other. She had never felt like this before in her life. Never had she felt a pull from the gut like she did when she saw him walking towards her. It was almost primitive, and she instinctively knew that this was real love, not kids playing about at grown-up feelings and emotions. As young as they were, they were both completely sure that they were destined to be together. It wasn't something they had ever really discussed—it just was.

Vincent was dressed well—he always dressed like a man. At weekends he was suited and booted; like all his contemporaries he knew the value of a decent bit of clobber. She tried to dress for him now with longer skirts, tailored jackets, decent high heels. One good thing about it all was her mother had stopped frowning at her these days, believing it was *her* good taste that had made her daughter opt for more conservative clothing. Good job she didn't know it was because she wanted to look older, more sophisticated, more adult and that meant not looking like Madonna or Cyndi Lauper. It meant looking like a grown woman should look. Clean, fresh and well appointed. She had read that in a magazine and it had become her mantra.

As Vincent O'Casey spotted Gabby sitting in the Golden Egg waiting for him, his heart soared with love and, he admitted, a great deal of lust. But this was Jonny P's niece and he was ever aware of that. This was also the daughter of Cynthia Tailor, a legend in her own lunchtime, and he was acutely aware of that too.

That aside, he loved this girl with all his being. At seventeen, and Gabby not yet fourteen, he knew he was playing with fire. But she was like a woman, a woman beyond her years, for all her schoolgirl chatter and smoking. She knew instinctively what he needed and she provided it for him. He knew that was rare in a couple and that what they had was special.

Vincent understood the loneliness Gabby felt inside, knew that her mother was the bane of her life, and everyone else's for that matter—his included. Because if Cynthia Tailor ever found out about him he knew he would be warned off, and not in a polite way either. He would get the kicking of a lifetime, which was why they were meeting so out of the way of their usual haunts. It was also why he was cultivating the friendship of certain young men who could give him an in to the kind of life he wanted to be a part of. If he could get some respect—and not just as a little local hard nut, but as an earner—Vincent knew it would sweeten the pot where her family was concerned. He had plans and he had dreams, and he was determined to see that they were fulfilled at some point in his life. Because this girl was going to be the mother of his children and that, he knew, was a fact.

As he walked over to the table, he saw the love shining out of her eyes and, like many a man before him, he believed that would be enough for them. He was still too young to know that determination was only the half of it. It was the hard graft that was the really difficult part. Life was like that, he would find out much too late. It let you think you had the upper hand when all along it knew you were heading for disaster.

For the moment, anything seemed possible. They were happy just to be together, and that was more than enough for them.

CHAPTER FORTY-NINE

Jonny Parker had spent a not entirely disagreeable afternoon with Cynthia, and was now on his way to visit one of his clubs. It was a very worthwhile enterprise which housed sixty different lap dancers over a two-week period. The girls were young, ultra fit and up for literally anything. Just the kind of girls needed for the West End of London. Even better, they were all well within the legal age, and had a vested interest in staying at that particular club. Jonny paid them *very* well, and they were in a position to meet men of all classes and colours who had one thing in common—serious amounts of dosh. Wonga was the girls' god, and they got it by the thankful. The men were vetted and they were, for one reason or another, interested in privacy more than the girls themselves.

A private club was a boon in many respects, because it afforded a level of safety that many of the men concerned needed in their daily lives—their work lives—and particularly in their night lives. Jonny had them all—from top businessmen to politicians and Old Bill to serious Faces, and he made sure any sojourn at the club was as secret as it was enjoyable. There was a lot of money in keeping people clean; he had tapped into a market that was not just lucrative money-wise but also gave him contacts who owed him.

This club was the first of many, and he was in negotiations to do the same thing in Liverpool, Manchester and Glasgow. The girls earned too much to open their traps, and they were also aware that one wrong word and they would never work anywhere again. This wasn't just a threat that they would be black-balled as such, but that their lives would be tragically cut short. No kiss-and-tell from *his* lap dancers. If they did, it would be the last thing they ever said and they were well aware of that.

Tonight he had a meeting with a local up-and-coming Face by the name of Derek Greene. Derek was also known as 'Derek the Red' because he had no trouble spilling blood. He was thirty-one years old, built like the proverbial brick shithouse and had been educated at a private school thanks to his father, a notorious bank robber who thought his son should grow up in the straight world. Derek Senior was now doing a twenty-five, and his son, then seventeen, had been left penniless and with no real qualifications except his extreme strength, his short temper and the nous that living around a villain had ingrained into him. He had risen in the ranks and become a man to be reckoned with.

Now he wanted a meet, and Jonny was very interested in what he had to say. The boy had a good rep, and he liked him. Always open for a bit of naughty, he was happy enough as he walked into the dim foyer of the Madison Avenue Private Members Club. It was a great space and it looked fantastic—understated and with an abundance of glass and chrome. No one looking inside would believe what its respectable façade hid. It could be the offices of a banking corporation, but once through the heavy wooden doors it was the epitome of sexual gratification. All reds, purples and creams, the girls' outfits, albeit very small, were colour-coordinated to match the surroundings that were reminiscent of a brothel the Pre-Raphaelites would have frequented. It was upmarket trash, and it was making Jonny untold money.

It was quiet now, though. Early evening just had the serious drinkers in, the ones who needed the Dutch courage to actually approach the girls, and a few of the local Faces ready to have a meet in more luxurious surroundings than their local boozers, where everything they said was overheard and repeated. The club was for people who had an agenda, and that agenda was wholly their own.

Jonny spied young Derek sitting alone and smiled to himself; the boy was learning the art of confidence. Never discuss business in front of anyone who might have an interest in it, either for themselves or other people. It was a good rule to live by and he liked that the younger man had appreciated his need for privacy in all his dealings.

He motioned for a bottle of Scotch and two glasses and, when the drinks were poured and the ice was clinking amiably, they began their meeting.

'So, young Derek, what can I do you for?'

Derek smiled, his huge face handsome in a dangerous kind of way. Jonny knew certain women would be attracted to it because looking at Derek you could tell this was a man capable of great cruelty and there were women who admired that.

'Nice set up, Mr Parker, really fucking impressive.'

It was said with genuine approval and Jonny felt himself relax. He liked this kid, though, in reality, he wasn't a kid, he was a large and very dangerous man. 'Glad you approve, Derek. And how goes your businesses? I hear tell you're knocking over more banks than the Luftwaffe.'

Derek grinned. 'Not too bad a business as it goes, Mr Parker. With my old man it stands to reason I would know the general economics of such an industry.'

They both laughed at his choice of words.

'True. I hear your little ones are well too.'

160

Derek almost blushed then; it was true what Jonny had heard—this was a family man beyond excellence. He had a lovely wife and three little ones, all daughters, who he doted on with a passion. The youngest had been born brain-damaged and it was rumoured that he had moved heaven and earth and serious amounts of poke to make sure she got the best treatment on offer. This was not seen as a weakness by the men in their world, but as a strength. You looked after your own before and above anyone else. It was another reason that Jonny felt he could work with the lad. He was decent and kind when appropriate, and a ruthless fucker when required. A lethal but necessary combination in a business partner.

Jonny hoped that the lad had a good proposition for him, one that would make it worth his while to take an interest in this fellow, because he would rather have him where he could keep an eye on him. There wasn't that much difference in their ages but, whereas Jonny had his creds, this boy was still paving the way for his own. If it was a bollocks proposition he would make a point of giving him a bit of collar—nothing too important but enough to give him a good earn. That way he could keep him close.

'So, back to where we began, what can I do for you?'

Derek smiled and it changed his whole face, he looked almost affable. 'It's holiday villas. Spain, Portugal, Florida. All above board and legal, and none of it really exists, at least it only does on paper. You need do fuck-all except advance me a few quid, and there is minimal risk as the businesses are owned off-shore by private investors. I have the

161

people to sell, I have the wherewithal to get the relevant paperwork to make us kosher. I also know that, when we have enough poke, we shut down and start up again somewhere else. The Spanish are good like that; you can rip off anyone, as long as you have the relevant paperwork. I have the land, I own the fucking land and, one day, I will build on it, but no villas or apartment blocks naturally. It would take the average Joe twenty years of his life to follow the paper trails and, when they find the end of that particular rainbow, we will all be long gone.' He sat back in his seat and sipped delicately at his Scotch and water.

'Can I see an outline?'

'I had it biked to your offices this morning. I have also taken the liberty of enclosing a share scheme showing you exactly how much your investment will bring you on return, depending on your initial outlay, of course. You have my word that I am in this in a serious capacity and just want us all to earn a good crust, and walk away with the minimum of fuss.'

Jonny Parker liked this kid more and more. He had some initiative and didn't sit there with his plans in his hands explaining it all in an hour. He had biked the details over and now Jonny could peruse them at his leisure. He had made a good judgement call on this Derek Greene, and he was pleased.

'Fair enough, Derek, I'll look them over and I'll speak to you soon. Now, how's your old man?'

Derek shrugged. 'Truth is, Mr Parker, fifteen years behind the door takes its toll on a man but, all in all, he's doing OK. He's happy enough with his lot, swallowed his knob, can't do anything else, can he? We all visit. Me mum's waited, bless her heart. She spent the best years of her life travelling all over the fucking country. But she's a good old bird, and she deserves to see him home at some point. Brief reckons another two, three years, he'll be back in the bosom of his family.'

'Fucking harsh the sentences handed down. Fucking rapist would have been out now.'

'At least then he would have had a unit where he could wander about and watch telly in his cell. Fucking nonces and their VPUs. Vulnerable Prisoners Units—have you ever heard the fucking like? 'Course they're vulnerable, who wouldn't want to kick their fucking heads in?'

They both nodded, pondering the futility of a legal system that protected the scum of society, and locked away men like Derek's father for the duration. It was a fucking melon scratcher all right.

CHAPTER FIFTY

'Go away, you weirdo.'

Cynthia Tailor rolled her eyes at the ceiling as she bellowed, 'Stop calling your brother a weirdo!'

Gabby grinned. 'But he is, Mum. Even his shrink thinks so.'

Cynthia wanted to laugh then; Gabriella was funny when she wanted to be.

James Junior looked around the table at his family silently. He was a large lad, and he had the look of his father's family. Staring at his sister, he smiled sneakily. 'How's Vincent O'Casey, Gabby?'

Cynthia looked at her son in shock, and he

laughed at her as he said, 'Didn't you know, Mum? It's the romance of the century by all accounts.'

Cynthia looked at this son of hers that she was finding it increasingly difficult to like and said coldly, 'Not Bridie O'Casey's Vincent?'

Gabby thought she was going to faint with fright at her mother's words, and her eyes pleaded with her brother to not do this.

He grinned nastily as he said loudly, 'The very same.'

Gabby was out of her chair in a second, screaming at her brother, 'You cat-killing ponce! You rotten little bugger!'

Cynthia looked at her two children and wondered which one to slap first. Her instincts won and she knocked her son off his chair with a sideswipe. 'Get out of my sight, you.' Then, when he had scrambled up off the floor and fled the scene of his crime, she turned to her daughter and said quietly, 'Is this true?'

Gabby knew it was pointless denying it, and so she nodded her head slowly.

When her mother's hand shot out and grabbed her hair she stifled a scream, knowing it was best to take whatever she dished out as quietly as possible. Begging annoyed her, as did screaming in agony, trying to escape, and attempting to talk your way out of things. Once her mother had you by the hair, you were all but finished.

'How long? How long have you been going behind my back?' This was her mother all over, not 'how long have you been seeing him' but 'how long have you been going behind my back'.

'A while, nearly a year . . .' Gabby had to be honest now she'd been caught; it was the only way out for her. If she lied now she was as good as dead. Her mother was not a woman to buy lies of any description. Once sussed out, all that you had left to redeem yourself in any way was the truth.

Cynthia screwed up her face in complete and utter amazement. A year! This had been going on for a *year*, and no one had guessed? No one had told her more like. The bastards. An O'Casey—a family so low down on the social stratum they might as well be fucking cavemen. Bridie O'Casey was a lazy, feckless trollop who couldn't even keep her kids clean, let alone her home. And the father! Paddy O'Casey, the local drunkard. It was beyond her comprehension.

'All I've done for you kids, and this is how you repay me? Your brother up there on the road to becoming a fucking serial killer and you well on your way to whoring! Well, lady, this stops here. You're coming home for good. No wonder you're always round your nana's! I bet she's encouraging him, fucking vicious old bag that she is . . .'

She punched her daughter in the mouth, sending her reeling across the room. Gabby landed on the floor by the dining-room door, and it was as if Cynthia was seeing her properly for the first time in years. The long, shapely legs, the high breasts, the tiny waist. This was a woman in the making and, if her boyfriend had seen his way fit to helping her along the road, she would kill the fucker with her bare hands.

Terrified, Gabby pulled herself up off the floor. She knew from experience that this was now about damage limitation. Taking a deep breath she said in her most humble voice, 'I'm sorry, Mum, I should have told you, but I knew how you would react . . .'

Cynthia was shaking her head at the two-faced skulduggery of this daughter of hers. 'A fucking O'Casey? Is that your fucking limit? Barbie's Ken has got more brains than him! The whole family is a bit touched. And you are going out with him! You shouldn't be out with *any* boys, you're too young.'

The slap was resounding, and Gabby felt the fury coming out of her mother's pores. She also felt her own anger mounting; she would not give him up no matter what her mother said.

'Who's next, Benny fucking Hill? You stupid little mare, you better not have been doing something you shouldn't! If he's mounted you I'll cut his fucking throat.'

Even Cynthia in her rage could see the absolute shock on her daughter's face at the suggestion and thanked the powers-that-be that at least the girl hadn't gone that far. But she could also see that her daughter had no intention of giving this idiot up, and that was what was really upsetting her. She would make sure this family of hers would not go to the bad, and would not show her up.

Such was the thinking of Cynthia Tailor.

CHAPTER FIFTY-ONE

Mary and Jack Callahan listened to their granddaughter, Mary with a sympathy that belied the fact she agreed, in part, with Cynthia's take on this state of affairs. Gabby was well and truly older than her years in looks, but not in any emotional capacity. She was all legs and make-up at the moment, and that was to be expected at her age.

What the girl couldn't see was that a few choice words on Vincent's part, and her life as she knew it could be over and she'd be left holding a baby. Mary had never thought she would agree with that mad bitch of a daughter of hers, but on this she was right behind her. The boy was too old and too knowing by half. He was also too good-looking for his own good.

It would do Gabby good to go home for a while. In all honesty, since the episode with the kitten, Mary didn't want the lad here either. He was a strange boy, with his vicious trouble-making, and she pondered long and hard at how he had become so callous without her or anyone noticing. She supposed that was the way of the world these days. TV was to blame in her opinion. It made children adults before they were ready—even the soap operas were full of sex and violence, and the kids watched them as avidly as she did herself. Though, at least she was scandalised by what she saw. Mary closed her eyes; she felt very tired suddenly and her granddaughter's voice was going through her head like a ninety-pound hammer.

'Well, you should have thought of all this, Gabby, when you were sneaking around meeting that lad.'

'But it's so unfair, Nana, my mum is the . . .'

'Don't say it, Gabby, she's still your mother.'

'I hate her, I hate her guts.'

Jack heard his granddaughter ranting and raving about her mother, his daughter, and he felt a terrible urge to join in with her. But he didn't. How they had come to this state of affairs he didn't know, all he knew was it was Cynthia's fault. Everything she touched she destroyed. Her own children included.

167

CHAPTER FIFTY-TWO

Derek Greene was a happy man. He had had the go ahead from Jonny P, and he knew his future was secure. He also knew that, if he played his cards right, his father's future would be secure too. He loved a bit of skulduggery, thrived on it in fact. 'Walk Like An Egyptian' by The Bangles came on Melody FM and he turned it up; he liked the beat of the record.

In the back of his car he had a small armoury, and he was delivering it to a friend in need. He was, therefore, driving within the speed limit, with his seat belt on, and his face a mask of pure innocence. It annoyed him when people got a tug for a stupid traffic violation while endeavouring to carry out their illegal business. It was a pointless nicking and it led to far too much trouble. While he was pursuing his nefarious businesses, he acted, drove and lived by the letter of the law. Why attract unwanted attention to yourself?

Pulling up at the scrapyard in Bow, he got out of the car and stretched for a few seconds. The Bangles had been replaced by David Bowie singing 'Ashes To Ashes' and he hummed along for a few seconds before walking nonchalantly to the Portakabins that served as offices.

He liked the yard. It was a place he had played in as a kid, and it was owned by his dad's old mate Phillip Gardener, a prince among men. He had come to Derek's rescue after his father's untimely nicking, having heard about their financial position, and he had stepped in to help them out. Derek had a feeling Phillip would have liked to help his mother out in a more personal fashion and she had knocked him back. He didn't blame the man for trying, and he respected his mother for her refusal; she was a decent old bird when all was said and done. His father had better remember that when he finally got out. Derek remembered his father had liked a bit of extra-marital interest, and that would *not* be tolerated this time round—his mother should be treated better than that. He would see she got the respect she deserved.

Phillip was a nice geezer, all bonhomie and kind nature most of the time, but he could also kick the shit out of men three times his size and he wasn't small by any standards. What Phillip had was a refusal to admit defeat, and young Derek understood that because he had a similar trait running through his veins. No matter how many times he was knocked down, he would get up again, making the opponent wonder just how long the fight would have to go on, and worrying how long they could keep up with the nutter in front of them.

Phillip watched Derek walking towards the offices and put the kettle on, he knew the lad liked a cup of tea. He drank gallons of the stuff day and night. He heard him come into the Portakabin and called out a greeting from the little cubby hole where drinks were made and hands were washed. Unhygienic, but unfortunately needs must and all that. Phillip was quite a fastidious man in his own way.

Phillip was a fixer. He fixed things for people and he had a knack of knowing how a fix should be executed. It was a very lucrative living for him and, when anyone was in a position they were not sure of, they came to him for advice—for a price of course. He was like the grave—he never discussed his own business so it was only right he never discussed anyone else's. He knew where the bodies were buried, and that meant literally as well as theoretically, so he was left alone, but was very well respected. No kids or wife had come his way—he had a large house that was looked after by his large, ugly, kind and very capable cousin, Marge. He quite liked his solitary existence, loving Belinda Greene from a distance and treating her son as his own.

The lad was a good study, and he learned quickly. He would make a good fixer himself one day, but first he had to learn the economics of this kind of work. One wrong word and the world he had so carefully constructed could tumble down on him in an instant.

Now they had a bit of work and they needed to make sure it was planned out and executed properly. Derek knew a small part of what was being undertaken, but that was all; even in his honoured position he would not get the full facts until it was deemed necessary. Phillip brought out the two teas and, as was his wont, he poured a small amount of brandy into his own mug.

Derek was sitting on the leather banquette, patiently as always, his face a study of earnest concentration. Oh, Phillip liked this kid. He was a pleasure to teach and a fine example of how a young man could be trained if under the right guidance.

'Did he swallow it?'

Derek smiled, a wide, amiable smile. 'Hook, line and fucking sinker.'

'He's a slippery cunt Jonny P, and he can smile

while he cuts your nuts off, so don't let your guard down even once, you hear me?'

Derek nodded, exasperated at how careful Phillip could be at times, even as he understood why the man was chary. Jonny P was a force in his own right, but not for much longer.

'Let him stew a while, and get him onside, then we'll arrange the final meeting.'

Derek nodded his assent. 'My thoughts entirely, Phillip. Then we can meet our mutual friend and get the deal done sooner rather than later.'

'It's going to cause chaos, you know that, don't you?'

Derek nodded.

'You can walk away any time you like, son. This is a dangerous operation, and you have a young family.'

'I know, mate, but I'm in over me head now, and I feel confident we can pull it off.'

Phillip smiled, one of his rare, real smiles. 'Good lad. I knew you wouldn't let me down.'

CHAPTER FIFTY-THREE

'Well, maybe if you took more notice of him he might not be such a fucking strange one, James. If you didn't snort up that shit like there's no tomorrow . . .'

Jimmy Tailor looked at his wife and wondered as he often did what she would do if he slapped her across her lovely mouth. He never would, but it didn't stop him dreaming about it. 'Shut up, Cynth, for once in your fucking life, just shut up.'

171

It was evident that she was momentarily shocked at his words, but she recovered her composure in about three seconds. Her shouting could be heard all over the house and, in her bedroom, Gabby put her hands over her ears. She was sick of it, and she was sick of being held prisoner like she had done something wrong. She could hear James Junior next door, kicking the wall as loudly as possible, and wondered at how she wasn't as mental as him.

She turned her CD player up to drown out the noise of her family's madness. She lay on her bed and thought about Vincent, which was all she did these days—even her schoolwork was suffering. But he was like an obsession, growing more powerful by the day. She wondered if he would be at the school gates tomorrow? She hadn't seen him today and it had worried her. Maybe he was fed up with the situation. Who could blame him? It was all *her* fault. She couldn't bring herself to use the word mother, or mum. She was just *her* now, and Gabby hated her.

Downstairs, the shouting was reaching its crescendo.

'You! You're not a fucking man, James Tailor, you're a fucking *boy*, an innocent, a laughing stock as well!' Cynthia was in full screaming mode now, her life as she knew it was in tatters, and this idiot she had tied herself to was as much use as a handbrake on a canoe.

'He's fucking going, Cynthia. If it will help him he has to go, can't you see that?'

Cynthia was swallowing down the urge to smash this man over the head with the nearest chair. He was quite happy for their son, their child, to go into a psychiatric assessment centre, a place where he

172

would be labelled a nut-bag, and he thought she would happily say it was OK. What fucking planet was he on? As always, her mind was not on the poor child, but on what his actions would look like to the outside world, what people would think of her.

'It's only for a few weeks, and then he'll be home, and he'll get the help he needs.'

'Over my dead body.'

'Well, from what the shrink said that's an option, Cynth. She said he's on his way to becoming a full-blown Looney Tunes. Or, in her words, he has no idea of the effect his actions have on the people around him. He is only interested in the world as it pertains to him and his wants. He cannot empathise with others, and has no understanding of the needs of others. Quote, unquote. Remind you of anyone, Cynth?'

'You ponce! Don't blame me for all this! This comes from your side, all fucking weird your family. Your mother's about as with-it as a three-legged camel.'

Jimmy sighed heavily. 'Can't you see that he has to go away, before he does anything terrible. It's for his own good as well as everyone else's. Anyway, we ain't got no say in it. If we refuse, the social workers will intervene and we'll have no control over his life at all.'

In her heart, Cynthia knew what her husband was saying was true, but it hurt her to admit that her child was 'not right', and she knew that people would blame *her*. They always blamed the mother in these cases. She felt the tears stinging her eyes and blinked them away rapidly. Why was this happening to her? What had she ever done to deserve this?

She needed to see Jonny and she needed to see him soon. He was another one—she could feel he was different, knew that all this with James Junior had pissed him off. She had gone on about it too much but, in all honesty, she couldn't see what they were up in arms about. He was ten years old, and they were labelling him already. He was highly strung that was all, and now tomorrow morning, they were supposed to take him to a child psychiatric unit in Kent and leave him there. Suddenly that didn't seem such a bad thing; with James Junior gone all she had left was Gabriella—that had to make life easier surely? He was a handful was young James and, as his father said, he would be in the best place.

She smiled grudgingly suddenly. 'If you're sure, James.'

Jimmy sighed with relief. She had finally seen sense and now the boy could get the help he so desperately needed.

He poured them both a stiff drink and, as she took hers from her husband, Cynthia was pondering how she could get rid of her daughter as well. She could do with a break; after all, she was the first to admit, she wasn't really the maternal type, and now she had her job. She would board her daughter in a good, strict school, where they would watch the little mare like a hawk. That would put a stop to her gallop, and give her the time she needed to pursue her other interests. James Junior killing that cat was like a gift from the gods really, it had turned out to have unexpected benefits. She felt a rush of excitement at having her life to herself once more, and it was very hard not to stop a wide grin from splitting her seriously concerned face.

Jimmy guessed what was really going through her mind; he knew her better than anyone. But he didn't say a word, all he could do was make sure his son got the best treatment available and hope against hope that it worked. Being brought up by Cynthia Tailor had to have some kind of repercussions, and he had a feeling this was just the start of them for both his children. He didn't worry as much about Gabby though. She had a thick skin where her mother was concerned, and he was glad about that. She was going to need that thick skin for a while yet; she was growing up and turning into a beautiful girl and it wasn't something his wife was going to accept graciously. That Cynthia was jealous of the girl was evident—not that she would ever admit it—but Gabby was really going to be a beauty, and that was something Cynthia was going to find difficult to tolerate. It was her way or no way—how many times had he heard her say that to the kids over the years?

Well, this was the upshot of her mothering and, while he hoped that it taught her a lesson, he doubted very much that it would. Cynthia didn't care about anyone or anything enough to change her ways, and that thought, along with his kids' problems, depressed Jimmy further still. He knew he should leave, take his daughter now and go, but where? Cynthia would let them go, of that he had no doubt, but he knew that with his lifestyle and his little habit, he wasn't going to be much use to his kids. It was a cop-out, but he didn't want the responsibility of those two by himself. Like his wife, he was too caught up in the world he lived in to make those kind of changes. It was a vicious circle, and every one of them was caught up in it.

175

The kids more than any of them, because they lived at the whim of their parents, and he knew he and Cynthia were not parents anyone would choose to be lumbered with.

Still, he consoled himself with the fact he had fought her to get James Junior the help he so desperately needed, so at least he had done that much. A voice in his head was telling him it was too little, too late. But he ignored that, and left the house quick smart. Cynthia could do the boy's packing—she was better at things like that than he was.

An hour later he was coked out of his nut, and working on long columns of figures. Only numbers made any sense to him these days, and he lost himself in them like a drowning man grabbing on to a lifeboat.

CHAPTER FIFTY-FOUR

Vincent O'Casey was waiting for Gabby outside the school gates the next morning and, seeing him, her heart rose in her chest.

'How's everything?' He genuinely cared, and that meant so much to her.

'I'm on me own today because me mum has to take me brother to some kind of kids' looney bin in Kent. I'll skip school, shall I? We can go somewhere and be together.'

Vincent knew he should refuse, but he missed her. Never had he felt like this about a girl before. Gabby was under his skin and, with the certainty of young love, he knew she always would be. She came from a dangerous family, and he was nervous about that, but it was her, Gabby, who filled his days and his nights. If he was honest, she was like a virus infecting every part of him, and he knew that she felt the same about him.

'I've got a motor round the corner, borrowed it off me mate Petey. He's working for your uncle Jonny actually, and he might get me onboard. I'm thinking of going into the banking business.'

Gabby smiled with pride. Once settled in the rather knackered Ford Capri Ghia, Gabby lit a cigarette and said earnestly, 'What bank will you work for? Barclays?'

Vincent grinned then and said mischievously, 'Sometimes, depends what bank we'll be robbing, don't it!'

Gabby laughed, but she felt the first fingers of fear inside her belly. She forced it away; he was older than her, and he knew what he was about. It was too late for her now, he was in her blood, and nothing he did would make her feel anything other than love for him.

'What, with guns?'

He nodded as he pulled out into the traffic. ''Course. Bit pointless trying to rob a bank with a fucking lolly stick!'

'But what if you get caught?'

'I won't get caught, it's a doddle really. Now, let's drop that, shall we? Where do you want to go? Victoria Park? How about Barking Park? We can go on the boats.'

She grinned shyly. 'How about Southend? I love Southend.'

'Southend it is.'

As they picked up the A13, she was quiet for a

few moments. 'I know this ain't been easy, Vince, but my mum's a tough one you know.'

Vincent laughed then. 'Fucking understatement of the year that! She's harder than most blokes. I mean, you have to admire her, don't you? She saved her sister from certain death, girl, and, from what I heard, she took out Kevin Bryant quick as anything.'

Gabby didn't answer; she had heard the stories, and they all differed in some way. She was astute enough to know that the whole truth had been scrubbed out a long time ago. She also knew her mother was capable of anything. And not in a good way. It occurred to her that maybe Vincent was with her for her family connections. She could see that her family could be a big draw to a certain kind of people. The thought saddened her, and she wondered if this man, this young boy who she loved so much, was seeing her as a way into the firm. She felt she had to say something.

'I wouldn't give stories too much credence, Vince. Me mum's got a hard side, and she don't like you. So any thoughts you've got about getting an in with her and me uncle Jonny through me won't happen. She thinks you're leading me astray.'

Vincent was serious now. 'Listen, Gabby, I've got in with a nice little firm, and they ain't nowhere in your uncle's league, or your mother's come to that. But I can tell you this, I know I won't be welcomed with open arms by your mum and dad. I'll sit it out until you're old enough to make your own mind up, and we can tip them bollocks, OK?'

At his words, Gabby felt the sun come out for her once more. He wanted her for *herself*, she was sure of that. She laughed gently and turned up the radio; Simply Red were singing 'Remembering The First Time', and they both grinned.

'Our record, eh?'

She laughed with him, happy to be beside him, happy to forget that she was playing truant and happy to forget about her mother. Today was just for them, and they were going to enjoy it.

CHAPTER FIFTY-FIVE

Jonny Parker was pleased with the villa scam. Everyone he had spoken to was of the same opinion—it was a good time for something like this. Package holidays were affordable for most people these days and Spain was booming. From Calpe to Marbella, Brits were flocking in their thousands, and they all wanted a little bit of Spain for themselves. 'The Dorm', as Benidorm was affectionately known, was kicking nine months of the year. It was cheap, and it was crowded, and that was exactly what the punters wanted.

So, as he drove to Cynthia's house, he was a happy man. It was as if he could do no wrong, and everything he touched turned into golden coins. In this case, of course, it was pesetas, but the principle was the same. He was glad they were meeting at her house; it wasn't far for him to go home from there, and he was knackered.

As he pulled up outside the door, he felt a small twinge of apprehension. Cynthia was getting more and more insistent about their 'relationship' as she called it, and he had a feeling she would soon be asking him to call time on his marriage, and that

179

was never going to happen. But, ever the optimist, he hoped he was wrong; they still had great sex and that was basically what their 'relationship' had always been about. Knowing what she was capable of still rocked his boat, and he knew that he was playing with a very dangerous adversary. That was part of the thrill. But he knew, when all was said and done, that as hard as she was, he was harder and, if necessary, he would show her that, and put the frighteners on her once and for all. He hoped it wouldn't come to that of course, but he had to watch his back.

As he walked through the door he had to smile. She had more front than Brighton, sitting on the kitchen table, legs splayed and a beatific smile on her face.

'I thought you'd never get here!'

'It's your birthday tomorrow—as if I would forget that.' He was undoing his trousers as he spoke and she laughed with him.

An hour earlier she had fed her husband and daughter at this very table, knowing that once they were out for the evening, she would be entertaining Jonny. James had taken Gabriella out late-night shopping to get her birthday present—like she believed they were going to the pictures!—but it was sweet of James to still play the part of the caring husband. She knew that her daughter didn't want to go. Gabriella's idea of a birthday present for her mother would be a milkshake full to the brim with deadly night-shade if it had been left to her. After all, today she had found out about the boarding school; the look on her daughter's face! It was true a picture was worth a thousand words— Gabriella's face had been worth that and more.

But that was forgotten now her Jonny was inside her and, as always, for both of them, it was all they really needed. When they were together like this, it was as if the rest of the world had disappeared, and it was just them.

Unfortunately, Jimmy Tailor had only had to go as far as his mother-in-law's to collect his wife's very expensive Rolex watch. Jack had got it for him cheap and, having spotted Jonny's car outside, as he and Gabby walked back through the front door, he expected to see Jonny Parker in his front room sipping a drink. But, strangely, it was in darkness. Moving through to the kitchen, his daughter by his side, Jimmy instead walked into a scene he would never in a million years have envisaged.

Even in his own distress, he still knew he should remove his daughter from the kitchen and get her away from what was happening on his kitchen table. The table where an hour earlier they had all eaten together like a normal family, like a real family. As if that had any truth in it. But, instead, he grabbed his wife's hair and dragged her off the table, and on to the floor.

He could hear screaming, but was that Cynthia or was it Gabby?

It was all happening so fast.

CHAPTER FIFTY-SIX

'Calm down, child, and tell me what's happened. Is it James Junior? Has something happened to him?'

'It's me dad, he's attacked me mum . . . You've got to come, Granddad.' Gabby was imploring Jack with her eyes while her nana tried to get some sense out of her.

'Me mum was on the table with . . . Me dad's gone berserk.'

Suddenly her words hit home and her grandparents both groaned as if in pain.

'Jesus Christ, what was she thinking! In her own home, the fucking whore.' Jack Callahan was fuming. 'I knew this would happen one day! I knew it. I warned her about being so brazen, I only wish I'd talked to him too. But you know Jonny Parker, no talking to *him*, is there? Too high and mighty for the likes of us . . .'

'Will you shut up, Jack!' hissed Mary.

It was only then he remembered that Celeste was there too, and she was looking at them as if they had all miraculously appeared before her in a vision.

Gabby looked from one to the other, and realised just how far-reaching the repercussions of her mother's actions would be. She had stopped herself saying Jonny's name, because her aunt had enough on her plate as it was. This was the night Celeste came round here for her dinner, and what her nana referred to as a 'catch up'. Now it was out, and Gabby felt it was her fault, but she had not known where else to go.

Her father had been like a maniac and, when she had left, her uncle Jonny was beating down on her dad in order to get him away from her mum. It was like a nightmare, only she was wide awake and it was really happening, and her dad would never be the same again. She had seen and heard the hurt inside him. The strange thing was, he seemed more upset with her uncle Jonny. And her uncle

Jonny she could tell was ashamed, ashamed and frightened. But then so he should be, he had done the dirty on them all. She hated him now just as much as she did her mother. They were both of a kind, both selfish, both believing that the world was only there for *them* and what *they* wanted.

Celeste was in her nana's arms now, and she followed her granddad out of the house, wondering what this night would bring them all, and aware that it wouldn't be anything good, that much was for sure. It never was with her mother. She was sending *her* away to school in the middle of nowhere so she couldn't be with Vincent, and all the time *she* was having an affair with her uncle Jonny!

Gabby still couldn't believe what she had seen, still couldn't get over her father's reaction. Her poor dad, her poor, poor dad. She was crying again, and she hoped that her mum was dead on the floor when they got back home. She wanted her dead so badly. If she died she couldn't hurt them any more.

Even James Junior might be in with a chance if *she* was gone, because her mother infected everyone and everything around her, and she destroyed anyone who stood in her way, just as she beat down anyone who disagreed with her.

Gabby hated her, even more than before if that was possible. Her mother had more or less called her a whore today, smugly telling her she was going away to school, where there would be no boys. Well, she herself would know what a whore was— no one could know better. In fact, she was worse than a whore, because she had done the dirty on her own sister, and that was something only the lowest of the low could be capable of.

Gabby hoped her dad killed her, she hoped he

had killed them both. They deserved it, the pair of them.

CHAPTER FIFTY-SEVEN

'Oh, shut up, Cynthia. Shut the fuck up!' Jack Callahan was disgusted with them, both Cynthia and Jonny, and it showed. He looked at his son-in-law and, sneering, he said, 'Where's Jimmy gone?'

Jonny had the grace to look shamefaced and that placated Jack a little bit. Even his son-in-law's fearsome reputation wasn't cutting any ice with him this night. He thought these two before him were lower than the lowest, they were carrion to him now. If he never saw either of them again it would be too soon.

'I don't know, Dad.'

'Don't you call me "Dad", you fucking slag! After this night is over I never want to see your face again. All this time you were fucking him did you think of your sister?' He looked pointedly at Jonny then. 'That's my daughter Celeste, your fucking wife, in case you forgot her name. Did either of you think about that poor girl, eh? Between you you've sent her off her chump, but then you sent your little James off his head and all, didn't you, Cynthia? Quite a track record you've got now. Well, you better find your husband. Who knows what he's capable of in his state of mind! He might be sitting with Lily Law bringing you down. Funny what a man's capable of when he's been fucked over by his mate and his wife.'

Jonny Parker was looking around him as if he

184

was drunk; he felt as if he was in a stupor. 'Does Celeste . . .'

'Oh, she knows, Jonny. You'll have a job talking her round after this little debacle.'

Jonny Parker felt physically sick at what he had caused. Looking at Cynthia now, her eye black, dried blood on her face from her husband's fists and boots, the ferocity of the attack was what had shocked him more than anything. Jimmy was a big man, and he had shown that he wasn't as docile as his wife had believed. He had even given Jonny a few good thumps before he had left the house, his car roaring off like something from the Grand Prix.

But it was young Gabby who really made him see what damage they had caused. Her eyes were on him and, if hate had been a tangible thing, he would have been knocked to the floor by now. And Celeste! His Celeste! She knew!

'Celeste . . . Is she still at yours, Jack?'

'If you mean does she know *everything*, yes, she does. Now maybe she'll get away from you and start living her life. As for you, Cynthia, you keep away from her. She thought the world of you, always did.' He looked at his elder daughter then, before saying, 'I hope you never know another happy day, Cynth. I hope you stew in your own hate and your own greed. You wanted what she had. Couldn't stand it, could you, that she got him, and you got poor Jimmy. Well, you're welcome to each other now, because I'm finished with you, lady. Finished with the pair of you.' With that he walked out of the house.

Cynthia was quiet as she watched her father walk away from her. Then, turning to Jonny, she said defiantly, 'I'm glad it's come out, now we can be

185

together . . .'

Jonny was looking at her in utter amazement now. 'What the fuck are you on about, you silly bitch? Glad it's come out! Are you off your fucking trolley? If you were the only woman left in the world, I wouldn't have you now. Can't you see what *we've* done? What *we've* caused? I love Celeste, I always will. I couldn't love you . . . No one could. Face it, Cynth, you're a lot of things, girl, but lovable ain't one of them.' He looked at the woman who had been like an itch to him for so long, and was pleased to see that it was one itch that had well and truly been scratched raw. 'I need to find Jimmy, and make sure he doesn't do what your father suggested. But first I need to see my wife, and try and repair some of the damage I've done to her.' He looked at Gabby. 'Look after your mum . . .'

Gabby laughed, and she looked years older than fourteen as she said, '*You* look after her. As far as I'm concerned me granddad has the right idea, she's dead to me and all.'

She left the house, and ran to catch up with her granddad who, putting his arm around her, said sadly, 'I shouldn't have left you there, Gabby; I'm not thinking right tonight.'

She slipped her hand into his, and together they walked back to her nana's in silence.

CHAPTER FIFTY-EIGHT

'Did you know about all this, Mum?'

Mary Callahan looked at this lovely daughter of hers and decided that only the truth would suffice

186

now. 'Everyone knew, I think. But how could we interfere, lovie? I kept hoping it would burn itself out . . .'

Celeste nodded; inside her brain somewhere she realised she had known too—not about Cynthia, but she had always known there was someone else. Jonny wasn't a man to go without anything he wanted, it was what had attracted her to him and, if it hadn't been for that night when Kevin Bryant had come gunning for her, she knew instinctively that none of this with Cynthia would ever have happened. That night had changed them all somehow, her more than any of them. For Cynthia it had been her re-entry into the world she loved, the world Celeste had only ever really tolerated. But she had loved her sister so much, had felt so grateful to her, and all the while she had been sleeping with her husband.

Celeste felt the bile rising up inside her, wondering how many times he had slipped into their bed and held her, when earlier he had been holding her sister. Touching Cynthia, tasting her. It was sickening. She was actually heaving now, and her mother led her into the toilet, and held her daughter's head as she brought up everything she had eaten and drunk over the last twenty-four hours.

Mary Callahan knew that if she had her elder daughter in front of her now she would take her out without a moment's hesitation. Cynthia had always been trouble and she knew she had always been jealous of this sister of hers despite the fact that Celeste was a watered-down version of her in every respect. Where Cynthia was beautiful, Celeste was pretty; where Cynthia had the body of an Amazon,

187

Celeste, bless her, was only half the woman her sister had ever been. Yet, where it really counted, Celeste was worth a hundred of Cynthia, a thousand of her, because Celeste was a good girl, a decent, kind girl.

She rued the day Jonny Parker had met both her daughters. He had brought them nothing but trouble and heartache.

CHAPTER FIFTY-NINE

Left alone after Gabby had followed Jack, Jonny Parker looked at Cynthia and it was as if he was really seeing her for the first time ever. She looked awful, and he could see the lines around her eyes and mouth, see the bitterness and ugliness that was inside her. He shook his head and turned to go.

'You're not walking away from me, Jonny. No one walks away from me,' Cynthia spat. Even now, after all this, she still couldn't bow her head in shame and hold her hand up to what they had done.

'No one walks away from you! Who the fuck do you think you are?'

'I'm the woman who took out fucking Bryant, that's who I am, mate—and don't you ever forget it.'

Jonny grinned. 'Who the fuck cares, eh? Can't you just once in your miserable life admit to being in the wrong? I would give anything for this not to have happened. My Celeste is everything to me and between us we've destroyed her. Could you honestly see her dragged down even further?'

Cynthia nodded, and said with her usual

arrogant honesty, 'Yeah, why not? Pity is no basis for a marriage. You need a woman who is as strong as you, you need a woman who knows the score . . .'

Jonny looked at her for long moments before saying, 'You're off your fucking head if you think I would ever contemplate throwing my hat in the ring for you. Celeste means the world to me, and I thought you were sensible enough to know that. I have fucked you for years, but that's it, Cynth. We *fucked*. If Celeste outs me, and I wouldn't blame her if she did, I still wouldn't want you and all you entail.'

That was when she attacked him, when he knew the sooner he got away from her, and sorted out his life, the better it would be for them all.

Her strength was no match for his and, violently shoving her away from him, he said, 'Now I'm going to my wife, and I hope to Christ she forgives me, Cynthia, because until now I never realised just how much I needed her, how much she meant to me.'

Cynthia heard the front door close behind him and then she finally cried. She knew that her Jonny, her Jonny Parker, was gone from her for good. Other than herself, he was the only person she had ever cared about in her whole life. Jonny Parker was her true mate, her perfect match, and she had believed, in her heart of hearts, that he felt the same as she did.

Looking around her at the ruin that had been her kitchen, she experienced for the first time ever a feeling of loss—deep, emotional loss—and she was surprised at how badly it was affecting her. She knew that her old life was over, that from now on she would be alone, and that frightened her. But she also understood that it was somehow her own doing.

All her life she had taken whatever she wanted, without a real thought for the consequences. Now, though, she knew that her mother's words were true. Everything in life had to be paid for, and mostly it was paid for with bitter tears. She had never believed that those words could ever be used in conjunction with her, but she saw now how true they were. And, for the first time ever, she cried those bitter tears.

CHAPTER SIXTY

Jimmy was drunker than he had ever been before and, to make things worse, he realised he had run out of gear. He searched his car until he found half a gram under the driver's seat mat. He snorted it straight from the wrap, and felt the tingling in his nose which told him it was good stuff. He laughed pitifully to himself. Then he took another long pull on the bottle of vodka. It was nearly empty.

He staggered out of the car, and the smell of his vomit hit him; he remembered vaguely throwing up earlier. He realised now he had knelt in his own vomit and felt the urge to throw up once again.

He looked around him then, and saw the lights of London twinkling everywhere. He was at the top of a multi-storey car park, and he felt the breeze as it brushed gently against him. His gaze drifted to the night sky, and he saw the Plough. He remembered his dad teaching him about the stars on a camping trip to France. He smiled at the memory. He had been lucky in that anyway—he had had a good childhood, not like his poor kids, dragged up by that cunt he had married.

Why had he stayed? He knew why really. Somewhere deep down he had always loved her, had hoped that inside her there was a nice person trying to escape. The last few years had been bearable. She had seemed happier, but now he knew the reason for that; she was trumping dear old Jonny Parker. Mate, family friend, brother-in-law and two-faced piece of shit. On his table where they ate their dinner every night, for Christ's sakes.

He heaved again at the thought. How often had they fucked on that table? Her calmly feeding them, knowing what she had done. She was beyond being a whore even—at least they didn't pretend to be other than they were. What she had done was so outrageous it was unbelievable. And the worst of it was the fact he had never even suspected anything, so what did that make him? Did they laugh at him behind his back? Did they joke about what a fucking fool he was? He had trusted them—well, Jonny; he had trusted Jonny.

He could hear music floating on the wind, and he strained to hear the song, he knew the melody, and then it came to him. Eddy Grant singing 'Baby, Come Back'. The irony was not lost on him, and he grinned then. He hated her now, really hated her for what she had done to him. Done to them all. Poor Celeste—she was not good at the best of times. Now she would have to deal with all this. He wondered if Mary and Jack had known about it all along. In fact, did everyone know, except him? He felt the shame burning through him as he thought of the people he knew, all of them aware he was being cuckolded, and not by just anyone, but by the most dangerous man in London.

Jimmy looked over the edge of the concrete barrier. The ground was a long way away. It was funny really—all this time he had believed he was a man, if not of renown, at least to be respected. But it seemed he had been wrong about that, as he had been about so many things.

He was sitting on the barrier now and, sighing deeply, he dropped off the side. His last thought as he plummeted was whether or not his son was actually his child.

He hoped not.

CHAPTER SIXTY-ONE

'You happy now, Mum? He's dead, me dad's dead.'

Gabby was in tears, weeping silently. She felt as if her heart had been ripped from her body, and the only thing inside her was this deep, dark sorrow. She had loved her dad. He had been good to her, and he had loved her, genuinely loved her. Now he was gone. He had killed himself because of her mother, her mother who had never cared for anyone or anybody in her whole life except herself.

'Get your stuff, Gabriella, you're coming home with me.'

Mary Callahan looked at her elder daughter and wondered for the thousandth time how she had ever bred this excuse for a woman.

'Get yourself away, Cynth, you're not welcome here any more.'

'I want my daughter, Mum.'

'Well, you can't have her. She doesn't want to go

192

with you.'

Cynthia looked at the woman who had borne her, and who she had loved and hated throughout her life, and she said snidely, 'Well, we'll have to see about that, won't we?'

Shutting the door in her daughter's face, Mary said sadly, 'Yes, Cynthia, I suppose we will.'

She put her arm around her granddaughter then and, hugging her, she said kindly, 'Come on, lovie, I'll make us a hot chocolate.'

'I ain't got to go back there, Nana, have I?'

Mary sighed heavily, then said in all honesty, 'I hope not, Gabby. I hope not.'

Jack Callahan was sitting drinking his beer; the telly was off, and the room was quieter than Gabby had ever experienced before. It was as if the events of the last few days had wiped out every bit of their energy and their happiness. Her auntie Celeste was back at home with her husband; he had, as always, talked her round. Jonny was sorry, there was no doubt about that, but her dad was dead because of him, and that wasn't something that could be forgotten overnight. She would never forgive either of them. Her dad had been one of the few people who had ever really cared for her, and she wished now, more than anything, that she had told him just how much he had meant to her. Now her mother was determined to get her back home, and had not shown even the slightest remorse at her husband's suicide, or acknowledged that she was the cause of it. As always it was about her mother, not anyone else. Her granddad and nana had aged before her eyes, and even James Junior was out of the picture. It felt as if her family had been dismembered, and she didn't know how to cope with it all.

The only bright spot was Vincent; he had been fantastic. Her granddad said he could come to the house, and that was wonderful. Just being near him, and feeling his love for her, was enough to make her feel she might, just might, get through all this heartache one day.

Her mum was bad, toxic—she destroyed everything she touched, and she didn't care who she hurt in her quest to get what she wanted. Gabby knew that she had been trying to get her uncle Jonny to go and see her. Phoning the house at all hours, until he had changed the number. It had made her nana and granddad furious. Her granddad said that it was common knowledge now, that the neighbours were having a field day. He also said that, if Jonny Parker had any sense, he would shoot Cynthia Tailor down like a rabid dog, and do them all a favour. She agreed with her granddad about that; she would gladly shoot her mother herself.

That Jonny was back in favour didn't surprise Gabby. She understood that her grandparents had turned their back on one daughter, but that they could never do it to the other one. Celeste needed her family, and they needed her. It galled her, though, that Jonny Parker had walked away more or less scot-free—that wasn't right. He was as much to blame for her dad's death as her mother was.

Her poor dad, that he would kill himself like that! She felt the tears once more. It seemed as though her whole life had suddenly been destroyed, and she didn't know how to make it better. She would never see her dad's face again, never hear his voice. While her mother, the main cause of it all, seemed no different than usual. She was acting like her life hadn't even really been affected. Even today, she didn't look remotely bothered that her husband was dead, that he had dropped six storeys and landed on a set of metal railings. She looked like she always looked—angry, dissatisfied and bitter. It was so unfair.

CHAPTER SIXTY-TWO

Derek Greene was chatting to Vincent O'Casey, and they were getting on very well indeed. That young Vincent was seeing the teenage daughter of Cynthia Tailor was common knowledge, as was the fact that he wanted an in with Derek and his crew. The boy had potential, that much was evident. He could steal almost any car to order, and he had a natural knack with engines of any kind. He would make a good driver, and that was a very important part of the bank robber's plans.

A good driver knew the roads like the back of his hands—the side streets and short cuts—and would not get flustered under pressure. Three burly blokes with sawn-off shotguns and a pile of cash, high on adrenaline, were not liable to be too kind to someone who didn't know where he was going. So a good driver was considered an asset.

From what Derek had seen and heard about this kid, he seemed like just the kind of lad they were looking for. More to the point, he had first-hand knowledge of what was going down with Jonny Parker, and that alone gave him an in where Derek Greene was concerned.

Vincent O'Casey, for his part, was only too

happy to tell Derek Greene anything he wanted to know. He was flattered by the man's interest, and pleased that he had finally found himself a proper in to the world he so admired, the world he was determined to make his own one day. Jonny Parker's indiscretion with his wife's sister was the main topic of conversation around the campfires. It seemed he was not as clever as he thought and people were picking up on his skulduggery.

As far as Vincent was concerned, seeing his Gabby so torn up inside was like a physical pain to him. He loved the girl and, as young as they were, he knew in his heart that they would be together for ever.

'I hear that Jonny Parker's old woman has had him back?'

Vincent nodded. 'Yeah, she ain't all the ticket though, by all accounts. But Cynthia Tailor's out of the loop for good now. Even her own kids don't want her.'

Derek nodded sagely. 'And who could blame them? Six fucking storeys! That was not a cry for help—he was determined to top himself.'

'My thoughts entirely, Derek. It's my Gabby I feel sorry for. She's lost her dad, her brother's away in a nut-house, and her mother is about as much use as a fucking pork chop in a mosque. Her life as she knew it is over, and now she's got to try and pick up the pieces. Did I tell you her mother is having her put into care? Won't even let her go to her nana's. She's arguing that Gabby's out of control and that her grandparents aren't strong enough to cope with her.'

After shaking his head at the shocking revelation, Derek said conversationally, 'Could you find out Jonny Parker's movements next Friday for me? I have to have a meeting with him, and I could do with a heads up. On the QT, like.'

Vincent O'Casey almost swelled up physically with pride as he answered, ''Course I can, my Gabby can find that out for me.'

Derek Greene grinned then. 'I was hoping you'd say that.'

CHAPTER SIXTY-THREE

Gabriella Tailor was heartbroken; they had finally buried her father, and it had been a distressing few hours. Seeing her mother, in full make-up, her head covered with a black lace mantilla and her body encased in a figure-hugging black silk sheath dress, Gabby had felt the urge to tear her apart. *She* had played the part of the grieving widow to perfection, and it was just that—a part she played. Her whole life was an act.

Now, back at her nana's, Gabby wondered at parents in general. Her father's family had not shown, but then they never really had much to do with them anyway, her mother had seen to that. Suicide was a strange thing; people seemed ashamed of it. Some would rather see their loved ones waste away with cancer, or get killed in a car. To Gabby, suicide meant her father finally bailing out on her, once and for all.

She had felt so lonely, so vulnerable in the crematorium, unused to the strange smells and subdued chatter. Quite a few people had turned out, but the majority of them were what her nana

197

termed 'sightseers'. People who came to tragic events out of a morbid fascination with other people's troubles. But her heart had soared when Vincent had slipped into the back pew, and the wink he had given her had lifted her troubled spirits.

Her mother, though, had stood alone, and she had wept alone. A forlorn figure, who wasn't fooling anyone who really knew what she was like. Not one person had acknowledged her, and that must have shown her what people really thought of her. Still, knowing her mother, Gabby supposed she probably didn't give a shit. Why change the habits of a lifetime?

Now she had to face the truth of the situation, because a social worker, a Miss Bellamy, was telling her grandmother that her daughter, Mrs Tailor, had signed the papers to put her daughter into care. Her nana and granddad were arguing with her, but somehow she knew there was nothing they could do—not at the moment anyway. By the sounds of it, they had to go to court and get a judge to grant a temporary custody order, and *then* they might get their granddaughter back. It wasn't a surprise to any of them; it was as if her mother had decided that if *she* couldn't have her family then *no one* could have them.

Still dazed from the events of the last few weeks, Gabby didn't have the strength to argue that she didn't want to go. Instinctively, she knew that if she caused problems with Miss Bellamy now it would affect her in the future.

She seemed a nice woman—well, girl. She looked a cliché of a social worker, all flat sandals and fat ankles. Her thick dark hair looked like a furze bush, but she had kind brown eyes, and that gave Gabby hope.

'Do I have to go?'

Miss Bellamy looked at the pretty girl with the long blond hair and blue eyes and sighed inwardly. She had not liked the mother of this child, who had seemed overly adamant that the child should not be left with her grandparents. Most parents would prefer their children with family—it was rare that they opposed that—but Mrs Cynthia Tailor had been convinced she was in no fit state to care for the child herself. Since her husband's suicide she had been on medication and suffering from depression—understandable, of course. But she had also stipulated that *her* parents were not fit role models; as well as their advanced ages, they were also supposedly drinkers, smokers and gamblers, among other more sinister things, not said but hinted at.

So, as always, these cases had to be investigated and, in the interim, the child would be taken into the care of the local authority. Just going on this initial visit though, Miss Bellamy felt the girl would be all right here. The house was clean and well kept, the couple, though old and smokers, were agile enough, and there was genuine affection between them. There was also undisguised animosity against the child's mother, and that was coming from every one of them.

That there was a brother in a secure unit also had to be taken into the equation. The mother had washed her hands of him, saying he was far too disturbed for her to deal with under the present circumstances. James Junior had had a meltdown when told about his father's death and had attacked everyone around him. And the next day he had knifed an orderly. He would not be going anywhere for a good while.

Miss Bellamy shook her head at the state of some people's lives. There was money in this family, good looks and wonderful homes, yet she wouldn't leave her dog with any of them for the day, let alone allow them to procreate. But such was life; you needed a licence to own a dog or a TV, and you were fined if you didn't have one, whereas there wasn't anything to regulate who had a child. It was scandalous really, but there was nothing she could do about any of it. Except pick up the pieces when it went wrong.

'Who would you like to stay with, Gabriella?'

Gabby smiled then. 'I'd like to stay here. I've been here for the best part of my life—I only lived at home recently.'

Mary chimed in then as if on cue, 'My daughter was never what you would call the maternal type, if you know what I mean.'

'That's an understatement, girl. A rat could do a better job of rearing its young than her.' Jack's voice was low and hard.

'She killed my dad, you know that, don't you?' Gabby added. 'He caught her with her boyfriend, my auntie's husband, her own *sister*'s husband. I was there, and they were on the kitchen table . . .'

Miss Bellamy had heard the gossip; who hadn't? It had lit up the offices for days. It was the talk of East London, and the man Mrs Tailor had been caught with was a local villain, so that just added grist to the mill. Not that there were any laws against villains having families, in fact many of the so-called villains were good parents. It was a contradiction in terms really.

'Please let me stay here.'

It was a genuine plea and, smiling, Miss Bellamy said gently, 'I'll do all I can, but you need to go through the proper channels. Can you pack a few things, Gabriella? Then we'll be on our way.'

'But I ain't long cremated my dad, I won't know anyone . . . I'm frightened, I want to stay here with my nana and granddad . . .' Gabby could hear the panic entering her voice. She didn't want to leave here, this was her home, the only home she had ever really wanted to be in. It was so unfair—once more her mother was controlling them all, even when she wasn't around she could still call the shots. Gabby ran into her grandmother's arms and Mary held her, soothing her as if she was a small child, not a growing girl.

'It won't be for long, if we cause trouble now it will go against us. Look at poor Hannah from across the road, they took all hers away because she fought with them. You do as you're told, child, and we'll have you back home quick smart. I'll let Vince know where you are, child, so don't fret.'

That was what she wanted, needed to hear and, after a little cry and a few more hugs, Gabby did as she was bidden, but with a heavy heart.

CHAPTER SIXTY-FOUR

'Listen, Celeste, it was madness—I was caught up in a madness. You know what Cynthia can be like.'

Celeste still hadn't spoken to Jonny, not a word since Jimmy's funeral. It was as if she had left her body behind and gone some place no one could reach her.

'Please talk to me, love.'

She stared at him, her eyes unblinking. It was a clear, honest gaze and it made him feel even more ashamed than he already did. Celeste could do that, she could make a person feel they were in the wrong with a look, a look that was more powerful than a politician's maiden speech. He knew it was because of her and the way she lived her life. Straight as a die was his Celeste. Decent, *honourable*. He had thought he was honourable too, once. Now, with the flak coming at him from all sides, he knew that word would never be used about him again, ever.

Jimmy's death had caused him a lot of problems. Men were wary of dealing with him now. A thief was acceptable, though not a gas-meter bandit or a robber of council houses or sheltered accommodation. But an honest to goodness blagger—a bank robber—was respected for the time and effort that went into such an enterprise. Liars were never welcome. Liars were dangerous people you avoided at all costs, because eventually their lies caught up with them, and everyone around them was tarred with the same brush. Even the Bible had a section about liars, as it did about adulterers.

Many people had guessed about Jonny and his sister-in-law—the delectable but definitely off-her-rocker Cynthia—and they had not voiced their opinions, not in public anyway. After all, it *was* Jonny P they were talking about.

But Jimmy topping himself had left a bad taste with all and sundry. Suicide was not something the

202

criminal world embraced—unless it was a grass, of course. *They* were expected to do it; it was a much easier death than if they were found by the people they had grassed. But that was beside the point. Since Jimmy's death, people had begun to question Jonny P's other activities, the general consensus being if you were capable of something *that* sleazy you were capable of anything. To add fuel to the fire, there were a few new kids on the block and they were not helping by questioning the integrity of Jonny Parker.

Jonny had made many enemies on his way up the criminal ladder, and it was these people who were only too glad to see him reap what he had sown. The wives whispered about a man who could treat his wife so, a man who could happily cuckold someone who worked for him. Jimmy was now remembered as a paragon. People said that it was no wonder he had been a drunk and a cokehead with a wife like Cynthia, and her up to all sorts with her sister's husband, the man who employed him and paid his wages. That her children were now in care was the most scandalising thing of all. The boy, it was rumoured, was not all the ticket; he had killed a neighbour's cat, cut its throat of all things! The girl was supposedly a nice little thing. Now that she was in a home, some of the women speculated that Cynthia hadn't liked the competition from her daughter. The girl was a beauty and that hard-faced bitch had unloaded her like she did everyone who got in her way, her husband included. Some even hinted that it was planned, that finding them like that on the kitchen table had been deliberate.

It didn't take long for Jonny Parker's carefully garnered reputation as a good guy to be forgotten.

He was now definitely deemed to have become too big for his boots or, as some of the cruder men said, he thought his shit didn't stink, and that could only cause him problems in his various enterprises.

It had shocked him as well that many of the Eastern Europeans he worked with, especially the Russians, saw what he had done as something akin to genocide. They were actively cold-shouldering him, and that was a worry in itself.

Yes, he had had an affair. So what? It wasn't his finest hour, even he admitted that, but the backlash had been astronomical. Jimmy Tailor killing himself had really sealed his fate, and he felt the weight of his guilt pressing down on him more and more each day.

Now he had the added torture of seeing Celeste, who he loved, really cared about, become, through his machinations, a shadow of her former self.

He wondered at times how the fuck he had allowed this to happen. But he knew the answer as well as the next man. He had always taken what he wanted, that was the trouble, and where that had once been seen as a strength, now it was a weakness. All he could do now was try and live it down. It was harsh and it was not going to be easy, but that was what he had to do. He had to get up and go to work as usual, look his critics in the eye and earn back his reputation little by little.

Celeste was still staring at him as he said slowly, smiling crookedly, 'I'm sorry, love. I'm so very sorry.'

She put her hand out and laid it on top of his. 'I know.'

He lowered his head and fought back the urge to cry.

CHAPTER SIXTY-FIVE

Derek Greene was happy, but then he was a man with a happy disposition. He had a lovely family, a nice life, and he had a shrewd head on his rather large shoulders. Today he was happier than ever. Today was the day he finally came into his own, and he couldn't wait for the fireworks to start. It had been a long haul, but he was content enough to wait a few more days to get his bonus. And what a bonus.

Jonny Parker was champing at the bit, and that was *exactly* where Derek wanted him. Considering the man's troubles, he was conducting his business with his usual acumen and Derek had to admire that, even if he did think Jonny needed a moral compass for his dinner now and again to remind him what was acceptable behaviour and what wasn't. But that was then and this was now.

'You look happy, Del Boy.'

He grinned at his wife. 'That's because I am, my princess.'

She looked at him shrewdly; they had been together since they were thirteen and she knew him better than he knew himself. 'What you up to?' She was suspicious now; her biggest fear was that he would do something silly and get a serious lump like his father.

'Just a bit of graft, nothing too serious but a good earner. Who are you then, the police?'

She grinned back. She loved her husband with all her being, and she knew, without a shadow of a doubt, that he loved her back. Three kids, numerous stretch marks, and a boob job later, she and Derek were still together. She knew she was lucky and she appreciated her luck. She would never take him for granted—that was how you lost your man. She still ran his bath for him, and massaged his shoulders, he was a king in his domain. That was how you kept your man in his home, and stopped him from being tempted to visit someone else's. Men were like kids—when they got bored they moved on to the next game. Well, that wasn't going to happen to her and Derek; she would see to that.

'You going to be late tonight?'

He shrugged. 'Depends, love, but if I'm gonna be later than usual I'll call, OK?'

She nodded. She knew he would call, and that was enough for her.

CHAPTER SIXTY-SIX

'Come on, Linford, you know it makes sense.'

Linford Fargas grinned, but it wasn't his usual friendly grin, and Jonny knew it would be a long while before they were once more back on their old footing. Linford had worked often with Jimmy; he had liked him and had been grieved at Jimmy's demise. To kill yourself was a terrible thing, and Linford had first-hand knowledge of that as his brother had hanged himself in Brixton while on remand. It was still a sore point with him, and he believed whole-heartedly that nothing could ever be so bad that you would take your own life. Life was something precious—your own life especially. You had one crack at it and you had a duty to yourself to make that life the best it could be. He resented Jonny's part in Jimmy's death, and that resentment lingered, unspoken, between them now.

All Jonny could do was make up for what he had done by carrying on and not rocking anyone's boats.

'It's a scam, ain't it?'

Jonny nodded. He felt Linford's anger bubbling away beneath the surface. 'Yes but we can rake it in with minimal outlay, and that can only be a good thing.'

Linford shrugged. 'Sounds good. The figures look good, Jimmy said—'

He stopped himself then, and Jonny said quietly, 'Yes, Jimmy said it was a good earner. We can mention his name, you know.'

Linford shrugged again. 'I liked him, he was a good man. But, like all good people, he didn't understand how bad the world could be.' This was the closest Linford had ever come to insulting his boss and they both knew it.

Jonny was silent for a few moments before saying earnestly, 'Look, Linford, if I could turn the clock back, don't you think I would? I lie awake at night pondering how the fuck I let her get under my skin like that. Truth be told, I never even really *liked* her. I can't explain the hold she had over me, and I know that sounds weak, and it sounds like I'm blaming her, and I'm not. After she outed Bryant, she fascinated me; she's dangerous, seriously fucking dangerous. She looks like an angel, but she's base. She fucks like an animal—it's almost primal. And I liked that. I know it sounds terrible, but I really liked that about her. She's like one of those devil dogs—you know, those fighting dogs? They can turn on you at any moment, but you still want to own one. I knew no good could come of it, but it didn't stop me. All I can say now is that my attraction to her is well and truly buried. I can't even stand the sight of her. Did you know she had the fucking audacity to turn up for work as if nothing had happened?'

Linford nodded.

'I think that was it. Her turning up at the betting shop really made me realise what I was dealing with. I know her, I know how she thinks, she is capable of anything. Literally anything. I've paid her off, what else could I do? She had to be given something, but it galled me. In my heart, I'd like to see her scrabbling in the fucking dirt, but then I can't talk, because I'm as bad as her—worse really—because I actually do genuinely love my wife. Celeste's forgiven me—well, sort of—and now I have to prove to her that she hasn't backed a loser. And I will. If it's the last thing I do, I'll make her see that the only person I will ever want is her.'

Linford believed Jonny was speaking the truth and, in a strange way, he almost understood where he was coming from. But Linford also knew that, for all Jonny's protestations, there had also been an element of 'I want her, so I'll have her' to it as well. He had taken her because he could, and he had not cared about the consequences until they had jumped up and bitten him on the arse. *Jonny* was responsible for all this mess, because it was believed in their world that men were stronger than women. That men should have the strength to turn away from temptation, whereas women were too weak to resist.

'Well, she turned out to be a very expensive pastime, Jonny. She cost Jimmy his life, and everyone else around you two has been infected with your games. You more than anyone, because this has cost you your good name. You're the butt of jokes and the cause of idle gossip. It will die down, but it will always be there, and you have to live with that knowledge. People love nothing more than to see the mighty fall, and you have fallen a fucking long way in people's estimation.'

Jonny sighed heavily. Linford was honest, he'd give him that. Whoever said the truth hurt was a clever fucker, but he would ride this storm as he had others. Look at Kevin Bryant—he had taken that on, and it had worked for him up until the end. He would get through this, he was determined.

'Well, now we've got that out of the way, shall we get back to work? I'm meeting with the villa geezers tonight. Are you coming or not?'

Linford nodded. 'I'll be there, don't worry.'

'Good. Now what's next on the agenda?' Jonny felt depressed, but he knew what he had to do was show his face and act as if everything was normal, then eventually, in the not too distant future, it would be. At least, that's what he hoped anyway, although the way things were going, he worried it might take longer than he had first believed.

CHAPTER SIXTY-SEVEN

Vincent O'Casey was thrilled to be in on his first ever piece of real skulduggery. He just hoped it all went as planned. At eighteen, he was a good-looking lad, and he had a nice way about him—not pushy, but not passive either. Anyone looking at him would know he could take care of himself if the situation demanded it. He was very respectful, called people 'Mr' when appropriate, and he had a reputation for being good with cars, and reliable into the bargain.

Derek Greene had seen his potential and, for that reason alone, he would always have young Vincent's loyalty and appreciation.

Vincent liked Derek. He was a man who was going places, but he listened to Vincent, and advised him on the many pitfalls of the criminal lifestyle. Vincent O'Casey came from a family of no-hopers—his father and brothers were nothing more than ice-cream freezers. Local geezers, thieves, sold a bit of knock-off, played the hard men to the neighbours. Talked the talk, but would need a glass to hand in a real fight. They were the kind of people that Vincent was determined *not* to be—local bully boys who thought the world began and ended on their council estate. He wanted more than that. Vincent knew he had the nous, the inborn cunning, necessary to achieve in the world he wanted to be a part of. Now he had a champion of sorts in Derek Greene, and this was his one and only chance of breaking free of his background and environment. If this all went tits up he would be like his father and brothers—just another fucking mook from East London, a blockhead, and he was not going to let that happen without a fight.

Tonight he was washed, shaved and in his best clobber, ready for literally anything. As he drove into the scrapyard in Bow, he was whistling with suppressed excitement. He was driving an old but spotless 2.8 litre Ford Capri, which had been a nice silver colour, until he had stolen it three nights previously. Now it was dark blue, and the plates were not the originals. The plates were actually off a 4.2 litre Jag, but that was nothing to worry about.

He parked up as arranged by the side of the Portakabin and, shutting the engine off, he waited as he had been told to do. He didn't even light a cigarette, unsure whether it would attract attention.

There were already a couple of cars there, and the lights were on inside. He felt a rush of adrenaline as he realised he was finally a real part of this world, and the pride he felt inside him was overpowering. If only his family could see him! He was on the periphery, he knew, but this was just a start for him. Once he proved himself, he would be given bigger and better jobs, and with those jobs would come the wonga and the prestige. He would make sure the O'Casey name would become something to be reckoned with.

When his Gabby was old enough, he would marry her and give her the life that she deserved. He hoped she was all right in that care home. He still felt enraged at what her mother was capable of. Even his mum—and she wasn't up to much— looked like the mother of Our Lady by comparison. At least *his* mother was loyal to her family, would lie to the Old Bill for them, would even stand up in court and do so if need be. Not like that unnatural whore poor Gabby was lumbered with.

No, he would see to it that Gabby had a good, decent life, and he would make that his purpose. He wanted a nice little house, and a nice little family, in a nice neighbourhood, where the kids would go to a good school, and have a bit of a chance in life. He worried about Gabby and where she was. He knew about care homes, had seen the inside of a few himself over the years. But that had

211

been his own fault not his mum's; he had been a bit of a tearaway as a youngster, and that had been the cause of him being put away. That wouldn't happen to *his* kids, not on your Nelly. He would be there for his little ones, not half-pissed all the time, or in the betting shop like his old man.

So intent was Vincent on his day-dreaming that he didn't notice that the Portakabin was gradually filling with people.

CHAPTER SIXTY-EIGHT

Cynthia Tailor was home alone, but that didn't bother her—she liked being alone. She glanced around the room, and felt the anger burning once more. She would have to sell up; the house was mortgaged to the hilt, and the insurance wasn't going to pay out.

She couldn't believe that she was in this position, and she blamed her husband and Jonny Parker. Thinking of her sister in that enormous house, with Jonny dancing to her every whim, made her almost apoplectic with rage. Everyone was acting as if it was *her* fault—he had walked away from it without any real damage. It was so unfair. She had wanted him like she had wanted no one else in her life and she had him for a time as well. But he had been a flake, just like the rest. Now where was she? He had paid her off, but it was a pittance considering what she was used to. She would have to get rid of this place and start again. Even Cynthia knew she couldn't stay around here after what had happened. But then maybe getting a fresh start was what she needed. She could buy a nice flat somewhere while she was still young enough and still good-looking enough to attract attention from men.

As for that daughter of hers, *she* would need her one day and, when she did, Cynthia would take great pleasure in shutting the door in her face, just like it had been shut in hers. Her mother and father were dead to her—they had acted as though *she* was the main culprit. But then Jonny was still keeping them, so they *would* have to take his part in it all. Like Celeste, they would do whatever he told them to do. Well, he would rue the day he dumped her as well. Just who the hell did he think he was? She still loved him, though. He was the only man to ever make her feel alive, and she would miss that more than anything.

She could feel the tears coursing down her cheeks, and she brushed them away angrily. For the first time in her life she knew what it was to lose someone she cared about, and she didn't like the feeling one bit.

Cynthia glanced around the room, remembering when they first came here, seeing the kids when they were still small enough to do as they were told, before they turned into a pair of scheming bastards like their father.

James had killed himself to spite her, she was convinced of that. Deep down she thought he had done it to teach her a lesson. She grimaced through her tears. Well, he had wasted his time, because she felt no guilt where he was concerned. None whatsoever.

She wiped her eyes carefully, then she went up her beautiful staircase and ran herself a bath. She had never been one for regrets. Instead, she would do what she had always done—look after number one.

Smiling now, she sank into the scented water, and planned her next move. The past was the past—she had a future to look forward to, and that future was going to be as a young widow with no kids, no ties, no nothing.

Fuck Jonny Parker, and fuck her family. She could get along without any of them, and that was exactly what she intended to do.

CHAPTER SIXTY-NINE

Jonny had always enjoyed the food at the Greek restaurant in Dagenham. He liked the owners and it served good food. He particularly loved the kleftiko. As he ate there with Linford Fargas before their meet about the villa scam, he pondered on how a life could change overnight, and not always for the good either.

'Do you reckon she'll go on the trot, Jonny?' Linford asked.

He shrugged. 'Who? Cynthia? Yeah, I do. She won't stick around where she ain't wanted. Anyway, if she doesn't, I'll give her a nudge in the right direction.'

Linford nodded. 'I'll nudge her if you like, with my boot in her arse!'

Jonny grinned. 'She did have a great arse, I'll give her that.'

Linford snorted, saying disdainfully, 'No arse is worth all that, mate, not even Madonna's.'

They were quiet again for a few moments before

Linford said, 'When's the meet in Bow again?'

'For fuck's sake, Linford, how many times? Eleven thirty, at a scrapyard. We meet all the other investors then, and get the run down on how much is in place. I think there's a chance of shifting some more gear as well. That little Derek was asking me about puff and I told him we could accommodate anyone for any amount. He seemed interested. Nice young fella, he is—I like him. But then his old man was on the up—well liked, by all accounts. Should get a walk in the next few years.'

Linford grimaced. 'All that time behind the door. Fucking disgraceful really. I couldn't do it.'

''Course you could. It's just getting your head around it, that's all.'

Linford didn't answer, but he wondered how well Jonny Parker would do in the same position. The *threat* of a great big lump and actually having to *do* a great big lump were two completely different things altogether. Jonny would have an easy ride being who he was. But Linford wondered at how well he would take his liberty being curtailed. That was why his brother hanged himself, he was sure of it. He had been looking at a twenty at least, and funky Brixton wasn't exactly hotel standard. But Jonny Parker was like a lot of the men in the game; they were too far removed to ever get a big capture. Too many smaller fish to catch before them. In a way, Linford supposed, he was in a similar position.

'Derek's dad was a real hard case in his day, wasn't he?'

'So the stories go, real, serious hard man—took no prisoners.'

Linford remembered hearing a story about him, but he couldn't remember what it was. Shrugging, he said carefully, 'As long as you're sure about this scam, that's all. Derek is young, and he hasn't got any real reputation yet. From what I've heard, he was only a whipping boy for a long time.'

Jonny sighed. Linford could be an old woman at times. 'Look, I've done me homework, and he's a kosher kid, OK? He's had a few good earns and this is his big one. He's getting a good little rep and I want him where I can see him, and that means working for me.' Jonny was getting pissed off now and, seeing two young men at another table watching him, he snapped at them, 'Had your fucking look? Want a photograph do you?'

The young men looked away. They knew who he was, and that was what had aroused their interest. Jonny was a name to them, he was famous. They dreamt of being him one day. The difference was that, at their age, Jonny would have challenged anyone who had spoken to him like he just had, no matter who they were.

The owner of the restaurant came over then. 'Everything all right, gents?'

Jonny nodded. 'Yeah, sorry, mate, feeling a bit fragile today.'

The owner smiled coldly. 'Well, that's understandable, ain't it?'

Jonny's fist, when it hit him, was so unexpected he took the full force of it. Linford was out of his chair and holding his friend back in seconds. The other diners in the restaurant were watching in fascination and terror.

Jonny knew he had done a wrong one, but he was sick of the way people were judging him; they didn't know him, they didn't know the half of it. This little story would be all over Silvertown by the

216

morning and he was glad. It was about time people remembered just who they were dealing with. He was sick to death of it and, right now, anyone was fair game. He had been too nice; he should have shown his strength from the off. He had tried to play Mr Nice Guy because he had been feeling guilty. Well, that was then and this was now, and he wasn't going to take it lying down any more.

Outside the restaurant, Jonny looked over the A13 towards the concrete jungle that was Ford Motor Works and, spitting on to the pavement, he said angrily, 'Fucking shithole this place, can't believe we even bother to come out this far.'

Linford opened the car doors and, once inside, said calmly, 'Like we've said before, things like what you've done leave a nasty taste, and thumping all and sundry ain't going to help matters, is it?'

Jonny laughed. It was his old laugh, loud and raucous. 'Fuck them, Linford my boy. Fuck them all. Now let's get to Bow and be done with this lot. I've had enough.'

'Whatever you say, boss.'

Linford started the car and they made their way to their meeting with Derek, neither of them saying a word, both lost in their own thoughts.

CHAPTER SEVENTY

Jack Callahan was laughing to himself as Mary watched him in amazement.

'Are you feeling the ticket, Jack? Laughing away there all on your Jack Jones.' She was pleased to see him happy if she was honest; it was a long time since there had been any merriment in this house.

Jack looked at his wife and said seriously, 'I have a lot to be cheerful about, my lovely, but I can't say too much just yet. Once it's over you'll know soon enough.'

Mary was nonplussed at his answer, but she kept her own counsel; there were some things you were better off not knowing, and this sounded like one of those things. Jack had not been right since he had seen young Vincent earlier in the day, and whatever they had been talking about had cheered him up no end.

She smiled to herself; young Vincent was a nice boy and now she was pleased he was seeing her granddaughter. She had revised her earlier opinion of him. She had met Jack when they were teenagers and they were still together, so she wasn't against young lovers like Cynthia was.

She pushed thoughts of Cynthia out of her mind; she was done with her and she didn't want her taking up any more of her time or her life. It was the shame that was the hardest to bear, although the fact that people knew she had outed her daughter permanently had helped them get over that. But it was the effect this had had on her grandchildren that really rankled. James Junior was still locked up in a secure unit. She didn't even know what that meant until Miss Bellamy had told her, and the shock had really knocked her for six. But it was the best place for him. He wasn't right that child; to do what he had done was not natural.

Still, at least Mary had heard from Gabby. She didn't sound thrilled at her new accommodation but she didn't sound too down about it. She was going to school at least, and she said it wasn't

218

that bad. Well, it wouldn't be for very long. Miss Bellamy thought they had a good chance of getting custody of her, but it was down to the courts now. Mary sighed; she was too old for this drama.

It was Jack she really felt for though. He had taken it much worse than she had believed possible. He had liked Jimmy, despite his weaknesses. For all he came from a different background and environment, they had got on very well together. She suspected that Jack had felt sorry for the man, but then hadn't they all? They would have felt sorry for anyone who had taken on Cynthia knowing her as they did.

And then there was Celeste to worry about. Mary had hoped she would finally walk away from Jonny after the last little lot, but it wasn't to be. She thought Celeste should have seen him for what he really was, but the girl wasn't right and hadn't been right for many a long year.

As Mary walked into the kitchen, she felt an enormous pain. It hit her chest and travelled down her left arm. She was suddenly breathless and, as she leant out to grab hold of a chair for support, she collapsed on to the floor, knocking over the tea things on her way.

Jack rushed out to see what the commotion was and, seeing his wife's grey face and shallow breathing, he phoned immediately for an ambulance, all the time cursing his elder daughter, and blaming her for her mother's collapse. It was a wonder this hadn't happened before now; she'd had more than enough on her plate the last few years, and this was the upshot. If he lost his Mary, he would do for that whore of a daughter himself, and that was a promise.

219

CHAPTER SEVENTY-ONE

Linford pulled in to the scrapyard in Bow, and parked between a new Daimler Sovereign, and an old stacked-head Mercedes. The Portakabin was ablaze with lights and, for a few seconds, Linford felt apprehension envelop him. He didn't know what it was, but something about this whole set up stank.

He had tried to voice his opinion to Jonny but he wouldn't budge. He was gagging for this villa lark, and who could blame him? It was the maximum return for the minimum outlay. It was all about renting offices, and looking the part. Once people parted with their dosh that was that. Over, done with, gone.

But it was Derek Greene who bothered him, and he could not for the life of him work out why. Then, as they walked into the Portakabin, it became as clear as day what had been niggling at the back of his mind. Now it was too late to do anything about it.

CHAPTER SEVENTY-TWO

As she sat with her father by her mother's hospital bed, Celeste breathed a sigh of relief. She was bad, but she would pull through. A heart attack the doctors said and, looking at her mother now, tubes everywhere and her face devoid of colour, Celeste wondered at how vulnerable she suddenly looked.

Her mum had always been there for her. She had been a good mum, had loved her and cared for her, made her smile when she was down, gone without so her daughters could have things. Celeste felt the tears once more and choked them back. How had everything gone so wrong?

Her mum and dad blamed Cynthia but, although she was a part of it, in reality it was Jonny who had caused the trouble. As much as she had loved him—and she realised the significance of the past tense—she should have known that he was trouble. He was a violent criminal and she had swallowed that, believing love could conquer all. Well, it couldn't. He had taken her sister and he had destroyed many lives.

She had gone back to him out of fear, fear of being alone, of having to earn a living, of going back out into the world; the world frightened her, the world was dangerous. Well, so was being in your own home she had learnt. Her house scared her; it was too big, too empty, and she longed for the bedroom of her youth.

She would give anything to be able to go back and do it all again, but that was impossible. She knew that if she had not married Jonny Parker her mother wouldn't be lying in this bed, and her father wouldn't be sitting opposite her, terrified of losing the person he had loved his whole life. Poor Gabby wouldn't be in care, and young James wouldn't be in a lock-up unit for kids.

She had brought this down on their heads by bringing Jonny into their lives. Celeste wasn't sure she would ever be able to forgive herself, but one thing she did know was that she would not go back to that house. She would go home and look after her dad, and then her mum when she finally came back from hospital. Jonny thought that he had done everything for the best reasons, but she knew that he had done everything he had for no other reason than that he could. Seeing her mother like this brought home to her just how useless her life had been up until this moment. It was time to grow up and take responsibility for herself, and those around her who she cared about, starting now.

'Can I get you a cup of tea, Dad?'

Jack looked at his daughter as if he'd forgotten she was there, then he just shook his head sadly and went back to watching his wife.

Jack knew that without Mary he would have nothing; he remembered everything she had done for him over the years, and was ashamed that he had never even made her a cup of tea. She had slogged and grafted to keep them all clean, fed and watered. He wondered how many meals she had cooked everyone over the years, how many beds she had made, how many shirts she had ironed. It was true what they said—you didn't know what you had till it was gone. Never was a truer word spoken.

He glanced at his daughter and saw the fear in her eyes that he knew was mirrored in his own; like him, she had taken her mother's presence in her life for granted. They all had at one time or another, especially that Cynthia—Mary had brought her children up for her, been there for her in the good times and the bad. He knew how hard it had been for his Mary to turn her back on her elder child, and the result of their daughter's actions was this heart attack.

Well, things were going to change, he was going to see to that himself. He never wanted to live through anything like this ever again, because he knew that if she went he would not be far behind her. A world without his Mary in it would be no world at all.

CHAPTER SEVENTY-THREE

Bertie Warner was smiling, but it did not make him look in any way amiable. Jonny Parker's shock was apparent, and that made Bertie a very happy man.

'Surprised to see me, are you, Jonny?'

Jonny looked around him and, seeing the serious looks on the men's faces, he felt truly afraid for the first time in years. Not that he would let this lot know that.

'Well, well, well, if it ain't Bertie Warner back from the dead.' He injected as much humour as he could into the words.

But it was Bertie who got the laugh when he said, 'No, not the dead, Jonny, me old son. Grenada.' He looked at Linford then as he said seriously, 'You'd like it there, son. A lot of fucking machetes, if you know what I mean.'

Jonny knew then he was on borrowed time and he said nonchalantly, 'So you had a swerve. That's all water under the bloody bridge now. What are you back for, fucking revenge?'

Bertie laughed now himself. 'Oh yes, revenge, and to take back what was mine. Well, mine and Kevin's anyway. He was my best mate, was Kevin. Me and him even did our National Service together, bet you didn't know that? Back in the fifties when we were only kids. That's where he

223

got the nickname "No Face". Playing poker in the stockade. But he was a good mate, a loyal friend, which is why you never approached me to have him over, you knew I wouldn't swallow that. You knew I would chop your arms off, and then put you in the boot of a scrapped car and crush you alive.'

Jonny laughed at Bertie but it was a thin laugh. 'You're joking! That kind of thing went out in the sixties with all the old Mustache Petes. You can't touch me without recriminations, you stupid old cunt.'

'Oooh, hark at her! I can do what the fuck I like, mate, and the sooner you get your fucking thick head around that the better.'

Jonny Parker had forgotten how ferocious Bertie Warner could be. Bertie was a known headcase; he also had a taste for torture, and that had always been his ace card. No one had ever wanted to cross him, because the consequences were dire. He had once burnt a man alive for cutting him up in his motor. Linford was worried, Jonny could tell, and it seemed that history was repeating itself. Young Derek wanted what *he* had, so he was teaming up with the man that he had originally taken it from. It was like a fucking nightmare, and Jonny knew the chances of him leaving this room alive were minimal at best. But he was not going out without a fight, that was for sure.

He glanced around him at the men in the room; all were heavies, ready for anything, especially young Derek Greene. How could he have been so dense? Linford had smelled a rat and he should have listened to his friend's instincts. But, in fairness, it had been an eventful few weeks, and he was not exactly at the top of his game because of that.

Bertie grinned, and he looked like a death's head. 'Come on then, Jonny, if you think you're hard enough.' He looked at the men around him and said almost gleefully, 'You can see his brain working, can't you? He's wondering which one of us to take out first. Then he's planning how to get out that door, and do a runner. Well, Jonny, me old son, that ain't going to happen. Sorry for the inconvenience and all that.' He walked behind the small wooden desk which was used by the secretary three days a week, and picked up a large machete. 'See this? See the irony of it, do you? Well, this is going to remove your arms, and then you are going into a motor, and you are going to be crushed. I've been planning this for fucking years, Jonny Boy, and, now the time has come, I feel quite excited about it.'

Derek Greene's eyes were glittering with the prospect of serious violence. Like Jonny before him, he believed they would take it all over and there would never be any pretenders to their thrones.

Jonny read what was going on in Derek's head and laughed. There would always be another young buck like Derek, waiting in the sidelines for what he saw as his golden opportunity. Just as Jonny was finding out. That, unfortunately, was the way of the world they had chosen, and it was a foolish man who didn't watch out for it, and expect it, even from his closest allies. And foolish he had been.

'Look, man, it was nothing personal . . .'

Bertie's voice cut him off. 'Nothing fucking personal? Is this cunt for real? You murdered my mate, well, not you as such. That little matter was

225

done by a *female*, a woman who was protecting her sister, that I can swallow. She was doing what anyone would have done, and my Kevin, as much as I loved him, and love him I did, done a wrong 'un going to your house. I hold me hands up to that. I didn't like it, but I had no choice—he was determined. What I am so irritated about is that you challenged us like we were *nothing*. You treated us like we were amateurs. Well, I'm back, lads, and you two are over with. You're finished, you're fucking done!'

As Jonny looked at Bertie and saw the maniacal look in his eyes, he knew this was it. His life would end in a Portakabin in Bow. Not the most salubrious ending to a life, but an ending all the same.

'Shove it up your arse, you silly old cunt! Bring it on! I ain't going without a fucking tear up.'

'I was hoping you would say that!'

Bertie swung the machete, a machete which had been sharpened into a lethal blade. It landed on Jonny's shoulder and, as Bertie had promised, it took his arm off.

The blood was spraying everywhere, and Derek Greene felt the thrill that hunters feel when they finally take an animal down.

Linford watched in horror as his friend was butchered before his eyes. One thing in Jonny's favour though, was he never screamed once, and that was remarked upon by all the men in the room. Even as they carried him, still alive, to the waiting car that was to be his tomb. He was slung into the boot like rubbish, and he was still cursing them loudly as they put the crushing machine in motion.

Linford watched every second with mounting

dread; he had known this was not a kosher operation, had felt it in his water. It had all seemed too glib, too structured to be real. He looked into the blood-spattered face of Bertie Warner and accepted the inevitable.

Bertie took Linford's head off his shoulders with one hefty slice of the machete. As it rolled across the dirty ground of the scrapyard and eventually stopped in a small hole, Bertie shouted gleefully, 'Look, guys, a fucking hole in one!'

They were all laughing now, stacked up on adrenaline and the knowledge that their main adversaries were out of the picture. All that was left now was for them to take what they felt was rightfully theirs.

Young Vincent had watched it from the sidelines, and he felt the nausea rising up inside him. Of all the things he had expected of the night, this was not one of them. He was party to murder now, and he knew then and there that this kind of skulduggery wasn't for him. He just wanted to be a blagger, a bank robber, nothing more and nothing less.

Linford's body, minus its head, was bundled into the boot of Vincent's car, and Derek Greene climbed in the passenger seat, saying happily, 'We're gonna dump this outside their main offices, then we lose the motor and get as far away from the scene as possible, OK?'

Vincent nodded.

'You are part of a new guard tonight, mate, in on the ground floor.'

And, as Vincent thanked Derek, he wondered at just what he had signed himself up for. This was far too much for him; all he had wanted was to drive a few getaway cars. Now he was a witness to the murders of two of the most dangerous men in London. Life could be such shit at times.

It was only later on, lying in his bed at his mum and dad's flat, that it occurred to him he had been used; he had told Derek Greene everything he had needed to know about Jonny Parker, but he didn't know the half of what Derek was planning. It wouldn't be the first time he was used, and it would not be the last, of that much he was sure. He was in over his head, and he knew that he could not walk away from any of it. This had been far too big a night for him to be able to pretend it had never happened. It would go down in East-End folklore and, in a way, he knew that he would enjoy people knowing he had been a part of it. Derek Greene had hand picked him for the job and that was a compliment, surely? If he used his loaf he could get a fucking decent earn, and be a part of a new regime.

He was aware he was trying to convince himself that everything would be all right. But another thing he had found out this night was that he had no stomach for murder and, no matter what the score, that had been murder at its worst; cold-blooded and messy. He was part of it now, and he knew he had to do what was expected of him. But he regretted getting involved in it all. Whatever Jonny Parker was or he wasn't, it didn't change the fact that Vincent had been a part of the crew who had outed his Gabby's uncle.

CHAPTER SEVENTY-FOUR

Celeste didn't report her husband missing for three days, but she knew, like everyone else, including the police, that he was dead. Linford's headless torso had been a message, and that message had been received and understood. She had thought the news would destroy her, but instead, for the first time in years, she felt free. The house and most of the other properties were in her name, as were a majority of the bank accounts, so she was a very wealthy woman. Jonny being gone didn't really affect her that much in the long run.

She also knew intuitively that her father had guessed what was going to happen; he had not seemed surprised by the turn of events. She wondered how Cynthia was feeling and if she mourned Jonny. Celeste hoped so, because *she* couldn't mourn him. She was glad he was gone, glad he was away from her, glad she was finally able to walk away from the life he had given them. Her mum was on the mend, and her life was once more her own.

She had loved Jonny Parker once with all her heart, but she had not loved what he had become. What he had tried to be. The violence he had embraced had finally turned back on him. What goes around comes around, how many times had she heard that expression? She knew his body would turn up one day and, until then, she would live her life as quietly and as decently as humanly possible with her mum and dad. She had had enough of the so-called good life; it had never been much good to her.

From that day, Celeste Parker never left her mother's home, not even for a few hours.

Book Three

As is the mother, so is her daughter

Ezekiel 16:44

It is not what a lawyer tells me I may do; but what humanity, reason, and justice tell me I ought to do

Edmund Burke (1729–97)

CHAPTER SEVENTY-FIVE

1998

'What's the matter with you, child?' Mary was worried about her granddaughter, she was very quiet these days, as if the light had gone out of her, and had been ever since coming out of care.

'I'm all right, Nana, I just don't feel that great lately.'

'You're not sickening for anything, are you?'

Gabby laughed at that. It was Irish for 'Are you pregnant?'

'Don't worry, Nana, *that's* not what's wrong with me.'

She saw the palpable relief on her grandmother's face and sighed inwardly. She wished she *was* pregnant; it would be lovely to have a baby of her own. Something to love and care for. A little person who loved you back unconditionally. Gabby craved love like other people craved water or food. It was because of her upbringing—God knows, the new social worker had told her that enough times. She grimaced at the thought of Miss Byrne; though she liked the woman, she could be hard work.

But that wasn't what was bothering her. How could she tell her grandmother that after nearly three years her mother wanted contact again? Of all the things she had expected that had not been one of them. And Miss Byrne was all for it! She said it would give Gabby 'closure'. What a crock of shit! What it would give her was untold aggravation, which was all her mother had ever brought to anyone in her life.

233

Still, she couldn't deny her interest was piqued. She was curious to see how her mother had fared since she had disappeared, and she would love to ask her how she could have dumped her two kids so unceremoniously without a second's thought. Then why ask the road you know? She knew the answer to that question already. Cynthia had walked away because that is what she did; she made a mess and she ran from it as soon as it got out of hand. Her husband had killed himself and what had she done? Left her children to cope with the fall-out.

'Are you going to answer me, madam?'

Gabby was brought back to the present by her grandmother's harsh words.

'Am I talking to myself here or what?' Mary was clearly irritated.

'Sorry, Nana, I was miles away.'

Kissing her nana's cheek, Gabby left the room and went to her bedroom. She sat on her bed and looked around. It was pretty enough; she liked the pale pinks and greens in the curtains and bedspread, the cream walls left unadorned—not a pop star or film star to be seen. She'd made it almost clinical, and she knew that was the result of years of being in her mother's house where there was *never* any mess whatsoever. She could still hear her mother's voice: 'Do you know how much that wallpaper cost a roll? And you want to put fucking Sellotape on it!' She had heard it many times, and it had always made her angry inside. Other girls had posters, pictures of ponies, whatever on their walls, but not her.

She pushed the thoughts from her mind; she was only thinking about her mother because the social worker had told her she wanted to see her.

That was it. It was a natural reaction but, still, it was stirring up unpleasant memories.

Gabby looked in the small dressing-table mirror at herself, wondering what her mother would think of her now. At sixteen she was a beauty, or so everyone kept telling her. She was also the living image of Cynthia. She stared into her deep-blue eyes, framed by dark lashes, and looked at her mouth, the wide-lipped mouth that was so fashionable at the moment. She was prettier than most girls, and that wasn't her being big-headed— it was a fact. Anyway, she knew that looks really meant nothing in the grand scheme of things—it was brains and contentment that mattered. And being loved.

She *was* loved, by her nana and granddad and by Vince, and even her auntie Celeste—though *she* was getting stranger by the day. She had never left this house since the day she had walked back into it after Jonny was killed. Agoraphobia, the doctors called it though Auntie Celeste said that was shite, she just didn't like going out and that was her human right. She had a point, albeit in a weird and wonderful way. All she did was eat and watch TV. She was rich as Croesus by all accounts, but even that didn't have any impact on her; she gave most of her money away to charity or anyone who came and told her a sob story.

Gabby knew it drove her granddad mad, but he was powerless to do anything about it. Celeste was as right as the mail; that was an undisputed fact, even the doctors had told them. She had 'retired' from the world, that was how her nana put it, adding that that didn't mean Celeste was a nut-job. But could she eat! She was half the size of the house nowadays, all chins and chafed thighs, but she had a good heart, and her eyes were alive with love when she looked at her family. In fact, if Gabby was honest, she actually believed that her auntie was one of the happiest people she knew. Go figure that one, Oprah.

But it was still her mother who was occupying Gabby's thoughts now. She couldn't rid herself of the terrible urge to meet with her, just to see what she was like now. Maybe she *had* changed, maybe she *was* a different kind of person, and if Gabby didn't go to see her she would never know.

Gabby didn't actually believe that for a moment, but it was a nice fantasy. Other kids took parental love for granted; some mothers stood by their kids through everything—even a rapist or a murderer often had the support of their parents, though Gabby suspected that was because they didn't want to believe their child was capable of such heinous crimes. But neither she nor James Junior had ever had their mother's love, and that hurt. Look at what had happened with poor James. He had got even worse and had ended up being sectioned. Gabby wondered if *she* had been in touch with him as well.

She sighed heavily again, and lay back on her bed. This had stirred her up inside, and made her think of times gone by that she would rather not remember. She turned her head and looked at the photo of her and her father she kept on her night table. It had been taken the Christmas before he died and he had his arm around her and they were both laughing into the camera. It was a lovely photo and anyone looking at it would never guess at the real Christmas they had endured that year—had endured every year with her mother in control, telling them what Christmas *should* be like. Cynthia thought Christmas was about having all the trappings. With all the wisdom of her age, Gabby knew that was where her mother always went wrong. Christmas was about people, about family— not things, not well-dressed trees and expensive presents, and a roast turkey that could feed a family of fifteen and still have enough left over for sandwiches. It was about enjoying the day, enjoying your family. Her mother had never known what it was to enjoy being with her family, that had always been the trouble.

Now she wanted to see Gabby, and Gabby didn't know what to do about it.

She was meeting Vincent later, so she would ask his advice; he might not be the sharpest knife in the drawer but he had a good heart. And he loved her, and she loved him, and that was what really mattered.

CHAPTER SEVENTY-SIX

Vincent was thrilled. He had a good little earner thanks to Derek Greene, and he had just been recruited as a driver on his first ever bank job. He was almost sick with excitement, though he had been sure not to let that show. He had driven Derek and a few of his cronies over the last few years and he had made a name for himself as a good little runner. He always canvassed where they were going beforehand, making sure he knew the route better than anyone who was born and bred there. They never got lost on their way there, or their way

237

home, and he knew that was valued. Some of the meetings had been in very out-of-the-way locations, that being the nature of the job involved, and he had always done his homework. It had been much appreciated, and he had got himself quite the reputation.

Well, it was paying off now; he was going to do such a fuck-off job he would soon be in demand. That was his goal in life—to be the best driver in London. Good drivers had a very important place in the scheme of things, and they were paid handsomely for their abilities. Another year or two and he could marry his Gabby, and they could start the family they were both looking forward to. They talked about it all the time; how they would decorate their house, what names they would give their kids, what kind of schools they would attend. They were going to have children who would be somebody in the straight world, and they would both work their arses off to achieve that for them.

As he parked his BMW convertible in the scrapyard, the same scrapyard where he had witnessed the demise of Linford and Jonny P, Vincent shuddered. It didn't matter how many times he came here—and that was frequently since Derek now owned it—he still felt the chill of apprehension as he drove through the large wrought-iron gates. It amazed him that the machinery in here was worth millions—it looked like a load of old tat. But he supposed it cost a fair bit to buy a machine that could gobble up cars— and people—and turn a large vehicle into a small block of metal, two foot by two foot.

He walked into the Portakabin, a large smile on his handsome face.

'All right, Del Boy?'

Derek Greene smiled back widely. He'd always liked Vincent O'Casey, and it had been a pleasure watching the boy flourish under his watchful eye. He was trustworthy and loyal, all the assets needed for this kind of life. Not exactly a contender for *The Krypton Factor*, but a shrewdie just the same.

'Sit down, mate, the others will be here soon. They're a little firm out of Manchester, and I have talked you up, so don't let me down, OK?'

It was a friendly warning and Vincent swallowed down his nerves as he said nonchalantly, 'I'm easy, looking forward to it. It's been a long time coming.'

Derek grinned again. 'Easy, tiger! I had to make sure you were ready before I sent you out into the big bad world!' Then, in a kinder voice, he said seriously, 'Look, everyone gets nervous, it's what gives you the edge. The day you don't get nervous on a jump is the day it goes wrong. I read a book once about Laurence Olivier, a very talented actor, but he said that he threw up every time he went on stage. See what I'm saying? It's the nerves that give people the edge. You'll be all right, Vince, you'll do good.'

Vincent smiled with pleasure at the man's words.

'Now, did you find them a hotel where they can get tooled up?'

Vincent nodded. 'It's in Southend. Small place off the front, where a crowd of men from Manchester won't be too noticeable.'

Derek grinned his usual amiable grin, the one that hid the hard man inside him. 'Good lad. We can't have them noticed by Lily Law around this gaff, know what I mean? They want to get in and out in a few days. You know the route, and we'll talk them through it together, OK? But they are relying on you to get them away. Have you arranged the chop?'

Vincent nodded. He'd already put everything in place to exchange the main motor for a more sedate model that the police would not be looking for. It was an honest motor, a family saloon, but with a revved-up engine in case of emergencies, such as the police recognising them and giving chase. 'All sorted, and all in place.'

'Excellent. I think you're going to be a useful addition to this outfit, young Vincent.'

Vincent was beaming at the praise. 'Thanks for the chance, Derek, I appreciate it.'

As he spoke, Bertie Warner pulled up outside. Bertie had taken on the mantle of boss with ease, and he was now at the top of this very lucrative game. As he swaggered into the small Portakabin, he was all good-natured bonhomie.

'Afternoon, my old mockers! I heard a great joke today: Why do brides wear white? Because all fucking kitchen appliances are white!'

Vincent and Derek both laughed, as was expected.

'My mate Peter Bailey is a funny man, no doubt about it. Shame he didn't go on the stage really—he could give that Jimmy Jones a run for his money.'

The phone rang and Derek answered it; he listened for a few seconds then passed the phone to Vincent saying, 'Fucking hell, no wonder they need a good driver. They can't even find their way to the Bow Road!'

As Vincent directed the men to the Portakabin, he felt the rush of adrenaline. This was the life, this was the life he had always craved, and it was within his grasp at last. He felt like the luckiest man alive.

CHAPTER SEVENTY-SEVEN

Cynthia Callahan—she had dropped the name
Tailor after she had left East London—looked
around her flat and felt the rush of pride her
home always gave her. She was living in a new
development called Chafford Hundred, and she
had a penthouse that looked over the Thames.
She could see the boats plying their trades, and the
shores of Kent. It was a lovely setting.

She had bought this place for yet another new
start; as usual she had become involved with a man,
who had eventually walked out on her. But not until
she had bled him dry. She smiled to herself, the
smile that made her look like an angel, but actually
hid the fact she was a devil in disguise. Amoral as
ever, she had understood the need to leave the
South Downs, where she had been living previously,
sooner rather than later. She had bought this place
after reading the advertising blurb and was now
awaiting the sale of her small house in Sussex.

Sussex had been good to her; she had quite liked
it there—especially Brighton. Brighton had been
the nearest thing to London, so she felt at home
there. Now, out here in the Essex countryside, she
was near enough to London to visit, but not close
enough to be a part of it all. That suited her down
to the ground. She had the best of both worlds
really, and she did like her solitude.

She had already met a few of her neighbours.
In the penthouse opposite her was a man called

241

David. In his mid-fifties, he was getting over a bitter divorce—just the kind of man she liked. Old enough to appreciate her, and young enough to think they had a future together. He had a few quid, drove a decent car, and his furniture was expensive and tasteful. He would be her new conquest, and she was looking forward to the chase.

She opened her bedroom closets and looked at the large array of clothes. She would play the part of a retired career woman for him and, when she finally had him within her grasp, she would start borrowing money from him—just until her money arrived from the Cayman Islands of course. That would be her story. By the time he realised it was all lies, it would be too late.

She laughed with delight. It was so easy to get these men to part with their cash, and they never pressed charges—they were too embarrassed. Lying came easy to her, and she had discovered she was exemplary at it. It was said people who lied needed good memories, which was true! She had a patter, and she never deviated from it. She would talk in telephone numbers, insist on paying her half of any bills or holidays, and she would casually mention all the different business deals she had on the go. It was so easy she could con them in her sleep. Eventually she would need a cash injection, and they would give it to her unquestioningly.

It was only when it started to dawn on them that she wasn't all she said she was that the rot set in, but by then she was already making plans for her flight. She'd be unavailable on all her phone numbers and gone from her home that they eventually found out had been rented and not owned by her. The truth was she *did* own it, but through a holding company and she rented it to herself. Oh, she was a clever little girlie. No paper trails, no actual criminal act, she just borrowed money. It happened all the time. The police had never once interviewed her, and so she had no qualms about continuing. It was lucrative, and it was easy—perfect in fact.

So why had she felt this sudden longing to see her daughter? She truly *wanted* to see her, see what she looked like, how she had turned out. Gabriella would be sixteen now, on the cusp of womanhood. Did she look like her or did she now resemble James? Cynthia had a feeling it would be her; she always had, even from a baby.

Cynthia had no interest in James Junior; he was already too far gone from her to be of any interest. But Gabriella had possessed the same spark that she herself did. What she was feeling was in no way maternal, it was simply curiosity.

She knew Gabriella was with her mother and father, and she shuddered at the thought of how she would be living. They lived like tinkers—all TV sets and boiled food. Cynthia had hated it as a child, aspired to a better way of life than the working men's clubs they frequented. She felt almost sick with shame about her upbringing.

Yet Celeste had loved all that, so had James when she had taken him to the club for the first time. He said it was a great place for meeting up with friends—like he had ever had any friends! To her it had always felt like slumming, but then she was above all that kind of shit. A good restaurant, decent wine and intelligent conversation were beyond these people's comprehension—they had thought she was a snob, and she knew she was. She was proud to be one. Who in their right mind would

243

want to live like *them*? Hand to mouth, eating food that had more preservatives in it than Joan Collins? Their main topic of conversation was what was going on in *EastEnders*.

If she had one regret, it was leaving her daughter to live like that. But then what would she have done with her? She had her own life, and a good life it was. Neverthe—less she was curious to see her again. It never occurred to her though that her daughter might not *want* to see her, that what she had done to her family might not be forgiven, let alone forgotten. As far as Cynthia was concerned, she had summoned her daughter to her side and what else could her daughter do, but answer that call? To Cynthia Callahan, that was simple logic.

CHAPTER SEVENTY-EIGHT

'You're joking, Celly?'

Celeste shook her head, and said seriously, 'No, I'm not, Mum. She's frightened to tell you and Dad, and who can blame her?'

Mary felt sick at what she had heard, and if Jack found out there would be murder done. That Cynthia thought she could waltz back into her daughter's life after all this time was outrageous. 'She's not thinking of going, is she?'

Celeste, one eye on the *Trisha* show and one eye on her mother, said honestly, 'I think she's just curious, Mum, you know. But I don't think she wants to go for any other reason than that.'

Mary nodded, but her heart was beating too fast for her own good. She sat on the sofa and bit her lips in consternation. Her first thought was that Cynthia might have changed, but she dismissed that idea as soon as it arrived. This was something far more sinister, she knew that in her waters. If Cynthia wanted to see that child there *had* to be an agenda. So, what could it be? And why hadn't Gabby discussed it with her?

'When did this happen, Celeste?'

Celeste shrugged her huge shoulders. 'A few days ago.'

That explained the child's demeanour recently anyway. 'What do you think, love?'

Celeste closed her eyes for a few seconds before saying, 'I think she should run as far away from her mother as possible and, before you ask, I told her that.'

Mary nodded in agreement.

'Cynthia is trouble; she's a liar, and she's dangerous. But, at the end of the day, she *is* Gabby's mother.'

'More's the fucking pity. Well, I'll have to wait and see if she asks me about it, won't I?'

But Celeste wasn't listening any more; the woman on *Trisha* was confronting her demons, which were drink and drugs, and Trisha as always was sympathetic but firm. Celeste liked Trisha, she had a nice way about her.

Mary watched the screen blankly, her mind in turmoil. Cynthia plus Gabby added up to a disaster, and she knew she had to make sure that any meeting between them was monitored. By herself if possible. None of this was good for her heart, she knew, but it was something that had to be addressed and at the earliest possible opportunity. Her daughter Cynthia was like Jaws—just when you thought it was safe to go back into the water . . . back she came, like the proverbial bad penny.

One thing was for sure though—Jack must never know about any of this. He would see his elder daughter dead before he let her back in this family again.

CHAPTER SEVENTY-NINE

Terry Marchant was a Mancunian with a loud laugh and an even larger thirst. Vincent liked him and, along with his two cronies Patrick Miles and Anthony Dawes, he was good company. They were blaggers extraordinaire, and they roamed the country robbing banks and building societies with gay abandon. They did the stealing, and then relied on a good wheelman to get them out of the way. Which is where Vincent came in; he got ten per cent of the load, and all he had to do was drive. It was a doddle.

Now, sitting in a pub on Southend Seafront drinking orange juice, Vincent was getting a real insight into the men he would be dealing with. Terry Marchant was a hardcase, that was obvious to anyone. He had the look, the build and the carriage of a man who it would be foolish to mess with. Vincent had learnt that over the years—you could tell from looking at certain people whether or not you could fuck with them. Terry Marchant was a definite no-no in that respect. But he was a lot of fun, and he had a great personality. His two colleagues were small-time, but nice blokes all the same. Vincent felt he would enjoy working with

246

them.

Terry Marchant, for his part, was pleased to see that the lad was not drinking alcohol. Even though the blag wasn't for a few days, he appreciated that the kid wasn't stupid enough to get a tug for driving over the limit. It meant he was sensible, and unlikely to get himself on the police radar, so to speak. Derek had spoken highly of the boy, and that should have been enough for him, but Terry still preferred to look the drivers over and form his own opinion of them before he gave the nod. Buyer beware and all that. He was weighing out a nice wedge for Vincent, and their livelihoods depended on him doing a good job.

It was strange really; no one ever understood that robbing was the easy part—it was the disappearing act afterwards that was hard. Once people saw a sawn-off, they tended to do as they were told. The Old Bill, on the other hand, were not so amenable. They hated blaggers with a vengeance; there was nothing so annoying to a Filth than a bank being knocked over in their jurisdiction. Fucking muppets! What were banks for? Sitting there, full of wonga, and no real security. Done properly it was a piece of cake.

He and the boys had sussed out the lay of the land already. It was a good little set up and the bank would be full of dough as it had all the wages for the surrounding areas waiting to be picked up. It was on a quiet road too—just the kind of place he liked. They'd do a final check but he was sure they'd covered all the bases and they'd be in and out, quick as a flash.

Terry ordered more drinks and started to tell a story about an old mate from Warrington who

247

had robbed a bank while drunk as a cunt. It was a funny story but it was also a bit of an allegory. It showed the stupidity of people while in the throes of alcohol, and how badly things could go against you if you weren't careful.

He noticed that young Vincent listened raptly, and he knew then that he had got his point across with the minimum of fuss. He didn't like aggro and he didn't like heroes. He liked people to do their jobs and forget about it. Seemed that this kid had all the attributes he needed.

So, finally, Terry Marchant relaxed and was able to enjoy the rest of his stay in Southend.

CHAPTER EIGHTY

'I told the social worker I didn't want to see her, Nana.'

Mary relaxed, breathing out a heartfelt sigh of relief. 'You did the right thing, child. She wouldn't have wanted to see you for any other reason than trouble. God forgive me for saying that about my own daughter, but it's the truth. Everything she touches she destroys, and we both know that, don't we?'

Gabby nodded. 'I'm sorry I never told you, Nana. I didn't want to upset you. But when I came in and saw your face I knew then Auntie Celly had to have said something.'

Mary smiled sadly. 'She did it for the best, lovie.'

Gabby nodded, but her eyes were filling with unshed tears. 'I know, Nana, but I wanted to see her a bit, just a little bit. She *is* my mum.'

Mary held her granddaughter close and comforted her as best she could, all the time cursing her elder daughter. Why couldn't she have just stayed away? Why did she want to upend this child's life on a whim? With Cynthia she had no doubt it *would* be a whim. No good could come of it.

CHAPTER EIGHTY-ONE

Vincent was waiting patiently outside the bank in Essex. It was twenty past ten in the morning, and Terry Marchant and his two accomplices had just walked into the bank, ski masks over their heads and sawn-offs in their sports bags.

Vincent watched through the window. The bank didn't get busy until lunchtime and so at nearly ten thirty it was more or less empty with just the three tellers inside and a couple of young mums paying their electric bills. He watched the pantomime unfold inside and, five minutes later, the men were on their way to the car and he was already getting ready to drive away. It had been so easy—too easy really. He was around the roundabout and on his way to Basildon before the first sirens were even heard in the distance.

At Basildon he turned off towards the train station, and the three men, now devoid of ski masks and without their distinctive red tracksuit tops— which were all the bystanders would remember— were relaxed and laughing. The adrenaline rush was over, and their job was done without so much as a hiccough. They chopped the cars with the minimum of fuss, leaving everything behind them except the money, and they were back in Southend within the hour.

Never had Vincent O'Casey had such a spectacular day. And never had he believed that a blag could be that fucking simple. They had netted just under a hundred grand, and he went home ten thousand pounds better off; it was like all his Christmases and birthdays had come at once. The best thing had been that he had loved it, loved every second of it. And tonight he was going to have the greatest night out of his life.

CHAPTER EIGHTY-TWO

Gabby had never seen so much money before in her life, and her eyes widened in disbelief. Vincent loved seeing her reaction as he showed her his cut.

Gabby looked at him in amazement. 'Ten grand!'

He grinned. 'Yes, ten thousand pounds, and keep your voice down or we'll have your nana and granddad in on top of us in a minute.'

'They're out, you div—they've gone to bingo with Mrs Jacobs over the road. And Auntie Celly ain't gonna come in here, she's watching her soaps. A fucking bomb couldn't get her away from the telly when Grant Mitchell's on.'

Suddenly they were both quiet, realising what that meant. Then, grabbing her, Vincent started to kiss her, and it was unlike any kiss they had ever had before. Gabby was in her dressing gown and, as he slipped it off her shoulders, she knew that she wouldn't stop him, this time she would let him.

When he lay her down on her little single bed, and she felt the money beneath her body, she knew that this was meant to be, that they were meant to be together.

Two big events in one day, and Vincent felt like he was the king of the world.

CHAPTER EIGHTY-THREE

'I'm telling you, the kid's good, Del. He didn't even break a sweat, and I know more experienced men who still collapse under that kind of pressure.'

Derek Greene was pleased at Terry's praise of his protégé. He had a good nose for talent, and he prided himself on nurturing that talent and finding a role which suited the person best.

'No, Del, he's a good one. I was well impressed.'

'How was your hotel? All right?'

'Perfect—small, out of the way, and run by an old couple who couldn't describe their own arses without a picture of it in their hands. Nice grub and all. It was a good little overnighter.'

Derek was thrilled. Terry Marchant was a Face of Faces in Manchester, but he still liked to work. He was a natural-born blagger, it was in his blood. It wasn't as if he even needed the money—what Terry needed was the rush. Just like his own father, Terry Marchant liked the thought of getting one over on the banking system and the Old Bill.

'So you would use him again, then?'

'In a heartbeat. He's got a natural talent for it, and that's rare in this day and age. Too many young lads can't keep their fucking traps shut. Also, he's

251

a nice kid, easygoing, never saw him drink once, only orange juice. That tells me he has a bit of savvy about him. I'll spread the word when I get back to Manchester, you'll get more calls for him.'

Derek nodded, pleased with the result. He had his cut nicely stashed in the safe at the scrapyard—that was what he called his petty cash. His beer and entertainment money. He had a feeling he would be getting quite a bit more of that kind of money from hiring out young Vincent in the near future. He only hoped the kid didn't go splashing out on motors and watches he should not have been able to afford, thereby bringing down on him the interest of Lily Law.

The Filth were always aware when a local boy had a new car, or too much money in their pockets; it was what alerted them to potential Faces. Derek's dad had drummed that into his head—always have a legitimate business on the go. A real business could explain away houses, cars and holidays. It also let you live a legal life with mortgages, loans, etc. But he had explained that to young Vincent, and he was a sensible kid; Derek was sure he would have taken it onboard. But he knew better than anyone how money in the hand could burn a hole as big as the Ritz in certain people's pockets, so all he could do now was wait and see. He wasn't too bothered about it. He had a feeling that Vincent O'Casey had an agenda of his own, and that agenda was about that bird of his. Pretty little thing she was as well. Nice face, shame about her mother! He smiled at his own wit. Well, only time would tell with Vincent, and Derek Greene had all the time in the world.

CHAPTER EIGHTY-FOUR

Cynthia watched her daughter leave the house and get into Vincent O'Casey's car which was parked outside her parents' home. She was in her own car, a small BMW convertible, but she was wearing a scarf and it was dark, so she wasn't worried about being noticed.

Vincent, however, had parked under a lamppost, so she had a good view of her daughter and her beau. She was surprised it was still Vincent O'Casey—surprised and annoyed. Didn't Gabriella have any idea at all? Had she learned nothing from her mother? But then, this was *her* mother's influence, she was sure. Get the first boy that gives you any attention and marry him before someone else does. Cynthia was actually gritting her teeth with annoyance and she made a conscious effort to relax herself.

It was odd, being back in the old neighbourhood; she hated it even more now than she had then. It was so scruffy and so depressing, no wonder the women who lived here looked defeated and so *old*. It was as if they had given up on themselves, which of course they had. Cynthia prided herself on her skin, on her trim figure and she dressed to impress—these women dressed to go up the shops!

But her Gabriella was a beauty, she would give her that. She was just like Cynthia at the same age—all tits, legs and slim waist, and she held herself and walked well. That was important to a woman, walking well. Her old nanny used to say 'Walk into a room like you own it and the chances are one day you will.' Pity Mary had never listened to her own mother—how different things might have turned out. Imagine still living in the first house the council gave you! That was her mum and dad all over; no fucking ambition, no desire for something better. Just grateful for being alive. How she would love to knock on that door, and give them the fright of their lives. She knew it would be her mother who put the kibosh on her daughter seeing her. Her mother would not want to lose the girl now she had her.

In truth, Cynthia was amazed at how much the refusal had hurt her. Why should she care about it so much? Her pride had definitely been hurt. And that social worker had irritated her with her fake sympathy and platitudes. Silly bitch—like she gave a flying fuck what she thought.

Still, she had made the woman promise to keep her up-to-date on her daughter's life, and she had agreed to that. Fucking cheek! This was *her* child, *she* had given birth to her, not that fucking old bitch of a mother of hers, or that dried-up stick of a social worker. No, it had been her, Cynthia Tailor that was, who had endured nine months of hell and eighteen long, hard hours of labour. She bet her mother had had a field day, advising her granddaughter to keep away from her own flesh and blood.

Well, fuck them. This was all she had really wanted—a quick peek, just to see what the girl had turned out like. And wouldn't you know, she was exactly as she had expected. A foolish girl who had no desire to make anything of herself. She would live the life of her nana, without anything of real value, and without any idea of the world that was going on outside the confines of this council estate.

Cynthia lit a cigarette and pulled on it deeply; she allowed herself three a day, otherwise all the hours she spent in the gym keeping in shape were pointless. She had a better body now than before she had had her kids. But that was the beauty of living alone, you could do those kind of things; go to the gym, eat well, take yourself off to a health spa for long weekends. Children stopped that, like they stopped anything good in your life.

Gabriella and Vincent were kissing now, and Cynthia shook her head in consternation. What a fool she had bred, what a complete and utter fool! Gabriella would settle for a life of petty dramas and no money, a life of cleaning and cooking for a man who, once the initial sexual thrill eased off, would use her like an animal while in drink. It was so predictable really, and fucking irritating. She had brought this girl into the world, surely there had to be at least a little bit of her in the child? She reasoned her mum and dad would have made sure whatever spark the girl might have would be repressed. The last thing they would want was another child under their roof with a bit more liveliness than they could cope with, a girl with the chance to make something of her life, instead of emulating them, just existing.

Cynthia drove away quietly, not even glancing into the car where her daughter was telling her boyfriend that she thought she was pregnant and that her nana was going to kill her.

CHAPTER EIGHTY-FIVE

'Calm down, Gabby. It's a shock, but it ain't exactly unheard of in this day and age, is it?'

Gabby couldn't believe how well Vincent was taking the news. She had thought he would be furious with her. 'I'm only sixteen, Vince!'

He laughed. 'We'll get married, so stop worrying about it, OK? I'll tell your nana and granddad with you. They won't be too thrilled but they'll come round eventually. So please, stop worrying.'

Vincent made it sound so easy and, in a way, she supposed it was. She'd tell them and be damned. But she still felt that she had let them down somehow, had broken their trust. She had a bad feeling on her, although that could just be her hormones.

Vincent felt a rush of love for this girl of his. She was having his baby and she was frightened, but surely she knew that he would always look out for her, always take care of her? She meant everything to him, and she always would.

'Look, Gabby, once the balloon's been dropped, you can start planning the wedding, OK? Once your nana knows about that she'll see we're serious about each other.'

Gabby nodded, feeling slightly happier but still apprehensive. It was as if a weight was bearing down on her, almost as if her mother was nearby, watching and judging her. Yet she knew that was stupid—what would her mother be doing here? She hated it here, always had. But for a while there she had felt her presence nearby. It had reminded her of when she was a kid and she had wet her bed, and she knew her mother would be coming into her room. Her mum had a way of letting you know she was near; it was hard to explain but she had almost felt her mother's closeness. But that was gone now, and she shook herself back to reality.

Vincent was right—it had happened now, and they had to make the best of it. She wondered if it would be a girl or a boy? She didn't care, she just wanted something to love of her own.

'Come on, we'll go up and tell your auntie Celly. She'll be our buffer until your nana and granddad come round.'

'Do you think they will come round, Vince?'

He grinned. 'Take my word for it, once this baby arrives they'll be over the moon.'

She hoped he was right. She wanted this baby badly, and she *wanted* it to be wanted, not just by her, but by everyone. She knew what it was like to feel unloved, and she was determined no child of hers would feel like that, not ever. It was the worst feeling in the world.

CHAPTER EIGHTY-SIX

Mary was disappointed, as was Jack, but they both knew there was nothing they could do about any of it. At least Vincent was standing by her, and that was something they supposed. But Gabby was so young, and they both knew how hard it was rearing a child, especially in this day and age. And that social worker, Miss Byrne, had not even looked shocked— it was as if she had been expecting it. In fairness to

257

her, maybe she saw something they hadn't. She had more experience than they did with children of all kinds, at least that was Mary's reasoning.

At the moment, though, her main worry was Celeste. The weight was dropping off her, and that would have pleased Mary if she didn't look so unwell on it. What was strange was that the girl was eating as much as she ever did. She was like some kind of human waste disposal unit, her mouth constantly in motion. Crisps, chocolate, take-aways—she ate anything at any time. And, to crown it all, she would not even go to the hospital, assuring them she was fine. She certainly didn't look fine—she looked awful but, as the doctor said, there was little anyone could do.

Mary felt plagued with anxiety nowadays, and that was not good for her heart, not good for it at all. Still, she had her tablets, and she didn't overdo it if she could help it.

'That girl's not well, Mary, but she won't admit it.'

Mary just stopped herself from berating her husband for his uncanny ability to state the bleeding obvious. Instead she said gently, 'I know, Jack, but what can we do? Like Doctor Morgan says, if she doesn't want to see him there's nothing he can do about it, and neither can we.'

Jack nodded, and Mary saw that, like herself, he was getting old. They were only in their late sixties but they were both in poor health. It was their dirt over the years; smoking, drinking, but also the worry. Oh, they had had their fair share of worry all right. She wondered for the thousandth time if Celeste should be forced from the house; after all, the reason she wouldn't go to a hospital for tests was because she wouldn't leave the house. Even the thought of the outside world sent her into a panic. How had this happened to her family? It was a familiar refrain these days, and Mary lay all the blame with Jonny Parker and her elder daughter.

She remembered Celeste as a young girl. She had been full of life, a nice girl without big ambitions—not like her sister in that way. No, Celeste had been a decent kind of person—she still was. But she had never had the toughness needed to survive in a world peopled with the likes of Jonny Parker and Cynthia Tailor.

When she heard that Cynthia had gone back to her maiden name, Mary had wondered briefly if there was any way they could stop her from doing that. Callahan was a good, decent Irish name, and it was meant for better than the likes of Cynthia. At times she loathed her daughter so intensely she felt sure the girl must sense it, no matter how far away she was. She believed that hate could be felt, even if the person wasn't in the room with you. She hoped her daughter felt her contempt as if it was a living thing; that was what she prayed for.

Since she had tried to get back into Gabby's life, she had stirred them up in different ways. Gabby had wondered if her mother had changed and was now capable of loving her at least a little. Mary thought she had more chance of getting a wank off the Pope than *that* ever happening. Still, she knew the girl had wanted it badly—needed it, in fact. She wanted to feel that her mother loved her at least a little. Well, Cynthia wasn't capable of love. Even her relationship with Jonny Parker had not been about love—it had been about taking what her sister had, and believing she had got one over on

259

her in the process. Now, with Cynthia back in the picture, Celeste had been reminded of everything she had tried so hard to forget.

Celeste was tied to this house, frightened of the world itself. And it was understandable; after all, it had never done her any favours, had it? Now she lived in these few rooms content, in her own way, with her TV programmes and her films about other people's lives. Even the house in Spain which she had loved so much was now sold. It seemed she would travel only once more in her life, and that would be out of this house in a coffin.

Her daughter's existence caused Mary no small amount of pain. Knowing her lovely vibrant daughter had been reduced to this wreck of a woman was hard to bear at times. But bear it she did. What else could a mother do? Oh, Cynthia had a lot of things to answer for.

Even that poor demented boy, James Junior, was still in care. Mary didn't want to see him though, as she had explained to the social workers. She had more than enough on her plate to last her a lifetime. Plus, she had been a bit frightened of James Junior since the kitten incident. Gabby had been kind and written letters to him with all the news, he was her brother after all, despite everything. He had never replied though. But she hadn't given up.

'Can I make you a cuppa, girl?'

She nodded at Jack and smiled faintly. 'That would be lovely.'

Since her heart attack he was like the tea boy, always offering to make her a cup, or get her a few biscuits. She knew it was love and guilt, both of which, unlike Cynthia, he seemed to have in abundance.

CHAPTER EIGHTY-SEVEN

Vincent had done two more jobs for Derek and he had another couple lined up. Piece of piss, as his father would say. And that was just it—it was so easy. He drove like other people ate or slept—it came naturally to him. From the moment he drove his first stolen car at thirteen it had been instinctive. Now his talent was making him a fortune, and he would need it as well, what with the baby coming and everything else. He was considering buying into a garage; it would be a legitimate business, and explain away any money he weighed out. He had listened earnestly to Derek and he knew that the man was giving him sound advice. He wanted to be kosher, at least outwardly anyway, and a garage would be ideal for him. He loved nothing more than tampering with cars so, all in all, it would be a win-win situation.

As he sat in the pub in Wapping waiting for Derek Greene to bring his new employers to meet him, he saw a girl watching him. Smiling at her, he realised she was familiar, only he wasn't sure where he knew her from. She wasn't local anyway. Pleased that such a nice-looking girl was eyeing him, he sipped at his orange juice, before turning his attention to the door.

The girl was already gone by the time he looked back, and he forgot about her immediately and got on with waiting. He was a patient lad in that respect, and in his job that was what you had to

261

be—patient and calm. Luckily, he possessed both traits in spades.

It was ten minutes later when he saw Derek walk over that it came to him where he had seen the girl before. Getting up, he looked at Derek and said quietly, 'Fuck off *now*, Del Boy. I think I was just eyeballed by one of the staff of the bank we blagged in Essex. I'm sure I recognised her from our recce.'

Derek didn't need telling twice, and he left immediately. Phoning the other two people who should have been on the meet he told them it was off, grateful that Vincent had the nous not to drag everyone else into his business. He went back to the yard and telephoned Terry Marchant; he had to give him a heads-up, and assure him that young Vincent would not be swayed. He only hoped that what he was saying was the truth, and the lad didn't succumb to the police offering him a deal. He didn't think the boy was capable of that kind of treachery, but you never really knew anybody until the chips were down. Harder men than him had served up their mates at the thought of a big lump.

He was sorry for the kid really; he had a pregnant girlfriend and a promising career. It was the girlfriend that bothered him. Would Vincent keep it shut in the face of leaving her to fend for herself? They would soon know, of that much he was sure.

But it was a bastard of an inconvenience; Terry had a few good jobs lined up for him. On the bright side, maybe the girl didn't recognise him; after all, he was a nice enough looking lad to attract some female attention. But if she *had* seen him on his recce of the bank, and she remembered him, it was all over. And he had remembered her, so it was definitely related, as the Filth would say. One thing was for sure though. If Vincent fingered any of them, he was a dead man, and that was a promise.

CHAPTER EIGHTY-EIGHT

'What do you mean arrested?' Mary Callahan was looking at Vincent's father as if he was an attraction in a zoo.

'What I say, Mary. He's been nicked for bank robbery.'

'What! Vincent?'

Paddy O'Casey sighed in annoyance. 'Look, is Jack about?'

She opened the door wider and invited the man inside. What was she thinking keeping him on the step like that? It was the shock she supposed.

Jack Callahan was watching the news with his daughter. When he saw Paddy come into the room, he knew there and then that it was not good news. He stood up and shook the man's hand. 'What's up? Is it Vincent?'

Paddy nodded. 'He's been pinched, Jack, armed robbery.'

'When? He's been here every day . . .'

Paddy waved a hand in annoyance. 'It was ages ago. He was seen by one of the girls from the bank in a pub and the Filth have him on CCTV a few days before the robbery. Fucking eejit, he is. Anyway, he's bang to rights and, with a bit of luck, he might make bail. But the brief ain't too hopeful. The girl in the bank was not the only one to pick him out of a line up—the manager did too. He'll

263

keep stumm about who was in it with him and, if he pleads guilty, he might get off with a ten stretch.'

'Jesus, Mary and fucking Joseph, this will destroy Gabby! She's banking on him being there when the child's born.'

Paddy O'Casey sighed once more. 'I know, but we can't always have what we want in life. She might as well learn that lesson now—this is as good a time as any.'

Hearing the defeat in the man's voice, Mary Callahan felt an urge to slap him across the face. This was his son's life, and he was acting as if it was nothing more than an inconvenience. No wonder young Vincent spent so much time round here. Well, he wouldn't be coming back for a long time, and she had to tell her granddaughter that at some point this evening. She would be devastated, and rightly so. Why were they being plagued with this bad luck? It just seemed to be one thing after another. Now Gabby was pregnant and alone. What a state of affairs.

CHAPTER EIGHTY-NINE

'You've got to snap out of this, Gabby, it's not good for you or the baby.'

Gabby knew that her nana was right, but it was hard. She was eight months pregnant, and her baby's father was doing nine years in Parkhurst. He would be out in four with good behaviour. He had not grassed up or implicated anyone else and the men thought he was wonderful, a real mate, and a right diamond geezer. Well, Gabby didn't share that opinion. *She* thought he should have told the Filth everything he knew, and got himself out a lot sooner. She shook her head as if she was clearing it. She didn't really mean it; she knew he had to take the fall. Grasses were not welcome in their world. Grasses were not welcome anywhere.

On top of everything else, his dad and brothers had found his hidden stash of money and taken it for themselves, so she was also skint into the bargain. They had jumped on that money like a monkey on a banana tree, and that had hurt. They had basically taken the food out of her baby's mouth. The O'Caseys had had a new TV and a good few parties on what should have been *her* money. Vincent was furious. That money was for her and her baby. But there was nothing he could do about it. Not from where he was sitting.

'I just miss him, Nana.' Her voice was a plaintive cry now.

''Course you do, child, it wouldn't be natural if you didn't.'

Her nana's no-nonsense approach made her smile at times, even though it could annoy her too. Mary Callahan's attitude was, it's happened, get over it. But then her nana had had a lot of experience where being let down was concerned, she supposed. It didn't stop Gabby from feeling lonely and abandoned once again though.

Her baby kicked and she smiled; at least her child was strong and healthy, that was something she supposed. She was determined to be the antithesis of her own mother; everything her mother had done for her and James Junior, she would do the opposite. She figured that at least that way, she would have to be doing *something* right.

But having a baby was a scary thing. A little person was going to depend on her for everything, from being fed and changed, to being loved and wanted. Well, this child would have all of that and, even though its father wasn't around, it wasn't because he didn't want to be. It was legally impossible for him to be there, and she would explain it just like that when the time came. It was so much better than being told your father had been nicked.

She was due soon, and she knew it would not be pleasant. In all honesty, she was frightened of what it entailed. She wished she had a mum to turn to. Her nana was great, but she was so old and, in truth, Gabby didn't want to worry her more than she had to. Her nana and granddad seemed to have aged almost overnight, and she knew it was because of her auntie Celeste.

Celeste was a shadow of her former self, and the really worrying thing was she didn't eat a thing now, she just lay there, on her bed, watching her programmes. Her granddad called her the *Radio Times*, because she knew every TV schedule, even Sky's back to front, making them all wonder if she ever actually slept. She believed the BBC was quality programming, but she claimed to prefer the shows that didn't make her feel like they were being condescending to her. She loved American talk shows, especially *Oprah*, and believed Jerry Springer had a place in that society, albeit not at the top end. It was surreal talking to her, because unless she had watched it on a TV programme she wasn't sure it was really true. She talked about Dr Phil as if he had come to the house and diagnosed her himself. She was really big on self-diagnosis. According to an episode of *Oprah*, she was losing weight because her good angel was helping her. After all, angels were real, weren't they? Celeste bought it all, hook, line and fucking sinker. She claimed to understand forensic pathology as well as if she had studied it at university, and was sad that most murder cases she read about in the papers didn't have access to the same resources that they did on TV shows. And why not? she demanded. Where was Dr Sam Ryan when you needed her?

Did these programmers never allow for people like her aunt, who believed all that shit without question? Or did they depend on them? What came first; the TV or the viewer? Did the people really have a chance against those boffins at TV stations around the world? That, Gabby realised, remained to be seen.

Even her granddad Jack had to acknowledge that Celeste wasn't right these days, and seemed to be becoming more and more entrenched in her TV world by the minute. She talked about Trevor McDonald as if he was an old friend, and she argued that Michelle Collins was not a bad person, she was *just* Cindy Beale.

Now that she rarely got out of bed, the smell was not good. She was not even forty years old but she looked sixty at least.

As she went into her aunt's bedroom, Gabby wrinkled her nose at the odour; it was sweet, but overpoweringly so. Gabby knew it was the Parma Violets her aunt sucked all day long, but it still made her want to heave.

'Fancy a take-away, Auntie Cel? You name it, I'll eat it!' This was getting boring; she did the same thing every night now, and each time she got the same answer.

'Nothing for me, sweetie. How're you and junior doing?'

Gabby sat on the edge of her aunt's bed and she said sadly, 'We're doing fine. And you?'

Celeste looked into her niece's eyes and saw the beauty in her face; it was the same innocent beauty her mother had possessed, except with Cynthia, it had masked her true nature. 'I nearly had a baby once, but I lost it. I lost a few actually. I thought it was terrible at the time, but now, well, how lucky was I, eh? I never had to tell them the truth about their father, never had to lie to them either.' She coughed gently before saying earnestly, 'I'm dying, Gabs, I have cancer of the uterus. I told the doc not to tell your nana. You know how she flaps about everything. But I'm telling you in case I don't see this little one born. No, don't be sad, I *want* to go. What kind of life is this for anyone, eh? But I want you to know I will miss you, and I loved you like you were me own.'

Gabby looked down into her aunt's face which still held the vestiges of her former prettiness and, choking down a sob, she held her to her breast as if she was the mother and her aunt was the child.

'I'll miss you, Auntie Celeste.'

Celeste smiled through her tears. 'No, you won't. When I go it will be a relief for you all, but not as much as it will be for me. My life was a waste, don't let that be *your* life. Promise me, darling, you'll make your life mean something.'

'I'll try, Auntie, I'll try.'

But even as she said it her heart and her waters were breaking.

CHAPTER NINETY

Vincent O'Casey was tired out. He had been in the gym all morning and then cooked all afternoon. One good thing about Parkhurst—on the SSB unit at least you weren't on constant lock up. It was still hard though. Knowing that Gabby was due at any moment, he was like a cat on a hot tin roof. All the other lags were chafing him, but he took it in a good-natured way. The fact that he had not named names had gone a long way to making his stay in nick quite easy. It wasn't ideal, but it was bearable, and Derek Greene had made sure of that, as had Bertie Warner. The Manchester boys treated him like some kind of mascot, and he appreciated it—it showed him that what he was enduring was not for nothing. The hardest thing to bear was that his little baby would be born without him, and he knew his Gabby needed him. She had no one really, except her old grandparents and they were fucking ancient. Nice people, but not exactly in the first flush of youth.

It was pointless dwelling on it now. The first thing he had learned was that the outside world was something you had no control over, therefore you must not let it do your head in. He knew better now than to let his thoughts wander too far from the normal. But with his Gabby on the verge of giving birth to his first child, a child he would not see until visiting day, it was getting harder and harder to pretend it was happening to someone else.

He consoled himself with the thought that he had not dropped anyone in it, that he could hold his head up. But it still didn't make up for being banged up in here while his girl was alone and pregnant on the outside.

As he was walking back to his cell, a screw called his name and number. He stood to attention as was required and the screw, one of the few who was a nice enough geezer, said to him happily, 'You got a daughter, lad—eight pounds nine ounces. Congratulations!'

'A girl? Oh my God, I got a fucking daughter!' Vincent was jumping up and down, his face a picture of happiness, his voice louder than it had ever been before.

The commotion had brought all the lags out of their cells, and Vincent felt his hand being shaken, and his shoulders being hugged, but it was like a dream to him. A little girl—he had a little girl. He hoped his Gabby had not had too bad a time of it. According to half the men in here, the first one was a piece of piss—except George Palmer whose wife had died in childbirth, but that was twenty-five years ago. Things were so much different these days.

The screws congratulated him, and one gave him a pack of cigars, while another gave him two bottles of decent Scotch. He knew this lot was really from Derek Greene but he was grateful nonetheless. When all was said and done, he would much rather have been beside Gabby and seen his little baby for himself. The men on the wing understood that, and they did their best to help him forget. He was grateful to them because he wasn't sure he could have coped with it alone.

CHAPTER NINETY-ONE

Celeste died just two hours after Gabby's baby was born. Little Cherie Celeste Mary Tailor entered the world screaming, and it was a sound that her mother cherished from the first moment. She was a big lusty child with thick blond hair and the Callahan blue eyes. She was adorable, and Gabby fell instantly in love with her, as did her great-nana and granddad.

Jack looked at the child as if he had never seen a baby before. He wondered if it was the fact she was a great-granddaughter and he never thought he would live that long, or if it was because the baby was exquisite. He decided it was most probably a mixture of the two.

It was a night of celebration, and a night of mourning. As his Mary had pointed out, God takes one and leaves another in its place. A load of old cobblers really, but he wanted to believe it this night. Wanted to believe that his poor Celeste might live again through this child. He sat there for a long moment, the child in his arms, the fourth living generation of Callahans, and he wondered what kind of life this child would have. He prayed it would be a good life, a really good life. His old mum had often said, 'Life at its longest is short, make the most of it while you still can.' How true that was. But with this baby's start in life, a very young mother and her father doing a big lump for armed robbery, he couldn't really see any good coming of it. He hoped against hope that he was wrong.

CHAPTER NINETY-TWO

Cynthia looked down at the baby who was, to all intents and purposes, her grandchild. She had taken the call about the birth from a girl she had known at school, and with whom she had resumed a rather sketchy relationship. The girl was a drinker and she supplied a few quid in exchange for news about Cynthia's family. Now she was at the hospital, and looking at her daughter's little girl.

The baby was very pretty—a robust, yet delicate-featured little girl, with thick blond hair and what already promised to be strong blue eyes. Oh, she would have the Callahan eyes all right, not those insipid Tailor eyes that James Junior had inherited.

Looking through the glass of the baby unit, Cynthia Callahan felt, for the first time in her life, a stirring inside her. Try as she might to force it away, she knew she would never be able to deny it. This child affected her on a primal level. Even her own children had never made her feel this deep a connection.

The child was looking straight into her eyes as if it knew she was its grandmother. Never had she seen a child so beautiful, so utterly gorgeous. And she looked exactly like her! The child was Cynthia all over.

The strength of her emotions shocked her. It occurred to her now that this was the *next* generation. She had given birth to this child's mother and, if it wasn't for *her*, this child would never have even been here. That was a very powerful thought. It made her feel invincible, like

Methuselah in the Bible, who had lived for nine hundred years—well, *he* hadn't but his offspring had. She finally understood family, and it had taken this baby to make her see what that really meant.

Her first attempt had been lousy—she had been too young and she had had her children with the wrong man—but now, with this little one, she felt she had a chance to redeem herself, make her life mean something. She could turn this child into a good person. If she was left with her mother she would end up like her mother. A teenage unmarried mum, a fucking waster, worth nothing— nothing of value anyway. Not as far as Cynthia was concerned.

The baby was like a magnet, and she felt a pull that she had never felt before in her life. She wanted this child. And she would move heaven and earth to get it.

CHAPTER NINETY-THREE

'She was my sister, Mum. I have every right to be here.'

Mary looked into her daughter's face and wondered what was the real reason this girl of hers had turned up on her doorstep at Celeste's wake. She could hazard a guess, but she was sure she would be wrong. Cynthia had not even wanted her own children, so why would she want a grandchild? Mary had felt she had no choice but to let her into the house and then she had seen the naked hunger in Cynthia's eyes as she had looked at little Cherie in her bassinet.

When Cynthia marched into the sitting room and immediately bent over the cradle to pick the baby up somehow Mary knew that her daughter had seen the child before, and she had felt as if she was witnessing a crime. Never had Cynthia been that gentle with her own children.

'If you're feeling maternal why don't you go and visit your son? I'm sure *he* could do with a bit of motherly interest.'

Cynthia held the child to her as she said dreamily, 'Why don't you have a day off, Mum? I know I made mistakes, but this is my grandchild and, whether you like it or not, that is the truth of the matter. She reminds me of my Gabriella at the same age. She's such a lovely child.' Cynthia knew that Gabby could hear her from her bedroom and she continued in a hurt voice, 'I hope you don't alienate this child from Gabriella like you alienated her from me. I was already aware I had made a big mistake marrying James, but it was you my kids wanted, wasn't it, not me. You made sure of that.'

Mary was incensed. 'How dare you! I took your kids in when you got fed up with them. I loved them like my own.'

Cynthia knew that was the truth, but she ignored it and said in a placating manner, 'Please, Mum, it's Celeste's funeral. Have a bit of respect.'

Mary was so furious at the words of her daughter she was rendered speechless. How could she say that to her, after all she had done! Her daughter was a manipulator who used everyone around her. Well, she would not use *her* any more, those days were long gone.

'You are welcome only to pay your respects. After that you can piss off.'

274

'I must say, Mum, that is you all over.'

Cynthia hugged the child to her; from her first contact with it she knew that this was a child that was meant to be with her. She loved it. The child was perfect in every way, like her little Gabriella when she was born, except now Cynthia was older and wiser, and she finally understood what flesh and blood meant. What made women kill for their kids, and what life was all about. She had never realised until this moment. The moment she had held her grandchild in her arms.

Cynthia was looking at the child with such love that even Mary wondered if she had been wrong about her daughter. Could it be that she wanted a second chance at motherhood?

Watching Cynthia, Gabby was completely convinced that there was genuine love in her mother for this child of hers. It hurt, knowing that she hadn't felt that way about her or her brother, but she was glad she felt like that about little Cherie. The baby had so few people in her little life—her father was banged up, his family had no interest, and this was the day of her great-auntie's funeral. Her family was shrinking by the day.

So, as useless as her mother was, Gabby would welcome her into her daughter's life and take whatever her mother had to offer, for as long as it lasted. Gabby was so desperately lonely, and she needed other people in her life. At this point, even her mother was preferable to no one. She knew her nana would think she was mad, but what could she do? This was Cherie's grandmother and she owed it to her to try and build a few bridges. As bad as her mother could be, she appeared to be enamoured of her grandchild. That was enough for Gabby, who, alone in the world with a new baby, was desperate to have a family again.

They had buried Celeste, and they felt her loss keenly, especially Mary who had always had a soft spot for her younger child. She had tried, in her own way, to make their lives easier. Now Mary had to watch her granddaughter forge some kind of relationship with her mother—the same woman who was responsible for the death of the daughter Mary had buried this day.

CHAPTER NINETY-FOUR

'It's not like that, Nana!'

Mary shrugged aggressively. 'How is it then, Gabby? Tell me and your granddad. We're interested. Only your mother was never what we would call a frequent presence in your life, so we're amazed at how often you seem to be seeing her.'

Gabby couldn't explain how hard it was to walk away from her mother these days. She believed she had genuinely changed, and she wanted to make amends. But her nana and granddad couldn't see that. She knew they had reason to feel like they did, but this was still her mother they were talking about, Cherie's nanny. In producing this child she felt, for the first time in her life, like she had done something good in her mother's eyes, and she was enjoying that feeling. It was almost as if Cynthia was loving *her* through her baby, and that felt good. All her life Gabby had felt there was something wrong with her; if her own mother couldn't love her, then who could?

276

'Oh, Nana, I know you think I'm wrong, but she *has* changed. She loves little Cherie like we do! Please, Nana, don't ruin this for me.'

Mary was shocked at those words. As if *she* would ever ruin anything for this girl, or the child she had produced. The only person who had ever ruined anything for her she was now welcoming back into her life with wide open arms. And no good could come of it, she would lay money on that.

She understood why Gabby was desperate to make some kind of connection with her mother, even after everything had happened. When all was said and done she was her closest kin. Mary was being forced to sit back and wait and then eventually pick up the pieces, because unfortunately she knew, as sure as she knew her own name, that this reunion could only end in tears.

CHAPTER NINETY-FIVE

As Jack Callahan looked at his wife, he felt the power of her, as he always had. She was stronger than he would ever be and it had taken her heart attack to make him appreciate just what a good woman he had bagged all those years ago.

Now he could see she was hurting. She had buried a child—something no parent should ever do. It was the wrong order of things; a child should bury its parents, not vice versa. And it had upset her that Gabby was all over her mother like a cheap suit.

'It can't last, Mary. You know Cynthia like I do—she'll fuck it up and Gabby will see her for what she is.'

Mary shook her head sadly; if only that was the case. But she had seen Cynthia looking at her grandchild, and she recognised that look. She had felt it herself many years ago. Cynthia saw an opportunity to make up for her mistakes; all the wrongs she had committed counted for nothing now that child was there. She thought of that baby as a new page to be written on, a new canvas to paint in her own image. Cynthia would not let this baby go, not now. Not when she had an in on its life.

Mary had felt the same when Cynthia had produced Gabby and James Junior. It was like a second chance at motherhood. When you became a grandparent, it was like God handing you a child without the pain of bearing it. And you were given something that was even more precious than your own kids, because it was *your* kids who had produced it in the first place.

It hurt a great deal to see Gabby forgetting what her mother was capable of and welcoming her with open arms. But what could she do?

Cynthia was on full charm offensive, and that was not an easy thing to ignore. She was playing on the fact that Gabby needed her mother, but Mary knew that Cynthia would soon lose interest. She always did, leaving a trail of death and destruction wherever she went.

Life was hard for a lot of people, Mary knew, but it seemed at times her family had it much harder than most. Cynthia saw to that; she had always been responsible for their problems.

'She will eat her up and spit her out, Jack. Cynthia wants that child, but she doesn't want its mother.'

Jack nodded in agreement. "Course she does. Think about it—she's kicking forty, she has nothing in her life—*never* had anything in her life if she's honest with herself. A baby will be something new to her; after all, it won't know her, will it? Not like everyone else does. A baby loves whoever feeds it.'

'That's what worries me, Jack. Not the baby so much, but our Gabby—she has always wanted her mother to love her, admire her, care for her.'

'That's human nature, Mary. But Gabby ain't a mug—she will see that this is all a fucking act, and she'll aim her out of it.'

'But I'm not so sure she will, Jack. She needs Vincent, needs him by her side. She's missing him, she's all hormones and wanting. She wants to be loved, and she wants to be loved by the people who matter. But I hope you are right, mate. I really hope you are right.'

CHAPTER NINETY-SIX

'Look at her go! She is as clever as a bag of fucking monkeys.'

Gabby could hear the pride in her mother's voice and she swelled with pride herself. Seeing her mother with her little daughter made her wish that she had been like that with her once. Cynthia certainly seemed a happier person now though. In fact, Gabby had never seen her mother like this before. She was lighter in herself, almost like a normal person. She *almost* seemed to enjoy her daughter's company, and it was no secret she couldn't get enough of her granddaughter's. Gabby knew her nana didn't like it, but she couldn't help herself—the pull of her mother was too strong. She had dreamt of having this kind of relationship with her for years. Daydreamed that they went shopping together for clothes, had lunch together, had fun together. Now they were finally doing those things, and it was all because of Cherie.

Cherie was gorgeous. She had a wonderful smile as well and, now she was crawling, she was becoming a little person—a little person who looked at her grandmother with love and happiness.

'Come to me, my little angel.' Cynthia picked the child up and carefully laid her on the changing table. As she expertly changed her nappy, she crooned away in her own particular brand of baby talk, before saying to Gabby, 'Leave her here tonight and have a night off, love. Go and visit your mates, have a few hours to yourself—young mums need that.'

Gabby wasn't sure.

'Look, Gabs.'

Her mother had taken to calling her that again and she liked it, it made her feel she was finally a part of Cynthia's life.

'You can have a nice bath in peace, do your hair and, best of all, you can have a full night's sleep. This little one is teething, and I haven't got any plans tonight. You can pick her up tomorrow.'

It did sound tempting, she had to admit. Gabby looked around the spare room in her mother's penthouse, which was kitted out like a movie star's nursery, and she was awed by it. It was pale lemon and white, and it even had stencilling on the walls.

It looked wonderful. A lot nicer than the bedroom the baby shared with her at her nana's. She knew that Cherie would be OK here, but she still wasn't sure about leaving her. Her nana would go mad if she left her overnight; she seemed to think Cynthia was up to no good. She wished they could see her and Cherie together—it was sweet to watch.

Cynthia was not going to take no for an answer. 'When was the last time you were a young girl, eh? When was the last time you got your glad rags on and had a night out with your mates? Had a few drinks, let your hair down? It's not good for you being stuck in with a baby all the time, even one as lovely as our Cherie. We'll be here waiting for you.' She smiled at the baby in her arms. 'Won't we, darling? We'll wait for mummy, won't we? How's that mate of yours, the one I always thought was a bad influence?'

'Christine Carter? Oh, she's still around, pops in to see me sometimes. Now *she* is always out somewhere!'

Cynthia laughed with her daughter. She knew exactly what Christine Carter got up to—she was a byword for whoring and drug-taking, by all accounts.

'You should ring her, go out with her. You're not a kid any more, are you? I bet she'll show you a good time!'

'I could I suppose, she does love a night out. But Vince . . .'

'*Vince* is in the nick, love, and I'm sure that if *he* had the chance of a night out he would take it without a second's thought for you or anyone. Blokes are like that, love. Anyway, you're not married to him and, while he's away, why should you be locked up too? He should have thought of that, love; if you want *my* opinion, I think you *deserve* a night out.'

Cherie gave one of her big gummy grins and the matter was sealed.

A little later on, Cynthia handed her daughter fifty pounds in cash. 'Have a good night, sweetheart, and don't worry about little Cherie— she'll be safe as houses.'

Gabby hugged her mother then, overwhelmed by her generosity and, when her mother hugged her back, she felt as if she had won the rollover on the lottery.

CHAPTER NINETY-SEVEN

'Where the hell have you been?'

Mary's voice was angrier than Gabby had ever heard it and, putting the pillow over her head, she groaned. 'Not now, Nana, I'm tired out.'

Mary opened the curtains and dragged the quilt and pillow from her granddaughter's bed. ''Course you're tired out—you've been out on the lash for two days. It's Sunday, love, and you are getting up and you are going to go to your mother's and you are going to get your baby. Remember your baby? *Cherie*, ten months old, little bundle of happiness?'

Mary saw the ravaged look on the girl's face and sighed heavily. The last few months she had started going clubbing—whatever the fuck that was—and Gabby had apparently taken to it like a duck to water. She was out more than she was in, and the upshot was that Cherie now spent more time with her grandmother than she did with her own mother.

That Cynthia was behind this newfound freedom, Mary had no doubt but, at the moment, Cynthia could do no wrong in Gabby's eyes. She was all 'me mum this', and 'me mum that'. Like Cynthia was suddenly the fucking oracle or something.

Mary was even more worried because she had found little pills in Gabby's bedroom drawer, and she guessed they were those things called Es they were always talking about on the news. They were dangerous—people had died taking them.

She looked at her granddaughter's emaciated body; she had lost a lot of weight, and she often appeared spaced out, that was the only way she could describe the vacant look on the girl's face. That was Christine fucking Carter's fault; she was known on the estate for everything from drugs to thieving. Now Gabby thought that Christine Carter was the epitome of council house chic.

Gabby was already asleep again, and Mary sighed, knowing it was pointless trying to talk to her while she was like this. In a way she sympathised. Gabby was little more than a child herself and she was tied down with a baby, with the father locked up on the Isle of Wight. With her mother on the scene, she felt her baby was being well looked after—it was with its nanny after all who doted on the child—so Gabby could go out and have a good time. Mary wasn't so old she didn't understand human nature, and if it was once a week she would have encouraged it. But it was now nearly every night. It was as if once Gabby had tasted freedom, she was hooked and wanted more and more of it, but at the expense of her baby daughter. Cherie had not been to their house in ten days, and that bothered Mary. The social worker was not impressed either, and that did not bode well.

She walked slowly from the room and, making a cup of tea, she wondered at how this would all finally pan out.

She didn't have long to wait for the answer to her question.

CHAPTER NINETY-EIGHT

'My mum's too old to have the baby full time and so Cherie would be much better off here. I think Gabriella would prefer it too.'

Miss Byrne nodded in resignation; as nice as this woman seemed there was something off about her that she couldn't quite put her finger on.

'Are the police sure *she* was selling the drugs?'

'Quite sure. She sold them to an undercover policewoman,' Miss Byrne responded bluntly.

Cynthia rolled her eyes in annoyance. 'For God's sake, what was she thinking! She has a little baby to care for and she does something that stupid. I admit I had my suspicions—I mean, she's always out. I knew she was taking something, I just didn't know what.' She gave the baby a rusk then fastened her into her high chair. 'She's so young, too young really to have a baby. I would have suggested an abortion but my mother would have none of that, of course. And now this little darling is here we wouldn't be without her, but . . .' She left the sentence unfinished but Miss Byrne actually felt herself agreeing with the woman's opinion.

'So you are happy to keep the child until we

deem Gabriella capable once more to take over as the primary carer?'

Cynthia wondered if the woman had swallowed a dictionary; she bet that kind of talk went down a bundle on the council estates. 'If you mean will I take on my granddaughter until my Gabriella is on her feet again, then yes.'

Miss Byrne agreed. 'Quite. Well, everything seems fine here and, I must say, the nursery is lovely. She really is a lucky little girl.'

Cynthia preened at the praise and, after she had shown Miss Byrne to the door, she picked up her granddaughter and said in an excited voice, 'It's just me and you, kid! Just me and you!'

Hugging the child to her, she made a mental note to give Christine Carter a few quid; after all, without her none of this would have been possible.

CHAPTER NINETY-NINE

'What possessed you, child?'

A couple of nights in the cells had certainly sobered Gabby up, no doubt about that. She looked terrified.

'Drug-dealing! That I should live to see the day!' Mary was heartbroken at the news, and it was this that made Gabby feel worse than ever.

'I wasn't, Nana—at least, that was the first time I've done it. Christine asked me to do it for her because she felt ill. I only did as I was asked, I know it was stupid . . .'

Mary shook her head in disbelief; how could this girl be so stupid? 'First time, or fiftieth time, it will make no difference to the courts. And you had drugs in your system—that's all come up on the blood tests. So you've lost your daughter. Guess who has her at this moment? Your mother, and I can tell you now you will have a hard time getting her back.'

Gabby groaned with shame and hurt. This was like a nightmare, a nightmare of her own making. Sitting in that stinking cell had made her think about her life, and she was not impressed with herself, so God knew what her mother must think of her. But then, her mother had encouraged her to go out and enjoy herself—she even gave her the money to go out and have a good time.

It was odd, but from that first night out clubbing, she had felt for the first time in years like a teenager. Surrounded by music and other young people, she had felt she belonged. This was what she *should* be doing. If she had used her head she could have been doing it without the responsibility of a baby and, as much as she loved little Cherie, she missed her freedom. She had known she was safe with her mum who loved the child. It wasn't wrong to leave the baby with its grandmother, was it?

But she had to be honest with herself now. It wasn't leaving her there that was the problem, it was that she left her there so often. Pretending that it was just because she knew her mother loved it, she had allowed her to become Cherie's main carer. Cherie didn't even want to come to Gabby any more, she just wanted her nanny. And who could blame her? Oh, she had been such a fool! And now she had a conviction for drug-dealing hanging over her. She felt sick.

'Will I go to prison, Nana?'

Mary shook her head in despair. 'I don't know, Gabby, I honestly don't know.'

CHAPTER ONE HUNDRED

Vincent O'Casey read the letter with growing anger and resentment. That his Gabby had been so foolish was one thing, but to find out that his child was now in the sole custody of Cynthia Callahan was quite another. After what Gabby had told him about her upbringing, he was not at all happy that his child was now at that woman's mercy. Yet, according to this letter, her mother was now a changed character, and she was helping her daughter to get back on her feet.

Gabby, he kept reminding himself, was very young, and she had made a very stupid mistake. He could forgive her that—of course he could—but he could *not* forgive her abandoning their child like this. She was promising to come and see him in a few weeks. She had missed the last few visits, and her letters had been sparse as well. Now he fucking well knew why.

He had missed Gabby, but he had also missed the baby. He hadn't seen her many times but he loved that child. She was a pretty contented little thing, always smiling and beautifully turned out.

This was the worst bit about being in prison; the world outside carried on, and there was nothing you could do about that. When things went wrong, like this trouble with Gabby, he couldn't help because he was stuck in here. Being helpless to do anything

287

for the people he loved was worse than anything else he could think of.

CHAPTER ONE HUNDRED AND ONE

'Look, Cherie, look at the pictures with Mummy.'

But Cherie wanted to get off her mother's lap, and sit with her nanny. Cynthia was holding a drink of apple juice, which she knew was Cherie's favourite treat at the moment. She picked up the child and sat her on her knee smiling at her daughter's crestfallen countenance.

'Listen to me, Gabriella—kids are amoral. They go to whoever feeds them. It's nothing personal, darling.'

Gabby smiled but her heart wasn't in it.

'I'll have to get her ready soon, love. She goes to a playgroup a few hours a day now, three times a week. She's making friends, bless her heart. While she's there, I nip up the shops, or go to the gym. I love her, darling, but she's a handful.'

Gabby felt she was being dismissed; she knew her mother was telling her she had better go soon. She made her feel as if she was holding the pair of them up somehow, was in the way. In fact, she realised that her mother had not even offered her a cup of coffee. She had only been there twenty minutes, if that, and she was already being asked, albeit politely, to leave.

'I can wait at the playgroup with her . . .'

'I don't think that's a good idea, Gabs, and, to be honest, I think you unsettle her. She has got into a routine, and Miss Byrne thinks she needs more structure in her life. Plus, I've arranged for her to go to tea with one of the little girls there. Dear little thing too, though not a patch on our Cherie!'

Gabby tried another tack. 'But I'm taking her to visit Vincent tomorrow—he'll expect to see her.'

Cynthia grinned then, and it was the old Cynthia for a few moments. 'Well, not a lot he can do about that, girl, is there? He should have thought of that before he got himself banged up.'

'But he wants to see her.'

'Well, then, in that case, he'll know what it's like to want, won't he? I promised Miss Byrne that I would do whatever is right for this baby and, at the moment, I don't think you should be around her. Not until you've sorted yourself out. Drug addicts are—'

Gabby interjected, shocked at her mother's choice of words, 'Drug addict! I ain't a fucking drug addict . . .'

Cynthia shrugged. 'Drug *dealer* then. Let's not split hairs, love. I don't think it's fair on this child to drag her from pillar to post, OK? It's not about what you want or what I want for that matter, it's about what is best for this little child.'

Gabby couldn't argue with that, but it was all wrong somehow. She was Cherie's mother, and she loved her baby. She had made a silly mistake, but she was already paying the price for that. Gabby was confused; her mother was pushing her away again, and she had a sneaking suspicion that somehow she had played right into Cynthia's hands and lost Cherie. Now her baby had a new mummy, and that was Cynthia Callahan. Suddenly, with stunning clarity, Gabby could see that her nana had been right—Cynthia had only wanted the baby, and she had used Gabby to get what she wanted. She felt as if someone had slapped her in the face.

'I'll ring you, Gabs, and we'll make arrangements for you to come over next week, eh?'

Cynthia was standing with the child in her arms, and Gabby knew she had been outfoxed, outmanoeuvred, and was now surplus to requirements.

CHAPTER ONE HUNDRED AND TWO

'She can't take our child for good, Gabby. Use your loaf.'

Gabby was sitting opposite Vincent and her heart felt like lead in her chest. 'But I realise now me nana was right about her. All her interest in me was for one reason only—to get Cherie.'

Vincent wasn't in the mood for this today. He was feeling out of sorts anyway; he had a cold coming, and he was suffering from cabin fever. It came on most long-timers two or three times a year. Especially the younger ones. Being banged up was hard work, and you had to get your head around it.

He took a deep breath and counted to ten like the gym instructor had told him to when he felt the urge to lash out. After he had exhaled slowly he said, 'I can't do this today, Gabby, I really can't deal with you moaning. You had a capture, you fucked up. We've all done it. All you can do now is make sure you sort it out, and sort yourself out while you're at it. But I can't help you, and the more you tell me, the harder it is for me, because I can't walk out that door and come to your aid.

And that is difficult for me to admit. You reckoned your mum had turned over a new leaf? Maybe she has. Maybe she has that child's best interests at heart. But Cherie's *our* daughter. So all I can say is get the court case over with, plead guilty and do a deal. Then work at getting Cherie back. Prove to your mum, the social workers, King Street Charlie if necessary, that you are back on track, and it will turn out right in the end. OK?'

She nodded then, her lovely face white with apprehension.

'Now, how's your nana and granddad?'

CHAPTER ONE HUNDRED AND THREE

David Duggan was very impressed with his neighbour Cynthia Callahan, especially when she told him her daughter was a recovering addict, and she now had to bring up her little granddaughter. From what she'd said, it seemed the daughter was like her father—weak willed and always looking for the easy option. Poor Cynthia told him she'd done everything she could, but the girl was a lost cause, and she could not allow that to happen to her granddaughter, which he thoroughly agreed with. The child was a delight too, and he felt they were becoming quite the little family unit.

He had taken to staying over a few nights a week; the sex was unbelievable, and the breakfasts the next morning with the little girl crowing and making them laugh had become the highlight of his existence. He didn't know what he would do without Cynthia now—she had become such a big part of his life. She was also a fabulous cook, and she had taken to letting herself into his flat and doing his washing and ironing for him.

That she used those opportunities to rifle through his desk, and get her hands on his bank books he had no idea. She always gave him back his keys, so he had no way of knowing she had already had a set made for herself.

David Duggan felt that he was a very lucky man to be given a second chance at happiness at this stage of his life. And he thanked God every day for bringing Cynthia Callahan into his comfortable, but rather dreary, life.

CHAPTER ONE HUNDRED AND FOUR

Cynthia adored her granddaughter and the feeling was entirely mutual. As she walked her in the park, Cynthia planned the child's life; a good school, private of course, and nice friends. Once she had fleeced David she would move on, this time to a nice London suburb. A place where the child would be surrounded by the finer things in life.

Oh, it was as if she had been given a second chance at happiness, and she was grateful to the powers-that-be for giving it to her. The only problem was Gabriella; she would always have to put up with her having some kind of role in the child's life, but she would make sure that her input was minimal at best. It irritated her but there wasn't a lot she could do about it. Well, not for a while anyway.

The social services thought she was the dog's

bollocks, and she had made sure of that by being the picture of kindness and generosity. They agreed that her daughter was still too immature to look after a child, and she pointed out how well Cherie had settled with her, which was not a lie either. Cherie was very happy, and why wouldn't she be? She was waited on hand and foot, clean and well fed. She had only the best clothes and shoes too; she was like a little doll, and Cynthia loved to dress her up.

The doorbell rang and she went to answer it; she hoped it wasn't David, expecting a cup of coffee and a quick feel—she really wasn't in the mood today. Opening the door, a smile plastered on her heavily made-up face, she was amazed to see her mother standing there.

'Hello, Cynth, aren't you going to invite me in? The social worker's just parking the car.'

Then, walking past her speechless daughter, Mary went into the large lounge and, kneeling down, she opened her arms to little Cherie and said happily, 'Hello, my little lovely, your great-nana's here to see you.'

CHAPTER ONE HUNDRED AND FIVE

Miss Byrne had a feeling that something was not right between Cynthia Callahan and her mother, but she couldn't put her finger on exactly what that might be. They were polite enough to each other, but it was forced, as if they were both playing a part. Which, of course, they were.

Mary couldn't help but be impressed with

Cynthia's home; although it was clean as clean could be, it still had the smell and feel of a real home. Cherie's toys were scattered all over the place, something that she had never seen in Cynthia's house when Gabby and James Junior were little. The poor things had been terrified of making a noise, let alone a mess.

Cherie looked well cared for and happy and that was what really hurt Mary Callahan. Why couldn't Cynthia have been that way with her own children? Watching how the girl put her arms up to her grandmother to be picked up, and seeing Cynthia, her daughter Cynthia, smiling at the child with genuine affection, even love, Mary knew then that Gabby was going to have a fight on her hands to get that baby back. Cynthia was besotted with the child, and she had never seen her besotted by anything or anyone before—except maybe Jonny Parker, and look at how that had turned out.

The social worker was watching the interplay with fascination; this was a mother and daughter who obviously had issues. At least contact had been established though. She felt she was reuniting this family, and was quite pleased with herself because of it. Suicide, she knew, could divide families, as had clearly been the case here, but with a little help and some counselling, who knew what might be achieved. When she said as much a few minutes later, she was amazed at the way the two women laughed as if they were never going to stop.

'Jesus, Jack, she's living like a fucking queen! The place is beautiful, and I hate to say this, but little Cherie is thriving. That's the only way I can put it— positively thriving.'

Jack Callahan listened with growing dismay. It seemed that his Mary had been right all along and, as he looked at young Gabby, he raised his eyes as if to say, well, you were warned this would happen.

Gabby swallowed back the tears that were threatening to fall. 'Did she look all right then, me mum? Was she all right about you going round there?'

Mary laughed gently. 'She had no choice. I had the social worker with me, and you know your mother—she could get an Oscar for her acting. I hate to say I told you so, but I did, didn't I? She wanted that child and now she's got her, and there ain't a thing you can do about it.'

'But *I'm* her mum!'

It was the petulant cry of a child, which, in reality, was all Gabby was. For the first time Mary Callahan wondered if Cherie might be better off where she was, but she forced that thought out of her head. Cynthia wasn't a person you could trust in the long term, she never had been.

'Well, all we can do is go through the proper channels and hope in the meantime that your mother gets fed up playing happy families. But I wouldn't bank on the latter, Gabby. I can honestly say I've never seen her so happy. I never saw a woman so obsessed with a child in my life. She won't let go easily.'

Gabby felt the weight of her mother crushing down on her; she felt like she had as a small child, unable to fight back against the might that was her mum, against the self-righteous-ness that her mother cloaked every word in. She knew she had been a very stupid girl. Caught up in Christine Carter's lifestyle, she had been too busy enjoy—ing herself and forgotten her responsibilities. She wouldn't lie to herself about that. Lonely without Vincent she had liked pretending to be a carefree young girl, clubbing, having a drink, a few laughs. She had also enjoyed taking the Es, and smoking a bit of dope with people her own age. She had even liked the attention she got from boys, although she had never succumbed to any of their advances—at least she had that going for her. She knew Vincent had heard rumours, and he was desperately disappointed in her, but she also knew he understood that she was young and she had been foolish and he had forgiven her.

Well, she had to get herself together—work towards getting Cherie back and creating some kind of life for them both. It wouldn't be easy, but she knew that if she tried, she could do it.

Jack Callahan hugged his granddaughter to him as if he knew exactly what she was thinking, and she wondered for the thousandth time how she could have been taken in by her mother. Even knowing everything she did about her, all she was capable of, she had still trusted her. Well, she would never make that mistake again.

CHAPTER ONE HUNDRED AND SEVEN

2003

Cherie looked at her mother and shook her head petulantly. 'I'm staying at Nanny's. We're going to a party tomorrow.'

Gabby, at twenty-one, was used to these kind of conversations with her little daughter; Cynthia always arranged lots of trips and parties when she was due to have her for the weekend. Gabby had learned a long time before to ignore the child's wide-eyed pleading. Once she was out of her mother's house, the girl was a different child.

'No, you're not. You're coming with Mummy.'

Cherie glowered at Gabby, saying loudly, 'But I hate it at your house, and Nana Mary smells bad.'

Gabby was itching to put her hand across her daughter's arse but she restrained herself with difficulty. Her mum would be straight on to the social workers, reporting child abuse, beatings and anything else she could think of.

Cynthia watched the exchange with a small satisfied smile on her lips. She had to give it to her daughter, Gabby was resolute. Well, she got that from her but, unlike her, she wouldn't be able to keep it up indefinitely.

'Nana Mary does not smell bad, and you know that.'

Cherie didn't answer, she was waiting to see what occurred between her mummy and her nanny first. She knew they didn't like one another. It worried her sometimes, but at other times it worked in her favour; it meant they vied with each other to give her what she wanted.

Gabby changed the subject. 'Your daddy will be home in a few weeks.'

Cherie brightened up then. She loved her daddy, and she truly believed that he was training to be a fighter pilot. Like a lot of kids she had been told that story, it explained away the uniforms everywhere on the visits. Cherie opened her mouth but, after a dark look from her nanny, she shut it again.

'The three of us will be together all the time then, and you can stay at Nanny's at weekends, *sometimes*.'

Stick that one up your arse, Mother, and smoke it.

Gabby knew that Vince was determined to get them back on track, and he had been a diamond. He had given Derek Greene a tug, and money had miraculously appeared every week, as had a nice council flat and new furniture. She was now established as a blagger's wife, and she was treated as one by everybody. It was amazing what the friendship of Greene and Warner could do for a body, and she was grateful for their help. She knew it bothered her mother as well, and she knew *why* it bothered her so much. But, as Vince said, he had earned his keep, he'd kept his trap shut and taken the fall for everyone. They *owed* him.

He was a very different Vincent these days; he was a man now, a big, handsome man and, like her, he had grown up quickly. She knew her mother would get the shock of her life when he came home, and she couldn't wait. He would put her well and truly in her place, and she wanted to be there when he did it.

The social workers were still hanging round like a bad smell, and she had heard through the grapevine that her mother told them exaggerated stories about Gabby's wild ways, and how she was still worried that her daughter was too immature to take care of Cherie on a regular basis. But Gabby was biding her time—she knew that fighting this woman was pointless. She knew the social workers wondered where all her money *really* came from, but they could go and fuck themselves; she was cleaner than a whistle. All she claimed was her Family Allowance and the minimum of benefits—that was it. But the drug conviction which, thanks to a good brief, had got her probation and one hundred and twenty hours community service, was still being held over her head like the sword of Damocles.

It was amazing really—if her mother had just kept out of it, she would be happily ensconced with her daughter now, and it would all be in the past. But that hadn't been her mother's plan. Right from the start, she had been determined to get the child, and she would stoop as low as she needed to make sure that happened. She had not allowed for the fact that Gabby was as stubborn as she was, when necessary, and so they were still playing this game.

'Has he got his release date, then?'

Gabby smiled, and Cynthia saw what a very beautiful young woman she was. It pained her to see herself as she had been twenty years earlier. She envied this girl her youth, and they both knew it.

'Yep.'

Cynthia would not lower herself to ask when that was; she would find out soon enough. 'Bet you can't wait.'

'Nope, I can't. You wait till you see him, Mum, you'll get the surprise of your life.' It wasn't exactly a threat as such, but she knew her mother was worried at the implication. 'Now come on, Cherie—I've got the car outside and we are going to Mackie D's for our dinner!'

Cherie was thrilled; she loved a McDonald's. Her nanny said they were too fattening and full of crap, but she didn't care. She was happy now to put her coat on and go with her mother, especially when she promised, 'Then we are going to watch whatever you want on TV.'

As her granddaughter got herself ready, Cynthia fought back the urge to take her daughter by the hair and batter her to death.

'Say bye bye to Nanny, darling.'

Cherie kissed and hugged her nanny, but it was obvious she was impatient now to be on her way.

'Don't let her watch anything frightening, she's too small.'

Gabby sighed heavily; this was a constant refrain. You'd think she let the child watch horror films day and night. 'As if I would.'

Cynthia replied, all self-righteous in her anger, 'Well, if I find out she's been glued to those American detective shows there'll be murders.'

'Well, you'd know all about that, wouldn't you, Mum?'

Cynthia was fuming at the inference, and the fact that her daughter felt confident enough to say it spoke volumes. The news of Vincent's return had given her girl an edge, an edge Cynthia would take great pleasure in blunting. She still had a few tricks up her sleeve.

Gabby smiled. 'See you.'

Cynthia smiled back, adding nastily, 'You can guarantee it.'

CHAPTER ONE HUNDRED AND EIGHT

'He's going to want a bit of work at some point.' Derek Greene was glad Vincent would soon be out.

Bertie Warner grinned. 'Well, of course he will, but not for a few months. He's got four years of shagging to catch up on first, as well as getting used to being on the out. We'll have a party for him; after all, the boy's been a fucking diamond. Bung him a few grand to tide him over and see what occurs—he might want to go straight.'

Derek laughed loudly at that one.

Bertie made a *moue* with his lips, then said in a serious manner, 'It has been known!'

'Not Vincent, it's in his blood. I've had great reports about him, done his time like a fucking man, and he's a big lad by all accounts. But then six hours a day in the gym will do that to a body. No, I think we should find him a good earner, get him back in the fold. He done a big favour for us and all concerned, and I respect him for that. Only eighteen and put on the island, and he made his mark there and all. Well liked, but didn't take any nonsense.'

Bertie agreed with his friend, and he said jovially, 'I bet that little bird of his is champing at the bit, eh? Four years with no nookie! Not heard a detrimental word about her either, have you?'

'Not for a long time. Had a bit of trouble when

he first went away, selling Es of all things, and to an undercover Filth. Something dodgy there—I could never put me finger on it, but it all smelt wrong, you know? That slag Christine Carter was behind it—she's a fucking skank, that bird.'

Bertie was quiet for a moment. 'Will young Vincent want to pay back any debts, do you think? You know, settle any scores?'

'Wouldn't blame him if he did. She nearly lost the kid over it.'

'Her mother's got the kid now, ain't she?'

'Most of the time, from what I can gather. Fucking Cynthia Callahan—Tailor, that was. Who would let that whore near an innocent child?'

Bertie shook his head at the stupidity of the social services; you read about those mad fuckers every day in the papers. They left kids with complete nut-bags who murdered them, starved them, or took them off nice people. No fucking sense in any of it. 'Well, if he wants to hammer the fuck out of Cynthia, I bagsy a ringside seat.'

Derek grinned at that. 'I'm with you there.'

'But, Del Boy, she was fuckable when she was young. Arse like two boiled eggs in a handkerchief, tits that pointed at the ceiling, and she had a walk which could reduce a grown man to his knees. Well, you would want her on *her* knees, if you get my drift.'

Derek was really laughing now. 'Young Gabby looks like her then, spitting image.'

Bertie grinned. 'Yeah, but she ain't got that air of danger that her mother always had. And she was one mad cunt—she shot my mate, and I could never get back at her, because she was only defending herself and her sister. It's a bastard, but it's the truth. If Parker had come after *my* old woman, I would have wanted Cynthia Tailor on her team, know what I mean? But he was a silly fucker was Kevin. He wanted revenge, and revenge is something you do at your leisure—not in the heat of the moment.'

Derek nodded at the truth of the other man's words. 'Well, none of them have had any real luck, have they? Jimmy Tailor killed himself, we removed Parker from the equation, and the son's in some kind of home for the mentally incapable. Fucking great family to be marrying into, that lot! Makes the fucking Borgias look like the Mickey Mouse Club.'

Bertie laughed. 'Well, young Vincent will soon make up his mind about them all once he's out from behind the door.'

Derek agreed with his old friend and said seriously, 'Amen to that.'

CHAPTER ONE HUNDRED AND NINE

Mary loved little Cherie, she was an endearing little thing, but she could see a lot of Cynthia in the child and she had to admit that bothered her. She had the same selfish streak and the same arrogance that had been Cynthia's trademark all her life. She had her great-grandfather twisted around her little finger, but Cherie, Mary knew, understood, even at four years old, that her great-nana Mary wasn't as enamoured of her as she should be. Consequently, the child was a bit offish towards her. She was a little manipulator, but then she would be; after all, she had a great teacher.

'You all right, Nana?'

Mary nodded. 'I'm fine, love, just tired that's all. Did Vincent phone today?'

Gabby nodded and grinned. 'This morning. I can't wait, Nana, I've missed him so much.'

'He's a lucky lad. He got a result when all was said and done. Only four years . . .' Jack's voice was full of pride and, hugging his granddaughter, he continued, 'I hear he is very well thought of. I went in the pub the other day and everyone, and I mean *everyone*, was buying me drinks, and asking about him. Saying what a diamond geezer he is. You done well there, Gabby—he's got a great future ahead of him, that boy.'

Gabby glowed at the praise and, smiling, she said happily, 'I know. Bertie Warner came round today and dropped off a few quid, as he put it, to get Vincent back on his feet. It was ten grand! They're having a party for him as well—Vince will love that.'

Mary sniffed disdainfully and said sarcastically, 'Ten grand, eh? What's that work out at? About two and a half grand a year? Vincent would have been better off getting a job as a postman—at least he would have been home every night.'

Gabby rolled her eyes in annoyance, 'All right, Nana, we get your drift, but what's done is done, and I just want to put it behind me. Once Vince comes home it will all be different.'

'Well, hopefully he'll sort your mother out.'

'I think we can guarantee that much, Granddad. He hates her.'

Jack Callahan laughed then. 'Like me then! The only way I'd talk to her now is if it was through

304

Doris Stokes!'

Even Mary laughed at that, though the joke saddened her. Cynthia had caused too much trouble for them, and she was still pulling their strings after all this time.

CHAPTER ONE HUNDRED AND TEN

James Tailor Junior looked around him with wary eyes, and wondered if the girl sitting in front of him on the bus was worth chatting up. She had nice hair, long and dark, seemingly her natural colour, but you could never tell, never be sure about anything.

As he stepped off the bus, he noticed the changes that had occurred in the area; if anything it looked even more run down than it had when he had come here as a child. Walking along the road, he saw that the traffic had increased twofold, and the shops were now all either take-aways or cheque-cashing facilities. He knew that when the pawn shops moved into an area, it meant the work was on the way out. It was common sense—rich people didn't need pawn shops. They suited him though; they would take a TV set without asking too many questions and, as for most junkies, those shops were a godsend.

He was smiling to himself now, and he wondered at what kind of reaction he would get at his nana's house. Not a fucking visit from them in years—a birthday card or Christmas card had been the sum total of their interest in him. Which, in fairness, was more than he could say about his mother. He had not heard a fucking peep out of her since he had been taken away. When they had said he could go home, she had said, 'No, thank you, he's not my responsibility any more.' What a fucking diabolical liberty! Who the fuck did she think she was? Well, he was going to go and see her as well, and when he did she would know about it.

The only one who had ever kept any real contact was his sister. Gabby had written to him at least three times a year, and he had appreciated that. In fact, sometimes he wished he had written back, but what could he tell her? That he was still on a lock down? Still in trouble? Still fighting everyone?

He had learned to play the game, though. Eventually it had occurred to him that he had to change to get out of that place and that is what he had done. He had acted the way they wanted him to act, and the psychiatrists had patted themselves on the back—look how well we've done with him, he can join the real world again, mix in society and blend in!

Fucking morons. He had gone from a group home to his own bedsit at sixteen. He was still classified as mentally ill, but not violent any more. It was in the bedsit he had first encountered heroin. He had not been able to believe it was illegal—it was the best thing he had ever experienced in his life! And he had been on more drugs than fucking Kurt Cobain! Anti-psychotics—you name them, he'd had them. He had spent most of his life higher than a jumbo jet. Now he knew what it was to be mellow, and he liked it. He still had violent fantasies, but the heroin helped to subdue them much better than those fucking pills they had shoved down his throat ever had.

So, finally, he was going to visit the family. He

was going to see just how the land lay and, more important than anything else, where that skank of a mother of his lived.

As he walked towards his nana and granddad's house, he saw Roy Brown, and nearly said hello. The cat incident had long been buried away in his mind, but now he remembered it and was sure his nana would remember it too; it wasn't exactly something you forgot, he supposed.

It all came back to him—the look on his nana's face when she had seen her bread knife, the precious antique bread knife she thought was so fucking marvellous. The memory made him laugh; she had looked so funny with that surprised look on her face.

Then he remembered the hammering his granddad had given him and suddenly he wasn't smiling any more. He was scowling, brooding. He'd like to see the old bastard try that now; he'd wipe the floor with him, and laugh while he did it.

James took a few deep breaths; he had to calm himself down, he had to look like he was a nice lad now. It was like pretending to the shrinks and the social workers—as long as you told them what they wanted to hear, and acted like they wanted you to act, you were all right.

Life, he had sussed out, was nothing more than an elaborate game; you played the role required, and you watched and waited for your opportunity. It was simple really.

As he approached his nana's house he felt the first stirrings of excitement mixed with apprehension. But it had been ten years since he had seen any of them, and that, he surmised, was to be expected.

CHAPTER ONE HUNDRED AND ELEVEN

'Come on, Mummy, I want to go to Mackie D's!'

Cherie was already bored with being at her great-nana Mary's. All her great-granddad wanted to do was watch the horse racing; she had picked out his winners for him and, as one had come in, she was now the queen of the horse world. At least that was what her great-grandad was calling her anyway. But it was stifling here, and she wanted to go out, go somewhere else. It smelt of cigarettes, chip fat and furniture polish, and she hated it. So did her nanny Cynthia; she had said the house was like a tomb, and then explained it was a place for dead people. Cherie didn't really understand that, but she imagined that the smell of her nana Mary's was that of a dead person's house and she didn't like the thought of that. Dead people were scary.

She liked it at her mummy's flat because it was bright and cheerful. But Nanny Cynthia said that her mummy wasn't a proper mummy, and the police wouldn't let her stay there all the time because her mummy sold drugs and her daddy was in prison. She didn't believe her daddy was in prison, and she tried to explain that he was training to be a fighter pilot and go to the war. But her nanny Cynthia said it was lies and she should remember that. It was confusing really; she had to remember so much and it was very hard to understand.

But one thing she did know for sure was that her nanny Cynthia loved her more than anyone else in the world. She knew that must be true, because her nanny Cynthia was the person she had to live with.

As they were leaving, the doorbell rang, and Gabby went to answer it. Cherie saw her mummy stumble backwards, and she was immediately alert to the fact something was happening. And she knew she had to tell her nanny Cynthia *anything* and *everything* that she heard or saw.

A large man was standing there, and Cherie looked at him with interest; he was smiling, but it looked wrong on his face. He had long, dark blond hair, and he was dressed like the boys who hung around on her nana Mary's estate. He had on a black Puffa jacket and baggy jeans, and on his feet were scuffed white Adidas trainers. Scruffy was what her nanny Cynthia would call him. He looked scary somehow, and the main thing she noticed about him was how bad his teeth looked.

She listened with rapt attention as the man said, 'Hello, Gabby, long time no see.'

CHAPTER ONE HUNDRED AND TWELVE

When Mary Callahan went to find out what was going on she thought she was going to pass out with the shock of seeing her grandson standing in her hallway. She knew she should tell him to go away but how could she do that to him? He must have been deemed all right, or they would not let him roam the streets surely?

'You look like you've seen a ghost, Nana.'

He was smiling at her and she saw that whatever else had changed about him, he still had those dead eyes. The smile looked genuine enough, but

309

it didn't reach his eyes. They reminded her of a dead fish, no emotion there whatsoever. He was the image of his father, but bigger somehow, she felt the threat of him invade her and she moved back instinctively.

She noticed that Gabby had moved behind her with little Cherie in her arms.

It was Jack who took over. He walked into the hallway and looked the boy up and down before saying quietly, 'What do you want?'

James grinned. 'I don't want nothing, Granddad. I was in the area . . .'

'You ain't welcome here, son. I'm sorry, but it's best to tell you straight off.'

Mary and Gabby both breathed a sigh of relief. James was not a person to invite into your life. It was sad, it was tragic, but they knew what was best. James was on medication, but that didn't guarantee anything. His 'psychotic episodes' as they called them—even though it was apparently some time since his last one—were still not something anyone in their right mind would want to be on the receiving end of.

James wasn't surprised at his granddad's words, but he had to swallow down the urge to take the old fucker by the throat and teach him a lesson. Instead he shrugged nonchalantly. 'Just as I expected, but I thought I would say a quick hello.' He turned his gaze to his sister and, smiling at Cherie, he said, 'She's beautiful, Gabs. Looks just like Mother, but I won't hold that against her. I'm thinking of visiting her next, but no one will give me her address. Don't suppose you've got it, have you?'

At that Jack Callahan laughed. 'I'll write it down for you, son, I'm sure you two have a lot of catching up to do.'

CHAPTER ONE HUNDRED AND THIRTEEN

Vincent lay in his cell and counted down the hours till he could walk out the doors of this dump and retake his place in society. It was a different lad who would be going home, and he knew that himself. He hoped that his Gabby was as excited as he was. Even though they had a child together, they had never actually spent the night in the same bed, let alone lived in the same house. It was going to take a bit of getting used to for them both.

He knew he had a lot of things to sort out. First and foremost, was that ponce Cynthia. His being banged up had been all the ammunition she needed to keep his daughter by her side. Well, she was going to get a fucking big shock once he was out from behind the door. Poor Gabby had been treated abominably, not just by that cunt, but by his own family. His dad and his brothers had skanked his dough and blown it, without even giving Gabby a few bob to tide her over. He had left her, a sixteen-year-old girl, to contend with it all and that had eaten at him like a cancer over the last four years.

He had done the right thing by keeping his mouth shut, but now he wanted compensation for that—and he intended to get it. It was true what they said in here—the last few weeks were the worst. At least when you didn't have a release date you didn't dwell on it too much. Once that date was set though, it was like time was crawling, every day was like a fucking month. But *tempus fugit* and all that, it *would* eventually fly for him, and he would be on the out.

The next cunt he was going to collar would be his old man. He was going to cut him, mark him for fucking life. That drunken Irish ponce had not even given him time to get sentenced before he had taken his stash and blown it. He intended to make them understand from day one that he was *not* a man to be mugged off, and that anyone who crossed him would pay the consequences. And they would pay dearly.

He had four long fucking years to plan it, and lying in the dark making those plans had kept him sane in this shithole. He was desperate to get out and make his mark in the world. He was a grown man now and, like the Bible said, he had put away childish things. He was determined to get a garage, a legit business, and he was going to become the best driver the Smoke had ever seen.

Derek Greene had already had a message delivered about how he would help him get on his feet, and he would see that the man followed through on his promises. Not many young lads would have been as tight-lipped as he had, leaving their little girlfriend alone and pregnant and prey to the world.

It had been hard watching poor Gabby try and get it together. He had understood her going off the rails a bit—she was a young girl and young girls needed someone to keep them on track. All that was forgiven and forgotten now. Her nana and granddad had been fucking diamond, and he would reward them for their kindness and their loyalty to his little family.

But he was itching to get out and start paying back the debts he knew were his and his alone. When he had finished with the people he felt had mugged him over, his name would be a byword for fucking retribution. And he would guarantee that no one, not *one* fucking person would ever think they could have him over ever again.

Prison was a strange place—it either broke you or it made you stronger. Well, he was stronger now both physically and mentally than he had ever been before in his life. He had read books until eventually he had understood them, he had trained daily to keep both his body and his mind from stagnating and he was ready for literally anything.

He thought of Gabby on her last visit; she was a fucking beautiful woman now, everything and more he would ever want. His feelings for her had never wavered. He would give her the earth on a plate, and he would enjoy giving it to her. Together they were capable of great things. Of that much at least he was sure.

CHAPTER ONE HUNDRED AND FOURTEEN

'I think we should have warned her.'

Jack Callahan had no such qualms and he said as much to his wife. 'Fuck her! He's *her* son, she sent him on the turn, so let her, for once in her life, deal with her own mess.'

'Supposing he hurts her . . .'

Jack shrugged nonchalantly. 'Well, we can only

hope, love. Now, make me a cup of tea, and stop worrying.'

Mary went to the kitchen and put the kettle on, but she was worried. There was no telling what James Junior was going to do and, whatever Cynthia might be, she herself would not want something like that on her conscience.

In her heart she had always known that James would one day turn up at their door. It was natural that he would eventually want to seek out his kin. She had just *hoped* that he wouldn't, if she was honest.

Many years ago someone had asked her if she thought tragedy stalked some people, and if that person asked her the same question now she would say yes. Tragedy and evil had plagued her family, and they were helpless in the face of it.

She made the tea and carried it through to her husband; he took the proffered mug and sipped on it without a care in the world. She admired him in many ways, nothing really fazed him. He saw everything in black and white, did her Jack. No grey spots for him.

CHAPTER ONE HUNDRED AND FIFTEEN

Bertie Warner decided to have the party for young Vincent at his pub on the Bow Road. He had arranged all the food and drink himself and it promised to be a great night. He couldn't wait to bring that young lad back into the fold.

As he looked at young Gabriella, who had come over to discuss the music for the party, he saw what

314

had attracted the boy to her. She was exquisite, and she had waited for him—that was always a good sign in a bird as far as he was concerned. She reminded him of his old woman, sensible and calm, which were good traits in a villain's wife. If the Filth kicked the door in at three in the morning with a search warrant in one hand and a sniffer dog in the other, it was always handy to have a wife who took it in her stride, and kept the kids away from it. Occupational hazards and all that—every job had them.

'You must be looking forward to seeing him back on the outside, love.'

Gabby nodded happily. 'It will be great! And I'd like to thank you, Mr Warner, for your help, it's really appreciated.'

He felt choked, and was surprised that he could still be touched like that after all these years. Most women in her position would be complaining they couldn't manage on what they were getting; after all, they owed the girl's old man a huge debt of gratitude. But this little lovely was actually grateful. Wonders would never cease.

'You're welcome, love. It doesn't even begin to cover it. You got a good one there in Vince.'

She beamed at the praise and said honestly, 'You don't need to tell me that, Mr Warner. I've always known my Vince was special. But I have missed him. I was only sixteen when he got banged up, we've never even spent the night together! And now he's finally coming home to live in our house! How mad is that?'

Bertie Warner felt the urge to actually break down and cry. This lovely little girl had shown him that no one was ever so hard they couldn't

315

appreciate a real sob story when they heard one. She wasn't even after a bit of sympathy, she was just being honest.

'He's a lucky man to have you, darling—I wish you both a long life of happiness.' She was smiling with excitement and he thought again how lovely she was. He envied young Vincent coming home to her. 'You book a DJ or whatever it is you have these days, and just bill it to the pub, all right, love?'

She nodded; this was like a dream to her, one she had been having for four very long years. And it was finally coming true.

CHAPTER ONE HUNDRED AND SIXTEEN

'Mum, listen to me. Vincent wants his daughter at home and, no matter what you tell the social workers, they are already putting in place a residential order for her to come back home full time. Now, if you push me on this, I will leave it to Vincent to sort you out.'

Cynthia knew that she was on the losing side. She had to take this well because if she kicked off now she would lose all contact with little Cherie and that must never happen. She just had to bide her time. This pair of fucking muppets would ruin it all by themselves and when that happened she would make sure she was there to pick up the pieces. So she plastered a fake smile on her face and said, 'I know, love, and I was going to say that now you are back together, you should be a proper family. The social worker has already explained that you are on track, and that they are confident that you will be able to cope with motherhood in an adult and confident way.'

She had mimicked Miss Byrne so well that even Gabby had to laugh at her.

'That is exactly what she said to me as well! In that exact voice!' She was so happy that Vincent was coming home she could even be nice to her mother.

'Look, Gabriella, it wasn't anything personal, you know, me having Cherie here. It was for your own good. You were sixteen and alone, and I know I wasn't the best mother in the world to you or your brother, but it was different with Cherie. I felt older and wiser. I was ready for the responsibility of a child and, truth be told, was trying to make up to you for everything that had happened in the past. If I had left her with you, you would have fucked up big time. You were just too young, love.'

Gabby smiled at her mother even though she didn't believe a word the woman was saying. She was backing off gracefully, and that meant she was more dangerous than ever, because she would be scheming. Well, let her scheme. Vincent would be there this time to protect her.

'Thanks, Mum. By the way, have you seen anything of James?'

For a second, Cynthia was nonplussed. Then Gabby watched as it dawned on her who she was talking about.

'No. Why, have you?'

Gabby enjoyed her mother's discomfort and that saddened her, because this was, after all, her mother. 'Yeah, he turned up at Nana's last week. He was asking after you. I didn't know if he'd been in touch.'

Cynthia shook her head violently, and Gabby could see she was rattled, far more than she had expected her to be.

'How did he look?'

'Scruffy, still strange. I think he was on something to be honest. His teeth were rotten. I was shocked at the sight of him—he looked really manic, but Granddad aimed him straight out the door. I felt a bit sorry for him.'

Cynthia didn't answer her.

'I tell you something, Mum, I'm glad my Vincent will be home soon. I wouldn't want James hanging around. Though I always wrote to him, a few times a year, like. He never answered a letter, but I still felt he should have some kind of contact with us, you know?'

Cynthia's mind was working overtime; on a couple of occasions lately she had felt as if she was being watched. Especially late at night when she parked her car, and now it seemed she might have been right to feel that way. Her son was back out on the streets, something she had not envisaged ever happening. After all, he was as mad as a fucking March hare. But so-called care in the community meant all sorts were let out these days. Cynthia, being Cynthia, did not see his condition as anything to do with her; as far as she was concerned, he was just born like it. And that, as she was wont to say, was that. But she knew that he had a particular dislike of her after his father's death. The doctors had warned her of that, and the feeling was mutual. She would keep her eyes open, and take the appropriate precautions. If he came on too strong she would report him without a moment's guilt. She had a baseball bat she kept for emergencies, and she would happily wrap it round his head if the need arose. She had known he was on the out, but it had not occurred to her he would want to see her or, more to the point, confront her. But at least she had a heads up now, thanks to this daughter of hers. The same daughter who was happily taking away from her the only person she had ever truly cared about.

She forced another smile on to her face. 'Well, he knows where I am, I suppose.'

'Oh yeah, he knows where you are all right, Granddad told him.' Gabby smiled at her mother, and the fear in her eyes was like a balm to her tortured soul. 'So, I will take the last bits of Cherie's stuff tomorrow, if that's OK?'

''Course it is. I hope you'll still let her stay here sometimes. I mean, once Vincent is home, he's going to want you to himself I should imagine.'

'Oh, he'll have me *and* his daughter. That's all he wants, Mum.'

'Of course.'

Gabby wondered why, after everything her mother had done to her over the years, she still felt bad when she scored a point over her. And no one was more shocked than her as she heard herself say, 'You're coming to his party, Mum, aren't you? It's going to be great.'

All the way home she could have kicked herself, because she knew that her mother, being her mother, would come to the party all right and it would be the fucking party's death knell. She sighed in frustration. It was always the same—her mother had a knack of making *her* feel in the wrong and, consequently, she felt she had to make it up to her. Well, Gabby decided, if she turned up, she would

319

act like she didn't know anything about it. That was pretty much all she could do.

Then it occurred to her that her brother could turn up too, and suddenly the whole thing just seemed too complicated and troublesome. James was her brother and she loved him. At least she loved the boy he had once been. He had serious mental issues, and when he wasn't taking his drugs he was violent. No one could have that kind of person too close to them. The thought of him near little Cherie made her blood run cold. He was so unpredictable. When he had suffered his violent bouts, the doctors had said there had been no warning, he had just snapped. And he had been like a steam train; whatever the person who'd supposedly wronged him had done, real or imagined, had made him almost murderous with his unsuppressed rage.

So why had they let him out? It made no sense. Her granddad said it was the arrogance of doctors—they believed they could tame people like James when in fact nothing could tame him. A chemical cosh only worked while the person involved was taking those chemicals. What happened if they decided to stop? Apparently James enjoyed hurting people, he *liked* it. So how on earth was he supposed to fit into normal society with normal people? He didn't know how to act, or what was acceptable behaviour.

Vincent would go mad if he caused any trouble, and she had a feeling that her brother would have met his match in her Vincent. She had to stop these negative thoughts. She had her daughter back, and her Vincent was coming home too. She had to stop looking for problems where there weren't any. The

320

trouble was, when your whole existence had been a struggle, you started to think that was all it would ever be.

Well, her life was picking up, and she was finally getting everything she had ever wanted from it. And that was a cause for celebration.

CHAPTER ONE HUNDRED AND SEVENTEEN

James Tailor had been watching his mother and, even though he hated her, she still fascinated him. She was still a good-looking woman, and she still had that walk she had always had, as if she was the only person in the world of any note. Which, in her eyes, was God's honest truth.

When he had been a little kid she had seemed almost omni-potent, but now, watching her, he realised she was nothing really, nothing to be scared of anyway. In fact, he thought she was quite sad these days. Ageing, which he knew would be killing her. Having seen how beautiful Gabby had become, he knew that would be like a knife in her ribs, and that pleased him. He hated her with a vengeance, even while he loved her.

He felt that disconnection with the world once more; it was the best feeling in the world to him. His trouble had always been that he cared *too* much. Things made him angry, really angry, and that anger all but consumed him. It was like a storm that raged in his blood, and the only way to settle it down was through a bout of violence.

But he knew his anger had been the cause

of him being locked away, so he had to try and control it. The heroin helped him enormously, and he was glad he had found something to dampen down those angry feelings. It couldn't quieten the voices completely, but it did calm them sometimes. He had stopped taking his medication, as it had interfered with his enjoyment of the drugs he injected into his body.

Watching his mother had become his hobby. The psychiatrist said he needed something to concentrate his mind on, and he was concentrating on her all right. He was watching her every move, and he found it enjoyable. He liked that he was spying on her and she didn't know he was there.

His dad had killed himself over her, which was sad because she really wasn't worth it. She was the shit on his shoes; his father had been worth fifty of her. She certainly wasn't worth dying for, but then his dad had never really understood just what he had lumbered himself with. But James could have explained—he understood it all now.

The psychiatrist had once asked him to describe his feelings for his mother, and he had thought about the question for a while before answering honestly that she was 'toxic'. She was like Agent Orange—it sounded quite nice but was full of hidden dangers, and it destroyed everything it touched. Just like Cynthia Tailor. Just like *him*. That was the one thing he had inherited from her; the urge to destroy things, destroy people.

Now it looked as if she was after Gabby's little girl, and that was something he could not allow to happen. Gabby was the only person he even remotely cared about; unlike the rest of his so-called family, she had always kept in touch with him, dropping him a line to tell him about herself and her life. Telling him everything he needed to know.

Gabby was a nice person and, although he thought she was a mug, she was the only person to have ever given him a thought. That was the worst of it, knowing they didn't even think about him, none of them did. Especially not his mother. She had dumped him faster than a cow dumped its pile of shit. She had walked away from him without even a backward glance.

Well, she would pay for her negligence, and she would pay dearly, of that much he was determined.

CHAPTER ONE HUNDRED AND EIGHTEEN

Vincent was packed and ready to go. It was amazing that after four years everything he owned fitted neatly into two carrier bags. But he didn't care about possessions; all he cared about was that he was on the out at last. In a few moments he would be outside, in the fresh air, in the real world. He felt almost sick with anticipation. Though underneath all the excitement ran a rich vein of apprehension; it was hard walking out of such a controlled environment. For four years he had not been on a bus or walked down a street, he had not even turned off a light switch. But he brushed away his nerves, and forced himself to relax. Not long now, and soon this would be a distant memory.

His Gabby was waiting out there for him and, for the first time ever, they could be together as adults, and that was heady stuff. He wanted to touch her, *really* touch her, feel her next to him, smell her hair . . . He felt almost dizzy with the thought.

He had been given a right royal send off, and for a moment he had almost been sorry he was leaving, but that had not lasted long. A couple of screws had arranged for a few bottles of Scotch and a bottle of brandy to arrive on the wing, courtesy of Derek Greene, and he had enjoyed the drink, appreciating the way his friends in there had been so glad that one of them was going on the outside.

It had been a great night; all the lags in there had reminisced about times past, about what they saw in their futures. And he had enjoyed listening to them as the Scotch loosened their tongues, and stories long forgotten had been told, and the laughter had been loud and free. That was the best bit—hearing that laughter, so uncontrolled and so natural. It was only then that he had realised that he had forgotten what laughter sounded like.

Usually on the wing everything was subdued some—how and people were always on their guard. You had to be—it was the way of this kind of world. Men banged up together could get into fights literally over nothing at all, small offences were allowed to fester until they became huge insults, and only violent retribution could assuage the injured party's ego. Men became different when they were isolated from family and friends; their children were growing up without them, and it was hard at times to deal with those kind of emotions.

Occasionally a man would come on to the wing who was an enemy on the outside for whatever reason, but the rule of thumb was you patched up your differences in nick. It was you against the screws, and it worked most of the time. But there was always the man who could not forget past mistakes, and then the wing became a subtle battleground. Tempers flared, and no one was safe. The main thing was learning to look after yourself. You had to watch your back constantly, watch what you said, and exercise a little diplomacy. He had seen the big mouths arrive, all bravado, with stories of how hard they were, only to become gofers within a week.

Gofers were the mugs who ended up doing the shit work—cleaning people's cells, making the tea. It was 'Go for this', or 'Go for that'. Vincent had found himself a niche there; it was well known he had been captured and had kept very quiet—not landing anyone in it but doing the time for them all. That had earned him a great deal of respect, especially as he had been so young. He had worked up from there, proving himself in small ways, and gaining a reputation for being a hard little fucker as well as a good companion. It was not an easy life, and it was hard for them all, but he had managed to overcome it. He had kept his head down, served his time and, now he had repaid his so-called debt to society, he was finally going home.

As he stepped out of the prison, he felt a rush of panic because, right up until this second, he had believed that it would go wrong somehow, and he would be stuck in there for good. As he acclimatised himself to the natural light, he saw a large black Bentley and, standing by it waving at him, dressed in a short black dress, was his Gabby.

He ran to her and picked her up in his arms. Her body fit into his perfectly as if they had been made for each other and, kissing her deeply, he felt at last like he was out. He was really on the other side of the wall.

'Oh, Gabby, you fucking gorgeous girl, this is like a fucking dream!'

Gabby was nearly speechless with happiness. 'Come on, mate, get in! We're finally going home.'

Vincent could feel her tears mingle with his as he kissed her over and over, afraid to let her go in case it all was a dream.

In the car, she handed him a bottle of champagne, and said shyly, 'You'd better open that, mate, it's from Bertie Warner. He's waiting for us—there's a big party, and it's all for you!' She was beside herself with excitement.

The driver, a large, usually dour man called Peter Bates, turned and shook his hand saying jovially, 'I am going to put the glass up. Nothing personal, but I think you two might like a bit of privacy.'

Two minutes later the glass divide was up, and the curtains were drawn. Looking at his Gabby, at how nervous she seemed, Vincent knew then that this would be the happiest day of his life. As he slipped her dress over her head, he felt how shy and timid she was, and he would always remember this moment. Because she was, without doubt, the love of his life, and he knew that she felt the same way about him. All his fears about them finally being together were gone. It felt as natural as walking or talking. He also knew that if anyone ever hurt her, he would kill them without hesitation. He had left behind a schoolgirl, and had come out to find a woman, his woman. His Gabriella.

CHAPTER ONE HUNDRED AND NINETEEN

'The motor's here, it's just driven into the car park.'

The pub was packed with people, and little Cherie was the queen of the night and loving every second of it. Her daddy was coming home at last, and she was thrilled at the prospect. It was like a dream to her; the noise, the people, the dancing! And it was all for her daddy.

Her great-nana Mary and her great-granddad Jack were sitting at a table proud as punch, and she picked up on the way people deferred to them. Nanny Cynthia though looked cross and she didn't know why. Her daddy's family was also there, and she sensed that they were *not* as welcome as everyone else. It was a wonderful night, and everyone was telling her how pretty she looked, and how lovely she was. It was a great feeling being so important, so special. Her daddy must be somebody to have all this done for him, and she was proud to be a part of it.

As Vincent walked into the pub with his arm around Gabby's shoulders, Cherie ran to him, and he picked her up and threw her into the air. She hugged him tightly, her slim little arms locked on to his neck, and he kissed her hair, savouring the clean smell of her, and the feel of her slight little body in his grasp. For the first time ever he felt that he had a family, a real family.

As he looked across the room he saw his father and brothers standing up toasting him, raising their glasses with everyone else and, passing his daughter to her mother, he walked straight over to the table that held his family.

'Welcome home, son.' Paddy O'Casey extended his hand to Vincent, but his brothers all hung back, shy now that he was finally home, and aware of how far he had come up in the world. They knew they had not been as good to his little girl as they should have been, and they were nervous.

Vincent sensed all this in a heartbeat and, ignoring his father's proffered hand, he grabbed the man by the scruff of his neck and, in front of everyone, physically dragged him across the small dance floor and out into the car park. There he proceeded to hammer his father with his fists until he was pulled off by Bertie Warner and Derek Greene.

Looking at his father lying in the dirt he said quietly, 'You robbed me, you treacherous old cunt. You took money that should have been for my Gabby and my baby. If I ever clap eyes on any of you I'll fucking kill you, you got that? And that goes for you lot as well,' he said to his brothers, who had followed him out to the car park.

The men nodded their heads, humiliated and ashamed.

Turning to Derek and Bertie, Vincent then said jovially, 'Come on, lads, we've got a party to go to!'

The two men followed him inside, acutely aware that a young boy might have been sent down, but a very dangerous man had returned in his place.

CHAPTER ONE HUNDRED AND TWENTY

'You must be mad, Gabby!' Cynthia was beside herself with anger and it showed. That her daughter could be pregnant again so quickly was a source of irritation to her.

'Thanks for the congratulations, Mum, really appreciate it.'

Cynthia stopped herself from retaliating, instead saying levelly, 'You're only young, why tie yourself down again?' But she didn't mean a word of it; her daughter's happiness was eating away at her, and the fact that Vincent was making a great name for himself was galling.

'My Vincent and me want another baby—he's missed so much of Cherie's life, and we want to be a family, a proper family.'

The inference was not lost on Cynthia and she seethed with indignation. Vincent, however, was not a man to fuck, as the Jamaicans would say. He had already put the hard word on her, told her that if she pushed her luck he would come after her without mercy. He had explained in a quiet and patient voice that if his Gabby did not get the respect due to her, he would hunt her down like a dog. Those had been his exact words, and it had been hard swallowing, but she knew she had to. If she wanted to see little Cherie she would really have to restrain herself, and she was willing to do that for the child. She adored that little girl, and she knew that Vincent saw this love as her only redeeming feature.

The social worker was well off the scene now

that Vincent had got his little garage, and was a productive member of society. She couldn't tattle in the social worker's ear any more about rumours and stories of her daughter's wild ways, and how worried she was about her granddaughter's moral welfare. Those days were long gone, and she knew it.

She forced herself to smile. If Gabby was pregnant she would need more help with Cherie, it stood to reason. This might actually work in her favour.

'I just don't want to see you losing your freedom, love, that's all. Old before your time.'

That made sense to Gabby, and she smiled faintly, her eyes softer now. 'It's what we both want, Mum. Vince is thrilled.'

Cynthia didn't answer; instead she put the kettle on. 'Well, why don't you leave Cherie with me, and have the weekend off to celebrate, eh?'

Gabby nodded. It was what she had hoped her mother would say, and she felt a hypocrite in many ways; after all, it wasn't that long ago that she didn't want the child anywhere near her mother. But that was before, when she didn't have Vince by her side, and was at this woman's mercy. Those days were long gone.

It would be nice to have a weekend alone with Vince. Cherie was a handful, constantly wanting her father's attention. But that was to be expected—he had not been in her life properly until now, and Cherie, the little madam, was making the most of him being there. For his part, Vince loved his pretty little daughter, and she knew he was happy at the prospect of another baby.

'Thanks, Mum. I'll pick her up on Sunday

330

afternoon.' Gabby walked into her daughter's bedroom which her mother had decorated to perfection, and hugged the little girl to her. 'You be a good girl for your nanny, OK?'

Cherie nodded happily. She loved it here; she was the centre of attention from the minute she opened her eyes until she fell asleep. For a child like Cherie that was heady stuff, and Cynthia indulged her shamelessly.

'Go on, get yourself away. I'm sure that man of yours is champing at the bit to see you.'

'He is, he always is.'

Gabby left the flat and walked to her car. As she unlocked it, she saw her brother standing at the corner of her mother's road, and felt troubled. After all, her Cherie was in the flat with her, and she didn't want James going there and causing trouble in front of her.

She drove to the corner and, stopping beside her brother, she said, 'What you doing here, James?'

He smiled absently at his sister, then he said, 'I hear your Vincent is doing well for himself.'

She ignored him and said again, 'What are you doing here, James? You know Mum doesn't want to see you.'

He shrugged and she saw how emaciated he had become. Vincent had heard he was an addict and, seeing him now, she believed it. He looked thin, drawn, and very run down. The weather was just turning cold and all he had on was a thin jacket over an even thinner T-shirt.

She looked into his face and was heart-sorry for the way his life had turned out. If he had not been her brother she certainly wouldn't have approached him. If she was honest, she had avoided him like the plague since he had been back on the scene. She had seen him from a distance a few times, and she had driven past him without stopping to even say hello. He made her nervous; anyone looking into his eyes could see that he was not quite right. He could easily be mistaken for a rapist, or a serial killer from a film. He was dirty, unkempt, and basically just odd. The trouble with James was that he was literally capable of anything, and she had to make sure he wasn't going near her mother's house while her daughter was there.

'My baby's in that flat, my Cherie, and if Vince finds out you've been near there, or that you scared her . . .' She left the sentence unfinished and she saw her brother's eyes widen. 'You are taking your medication, aren't you, James?'

The question threw him, and she could see it had also annoyed him.

'Are you?' she repeated.

He shuffled his feet for a few seconds, unable to meet her eyes. 'What do you care?'

She sighed then, a sad, drawn-out sigh. 'You're still my brother, James . . .'

He didn't answer her so she tried again.

'Where are you living? Locally?'

He shrugged. 'Why the interest suddenly?'

Gabby could smell the foetid breath of the junkie and she felt her stomach heave.

'Because you are hanging round Mum's street, and you aren't exactly her biggest fan, are you?'

He looked awful, like he had been sleeping on the streets, and she wondered at how her father would feel seeing him like this. Seeing what had happened to them all, for that matter. She wondered if, had he known what their fates would be, he would have left them like he had, at the mercy of a woman who had no real care for anyone except herself, and now also little Cherie.

Neither Gabby or James had had the best start in life. They had been little children at the mercy of an adult who had no real care for anyone or anything but what she herself wanted. It was an abortion really, all of it.

'It's a free country, Gabby. I can go where I like, and I like to watch Mother. I can promise you this though; if I decide to have a word with her, I'll make sure she's alone, OK? I can't be fairer than that, can I?'

Gabby looked at this man who was still her brother despite the fact they felt like strangers and, shaking her head, she said sadly, 'Please tell me where you're living, James. I just want to help you if I can.'

He didn't answer her; instead, he gave her his usual enigmatic smile and walked away.

She sat in the car for a while wondering if she should warn her mother about him. But she guessed that she knew he was there already. She wasn't a fool—she would have noticed him surely? Yet, turning the car around, she went back to her mother's flat anyway. While her Cherie was there she wanted to feel the girl was safe, and she made up her mind to tell Vincent about her worries.

CHAPTER ONE HUNDRED AND TWENTY-ONE

'I need a good earner, Bertie. I've got another baby on the way and, though the garage does OK, I need some real money to get a mortgage, et cetera.'

Bertie Warner grinned laconically; he had wondered how long it would be before Vincent wanted more. It was indisputable that he was on a fucking good earn, but he would still never feel he was getting enough money—that was just this boy's nature. He seemed to think the world owed him a living. True, he had done them all a big favour, but, by the same token, he had already been handsomely recompensed, and he had earned the respect of everyone into the bargain. It was too soon for Vincent to be out on the rob and Bertie said as much.

'Calm yourself down, lad. If you go out too soon you'll get another fucking capture. They will be keeping an eye on you for a good while yet. They will be aware of your known associates and they will even be monitoring your calls. Now, you remember what I told you about mobiles, don't you? Never, and I mean *never*, use your mobile for work— you always talk business from a fucking public phone or an untraceable pay as you go. The Filth are using scramblers and all sorts to listen in on conversations, so be aware.'

Vincent could barely keep the impatience out of his voice as he answered heavily, 'You have mentioned that before, Bertie.'

Bertie Warner, annoyed now, said sarcastically,

'I'm sure I have, clever bollocks, but just in case you are a bit dense I thought I would mention it again. Only you lot seem to think you are technological wizards because you can fucking dial a phone number. Well, *my* technological wizards, who are shrewder than you lot put together and then some, have warned me of the pitfalls of tapping. The signal is winging its way through the air, and can be intercepted at any time. Now, I may not be Alexander Graham fucking Bell, but I know enough to listen to the people who *do* know about these things. So if you ever ring me cold again like you did today, I will see to it that your fancy new mobile gets shoved so far up your jacksie you'll have to shove your hand down your throat to answer a call!'

He was bellowing now; he could be heard all over the scrapyard. And it took Vincent O'Casey all his considerable willpower not to knock the man on his arse. But he knew that for the mug's game it would be—Bertie would have him sliced and diced without a second's thought. Bertie was a lot of things, but even-tempered was not one of them. He could be moved to tears at the plight of a starving child in Africa one moment, only to become murderous if the noise of a child's actual crying interrupted him watching the news. He was a mass of contradictions, and it was best to let him get his anger out of his system.

'And for the fucking record, Mr Big fucking Earner, *you* work for *me*, and *I* say when, and if, you go back out on the street.'

Vincent licked his dry lips, and bit back the retort he was dying to make. Instead, he bowed his head, feeling like some kind of errant schoolboy.

Satisfied by the boy's outward deference, Bertie

335

lowered his voice and said amiably, 'I done a lump and half, son, and I know how you're feeling, but believe me when I say you have to lie low for a while. I mean, be honest, do you want to get captured again? Because this time, mate, it will be a lot longer than four years behind the door. Next time round you become what the courts call a serial offender, and they'll throw away the fucking key, son. So, tighten your belt. You're on a fucking decent earn—many men work a month to earn the poke you get a week—and the garage will pay off. Take my advice and stop giving it the large—you've plenty of time for all that when you're properly established.'

Although Vincent knew he was getting sound advice, he still couldn't let his wants go. He liked the life of a criminal; he liked the kudos and, most of all, he liked the money. He was determined to get some serious poke if it was the last thing he ever did in this life.

When he left, Bertie Warner sighed in annoyance. He had seen them all come and go—real hitters who, if they had a bit of patience, could have gone right to the top of their game. Impatience, Bertie had learned, was the scourge of the villain; it was the downside of easy money. So many of these young lads blew their wages in a week and were soon looking for another earn; if they saved a bit for the rainy days they would be quids in. He watched them in the pubs and clubs— big diamond Rolexes and eighty-grand motors and they were still signing on, for fuck's sake! The naivety of these young men was laughable. He blamed the education system—they taught them how to add up, but not how to invest their money and save the bastard, or at least some of it, anyway.

Bertie lived well, but not as well as he could, and that was because he knew the Old Bill loved nothing more than someone who lived it large with no real means of employment. A local Face driving a prestige car, with all the rent paid, while still on fucking Jobseeker's Allowance did tend to raise the red flag. But these young lads wouldn't listen, none of them.

Well, he had said his piece—it was up to Vincent O'Casey now. But he hoped the lad used his noodle. He really had a knack for the driving and, if he could just wait a while, he would be set like the proverbial jelly.

Bertie decided to have a talk with young Derek and see what he thought about the situation. If the boy got a tug, he didn't want it coming down on them. The trouble was, the mood Vincent was in, he was liable to go outside for his work if *they* didn't give it to him. Vincent was like all this generation, they wanted everything in five minutes, but they needed to learn that it took a long time and a lot of effort to bring off any decent job. Planning was the key, planning for every and any eventuality. That, unfortunately, was the bottom line. Haste meant mistakes, and a mistake on this lad's part could get him a big lump inside, and another kid meeting their father only once a month.

CHAPTER ONE HUNDRED AND TWENTY-TWO

James was squatting in Hoxton with three others—two girls in their late teens, and a man in his forties called Dougie McManus. As he looked at the three of them sprawled out on the floor, he wondered at how he had got himself in this mess.

Dougie was a hustler, a panhandler, and not a very good one. With his long straggly hair and beard, he resembled Christ in a good light. But he also looked like a junkie, and people either threw a few pence at him or told him to fuck off. But he could score anything from anyone.

The girls were relatively new, and would not last more than a week at most. They were runaways, drifters, and Dougie was already freaking them out; they were not interested in his sexual advances, and were already sick of his high stories. James had noticed that all junkies talked about was the last high, or a spectacular high from the past. Dougie's tales always involved a stash he had bought once, or stolen from someone, or found the Holy Grail of skag, always the best high ever.

Normally, James just tuned him out, but now he was getting angry, because the money he had hidden in the squat had miraculously disappeared, and Dougie and the girls were stoned out of their tiny—emphasis on the tiny—minds. So, putting two and two together, he made the usual four.

He looked down on their sleeping forms and thought about how he'd ended up in this place. He had left his bedsit because he had wanted to. He believed that the woman in the next house could read his mind through the walls and he could feel her interfering with his thoughts day and night. She was very old, and she had a foreign accent, but he knew that was all just an act. She was working for his mother and reporting back to her.

He had been very clever. He had got dressed one day, and walked out of his bedsit without anything, as if he was just going to the shops, and he had never gone back. That's when he had shaken off the authorities—they were all a part of the conspiracy anyway, giving him tablets to stop him knowing the truth. He was a lot of things but a moron wasn't one of them.

Ha! He had shown them all, and he would carry on showing them all. Now here he was in a den of thieves, living with *actual* thieves. What was it his father had always said? Never steal off your own— and yet that was exactly what this lot had done. As bad as they had tried to make him out, he had never stolen unless he was at rock bottom. He prided himself on that.

Now these pieces of scum had robbed him. He could smell the sourness of the girls' bodies and wrinkled his nose in distaste. One of the girls, Alicia, was quite nice. She was very posh and had gone to an expensive school, but her parents had washed their hands of her, and who could blame them? She was a thief, and thieves never prosper.

He sat down on the hearth of the old-fashioned fireplace; it was filthy, overflowing with cigarette butts, roaches, and the usual detritus of a junkie's lair. Needles, wraps, and sooty tinfoil burned and wrinkled, McDonald's wrappers, and sugar-laden drinks bottles. He looked at Dougie's narrow face, thin beyond belief, and his filthy beard full of food and grease. He wondered if they were really asleep—perhaps they were pretending, hoping he would go away so they could get their stash out behind his back. The stash he had paid for, that they had bought with his stolen money!

He stood up and went into the kitchen. Holding open the heavy door was a rusty old iron. It had once been a lovely piece of metalwork, burnished black, and it had probably ironed ladies' lawn handkerchiefs, or their knickerbockers; he smiled at the thought.

Picking it up, he walked back into the room and, raising the iron above his head, he brought it down with all the force he could muster on to Dougie's face.

Dougie, so full of heroin he couldn't feel a thing, was knocked out cold by the first blow. Ten blows later his face was gone and, placing the iron carefully on to the floor by the body, James Tailor methodically searched the man's clothes for anything of value—he wouldn't miss it now, after all—before leaving the flat. He had to get away. Far away.

CHAPTER ONE HUNDRED AND TWENTY-THREE

'But it's my scan, you said you'd come with me.'

At the other end of the line, Vincent could hear the disappointment in Gabby's voice.

'Look, babe, I can't do anything about it now.' He sighed. 'I have to go to this meet, it's important,

340

OK?' A few minutes later he put the phone down, and turned back to his two comrades. 'So are you in then?'

They both nodded. Geoff Gold was clearly thrilled, but his brother Micky was not as easily pleased.

'Hang on a minute, who told you all about this place?'

Vincent smiled; he had expected this question before now and, in hindsight, he would realise that it should have bothered him. He tapped his nose. 'Never you mind. It's enough that I trust the bloke. The fewer people who know our business the better, don't you think?'

The two men nodded, but he could see that Micky Gold was not that impressed, which annoyed him. The Golds were from Canning Town and they were a pair of blond Adonises. Both were tall, had thick wavy blond hair and dark blue eyes framed by long black lashes. Derek Greene said they attracted too much attention to be villains of any real note—women took too much notice of them for a start—but they would not be put off by that. Their father had been some Scandinavian seaman and their mother was a good-looking local girl who had often moonlighted as a brass in the various pubs of East London during the sixties and seventies. They loved their old mum and would do anything for her. She, in turn, supplied them with food, did their washing, and lied to everyone for them, from girlfriends to judges. They had a good little rep, but had never done the big one.

'Look, Micky, if you don't want in just fucking tell me and I'll stop wasting me breath.'

Geoff looked at his younger brother and said

hastily, 'Shut the fuck up! This is all kosher, and I want in.'

Micky shrugged but he was still chary and it showed.

Vincent wasn't bothered. If nothing else, this job would appeal to their greedy natures; after all, that's what had made *him* so interested. He poured the Scotch out and they sat down in his office at the garage he was beginning to make such a success of. Then he took them through the robbery that was being planned for a bank in Borough Green, Kent. By the time he had finished outlining the proposition, both were smiling widely, as he had known they would be.

'This, my friends, is what is known as a piece of piss.'

The Gold brothers were only too happy to drink to that.

CHAPTER ONE HUNDRED AND TWENTY-FOUR

Cynthia Callahan was looking at the two policemen in complete shock.

'He what!'

The elder of the two men took her gently by the arm and walked her through to her kitchen where he helped her into a chair at the scrubbed pine table. The younger man put the kettle on, knowing this was a cup of tea and a chat scenario; the poor woman looked mortified.

'I'm sorry to be the harbinger of such distressing news, but we feel we have to warn you. Your son has murdered a man called Dougie McManus, and we believe he may come here at some point. In the squat where he was living we found exercise books that were your son's, in which he detailed how he was going to harm you. Burn you out, in fact. So we need you to be on your guard.'

Cynthia nodded, but her mind was whirling. 'He's killed someone. He has finally killed someone.'

The policeman looked at his young counterpart to see how he was getting on with the pot of tea.

'I'm afraid that's true, Mrs Tailor—'

She interrupted him. 'I'm Callahan—Miss Callahan. I reverted to my maiden name after my husband's death.'

He made a note of that in his little book. 'Now, has he approached you?'

She shook her head. 'No, but I think he's been stalking me for a while. My daughter warned me about him the other day, funnily enough. You know he has severe mental problems?'

The policeman said he did.

'He was diagnosed schizophrenic at a very young age, after his father committed suicide. It's very sad. I need to know, have you any idea where he could be?'

'Well, Miss Callahan, I was going to ask you that very same thing.'

She shook her head again. 'I avoid him like the plague, to be honest. He's a very difficult person to deal with. He believes he is being watched by government forces. If you talk to his doctors they will explain it to you.'

He nodded—he had spoken to the doctors already.

'My daughter might know something, but I doubt it—same with my parents. He's not someone you encourage into your life, if you get my drift. Very violent, and very easily riled up. He cut a neighbour's cat's throat when he was just coming up to nine.'

The policemen were surprised to note that, as she described her son's problems, there was no real emotion there at all for him.

'My daughter seemed to think he was on drugs. She said he looked like he was on something when she saw him just down the road from my house. She stopped the car and spoke with him. I had her little daughter staying with me at the time so naturally she was worried in case he came here in front of the child . . .'

He waited until the teas were placed before them all, before saying gently, 'We believe he is on heroin—a lot of the mentally disturbed take that drug on the streets. We also found a crack pipe, and evidence that he'd used it, at the murder scene. Is there anyone you can think of that he might go to? Any friends?'

She shook her head. 'No, nobody. He's a loner, a strange boy. I wish I could help you more.'

Five minutes later they were ushered out of the front door and, seeing the number of locks she had on it, they realised that she had been preparing for her son coming for her long before they had arrived on the scene.

'You keep yourself safe now, Miss Callahan, and, if he comes near you, ring the police immediately. All the forces are looking for him, so try not to worry.'

Cynthia closed the door and locked it, every bolt

and chain, then she went around the house making sure everywhere was secure.

In the kitchen she poured herself a large vodka and tonic and then, smiling slightly, she wondered if he would have the guts to turn up here. Burn her out! She'd like to see the little fucker try.

Picking up the phone she rang her daughter. If he went near her grandchild, she'd skin him alive. The only good bit of all this aggravation was that they'd have to lock him up again and, hopefully, this time, they would throw away the bastard key.

CHAPTER ONE HUNDRED AND TWENTY-FIVE

'Look, Gabby, all men are the same, they get you pregnant but they have no real interest in the actual pregnancy—it's only the baby they are interested in, and even that wanes after a while.'

Gabby sighed. Did her mother really think she was helping? The worst thing of all was she had a feeling that what she was saying was true. She was heavily pregnant and Vincent was never in the house for any length of time. The garage was doing well, and that pleased her; they were beginning to save some money, and they were moving to a new council house before the baby was born. But he was out from early morning till late at night.

Cynthia looked at her daughter and felt the urge to shake her. What was it with this girl? She couldn't see what was under her nose—she had bagged herself a blagger, and blaggers were not known for their homing instincts. She should think herself lucky she had a man out grafting for her—not that she was that enamoured of her daughter's 'partner' as they called them nowadays. He looked down his nose at her, and did not bother to hide his indifference. Dislike she could cope with because it meant she'd made an impact at least. Indifference, on the other hand, meant she had not had any effect on the idiot in any way. He ignored her completely, which really pissed her off, and the fact that her daughter didn't even defend her to him really annoyed her as well.

'Any news on Nutty?'

Gabby rolled her eyes and said huffily, 'Will you stop referring to James like that? They haven't found him yet. God knows where he is by now.'

Cynthia snorted then. 'Fucking Broadmoor is where he should be, locked away for good.'

'He's your son, Mum!'

Cynthia snorted again. 'Stop fucking saying that, he's nothing to do with me! Anyway, he's over eighteen—he's his own person now, responsible for his own actions.'

Gabby didn't answer; it always amazed her that her mother could just push the blame away from herself without a second's thought. She rubbed her belly—she was feeling awful today.

Seeing her daughter's discomfort Cynthia said, 'Get your stuff, Cherie, you're coming home with Nanny.' She held a finger up to her daughter in protest. 'Not a word, you need your rest. Now, I've put a lasagne in the fridge, and I've got your ironing. So stop panicking and put your feet up.'

Gabby felt a rush of gratitude to this woman who she alternately loved and hated. Since Cynthia had seen how ill she had been with this baby she had been a diamond. She even talked about the baby as if she was looking forward to it, which Gabby thought she secretly was. Cynthia was buying little bits for it, and she had got out Cherie's old cot, so she must be expecting the child to stay there on occasion.

For the first time in years, Gabby felt a modicum of contentment in her mother's company as they chatted and laughed. It was as if the heavier she got with this baby the better her mum liked her. Her nana Mary thought she was mad, but they didn't see this side of Cynthia—so few people ever did. There was no doubt about it—as her mother got older, she was becoming more like a mother should be. OK, not where James was concerned maybe, but then he'd always been difficult, to say the least. Gabby hoped none of her kids inherited his mental illness, that would be too cruel. Whereas her mother had never been a loving mother exactly, Gabby was—she loved her family with all her heart.

She had tried to tell her nana and granddad about how her mum was behaving these days, but they both dismissed it out of hand, saying she was after something, just as she had been before. Gabby understood that they didn't trust Cynthia, but even if she was after Cherie, now that Vincent was back he would never let anything happen to them.

Having him there made her so happy—she just wished he was home more. She knew that it had taken lot of work to get the garage off the ground, and he wanted to make a success of it. It was all for them so she shouldn't really moan too much.

Cherie had her little bag packed, and was impatient to go with her nanny Cynthia now. She had brought all her drawing books with her; she loved drawing, and her nanny Cynthia had got her an easel which she loved painting on. She had a white smock just like the real painters in a book her nanny showed her.

Cynthia really thought the child had a talent, and she was determined to see her make the best of it. She could be the next Tracey Emin, that was Cynthia's belief. She knew with certainty that this little girl had a brilliant future ahead of her, and she would move the heavens to see she got the chances Cynthia felt had been denied to her. She saw herself in little Cherie, saw her as she would have been with different parents, with people who could have given her a proper start in life. Cynthia blamed her parents for the way her whole life had turned out, and her son's life as well. She believed with all her heart that her mother had had more say in James Junior's upbringing than she did and, consequently, the blame for his condition lay at her mother's door.

It never occurred to her that dumping her children at will, not loving either of them, and placing impossible demands on them might have had something to do with her son's illness and her daughter's desperate craving for love. In fact, Cynthia was proud of her Gabriella; she was doing all right, and so long as she let her have Cherie she would remain in her good books.

It was Vincent that Cynthia had the main problem with these days. He didn't like her having too much to do with the child. She knew she had to sort something out there. He needed taking down a peg or two. Since he had been released he thought he was the dog's gonads—well, what man didn't?

She smiled at the thought of bringing him down,

and she drove back to her house lighter in spirit, with her little Cherie chattering away beside her.

CHAPTER ONE HUNDRED AND TWENTY-SIX

The Golds had been watching the bank in Borough Green for the last few weeks and they knew down to the last detail who went in and who went out, at what times the bank was quiet, and when it was busy. On one specific day in every month, the bank held over one hundred thousand pounds before it was taken away by guards. Today they were sitting in a small coffee bar, watching the handover with interest.

There were three men outside the vehicle, and two inside—one driving, the other riding shotgun— so they were going to need to get the safety deposit box *before* they hit the inside of the back doors. It seemed to be a doddle.

The guards appeared very complacent, joking with the manager, and acting very relaxed. That was the beauty of carrying out robberies in small villages; they looked sleepy, and no one thought anything bad could happen in them. With sawn-off shotguns and the element of surprise to their advantage, this would be over in minutes.

Pleased with the day's findings, the Golds got into their nondescript car and drove away sedately, sure that this was going to go without a hitch.

CHAPTER ONE HUNDRED AND TWENTY-SEVEN

'Well, she's asleep. Surely you don't expect me to wake her up!' Cynthia's voice was low, but full of contempt. Vincent was on the phone asking why she had not brought his daughter back as arranged.

She had not said when she would be bringing her back for definite, she had just said maybe Sunday night. Anyway, she had rung her daughter earlier and left a message to say that Cherie was a bit under the weather and then she had put her to bed. It wasn't her fault that Gabriella had not checked her messages and she said as much. But Vincent was not a happy bunny.

'You know she should be here, Cynthia, she's got school tomorrow.'

Cynthia snapped right back at him, 'Not with a cold, she isn't. Plus, poor Gabby's just about ready to drop, she can't be running around after that lively little mare. Unless you're staying home, of course.' She knew she had him then and she smiled down the phone imagining how angry he was.

'Well, I want her back tomorrow, all right? She spends far too much time at your drum for my liking.'

Cynthia didn't answer him; she had won this battle and if it was left to her she would soon be winning the war.

When she put the phone down she went back into her kitchen and looked through Cherie's drawing case. She had found a piece of paper earlier, and on it, written in pencil, were the plans to rob a security van for a bank in a place called Borough Green, which was apparently in Kent.

Cherie had drawn a picture of a nice house, and she had been admiring it when she had spotted the little diagram on the back. This was how you planned any robbery, Cynthia knew, from her time in Jonny's circle. You used Ordnance Survey maps and you always used pencil—never pen. Then, once the route was established, the map was destroyed, along with anything else incriminating. Cynthia knew that this would have been destroyed eventually, but Little Miss Trouble had got to it first, unaware that it was her father's blueprint for his next job. She laughed with glee. That Vincent really should be more careful about what he left in his office at the garage.

She hugged the paper to her chest. Oh, the old saying was right: God really did pay back debts without money; of that she was now sure. In her hands was the fate of Cherie's interfering fuck of a father, and she knew *exactly* what she was going to do with it.

CHAPTER ONE HUNDRED AND TWENTY-EIGHT

Mary Callahan wasn't well, and Jack knew it. She was having trouble breathing, and she seemed to spend longer and longer having a 'bit of a lie down', as she called it.

He looked at her now as she slept next to him in their bed. Her face still held some of the beauty that had attracted him all those years ago. In

351

repose, the lines were not so harsh, and she seemed younger somehow, more how he liked to think of her. She had been an eyeful all right, like their Celeste. Hers had been an understated beauty, as opposed to Cynthia's in-your-face sexuality. Mary had aged prematurely; all the trouble that Cynthia had brought to their door over the years had certainly taken its toll on her as, he supposed, it had on him too. But, for all their trials, he still loved this woman, and he hoped to God that he died first, because he didn't think he would cope without her.

He decided to make her an appointment at the doctor's, but tell her it was for him—she would accompany him then to make sure he went. It was the only way he'd get her there—she spent so much time worrying over everyone else, but not a second did she waste on herself.

She had never been the same since their Celeste went. He knew that she blamed herself for her daughter's eventual decline but it wasn't her fault. Celeste, unlike her sister and indeed her own mother, hadn't had the strength of mind needed to cope with what life had thrown at her. It had finally worn this wife of his down too; she was losing weight by the day, and she had no appetite.

He was suddenly assailed by a memory of her having their Cynthia. She had given birth at home and he had been angry because his racing paper had been used to mop up after her waters had broken. It had made him feel slightly sick. Then, after what seemed like ages, he was presented with his little daughter. Even then, as a newborn, Cynthia had been absolutely gorgeous—everyone said so. And he remembered saying to his exhausted wife, 'She'll break some hearts, this one!'

If only he had known then that she would break not only hearts but also whole families apart, he would have drowned the evil cunt there and then. He remembered his Mary, tired but triumphant, looking down at that child as if she was the most precious thing in the world. Where had it all gone so wrong?

He felt near to tears, and told himself it was just his age creeping up on him. If truth be told, he wouldn't be too trashed about shaking off this mortal coil, and going for the long sleep. In fact, he would rather enjoy it.

He laid his wrinkled hand on to his wife's hair, and it was only then that he realised she was cold. His Mary had died in her sleep. She was past all the hurts that life had thrown at her. For the first time in years, Mary Callahan was really at peace.

Sitting up in bed, Jack Callahan held his wife's hand and cried bitter tears. He blamed Cynthia for this; Mary should have had years left to her. They should have had years left *together*. If Mary had not taken on the burden of her daughter's children and all their combined problems, they could have lived out their twilight years in peace and companionship. His Mary was but another casualty in the war that was Cynthia Callahan. She had never really stood a chance.

CHAPTER ONE HUNDRED AND TWENTY-NINE

Vincent held Gabby while she cried, and he knew it couldn't be good for her or the baby. Mary's passing

353

had hit her badly, very badly. She had been the only real mother she had ever known, and he had a lot to thank her for, he knew. Without Mary and Jack, his Gabs would have been alone in the world with his daughter and completely at the mercy of Cynthia Callahan. Things had been bad enough as it was, and the guilt he felt at leaving her was ever present. As was Cynthia. It felt like she was always round, helping out.

All he needed was a couple of robberies under his belt and he could get them a decent house of their own, bought and paid for, and then get on with his legit businesses. He would only go out for a drive every year or so. It was a foolproof plan, and he wanted to make sure that this girl of his— and the children, of course—had everything they needed for the rest of their lives. It was important to him that they were all well set up.

He wanted his Gabby in their own little house, his kids at the best schools available, and a place in the sun. That had been his dream throughout his prison sentence, and now he would make it all come true.

Fuck Greene and Warner, with their 'be patient' and 'bide your time' nonsense. He was a fucking shrewdie and he knew what he was doing. He was looking after his family; after all, that was a man's job.

Cynthia brought in a tray with tea for her and Vincent and a small brandy for Gabby.

'She can't have alcohol, she's pregnant.'

'One little shot won't hurt her, and it will make her sleep, calm her down. All this crying can't be good for her or the baby.'

He could see the sense in what she was saying.

Cynthia took Gabby from his arms and, holding her close, said gently, 'Come on, love, drink this up, eh? It'll make you feel better.'

Gabby did as she was told, and drank the brandy, coughing at the raw taste.

'There, that will make you feel better, love. Now come on, put your feet on the couch, darling. I'll make you some hot milk with honey in it, like my mum used to make for me when I was feeling ill. I bet she did it for you too, eh?'

Gabby smiled brokenly and nodded her head.

Twenty minutes later the milk had been drunk and she was asleep. Cynthia looked at Vincent and sighed. 'She's taken it bad, Vincent, but it's to be expected—my mum was more of a mother to her than I ever was.'

Vincent stayed silent; he didn't know how to answer that statement.

'Do you want me to take Cherie with me? I can take her to school, the usual—it's best to keep to a routine with kids. There's going to be a lot of running about with the funeral to arrange and everything. And, well, my dad isn't going to be much use, is he? My mother did everything—he can't even boil an egg.'

It was strange talking to Cynthia like this, she seemed almost normal, caring even. Vincent knew she loved his daughter, of that there could be no doubt. It was just a pity she had never felt like that about either of her own kids.

As if reading his mind, she said, 'I was never a good mother. I found the kids got on my nerves a lot of the time. I suppose being lumbered with James didn't help—he was hard work, Vincent. Not that he meant to be, but he was so weak. I

355

had to sort out everything, from the bills to the washing and the cooking. Everything. I think I just wanted to be free, you know? Free of all the responsibilities. And my mum, well, she wanted the kids there all the time, and I got into the habit of letting her have them.' She smiled and her whole face was transformed. 'I suppose that's where Gabby gets her mothering skills from—she certainly didn't get them from me!'

For the first time ever, Vincent felt himself warming to Cynthia, disarmed by her honesty.

But Cynthia on full charm offensive was hard to resist; many men had found that out to their cost. She saw him softening towards her. Well, when she was finished with him, he would be her best mate, she would see to that. Although he might not be around too long if she had anything to do with it. At least this way it would allay any suspicions he might have about her. She wanted him to believe that she had his Gabby's best interests at heart, that she had simply found her maternal instinct later than most women, and that she would always be there for his children, as well as Gabby.

It was so easy. Men were such fucking children—all you had to do was tell them what they wanted to hear, act the little housewife, and Bob really was your uncle and Fanny your aunt.

CHAPTER ONE HUNDRED AND THIRTY

'It's a lovely day—cold but sunny. A fine day to have a baby!'

The Jamaican midwife was trying to make

Gabby laugh and, to be nice, she smiled weakly. But she had only just buried her nana Mary, and now the pains were ripping her to pieces. She knew it would be worth it, that her baby would be born perfect, and she would have a proper little family. She wished her nana was here though; it was hard without her.

She saw Vincent walk into the room, and she smiled tragically. Then another pain gripped her and she grimaced as the noise of the air leaving her body sounded like a loud fart and she laughed with him, as he said, 'Fuck me, Gabs, what hole's this baby coming out of!'

She bore down, and felt the baby crowning, watching Vincent as the miracle of birth was revealed to him. She hoped he wouldn't be put off with all the blood. But far from being repulsed, he was entranced. Pleased as punch to be there and, as their second child, and their first son, slid into the world, she saw only pure joy and amazement on his face.

As he cradled their little boy in his huge arms, she was happier than she had ever been in her life. She finally had what she had always craved. Now she had a real family, and it felt good.

CHAPTER ONE HUNDRED AND THIRTY-ONE

As Cynthia held Vincent Mark Two, as his father referred to him, she was once again overwhelmed with the feeling of belonging he engendered in her. It was as if he was her child, the same emotion she had experienced when she had first seen little Cherie five years before. That her Gabriella could produce such perfect children with that dolt she had lumbered herself with was, in itself, amazing. But, once again, this child looked like her. It had her eyes and the same shaped face as her, as well as that sovereign-coloured hair—blond with red streaks—which had always made her stand out from the crowd.

'He's stunning, Gabriella, absolutely beautiful. Well done, you two.' She aimed her smile at Vincent and she saw the delight on his face at her words. Like his genes alone could have presented her with a grandson like this! It would take her time to stamp out the O'Casey traits, she was sure. This little boy would be someone, a banker, or a doctor; he was like a blank canvas waiting for her to colour him in. One thing was for sure—he wouldn't be a fucking bank robber like his old man, she would see to that. Her smile widened as she thought of what she had done. She had made sure that his father would not be around to interfere in his little life. It was her secret gift to her new grandson.

She smiled at Vincent Senior once more, aware that she would have to put up with it until he was captured trying to rob a bank in Borough Green. The police were watching them all, and she knew that the conspiracy to rob charge would keep him out of their lives for at least seven years.

Gabriella would be heartbroken, which was to be expected; after all, the girl loved him. Cynthia understood that, but she was more concerned that, if left with these two people, her grandchildren would never have anything in their lives, not anything worth having anyway. They would end

358

up labelled blaggers' kids, and they would go the way of all thieves' children, embracing that life as all that would be open to them. So she was pleased with herself, pleased at what she had done.

As Vincent took his son from her, and gazed down into his perfect little face, she did not feel an ounce of shame. She was saving these kids from a fate worse than death.

'He'll be someone this little lad, Gabby, I can feel it in my bones.'

Cynthia laughed with her daughter at the words and, looking at Vincent, she winked happily at him.

He winked back, oblivious that his fate, like that of his little family, was well and truly sealed.

CHAPTER ONE HUNDRED AND THIRTY-TWO

'What a fucking mug! But would he listen to anyone?'

Bertie Warner was incensed at the news young Vincent O'Casey had been captured as he and the Gold brothers were about to enter a bank in Kent. They were caught with guns, balaclavas, the works. A whisper had got out, and somehow the Filth had got wind of it. How, he didn't know, because it was the first *he* had heard about any of it. In fact, it seemed that no one had any idea about the fucking robbery at all. So either one of the Golds had become loose-lipped, which was very doubtful, or Vincent had mentioned it to someone. Not a chance of that; knowing how Bertie felt about him going back into the game too soon he would have kept it quiet. No, this had to be close to home. Micky Gold had just dumped his wife for a seventeen-year-old blonde, but then would he mention a piece of work to his old woman? It was a melon scratcher all right.

But they were bang to rights now, and they would be looking at a good few years behind the fucking door, before they would be out celebrating Christmas with their families. Stupid, stupid fuckers. Especially that young Vincent. Bertie had had such high hopes for him.

He thought about that girl of his. She had not long had her second baby—a lovely little boy—and she would be devastated by this news; after all, it was not the first time Vincent had left her literally holding the baby. The poor little whore. Some girls really were unlucky. Still, what was done was done, and life on the outside continued.

But all day he kept thinking about young Vincent and about what a waste of a life it was. The second stretch was always worse than the first—for a start, you knew what to expect. Bertie would grease a few palms, make it easier for him, pay out and get him his own cell, a bit of snout and a few luxuries. Vincent would be out one day, and Bertie wanted him to remember that they had not forgotten him. He would slip that little bird a few quid too, tide her over till she was sorted out. It was the least he could do.

CHAPTER ONE HUNDRED AND THIRTY-THREE

Vincent O'Casey sat in Brixton on remand and listened to the sounds that were once more his background music. Prisons were really noisy at night. Snoring, arguing, laughter, and often the sound of muffled sobs from the men who were desperately missing their families. The sound of the POs walking up and down, hearing the loud sliding noises of the slats opening and closing as they checked to make sure no one had topped themselves or were up to some kind of skulduggery such as digging their way out or making a shiv. This was to be his life again, and it would be his life for years and years.

He wished he had listened to Bertie and Derek, but it was too late. It was way too late for everything and anything now; his little lad would grow up without him like little Cherie had done. His poor Gabby would be left with two kids, and no visible means of employment—without him the garage would need to be sold, he knew that. Why had he been so determined to do it? If he had listened to men older and wiser than himself, he would be at home now holding his little son and, later on, holding his lovely Gabby in his arms. Instead all he had to look forward to was absolutely nothing. Nothing worth anything anyway. He hoped Gabby would be OK, but at least she had her mother. Love or loathe Cynthia, she adored those kids, and she wouldn't let anything happen to them.

He would kill the fucking Gold brothers! One

of them must have had a loose lip, because he had told no one, absolutely no one, about the blag. So it *had* to have been one of them. The worst of it was they had been nabbed before they had even got out of the fucking car. How humiliating was that?

Lying down, he put his face into the pillow and, like many a man before him, he cried like a baby; he cried for his family, for the life he had lost, and for the life he would now be living. But mostly he cried for Gabby and the knowledge he had left her high and dry for the second time in six years. That was what really hurt. Her world as she knew it was gone. The life they had planned was not to be. She had a baby less than three weeks old, and no one to tell her they loved her late at night. That, he knew, would be the hardest for her to bear.

CHAPTER ONE HUNDRED AND THIRTY-FOUR

2008

Cynthia was tired but pleasantly so. At three years old, little Vincent was a real handful, but she had enjoyed the day at the zoo as much as he had. With his sister Cherie loving the bones of him, and his nanny Cynthia treating him like a king, he was a very contented little boy.

As she put the pushchair away in her hall cupboard, and walked through to the lounge, she saw the children dutifully taking their coats off and removing their shoes. They were such good kids, did anything at all she asked without her having to yell or bully them into it. So different to her own son and daughter. The thought brought her back to Gabriella, and the news she had imparted earlier that day. It seemed that '*her* Vincent', as she sickeningly referred to him, might get early parole. A bit too bloody early for Cynthia's liking.

Cynthia had enjoyed three years of more or less complete autonomy over the children, but now her daughter, with the help of her antidepressants, was finally getting herself back on her feet. She had taken Vincent's departure very badly, and lost interest in everything and everyone—even her little boy. As Cynthia had pointed out, that ponce had left her holding the baby *twice*; any other woman would have legged it, but not her Gabriella. Cynthia conveniently ignored her own part in Vincent's arrest—she had long ago convinced herself she did everything for her daughter's own good. Gabriella would never have understood that it was for the best. She had taken losing Vincent very badly indeed. The doctors had blamed it on post-natal depression, and she had not disputed that.

Then, when little Vincent was five months old, Gabriella had had a complete nervous breakdown. She had needed to be hospitalised, and she had stayed there for eight months. Those had been the happiest eight months of Cynthia's life. She had moved into a house closer to Gabriella's and she had taken the children. She had made herself a lovely little family and, on top of all that, she had been given benefits, actual *money*, to look after them! This country was wonderful really, with its welfare state—she got more than her daughter would have, what with Carer's Allowance, and all the other perks. A right little scam if truth be known and it was easily abused—they even paid for her car! But, more than that, the money made them even more hers—she had the Child Benefit book, *everything* in her name. Legally, that was worth a fortune to her as they were in her custody. Possession, as they say, is nine tenths of the law.

Now Gabriella was being difficult, wanting them back home with her. Cynthia intended to make sure that didn't happen—these were *her* babies now, and she would fight to the death to keep them.

'Why are you scowling, Nanny?' This from nine-year-old Cherie who was very observant.

Cynthia forced a smile on her face as she said quietly, 'I was just wondering how you would both cope if you had to go back to your poor mummy.' Her voice sounded as if that was inevitable, and she was gratified to see the alarm in the child's eyes.

'They won't make us, will they, Nanny?'

Cynthia shrugged, as if it was in the hands of the fates, and walked out of the room, knowing she was leaving a very troubled and worried little girl behind her. It was exactly the kind of reaction she was hoping for. If the kids didn't *want* to go home, she knew that her daughter would not be the one to force them. Also, the social workers would not be too hard on them either—she had made sure that they knew the score—or her side of it anyway. After all, mental illness ran in the family, didn't it? Her son James was as mad as a box of frogs, and her sister Celeste had not been the full fucking shilling either. Then her daughter, the mother of these beautiful children, was not exactly a shining example of motherhood or normality. She had become hooked on the very pills that were meant to be helping her! She didn't eat, sleep or shit at regular intervals without them—she was basically a mess. Maybe she *was* trying to sort herself out, but Cynthia had told the appropriate authorities that, while her daughter could visit her children here as often as she liked, she despaired of their lives if forced to go back to their mother's home full time. It seemed that they agreed with her. They bloody better had in any case, or she would want to know the reason why.

Gabriella had been allowed to have them next weekend for a trial period, so Cynthia had until then to devise a plan to make sure that they never let her daughter within five foot of these kids in the future. She was doing this for the benefit of the children. At least that is what she told herself. Without her, the kids would not be able to cope, and Gabriella needed to accept that the children were no longer hers. The sooner she accepted that the better. She could start another family with that fucking oik Vincent O'Casey when they finally let him back out on the street but, as far as these two were concerned, there was no way Cynthia was giving them up.

CHAPTER ONE HUNDRED AND THIRTY-FIVE

Gabby spent the day cleaning and polishing the house; she had got in all the treats that kids loved, and she had rented a couple of Disney DVDs. Their rooms looked lovely, and she had also made sure she had lots of drawing paper for Cherie—she was showing a talent for art that made her really stand out at school. At least that's what her mother told her anyway.

She sighed as she thought of her mother. Cynthia, she knew, loved the kids—it was in a way her only saving grace—but she had moved heaven and earth to stop Gabby, their own mother, from being any part of their lives. Gabby blamed herself of course. After Vincent had been captured yet again, and she had seen herself once more on her own with another child, she had hit rock bottom. Coming so quickly after her nana's death, it had all but destroyed her. It had taken her three long years to get herself back on her feet, and she was determined to make sure that her children came back to her where they belonged. She had promised Vincent that she would get them back, and she intended to keep that promise. He had been a great help to her even though he was far away, and he gave her the confidence she needed to fight her mother. It was so hard fighting Cynthia because she always, *always*, seemed to be in the right.

Cynthia didn't seem to be particularly worried about her daughter's problems. She was so tied up with her grandchildren, she didn't have the time or inclination to care about her relationship with her own child—the very same child who had borne the only two people Cynthia loved. Gabby appreciated all that her mother had done, but then surely any mother would have done that for her daughter? So why couldn't Cynthia go the whole hog, and let her have the kids back? Why was she so determined to make sure that they had the least possible contact with her? It felt personal, as if her mother was punishing her for wrongs, real or imagined.

When she had spoken to her psychiatrist, something he had said had rung very true with

366

Gabby. 'Psychopathic personalities can emulate the emotions and actions of the people around them, even though they could never experience those actual emotions for themselves.' He had been talking about her brother but, for some reason, it had made her think of her mother. She had felt a deep disloyalty at that because, when all was said and done, her mother had stepped into the breech when she had been needed. But now she was no longer needed. It wasn't as if Gabby would stop Cynthia seeing them ever again—she knew how close they were to their nanny. She could only dream that one day they would love *her* that much. But for now she would be content to be a part of their lives. She wanted them back home with her and, eventually, with their father Vincent. Her mother was making it all so difficult, and that was what hurt her the most.

Gabby could not even risk arguing with her—if she did, her mother told the social workers that she had been 'aggressive', that she had 'frightened the children' and, as the social workers knew that her children were not exactly enamoured of Gabby, she had to tread very carefully indeed. Cynthia was ruthless and she would do anything in her power to keep these kids as she was demonstrating daily. No one else knew exactly what her mother was really capable of—especially the goody two-shoes social workers. They thought she was wonderful; a fucking martyr. Well, they obviously didn't spend much time with her, or they would have seen her other side by now.

Thankfully Vincent would be back soon, and he would not take any nonsense from her mother or anybody else. She had that much to look forward to at least. Her mother was wary of her Vincent, and so she should be—he was stronger than she realised. Strong enough for both of them and together they would face her down once and for all.

Gabby glanced at the clock and stopped her cleaning; she had to be around her granddad's at six to make sure he had something to eat, and have a bit of a chat with him. He was still missing her nana Mary and she knew that without her in his life he would just give up.

She would pop the kids round there—that's what she would do. They could all stay there Saturday night, and it would give him a thrill to see them. He loved it when they came round, which wasn't very often thanks to her mother. Her nana Mary had warned her years ago that Cynthia wanted her children. Gabby wished now that she had listened to her.

CHAPTER ONE HUNDRED AND THIRTY-SIX

'I love you too, Vincent. I'll be up the weekend, OK?' Gabby replaced the receiver and turned to Cherie and little Vince, who were looking at her as if waiting for her to do something. She had picked them up an hour ago from her mother's—not that they had been very enthusiastic about coming with her. Now they both seemed so uncomfortable around her it was breaking her heart.

'Did you like talking to your daddy?' She had hoped it would be a treat for them to speak to him.

Cherie shrugged. 'It was all right.'

'He'll be home soon, and you'll be able to see him all the time.'

Cherie gazed at her with her big, wide-spaced blue eyes, and the expression in them told her that was *not* something she was looking forward to.

Smiling with difficulty, she said gaily, 'So, what do you want to do?'

Cherie looked at her brother and they both said in unison, 'Go home.'

Gabby swallowed her disappointment; she knew she had to give it time, once they realised they could have fun with her as well as their nanny they would come round. But she could feel the ache of tears in her eyes and throat. 'Well, you can go,' she nearly said 'home', but quickly replaced it with, 'back to Nanny's soon. Now, who wants to go in the car?' She knew little Vince would want that; he loved cars, he had inherited that from his father all right.

When they arrived at her granddad's she saw Cherie sigh heavily. 'I don't like Great-Granddad Jack. He smells and so does his house.'

Gabby had had enough and, before she could stop herself, she said quietly but with emphasis, 'You know that's not true—that's just what Nanny Cynthia says. My advice to you is get out of the car now, and keep your opinions to yourself in future. I really can't believe some of the things you say, Cherie. You're nine now, not four. Stop parroting my mother.'

'I'm not parroting anyone. He smokes like you do and it stinks.' She curled her lip in disdain as she spoke.

Gabby replied angrily, 'Your nanny smokes.'

'Not near us, she don't. She knows it's bad for

369

us to breathe in all that crud and toxic fumes.' The inference being that her mother didn't care if she was poisoning them, because she didn't care, period.

'You keep your opinions to yourself, young lady. You are going in there and you are going to be a good girl. Do you hear me, madam? You will do what you are told for once in your life.'

If she had taken back her arm and beaten the child to the floor the effect could not have been more extreme. Cherie's eyes filled with tears and she started to shake and, as Gabby looked at her in alarm, it brought back a memory. That was how her mother would act when she didn't get what she wanted. She had seen her father buckle down at that stance, and she felt a chill of fear that this child was already too far gone from her. She emulated her nanny Cynthia in everything, and the poor thing believed that was right.

Gabby fought the panic she felt rising in her chest and, taking little Vince out of his car seat, she said as nonchalantly as possible, 'Now out of the car, and not another word, OK?'

She was dreading telling the child they were staying the night. Little Vince went into his great-granddad's happily but Cherie trailed behind. It occurred to Gabby that she *had* done the right thing; she spent too much time trying to please the child when she should be making her see who was the parent.

CHAPTER ONE HUNDRED AND THIRTY-SEVEN

Cynthia had got herself sorted early, and now she was ready to go. She wondered briefly if she was taking things too far, but she knew that if she didn't go far enough, it would be overlooked. Gabriella was gradually winning the social workers round to her side and, if that happened, Cynthia would be left with nothing. Surely they could see how well those children had blossomed under her care? So what if she was the grandparent? Their own mother couldn't have done a better job of raising them. In fact, she had all but deserted them and now Gabriella expected to walk in and take them back, as if all Cynthia had done was for nothing. The thought of those kids stuck in that place with her and Vincent made her blood boil. They would never have a chance at anything.

She understood then that she had to do what she had planned. It was for the good of the children and, at the end of the day, they were what really mattered. She would do anything, literally *anything*, to see that one day she would have them for ever. All she had needed was an opening and today it had come. She had had a phone call from her granddaughter saying that her mother was making them stay at her great-granddad Jack's and she wanted to come home.

As she had spoken to the child, Cynthia knew this was the perfect opportunity to prove her daughter's uselessness as a parent. This was like a gift from the gods, and she intended to take full advantage of it.

CHAPTER ONE HUNDRED AND THIRTY-EIGHT

Jack Callahan watched as his great-granddaughter turned her pretty little nose up at everything in his home. He was glad, for the first time, that Mary wasn't here to witness this; it would have broken her heart. Cherie had been a sweet little thing when she was born, but now she was Cynthia's spawn, there was no doubt of that. He was sorry that he could find nothing to like about the child—even her beauty wasn't enough to make up for her natural air of superiority over everyone around. Like Cynthia before her, she already thought she was the dog's gonads, and he was itching to put his hand across that spoilt face. The worst thing of all was seeing poor Gabby trying her hardest to win the spoilt little mare over and only managing to make the child respect her even less. It was obvious the child knew the state of play, and was happily making her poor mother jump through hoops.

The little boy, however, was too young for Cynthia to have done much damage. Either that or the lad had more of his father in him, and wasn't so easily swayed. Jack hoped so, because if not, a few years down the line, there was going to be another troubled boy, like that fucking looney James Junior. Jack watched a lot of daytime TV these days and he knew all the psychobabble, and the words 'mother-damaged' always sprang to mind where that boy was concerned. Cynthia was like a disease, a cancer which invaded everyone around her until they were all infected with her spite and hatred. Now Jack could see her all over again, reincarnated in this little girl before him. He wasn't sure he could take it any more and his plea to her was heartfelt.

'Please, Cherie, will you just for once stop your yammering! Let's all sit together in peace.'

Little Vince was watching in fascination; he always did what his sister wanted—it was easier that way. But he didn't want to watch a film about Barbie, he wanted to watch Buzz Lightyear. He liked him, he was funny. He wondered if his sister would get her own way—she usually did where their mummy was concerned. He liked his mummy, and he liked his great-granddad Jack, but he knew that his nanny Cynthia didn't like them, so that could be difficult sometimes. He had learned at a young age never to let his feelings show; it caused too much trouble.

'I don't want to watch that film, it's for boys.'

Jack decided he had really had enough of this one's attitude. He leant forward from his armchair then, and said firmly, 'Well, that's what is known as tough shit. *I* want to watch Buzz Lightyear, so does your mum, and so does your brother. Look up the word "democracy" in your dictionary, love. It means that the people with the most votes win! Now, put a sock in it, and let's get this show on the road.'

Vincent, thrilled at the turn of events, climbed on to his great-granddad's lap happily. But his enjoyment was short-lived. As the film began, his sister unleashed a tantrum which was, without doubt, her biggest and loudest to date. In short, pandemonium broke out.

They were back at their mother's by five past eight.

CHAPTER ONE HUNDRED AND THIRTY-NINE

Cynthia was nervous, but she felt sure she was doing the right thing. She had everything she needed to hand and all she had to do now was wait until it was late enough, and she could put her plan into action. As she waited patiently until she could safely leave her flat, she daydreamed of the life she would have with the kids she adored. And adore them she did, especially her Cherie, but then her little Vincent, though she hated the name the child bore, had stolen her heart as only a boy can. When she recalled the way he would climb up on to her lap and put his chubby little arms around her neck, she felt justified what she was doing for them was right. Anyone would do the same to save their grandchildren from a life of misery and degradation, she was sure of that.

Their father was a bloody blagger for starters! And, as she was always pointing out to the social services, caught not once but twice! She conveniently forgot her own past associations with the criminal classes and her part in them. She was good at rewriting history—she could wipe out anything that did not fit in with her version of events.

But now, thanks to Cherie, and the training she had been given to update her nanny on what they were doing with her mother, Cynthia had the opportunity to prove once and for all to the powers-that-be that her daughter was not fit to look after her own children.

Then they would be hers, and they would *stay* hers. Let Gabriella and Vincent make a new family, because there was no way they were going to get these kiddies. She would do whatever it took to get what she wanted. A little voice reminded her it wouldn't be the first time but, as always, she forced the thoughts away. Over the years she had become very good at that.

CHAPTER ONE HUNDRED AND FORTY

'No, Cherie, you can't go back to your nanny's. Look, you got what you wanted—we came back to my house. Your brother is asleep in the other room, and I'm very tired too. So come on, honey, you can sleep in here with me tonight.'

Cherie looked at her mother and decided that she had better do what she was told; after all, she had won the fight about staying at Great-Granddad Jack's. It wasn't really that he smelled—she didn't like it there because her great-granddad was all over little Vince. She used to be his favourite but that all changed when her brother came along. These days he hardly took *any* notice of her, except to say she was 'too much like Cynthia', and he said it as if it was a *bad* thing. Now she was lying in bed with her mummy, and she was feeling quite tired. Getting her own way could be exhausting.

'Can I have a story, Mummy?'

Gabby pulled her close, and said happily,

''Course you can, darling. What story do you want?'

'Little Red Riding Hood, please. The *long* version.'

Gabby laughed and started telling her the story. Cherie was asleep in no time and, holding her daughter to her own body, Gabby felt close to her for the first time. She couldn't wait for this to be her normal life. Soon she would have her babies back, and she would have her Vincent home. He had sworn he would go straight this time, that he would not do anything that would part him from his family. She knew that everyone thought she was mad, but she loved him, and she had to believe what he told her. It had been even harder when he had gone away this time and she had not coped well at all. And poor Vincent had been stuck on the island again, and unable to do anything to help her. She knew how hard that must have been for him, but that was all in the past now. She was on the mend, and he would be home at some point. All she could do was look to the future. She would not keep the kids away from her mum; after all, she had been there for them for a long time. But she wouldn't lose them to her. She would show them all that *she* was the best thing that could happen to her kids.

Gabby fell asleep smiling, thinking of how lovely it would be to have her family back together. Her, the kids, and her Vincent. It was the stuff that dreams were made of.

Three hours later, she awoke to a room full of smoke.

CHAPTER ONE HUNDRED AND FORTY-ONE

Cynthia let herself into her daughter's home and stood in the darkness of the kitchen, looking around her in the gloom. It was clean, she would give her daughter that, but it was still shabby. It was still council in her eyes. It broke her heart that her grandchildren would be reduced to this. Well, not for long.

She knew the best way to cause the fire was to start it from the front door, and let it take its own course, so that is exactly what she did. As she set to work, it did not cross her mind that she was destroying everything her daughter owned in the world—her photos, her clothes, all her personal effects. All she had to do was start the fire and then the Calor Gas heaters her daughter used for warmth would do the majority of the damage for her. She was grateful for the light from the street-lamp outside—she daren't put a light on, or make a noise. These places were like rabbit hutches, even a toilet flushing next door could be heard by all and sundry. She was smiling as she lit the match, and she slipped out as quietly as she had come in.

On the way home she was playing ABBA on her car stereo and singing at the top of her voice. This really was her Waterloo; she would play up her daughter's dangerous stupidity for all it was worth. A lit cigarette could cause untold damage—ten lit simultaneously could do even more! She guessed the washing basket full of clothes would be the first to really ignite, but the bin in the kitchen would also be a big help.

She would explain away the petrol by saying it was an insurance scam, that her daughter had hinted at money to come. She had covered all bases, and now she would have those kids until they sorted out accommodation and all the other shite that went with a major fire. Either way, this was a win-win situation for her.

CHAPTER ONE HUNDRED AND FORTY-TWO

Cherie was shaking Gabby, screaming at her to wake up.

'Mummy, Mummy, the house is on fire!'

Gabby could barely breathe; the bedroom was engulfed in smoke. Coughing, she jumped out of the bed. Vincent, the only thing she could think about was her baby Vincent, alone and afraid in his room.

She phoned the fire brigade in a panic and then, taking her daughter by the hand, she did the worst thing possible; she opened her bedroom door.

CHAPTER ONE HUNDRED AND FORTY-THREE

'Are you Cynthia Callahan?'

Cynthia, who had partaken of a few drinks to celebrate her late-night excursion, was bleary-eyed as she looked at the policeman and woman at her door.

'Yes, I am. What's going on? What's happened?'

Sergeant Proctor could hear a rising panic in her voice. He walked her through to her kitchen and, sitting her down, he nodded to the policewoman, who looked through Cynthia's cupboards until she found a bottle of brandy. Pouring out a large one, she placed it in front of the frightened woman.

All the time this was going on there was a panic rising inside Cynthia. This wasn't just about a burnt-out house. This was too ominous.

'Please, tell me! What's happened?'

Sergeant Proctor took her trembling hand in his and said gently, 'There's been a fire at your daughter's house. I'm very sorry to have to tell you that your grandson Vincent O'Casey died in it. The fire was too fierce for anyone to get to him and, believe me, your daughter tried. She's suffered third-degree burns on her hands as a result. Both she and your granddaughter are in the Old London. Your granddaughter is unharmed though—she's just being treated for smoke inhalation.'

Cynthia could hear the Sergeant's words, but she couldn't take in what he was saying. 'But they weren't in the house! *Why* were they in the house? They were staying at my dad's. Cherie told me on the phone that they were staying at my dad's . . .' She was shaking with shock. She looked into the Sergeant's eyes, pleading with him to tell her that none of it was true. When she had sneaked into the house, no one had been there—the house had been *empty*. She knew that because they were supposed to be at her fucking dad's! Oh, why could her daughter *never* do what she was supposed to! Now look what had happened. If that girl could only do what she was supposed to . . .

'You're wrong. You *must* be wrong. My daughter and my grandkids are at my dad's. You've got the wrong house, the wrong people . . .' Cynthia started to cry then. 'Please . . . Please tell me you've got the wrong people, please . . .'

Sergeant Proctor held her while she cried and, as he would say later back at the station, never had he heard crying like it. She had sounded like a wounded animal. It was only when the doctor finally arrived and sedated her that her raving abated and she dropped into a deep, troubled sleep.

CHAPTER ONE HUNDRED AND FORTY-FOUR

'It's like I'm cursed, Granddad. The first night they stay with me, and my little boy gets burned to death. My mum was right, I should never have been allowed to have them on my own—look what happened. Cherie had been on at me about smoking, she said she hated the smell of it. It's why I came home from your house. Why didn't I just stay at yours?'

Jack Callahan wished to God that he could ease his granddaughter's pain, but he knew no one could do that for her. Still, he hoped that what he had to tell her would relieve her of some of her guilt.

'Look, Gabby, there's something you should know. The police think the fire was started deliberately, and they think it was James who did it. Someone got into your house and lit cigarettes all over the place. It wasn't you. Whoever it was had placed piles of clothes under the fags, and your wastepaper basket and bin. I wasn't supposed to tell you this—they didn't want you to know until they thought you could cope with it, but your mother thinks it was James and so do the Old Bill now. She said he had turned up at her house a few days before and demanded money. I rarely agree with her, but I think this time Cynthia is right. It was James—it *had* to be. Who else would do something so fucking wicked?'

Gabby was thunderstruck. 'James? But why would James hurt me and my kids? It don't make sense!'

Jack shrugged. 'Why does that mad bastard do anything? There's no sense to be had out of this, and you'll drive yourself crazy trying to make some. He's a fucking nut-bag, always was, and always will be. So stop beating yourself up, love. I'll tell the police I've told you. Will you believe it if you hear it from them too?'

Gabby was numb; of all the explanations for what might have happened that night, her brother being the culprit was not one of them. But she supposed it had to be true—maybe he had thought they were out?

She felt the tears streaming down her face once more, and she looked at her heavily bandaged hands that had been burned down to the bone with her efforts to open her son's door. Her baby boy, her Vince, was dead, and it was her own brother who had killed him. There was no doubt about it—they were cursed, the whole family was cursed.

CHAPTER ONE HUNDRED AND FORTY-FIVE

Cynthia was not herself and everyone remarked on it. In the week following little Vincent's death the weight dropped off her and she looked older. People talked about how good she had been with those kids; she was hailed as a wonderful grandmother who had given up her life to raise her daughter's children. But she knew the truth, and it was eating at her like a cancer.

It had been quick thinking on her part, even in her distress, to say her son must have done it, and that had seemed to ring true. After all, *they* were the ones who'd told her about his threat to burn her out. He would eventually turn up like a bad penny, and they would charge him. It would do some good anyway; this time they would lock him up and throw away the key. They should have done that years ago.

It was the nights that were the worst for Cynthia. She thought she could hear little Vincent calling for her. And he would have called for *her* not his mum—it was Cynthia he would have wanted. She felt the sweat as it suffused her body, and the shortening of her breath that always accompanied it. Why had she done it? She had just wanted to make it seem as if her daughter was trying to fiddle the insurance and get herself a better house to live in into the bargain. Why had she not checked the bedrooms? She felt the tears once more, the tears that were never far from the surface. That little boy, that dear, handsome little boy . . .

As Cherie came and placed herself on her nanny's lap, Cynthia held her tightly, loving the feel of her small body, and remembering little Vince as he snuggled into her, his sweet baby smell of Johnson's powder. Now he was gone, burned to death, bless him, though the fireman said the smoke was what finished him off. He would have been lying in that cot, choking, and calling for his nanny Cynthia. He would have expected her to come and save him, she who had loved and cared for him all his life.

She leant forward and took a large swig of her whisky; it was the only thing that afforded her even a modicum of peace. She drank it whenever she needed solace, and that was all too often this past week. She needed its strength to help her forget for a few hours what she had done. Nothing in the world could ever wipe it out completely, but the Scotch helped and she drank it like water.

All she had left was her Cherie, and she could not lose her as well.

CHAPTER ONE HUNDRED AND FORTY-SIX

Vincent was devastated, and he knew that whatever he was feeling, his Gabby would be feeling it a hundredfold. Little Vincent, his namesake, was gone. It was hard to believe, because he had never really known him. But he had still been his son, the boy he watched being brought into the world, the boy he had such hopes and dreams for. His heart bled for Gabby, facing the worst that life could throw at a woman, and facing it alone, without him. It was like a nightmare.

Everyone in nick was being fantastic—even the POs had been sympathetic. One had even brought him in a bottle of Courvoisier brandy, courtesy of Bertie Warner and Derek Greene, and he had appreciated that. It was good of them to think of him, and he had been told they would stand the money for the funeral for which he was grateful. But he would pay them back every penny; the least a man could do was bury his own.

He was getting a day release to go to his son's funeral, how fucking fucked-up was that? Well, he would go and support his Gabby, then he would work at getting out of this dump and, when he did, he was going to hunt down that mad slag of a brother of hers, James fucking dead man Tailor, and he was going to kill him. He would kill him slowly and painfully; he would burn that skank alive, and let him know just how it felt, how his little lad had felt, choking and coughing, the room filling with black smoke and that cunt laughing about it. Because he would surely laugh about it would James, just like he apparently had when he had killed that poor fucking kitten.

Vincent poured himself another drink, and swallowed it quickly. He would give ten years off his life to be with poor Gabby now, holding her, and comforting her. They said her hands were very badly burned from trying to open the metal doorknob; burnt down to the bone. She was an incredible woman. She had taken their daughter to safety first, and then gone back inside to try and get her boy. She had done everything in her power to save him. Vincent couldn't hold back the tears

384

then. He felt the uselessness of his life, and the complete waste of these years he had spent away from his family. He could have been with them every day if he had just used his loaf. It was too late for recriminations now, all he had left inside him was a thirst for revenge.

He knelt down in his cell and, placing his hands together, he made a pledge to God; he was going to find James Tailor and he was going to kill him. That was the only thing keeping him sane.

CHAPTER ONE HUNDRED AND FORTY-SEVEN

Cynthia was awake. She knew she should at least try to sleep, but it was the child's funeral tomorrow and she couldn't stop thinking about it. She wondered if she would be able to face it. She knew she had to go, if for no other reason than to allay suspicion, but she was dreading standing at the grave, knowing that the little boy being buried was there through her fault alone.

She wondered at life and how it could sometimes hold up a mirror and make you see yourself as others see you. It could hurt more than any physical injury. If she could, she would do anything in her power to change the last few weeks.

She had always been faithless; the nuns, priests, all the people who believed in God were nothing more than fools to her. Now, though, she wondered if she had been too hasty in blowing *Him* off. God, her mother used to say, paid back debts without money, and she must owe *Him* more than most people.

She knew she had to face her daughter, and make her believe that she was only interested in what was good for her and the child. She would let Gabriella see Cherie often, she could not be any fairer than that. But, after this, she knew more than ever that she could not live alone now. She could not be without her Cherie—she was all that she had left.

CHAPTER ONE HUNDRED AND FORTY-EIGHT

Gabby was pleased it was a cold and grey day—it would have felt wrong to have been burying her baby in the sunshine. She knew that she would never feel any warmth again; it was as if a lump of ice had settled in her chest, and it would never budge.

She glanced at his little white coffin, and wondered at a god who could take away a child from its mother. What really hurt was that she had had him for only one night and now he was dead. It didn't matter that it was her brother not her who had burned them out—it had still happened on her watch, as her mother had so succinctly put it.

Maybe her mother was right. Gabby's life was a shambles in many respects, and that had been driven home to her more and more lately. The only man she had ever loved had been twice banged up for armed robbery—hardly a good role model in the eyes of the courts, or anyone else for that matter. She was not allowed access to her kids unless her mother deemed it OK, and *she* had the legal rights that should have been Gabby's. Life was unfair, but she had to accept the blame for a lot of what had happened to her and her children. She had been too young, too stupid to have a child alone the first time round, and with little Vince fate had interfered once more, and she had been left holding the baby again.

She saw her Vincent walking towards her, flanked by and handcuffed to two prison officers. She stepped towards him, the sight of him opening the floodgates, and she heard herself sobbing as if from a distance.

CHAPTER ONE HUNDRED AND FORTY-NINE

Cynthia was amazed at the reaction of the people at the funeral. She had been hugged and given condolences by people who would normally cross the road to avoid her.

She could see Gabriella, a beautiful name she had always felt was wasted on her daughter, standing with Vincent. The two POs with him looked suitably solemn and out of place at a child's funeral.

The sight of Vincent O'Casey in handcuffs angered her; he was bringing this lovely child's funeral down to the level of his family. They were there as well, though standing apart from everyone else, all looking like rejects from *The Jeremy Kyle Show*. They were just using the boy's death to worm their way back into Vincent's good books. She could easily walk over there and fell each and every one of them, punch and kick them to make them leave this place that was not supposed to be soiled by the likes of them. But she would leave that to Vincent; his opinion of his family was just about the only thing they could agree on. The irony was not lost on her.

Cherie was holding her hand tightly and, even though she knew she should make the child go to her mother and father, her innate cunning told her to keep her there. People would see that the child preferred her and that was the main thing. She had made a terrible mistake with little Vince, and she had paid dearly, but it had just made her all the more determined not to let this little one go from her. Without Cherie she had nothing, and that was wrong; after all, Gabriella could have more kids. She should have looked after the children she already had, not succumbed to her depressions and her pills. She was not fit to look after a child as intelligent and special as Cherie. She was wholly Cynthia's child, and that, she was determined, was never going to change.

CHAPTER ONE HUNDRED AND FIFTY

As Vincent listened to his Gabby sobbing, watched that piece of shite Cynthia keeping his daughter by her side, and saw poor old Jack Callahan aged and broken, he swore there and then that this was all going to change.

He had caught Cherie's eye and she had looked away, then up at her nanny Cynthia, as if asking permission to go to him. He allowed for the fact he was in handcuffs, but it wasn't as if she didn't know he was banged up—she had been to visit him. He knew it was Cynthia who had poisoned her, but he also accepted that Cynthia, whatever she was or she wasn't, had been there for the kids when poor Gabby couldn't be. He blamed himself for that; he had left her twice on her Jack Jones, twice holding the baby, *literally*.

He hadn't been there for either of his kids for any length of time, so was it any wonder his daughter didn't beat a path to his door? She was nervous of him and, from what Gabby had said, her mother had made them both out to be the bastards of the universe. They couldn't blame the child for that, though, in his heart, he hated Cynthia for the way she had manipulated them all, even him. At one time it was either Cynthia or care, and Cynthia was preferable to those kiddies being in the system. It was a fucking abortion and it was his fault.

That moron James had always been a few chips short of a McDonald's and, as Cynthia had been the cause of his fruit-caking, he was not impressed with her having too much authority over his daughter.

He felt powerless. He would never get used to it, yet he had been experiencing it for far too long. All he could think about was wiping out that bastard James; after that, everything else would fall into place, of that much he was sure. If he went away again, at least this time it would be for a good reason.

As the thoughts of revenge swirled around his head he held his Gabby as best he could under the circumstances.

CHAPTER ONE HUNDRED AND FIFTY-ONE

Jack Callahan had never felt so old and weak. He could not believe they were burying that lovely boy. Why had he let them go home that night? Why had fate chosen that night for James to have one of his rampages? And why couldn't the police find him? That's what he asked himself day and night—where could he be? If Jack had an inkling he would go and take the fucker out himself. It was as if James had disappeared off the face of the earth. Cynthia had said that when he had come to her house he had been high on drugs, accusing them all of ruining his life, accusing her of loving his sister's kids more than her own, a truth that must have hit home even to someone as thick-skinned as Cynthia.

He glanced at her and wondered how someone like her and her son could be allowed to roam the earth, when such a lovely little boy had died. It was all wrong.

Poor Gabby was beside herself with grief, and Jack was glad his Mary wasn't here to see this. As the priest himself had said to him, this would surely have killed her. It was a wrong day, in so many ways.

CHAPTER ONE HUNDRED AND FIFTY-TWO

Bertie Warner stood in the cemetery and watched the proceedings with a suitably respectful expression. He didn't like things like this at all; he saw death as an inevitable thing, but he hoped that he would go naturally when the time came and not by the hand of someone else. In his opinion, cancer was preferable to a bullet in the brain—at least then you had the opportunity to tie up loose ends and say your goodbyes.

A child's funeral was a bastard; it was the wrong order, and it made everyone who attended feel they were blessed because it wasn't *their* child who had died. There were times when he could launch his lot into the atmosphere, but he wouldn't part with them for the world. If one of them died he would be distraught, and that was exactly how poor young Vincent and Gabriella looked.

Truth be told, though, it was Cynthia who was the star turn at this funeral, stealing all the attention. She looked like something from an American mini-series; black fitted suit, high-heeled shoes, and a small hat with a lacey bit hiding her boat race from the world. She still had the looks, he had to admit—not that he would touch her if she begged him. Well, he might if she begged him *really* nicely.

It was a sad day and no mistake. So why did he feel that there was something awry—he liked that word, it was something an old-fashioned Filth would use. But his shit detector, and he prided himself on his shit detector, was telling him there was something fishy about all this. It *smelt* wrong and, even though that nutter James was capable of something this heinous, it all felt a bit too convenient for his liking.

Now, it was common knowledge that he hated Cynthia; she had outed a close friend of his, even if he couldn't fault her actions at the time. But that hatred he had for her also made him suspicious of her, and what she was capable of. Though, from what he could gather, she loved those kids, so he was most probably barking up the wrong tree.

Still, he liked a nice little snoop occasionally, and he had plenty of Filth who owed him favours. If nothing else he would be able to give Vincent a proper update on his son's murder case, because this was murder, whichever way you looked at it.

CHAPTER ONE HUNDRED AND FIFTY-THREE

As they lowered little Vincent's coffin into the grave, Cynthia's crying could be heard above everyone else's, and that only proved to the onlookers how much she had loved that child. The gossips speculated how that boy would still be alive if he had been at his nanny's where, in fairness, he had lived most of his life.

Gabriella was a lovely girl but she had been incapable of taking proper care of those children. She was like that Celeste and everyone knew *she* hadn't been the full shilling. No, the general consensus was that Cynthia, whatever people might think of her in the past, had proved herself in the end.

Cynthia felt the tide of good wishes and basked in their warmth and, as she stood by her daughter, hand on her arm, her granddaughter clutching her other hand, she knew that she had won, at least where public opinion was concerned.

Everyone watched her pull Gabby into her arms, and they said afterwards that when it came down to it, no matter what, you always wanted your mum when things were bad.

CHAPTER ONE HUNDRED AND FIFTY-FOUR

It was almost nine months since the funeral of little Vince, and Gabby was finally getting back to some kind of normality. It had not been the greatest of times, and she knew it would take a long while before she felt strong enough to feel anything close to happiness again.

Vincent was home, working at a garage in East London and they were gradually getting things together. It had been hard for them; he had never really known his son, but he had grieved for him as they both had. Cherie wasn't living with them, but they saw her a lot, and that was enough for Gabby these days. As Vincent said, it was a shame to take the child away from her nanny until they had replaced everything and had a proper home for her. But Gabby knew it was because Cherie didn't really bother with him. He had been away for so much of her life, she just didn't know him any more. It was sad but it was a fact of life.

Now she was pregnant again, although she was too frightened to get excited about it. Vincent was over the moon; he saw it as a chance for them to start again with the family they both had always longed for. Gabby wouldn't allow herself to get too caught up in his dreams. She had never been lucky in that way—every time she had believed her life was back on track it had been destroyed.

She had a lot of trouble with her hands still. It didn't bother her that they were scarred, but it was difficult to pick up small things, like pins or stamps. Even a knife could be quite difficult for her, but she was doing a lot of physio, and soon she would have another skin graft and then things would be even easier. She supposed they might put that off now until after the baby was born.

She hoped it was a girl; she didn't want to replace little Vince with another boy, but she knew that Vincent was hoping for a son he could take to the park and play football with. He wanted a little lad he could lavish all his time and energy on. She wouldn't begrudge him that—he had been her rock in so many ways, helping her through her grief and her guilt. Because she did feel guilty about what had happened, and would bear that guilt for the rest of her life.

It hurt that her own brother hated her so much he was willing to do that to them all, was capable of setting fire to her home, when she was the only one who had always tried to do what she could for him. In her own way she had kept in contact with him and, consequently, she had brought him into her children's lives. What a price they had paid for her stupidity!

It was hard getting through the days, and she still had very black moods when she wondered at what was going on with the world and she questioned everything. Why had this happened to her? Why she had been singled out for so much heartache? She had no answer. But it meant she would not celebrate this new baby until it was born—anything could happen between then and now.

As she combed her thick hair into place, the phone rang and she answered it carefully, making sure not to drop the receiver. It was the police. She listened for a few moments, before asking, 'Is this about James?'

She hoped they had found him; the thought of him out there after what he had done was worse than anything. Supposing he came back to finish the job? That was her nightmare—him sneaking back to burn them to death in their beds. He was capable of murder as they all knew—look at that Dougie person he had killed. She shuddered at the thought. Plus, if they caught him, then that meant her Vincent could not get his hands on him. Revenge wasn't worth doing life over. Her greatest fear was that Vincent would be banged up for the rest of his days. She knew he spent hours trying to track James down and had put a price on his head. Anyone with information could get twenty-five grand if it led to him being found. That was a big incentive, and she knew it.

'I beg your pardon, are you sure?' She listened for a few more seconds then she said in a dazed voice, 'No, I'll tell my mother, I don't think she should hear this over the phone.'

She put the receiver back in its cradle and went into her kitchen. Sitting at the kitchen table, she looked around her for a few moments, unable to get to grips with what she had just been told.

James was dead. He had been dead for over a year, although he had only just been found in a squat in Leicester. He had died of a heroin overdose, and he had been lying there all that time, undiscovered. They had deduced that it was James through his belongings, despite the body being in a state of decay. They would confirm with a DNA test, but they were more or less certain it was him.

If James was dead, then who had tried to burn her house down? Who had killed her little boy? And, more to the point, who had been at her mother's a few days before the fire? None of it made any sense. The person they had found could not have been James, surely? She decided to ring Vincent. He would know what to do.

CHAPTER ONE HUNDRED AND FIFTY-FIVE

Cynthia was happier than she had been for a long while. She was finally getting over losing that little child and his awful death. She still needed a drink to get her through the day—and especially the nights—but she was beginning to feel she had it all under control.

Vincent had not taken to his daughter, and she had not taken to him, thank God. Cherie looked down her nose at him, and so she should. Cynthia had drummed into the child to expect better in life and she would make sure she got it. It had worked out quite well for her. Well, it had worked out as well as could be expected, all things considered. At least she had Cherie who, at ten, was so like her at the same age it was uncanny.

Now that silly cow was pregnant again. Didn't she ever learn? The girl was a total bloody idiot where Vincent was concerned. She could not see further than his dick, and that was about the strength of their relationship. He fucked her, he got her in the club, and then he left her. Gabriella believed it was third time a charm. As if that oik would be able to keep out of prison long enough to fucking see it born! If only he could find James before the police did—that would make sure Vincent wasn't around to interfere for a *very* long time. Even if her daughter *was* once more pregnant by him, she would happily see him put away for good—especially if it meant James was out of the picture too.

She had made up her mind that she wasn't going to have too much to do with this new grandchild. She decided that, if she used her loaf, this would be the perfect opportunity to get Cherie away from them both for ever, and keep her for herself.

As she poured herself another of her 'black' teas—her euphemism for whisky and water—she pondered on how she could talk them into letting her move right away with Cherie. She couldn't stand to be in London any more—everywhere she looked she was haunted by memories of baby Vince. Every road, park and zoo reminded her of him and she could hear his voice asking her things, making her laugh. Oh, how he had made her laugh—he had been such a dear little fellow. She realised she needed to get as far away from those memories as possible.

Gabriella had phoned to say she would be here soon. She wondered what she had to talk to her about? Probably wanting help with that baby she had on the way.

CHAPTER ONE HUNDRED AND FIFTY-SIX

Gabby had parked her car by the new Somerfield's at Chrisp Street Market; she needed to pick up a few bits for Vincent's dinner, before calling at her mother's. She couldn't drive for long with her hands as they were but she could manage the automatic Vincent had got for her to get around locally. Vincent was as mystified as she was about the news about James. He said he'd dig around a bit for some more information. As she walked out with the trolley, she was startled from her thoughts when she heard someone call her name.

'Is that you, Gabby?'

Gabby looked into the woman's face, unable to place her. She grinned at her before saying in a friendly manner, 'Sorry, do I know you?'

The woman smiled; she was in her late forties and she had kind eyes and heavy legs. 'I'm Jeannie Proctor. I lived next door to you in Ilford when you were a nipper.'

Gabby smiled back. 'Oh, really? I'm sorry, I don't remember.'

The woman looked her over, and she said in wonderment, 'You are the living image of your mother—that's what made me recognise you. Beautiful, just like her. How is Cynth these days?'

Gabby nearly said, 'Well, she would not be happy

398

to be referred to as "Cynth"!' Instead she said, 'She's fine, you know me mum!'

It was meant in jest, but the woman nodded, then said seriously, 'Oh, I know Cynthia all right! Tell her she still owes me for the dry cleaning bill.'

Gabby laughed then. 'What dry cleaning bill?'

Jeannie Proctor paused for a few seconds as if she was wondering if she should speak, then she said candidly, 'It was a long time ago, so I don't suppose it matters now. She torched the house— for the insurance, like. She had spent so much on it that they could never get the price it was worth, so she torched it. Left fags all over the place, she did, and open cans of paint and turps. Looked like she was decorating, see. She was a fucking girl, her. Mind you, in those days you could get away with murder with insurance companies. Can't any more, they're wise to everything now.'

The woman was laughing, but Gabby could feel herself going cold.

'I had my bedroom windows open, and the smoke damage was atrocious, as you can imagine . . . Here, where you going?'

Jeannie Proctor watched as the girl hurried away from her. 'Well, what on earth rattled her cage?'

CHAPTER ONE HUNDRED AND FIFTY-SEVEN

Gabby sat in her car and thought back to what Jeannie Proctor had said to her. Somehow she knew that the woman was telling her the truth. But did that mean her mother had burned *her* house down

399

too? Had killed her baby boy? Somewhere inside she knew that was what had happened.

It was all falling into place now. She had been on the verge of getting the kids back, she had straightened herself out. In her heart she should have known her mother would not have countenanced that. Her mother had always wanted those children more than she had ever wanted anything in her life. Gabby had actually deemed that at one time her mother's saving grace—the undeniable love she had for those two little mites. It was the love she had never had for her own kids, but she had lavished it on her grandchildren. Gabby had been so grateful to her, had felt so indebted to her for all her help. She recalled how badly her mother had taken little Vince's death; Gabby had assumed, like everyone else, that it was because she had loved him and cared for him. But it had been guilt. The wicked bitch had been consumed with guilt.

Even as Gabby's heart was trying to deny what she was telling herself, her brain was telling her that it couldn't have been her brother who started the fire. The brother who her mother had said had visited her a few days before, and who she subsequently admitted had threatened them all with death, pain, torture and destruction, was well and truly dead by then.

Gabby remembered her mother's devastation at the kids having to leave her to go home to their terrible mummy. How she had kept saying Gabby wasn't ready to have the kids back yet, that she still needed to sort herself out. It was exactly what she had said about Cherie coming back to her after the fire. Gabby had believed her mother was doing her a favour by keeping Cherie with her then. Cherie, who could have died as well if she had not slept in her bed that night, who would have been in the same room as little Vince, who had been so determined to leave her great-granddad's house because of Cynthia's bad mouthing.

She could see that her mother hadn't intended to kill them. She had believed they were at her granddad's that night. Cynthia had burned the place down thinking it was empty, but she had done it to make it look like Gabby was incapable of looking after her own children. A big fire would make them think twice about letting the children come back home, especially when there was no fucking home for them to go to. Gabby could almost hear her mother saying to the social workers how irresponsible she was to have left a fag burning, and imagine if the children had been in there with her.

Well, they *were* in there with her. While her mother was creeping around her house with every intention of burning it down, she had been asleep upstairs with her babies. It all made perfect sense now—her mother would have had to keep the children at least until she was re-housed, and back on her feet. And that would have been months, if not years.

Cynthia had done it deliberately, and she had done it for no other reason than to get what she wanted, as she had always got what she wanted. Gabby had lost not only her little boy in that fire, but all her photos, the memorabilia of her life, of her kids' lives, of her nana Mary and her all-too-little time with Vincent. Her mother had been willing to leave her with *nothing* in her

401

determination to keep those kids, and instead she had murdered her little boy.

Gabby thought back to how her mother had always made sure she got whatever or whoever she wanted—by hook or by crook. Cynthia had taken Jonny from poor Celeste, she had taken the kids from her own daughter, and she had been the reason her husband had killed himself. She had murdered in cold blood once—to save her sister she claimed, but she had done that to save herself too. It would always be about *her*, and what *she* wanted. It would *never*, could never, be about anyone else.

And what about poor James Junior? Cynthia had blamed James from the get-go. She had put him in the frame with her lies about him going round there and threatening all sorts. Was there nothing she wasn't capable of?

Gabby was outside her mother's flat, parked up all neat and tidy, but she had no memory of driving there. She got out of the car, and she felt as if she was walking through water, so heavy and awkward did her limbs feel.

CHAPTER ONE HUNDRED AND FIFTY-EIGHT

Gabby was throwing up in her mother's toilet, and all she could hear was her mother's voice going on and on and on.

'I don't feel well, Mum. I feel ill and out of sorts.'

'Well, whose fault's that then? Pregnant again, aren't you? He'll leave you like he did the last two times. He won't keep out of the nick, love—it's all

402

he's fucking fit for. And I can tell you now, I'm not looking after any more kids either. You're on your own this time, lady. I told you when you met that idiot Vincent O'Casey, I said then, and I stand by my words, he has the brains of a fucking rocking horse and the face of a Tonka toy. But would you listen to me? You should get shot of that baby. How can you have another one? I mean, I ask you, how long before he'll be banged up again?'

Gabby was frightened of the hate spiralling inside her. She was terrified of the feelings consuming her, and the thoughts that were spinning out of control inside her head. She didn't want to hurt her mother, she *mustn't* hurt her—not yet anyway, not until she had found out the truth, no matter how painful it might be. But she had to know.

She took a deep breath and said calmly, 'Have the police spoken to you yet?'

Her mother went quiet at that, and then she asked warily, 'What about? Why would they want to speak to me? More likely they were after your old man. What's he gone and done this time?'

'*Vincent?* My Vincent ain't done nothing, but it seems they have found James.' She saw her mother's face pale, and she wanted to smile.

'Where? Where did they find him? Have they charged him? The murdering little fucker.'

She was good, Gabby would give her that. What was it the psychiatrist had said about mimicking emotions? Oh, that was her mother all over.

'Well, where is he? Is he in custody? Have they collared him or what?'

Gabby could almost feel the panic emanating from her mother, and she knew then that she would enjoy bringing her down, she would love every second of exposing her for the liar she was. 'He's in a morgue up in Leicester. He's been dead for over a year, Mum. You do realise what that means, don't you?' She saw Cynthia trying to take onboard what she had said to her. 'It means he couldn't have been the one who set fire to my house, and it also means that you couldn't have spoken to him a few days before like you said you did. Because he was dead then. Unless you saw him through a fucking medium, you lying, treacherous, fucking whore of a woman.'

Cynthia was taken aback by the vehemence of her daughter's accusations. She knew only too well that her daughter was telling the truth. Now she had to find a way out of her lies and subterfuge. Trust that fucking James to be dead! That was so like her kids—they always let her down.

'I know what I saw, and it was not long before the fire, but it might have been a few weeks before—I was confused, I was upset. For fuck's sake, Gabriella, it was a terrible time. What are you trying to prove here?'

Gabby laughed harshly. Oh, she was really good. Her acting was of Oscar standard. Move over, Dame Judi Dench, you are an amateur in comparison with Cynthia Callahan. 'What *I* am trying to prove? I am trying to prove who was responsible for the death of my little boy, Mum, that's what I am trying to prove. And, by all accounts, it wasn't my brother, your son, James, so who does *that* leave?'

Cynthia just shook her head in utter disbelief, stalling for time. She was thinking on her feet now, trying to work out how she was going to explain it all away. 'I don't know, darling—maybe he got someone else to do it, or it was someone after your Vincent. You know what villains are like—he probably fucked someone over in stir, and that door of yours was never safe, was it? One good push and it was open.'

Gabby just stared at her mother, the woman who had carried her in her belly, and who had never in her life given her a thing that was worth having. The very same woman who was now trying her hardest to talk her into believing that her house burning down and her son dying was all some kind of conspiracy by persons unknown, as the police would put it. *She* had burned that house down to stop Gabby having access to her own children. That was the truth of it all. Cynthia had done it to get what she wanted. Just as she had always got what she wanted all her life, no matter who suffered because of it. It was a wicked, calculated act that had been the cause of her little son dying, choking to death in thick black smoke. She could hear his voice calling for his nanny over and over—that made it even worse. He hadn't called for his mummy—only his nanny who had made sure he wanted her over his own mother. Even Cherie didn't want her, or her father either, come to that. She was a spoiled, rude and arrogant little girl who, if she had not been so fucking ruined, would not have made them all leave her granddad's house.

'It was Cherie, you know, who made us come back that night. She didn't like it at your dad's—she said it *stank*. You have always drummed into her how your mum and dad smelt, and were not nice people, and that I can't be trusted to take care of them. And so, to please her, to make her happy, I

405

brought them back to my house. The house where her brother died, because her adored nanny tried to burn the place down while we were sleeping in our beds. How the fuck do you sleep at night! Knowing what you did, how the fuck do you sleep a wink? Is that why you went on the drink? Because you drink a lot now, Mum, don't you? Does it drown out the knowledge that you fried your grandson in his cot?'

Cynthia tried not to react to that; it was a truth which ate away at her every day. She *had* to get Gabriella onside again. 'What would I know about starting fires, you silly girl. You're over-wrought, Gabriella, listen to yourself, for fuck's sake! You haven't been right since that child died, and I understand that, babe, I feel the same way . . .'

It was 'babe' now; Gabby could see she was really pulling out all the stops. 'No, you don't, Mum. You've never cared about anyone or anything in your life. You're a fucking leech. You take everything from people. You pretend you care, but you don't, you don't know how to. You'd even blame poor James—James who you sent off his fucking rocker in the first place . . .'

'You are not going to make me listen to this shit, Gabriella. You are wrong, *very* wrong. Use your bloody head, girl! I loved that little boy with all my heart . . . and, as for your brother . . . I don't believe a word of it—they must have the wrong person.'

But Gabby could see the fear in her mother's eyes and she knew that it was true. Every word of it.

'I met your old mate, Jeannie, today. That's how I know everything—she told me *all* about the house in Ilford.' She could see her mother's head working, trying to figure out exactly what she was saying, could almost hear her brain whirring as she tried to lie her way out of what they both knew was the truth.

'What the hell have you been taking this time, eh? What the fuck are you on, Gabriella, to make you come out with this shit?'

Gabby found she'd picked up a large bronze statue of a cat. As she held it in her scarred hands she felt the weight of it. Her mother kept talking. The world according to Cynthia Tailor who, along with God Himself, was almost omnipotent in the lives of her family, who ruled every—one around her with a rod of iron. She could see her mother's mouth moving constantly, but she couldn't hear what she was saying any more; all she was conscious of was a rushing noise in her ears. Then she struck her.

She lifted the bronze statue back over her head and hit her mother across the face with it, using all the force she could muster, and enjoying the feeling of total retaliation. For once it was her doing the hurting, and that felt good. She hit her over and over again, watching the spray of blood as it spurted from her mother's head, enjoying her mother's pain, and her mother's suffering.

She knew that this had been a long time coming, and that she should have done it years ago, should have done it when she was a young girl. She could have saved so many people so much heartache. She was determined now, determined to shut her mother up once and for all. Shut her up for good.

Cynthia fell sideways on to the white leather sofa. She could hear a gurgling noise that was almost comical. The blood was still spraying out everywhere like a crimson mist, and she was glad, glad the lying, two-faced, murdering whore was

407

finally shutting her big, filthy mouth up. She hoped she was in as much pain and terror as her little boy had been when he was fighting for his last breath, expecting to be saved by this woman who had started the fire in the first place so she could get what she wanted.

Gabby hit her mother again and again, each blow easing the knot inside her, each blow easing the hate she had inside her for this woman who had been the bane of her whole life.

She looked down at the bloodied form and, for the first time in years, she felt almost at peace. Her mother's face was unrecognisable, a deep red gash that was pumping out blood at an alarming rate.

Gabby looked at the woman she had hated nearly all her life. Then she sat down on the ladder-backed chair her mother was convinced was an antique, put her face into her bloodied hands and cried.

CHAPTER ONE HUNDRED AND FIFTY-NINE

'Fucking hell, Vince, when your lot go they don't muck about, I'll give them that!' Bertie Warner's voice held a tinge of admiration in it. 'Maybe I should give her a job on the firm!' Bertie laughed at his own joke.

Vincent looked around the room, and shook his head in amazement that his Gabby was capable of this kind of violence. But then, after what she had told him, he understood it to an extent. All her life Cynthia had done everything possible to destroy those around her, and it seemed that now, finally, one of those people had retaliated and in a spectacular fashion.

Gabby was still sitting on the ladder-backed chair. Her face and hair and clothes were sprayed with blood, but the strangest thing was, for the first time in years, she actually looked at peace.

'She did it, Vince, she fucking killed our baby. She torched our home so she could keep our kids with her. Keep them in her power. Everyone had to be in her power, had to do what she wanted; she would never be happy with anything else.'

Vincent went over and held her gently. She felt so frail, her body was so slender still, even with the pregnancy, and he knew that this had been coming for a long time. He blamed himself—if he had not been away so long, none of this would have happened. He should have been there for her and for his kids, instead of rotting away in prison. But that was the chance you took in his game, and you had to accept that or you would go off your head. His old cellmate used to say hindsight is a wonderful thing, but it was fucking foresight that people needed.

Bertie looked at young Vincent, as he still thought of him, and wondered at a man who could be so calm in the face of such carnage. Gabby had literally taken her mother's face off—this was the act of someone who had reached the end of their tether.

He nudged Cynthia's body with his foot none too gently; if she groaned he would finish the slag off himself. He smiled. Just as he thought—as dead as the proverbial dodo. Good riddance to bad rubbish, he was glad she was gone. He had had his own axe to grind with her; after all, she had taken out one of his closest friends. He cleared his throat noisily and said, 'We better get this place cleared up before Lily Law comes a-snooping! You take her home and sort her out, son. I'll deal with this little lot.' He sighed theatrically. 'Thank fuck she lived in this end house—bit more privacy, if you know what I mean!'

CHAPTER ONE HUNDRED AND SIXTY

Gabby was lying on the bed; such was her relief at the knowledge her mother could never interfere in her life again she almost felt lighter in her body. Even the pain of her hands couldn't bother her. It was as if the heavy weight she had carried all her life had been taken away from her and, consequently, she felt better than ever, mentally as well as physically. She felt no remorse for what she had done. Thank God that Cherie was having a sleepover at her friend's house; she was going straight from school, so no one would be any the wiser about Cynthia's disappearance until tomorrow when she didn't pick up Cherie from school. Vincent said it would all be sorted; all she had to say was that she went round there and she wasn't in, so she had left her a voicemail message and then come home again.

She pulled herself on to her back, and stretched her arms above her head. She felt a luxuriousness overwhelming her, as if she had finally found the secret to eternal happiness. Knowing that Cynthia was gone was like receiving the greatest gift ever. It meant that her life would change drastically in every way. She could do *what* she wanted, *when* she wanted; there would be no Cynthia to stick a spoke in the wheel, no Cynthia to shoot down her hopes and her aspirations, no Cynthia to make her feel inadequate any more. And no Cynthia to burn her children to death or turn them against her.

Her granddad Jack came in to the room with two cups of tea, and she smiled at him dreamily, 'She's gone, Granddad, and I don't feel an ounce of guilt.'

Jack sat on the bed carefully and, taking her hands very gently in his, he said seriously, 'Listen to me, love, you will. When this sinks in you will realise the enormity of what you have done. Now, I'm not saying that what you did was bad but, love her or loathe her, and I certainly loathed her, she was still your mother when all was said and done. That will be the thing that will play on your mind.'

Neither of them spoke for a while. Then Gabby said honestly, 'I won't let her ruin the rest of my life, Granddad. She's ruined so much of it already, I can't let her ruin the rest. I'm glad I did what I did; it's just a shame that someone didn't do it to her earlier, then my little boy would still be alive, and I wouldn't have her blood on my hands. She was not a person who had any right to decency or kindness, she was not a person to aspire to be. She was cruel, and she was evil in many ways. She took what she wanted from anyone, she was nasty, vindictive and she never threw me a kind word. She was the reason my dad killed himself, why Auntie Celeste went off her head, and why my brother never knew a happy day in his life. I don't feel a second's guilt over that bitch, so don't worry about me, OK? I'm fine, better in fact than I have been for many a long year. Me and Vince have a chance now, we can be a

411

real family and Cherie won't have her dripping her poison in her ears at every available opportunity. I am actually looking forward to the future now, and that is something I could never say before today.'

Jack picked up his tea from the bedside table and drank it quickly. He heard the truth in the girl's words. 'I'm glad to hear it, love, I just don't want her on your mind.'

Gabby laughed softly. 'No fear of that, Granddad. I feel free, really *free* for the first time in my life. It's as if I can finally breathe again. I paid her back for my boy, and for everyone she ever contaminated by her touch. So don't worry about me, mate, I have never felt better.'

CHAPTER ONE HUNDRED AND SIXTY-ONE

'"No, officer, I haven't seen or heard from her for days."' Detective Sergeant Smith laughed as he spoke. 'That's all we hear, sir. It's as if Cynthia Tailor has dropped off the face of the earth. There's nothing at her house—she's gone, lock, stock and barrel. The neighbours said a moving van turned up and was gone within an hour. It's as if she never existed.'

Detective Inspector Williams nodded. This was a really strange affair; he knew there was skulduggery afoot but actually proving it would be impossible.

DS Smith continued, 'It seemed she had scammed quite a few men over the years, sir—it could have been one of them she was running from. A David Duggan made a criminal complaint against her but she seemed to have swerved that with ease. But, on closer inspection, she wasn't what you would call a model citizen, if you know what I mean?'

DI Williams shook his head. 'I know exactly what you mean. Cynthia Tailor, Callahan that was, could start a fight in an empty house. But the point is now, where the fuck is she?'

DS Smith laughed then as he answered. 'Your guess, sir, is as good as mine.'

'What about the daughter? Didn't she have her children at one point?'

DS Smith nodded. 'From what we can gather, sir, the daughter is as baffled and bewildered as we are. Heavily pregnant now and lost her little boy in a fire. She seems to think her mother has done a moonlight flit. Her expression, not mine. She doesn't seem unduly worried about her and, as for Cynthia Tailor's father, he thinks she will turn up, as he said in his own words, like the proverbial bad penny.'

DI Williams sighed. 'Leave it with missing persons then, we've done all we can.'

DS Smith nodded once more and left the office of his superior. He was in line for a forty-grand bonus for this little piece of work, and he was absolutely thrilled about it. He wondered what part of the new M25 Cynthia was now resting in. He would put his money on a slip road, but she might be holding up a flyover. Either way, there was no way she was ever coming back, of that much he was sure.

CHAPTER ONE HUNDRED AND SIXTY-TWO

Vincent looked around his new house and smiled in satisfaction. It was lovely, and he knew that they would be very happy here. It was a new start for them, and that was something they needed desperately.

As he looked at Cherie's pretty face he smiled at her, and she tentatively smiled back. 'You can decorate your room any way you like, sweetheart.' She was only happy when she was getting something—mainly her own way. She was related to Cynthia all right. 'Go and help Mummy with the bags, would you?'

She skipped off to do as she was told. Since she had been away from Cynthia she was becoming easier to handle, but it was the change in his Gabby that was the real eye opener. She was like a young girl, laughing, easy with herself and everyone around her. It was as if Cynthia's death had unleashed the real Gabriella Tailor. He hoped that she stayed this happy always, because although he loved the old Gabby—always had and always would—now he felt as though he had been given another woman to love alongside the old one. This one made plans, had ideas, was sure of herself, whereas the old one had always been frightened to be happy because it had never lasted for her. Now she was strong, strong in every way. And he loved her with all his heart and soul. This was the beginning of the rest of their lives, lives without the burden of Cynthia Tailor and what she entailed.

Picking up Gabby, he carried her across the threshold and her high laughter drew the attention of the passers-by who could not help but smile at such complete and utter happiness.

EPILOGUE

Richard O'Casey, known affectionately as Ricky, was laughing his head off, and he was obviously enjoying his day out. His older sister Cherie was grinning at him, and he was grinning back. As they ran back to their parents, they were holding hands.

Richard had the unmistakable Callahan eyes, and the sovereign-coloured hair. He was a good-looking and a happy boy. Cherie was growing up and she could easily pass for older than she was, with the unmistakable Callahan femininity she exuded. Vincent watched her like a hawk, as did Gabby. Cherie knew all this and she had made sure that she acted how they wanted her to act; that way she got a lot more leeway, but she was already a terrible liar, who had an eye for the men, not boys, *men*. Gabby feared there was far too much of Cynthia in the girl, but that was to be expected—she had been her role model for so long. Gabby suspected she was a lost cause, but they were determined to do the best they could for her, and make her into a better person because they loved her in spite of everything. It was hard work though—if Vincent had not been as strong-minded as he was, Cherie would have been walking all over him by now. She already knew how to captivate any males in her vicinity.

Ricky, on the other hand, was a wonderful little boy, who enjoyed life, and understood the word 'no'. As he looked at the gravestone, he said sweetly, 'Great-Granddad Jack's down there.'

They smiled at his words. 'That he is, my little

417

lovely. He's with your great-nana Mary—she would have loved you!' Gabby wished her grandparents could see them now.

Vincent held Gabby's hand, and he squeezed it affectionately as she looked down at the grave of the only two people who had ever cared about her when she was growing up.

Cherie watched them both warily; she hated the way they were always hanging off each other. And how could her dad hold her mother's *hands*? They were awful—all scarred and deformed. If *she* had those hands she would wear gloves all the time.

She glanced across the cemetery at her uncle James's grave. They put flowers there as well, though why they would acknowledge a nutter like that she didn't know. She would never understand her family, not if she lived for a thousand years. Since her nanny Cynthia had gone on the trot they had all acted like it was Christmas every day. Well, *she* missed her nanny and she couldn't understand why she had not taken her with her. She said to her mum then, 'I wonder if we'll hear from Nanny Cynthia this year?'

Gabby shrugged. 'You never know, she could turn up out of the blue. I wouldn't put it past her.'

Vincent O'Casey looked at his family and felt that, after everything, they were finally getting on track. He had bought his garage back now, courtesy of Derek and Bertie. He tuned up certain motors for certain people for certain jobs; it was very lucrative, but nothing that could put him back in the nick. He loved his freedom too much to do anything to jeopardise it, and he loved his family too much to leave them ever again. As he looked at his wife, because they were married now, and

418

saw the little bump under her coat he felt a great wave of happiness. He hoped this baby was a girl. They were still young and they had their whole lives ahead of them.

Cynthia Callahan was dead and gone, buried all alone and far away from the people she was supposed to love. Her days of dictating other people's lives were past. It was just them now, and they were happy, really happy. Unlike Cynthia Callahan, they knew the value of love, and they knew the value of loyalty. And they were determined that they would be happy despite everything and every—one who had tried to destroy them. After all, as Mary Callahan had always said, what can't kill you can only make you stronger. They had faith in each other and in their ability to live a happy life, and that wasn't bad for starters, was it?

'Who fancies fish and chips?'

Richard was jumping up and down with sheer excitement and even Cherie looked keen. They walked away together as a family.

As they neared the cemetery gates, Gabby looked back to where her brother lay alone. Just for a few seconds in the autumn sunshine she thought she saw her, Cynthia, standing by his grave. She looked lost, unhappy, sorry. Gabby knew it was a trick of the light, but somehow it made her feel better. So she closed her eyes and said quietly, 'Goodbye, Mum.'

Then, smiling, she followed her husband and kids to the car.